"The City" and "The Fifth Face"

TWO CLASSIC ADVENTURES OF

by Walter B. Gibson
writing as Maxwell Grant

plus **"The Immortal Murderer"**
by Alfred Bester

Foreword by Harlan Ellison®

with new historical essays by
Will Murray and Anthony Tollin

Published by Sanctum Productions for
NOSTALGIA VENTURES, INC.
P.O. Box 231183; Encinitas, CA 92023-1183

Copyright © 1936, 1940, 1944 by Street & Smith Publications, Inc. Copyright © renewed 1963, 1967, 1971 by The Condé Nast Publications, Inc. All rights reserved.

The Shadow Volume 10 copyright © 2007 by Sanctum Productions/ Nostalgia Ventures, Inc.

The Shadow copyright © 2007 Advance Magazine Publishers Inc./The Condé Nast Publications. "The Shadow" and the phrase "Who knows what evil lurks in the hearts of men?" are registered trademarks of Advance Magazine Publishers Inc. d/b/a The Condé Nast Publications. The phrases "The Shadow Knows" and "The weed of crime bears bitter fruit" are trademarks owned by Advance Magazine Publishers Inc. d/b/a The Condé Nast Publications.

"For Every Action…" copyright © 2007 by The Kilimanjaro Corporation. All rights reserved. Harlan Ellison is a registered trademark of The Kilimanjaro Corporation.
"Rise of the Supervillain" copyright © 2007 by Will Murray.
"The Shadow of Alfred Bester" copyright © 2007 by Anthony Tollin.

This Nostalgia Ventures edition is an unabridged republication of the text and illustrations of two stories from *The Shadow Magazine,* as originally published by Street & Smith Publications, Inc., N.Y.: *The City of Doom* from the May 15, 1936 issue, and *The Fifth Face* from the August 15, 1940 issue, plus "The Immortal Murderer," broadcast December 10, 1944 on *The Shadow* radio series. Typographical errors have been tacitly corrected in this edition.

International Standard Book Numbers:
ISBN 1-932806-73-3   13 DIGIT 978-1-932806-73-1

First printing: August 2007

Series editor: Anthony Tollin
P.O. Box 761474
San Antonio, TX 78245-1474
sanctumotr@earthlink.net

Consulting editor: Will Murray

Copy editor: Joseph Wrzos

Cover restoration: Michael Piper

First printing: August 2007

The editor acknowledges the assistance of Dwight Fuhro, Ellen Kuhfeld, Michael Catron and Karl Schadow in the preparation of this volume.

Nostalgia Ventures, Inc.
P.O. Box 231183; Encinitas, CA 92023-1183

Visit The Shadow at www.shadowsanctum.com & www.nostalgiatown.com

Volume 10

The entire contents of this book are protected by copyright, and must not be reprinted without the publisher's permission.

CONTENTS

Two Complete Novels From The Shadow's Private Annals As told to Maxwell Grant

Thrilling Tales and Features

FOREWORD: FOR EVERY ACTION... by Harlan Ellison® .. 4

THE CITY OF DOOM by Walter B. Gibson
   (writing as "Maxwell Grant") 6

RISE OF THE SUPERVILLAIN by Will Murray 60

THE FIFTH FACE by Walter B. Gibson
   (writing as "Maxwell Grant") 62

**SPOTLIGHT ON THE SHADOW: THE
   SHADOW OF ALFRED BESTER** by Anthony Tollin ...116

THE IMMORTAL MURDERER by Alfred Bester 117

Cover art by George Rozen and Graves Gladney
**Interior illustrations by Tom Lovell, Earl Mayan
and Edd Cartier**

"FOR EVERY ACTION..." by Harlan Ellison®

It is, as we are given to comprehend the received universe, an immutable Law: "For every action there is an equal and opposite *re*action." Whether it is the dreamy tilting of the Jupiterlike gas giant that circles the star HD 189733 every 2.2 days, or the flipping of the bird and the cursing of the road-raged SUV driver when he cuts across three lanes of freeway traffic and you lay on the horn as he nearly takes off your side-view mirror; it is action and *re*action.

Not just opposite, but *equal*. Sometimes the push-back is unseen, lost in the dust-heaps of some faraway star cluster; and sometimes—as with The Shadow—the push is utterly unseen. You, I, everyone who passes us on the street, everyone we know, whether a Bach or a Tesla or a Willie Mays, has been pushed from day-one: the surly boss; the schoolyard bully; The System itself, no more kindly than a headless snake; the arrogant teen; the indolent public servant; the petty scam artist; the corrupt televangelist. You and I have always had to deal with them. As Dorothy Parker used to put it, "What fresh hell is this?"

And so, action/reaction, thus it is with Good vs. Evil, Right vs. Wrong. The push against you by abusive parents or impatient teachers or tunnel-opinioned politicians…the *re*action is a lifelong character tic: cowardice, fear of authority, failure to grasp opportunities or stand up for yourself. The great orbs swing in space, the meteors shower across the horizon, and you are bent under your own inadequacies.

Remember: I'm speaking here in the abstract about equal and opposite forces. Catch the trope. In the inspired stories of The Shadow—popular culture lit you should pray you never outgrow—because in its plots and naïvetes these stories are heavily freighted with that innocence of childhood or nature that too many of us seem to jettison when the Night of Maturity falls and we exchange our comic books for a five-year-old Cutlass—in the adventures of The Shadow we find the eternal immutable Law of equal and opposite. Good vs. Evil, Right vs. Wrong; and a rowdy, uncanny simulacrum of our Inner Hero. Oh, if we only had gone to Tibet, and learned the ways of Kent Allard. Oh, if only for a day, we could *be* The Shadow.

So whom would we fight, and it comes round again to equal and opposite? It is not fit and proper for Superman to duke it out with carjacking punks or litterbugs. He has to take on doom-providing supervillains. Sherlock Holmes had to have his Moriarty. Nayland Smith took on Fu Manchu. Brown was von Richthofen's equal, his opposite. Precisely so, The Shadow might—in the course of business—lay out or plug a yegg, a thug, an assassin, a chowderheaded gofer, but he *must* have his equal and opposite. Which brings us to *City of Doom* (I hate that "The" in front of *City*). Mocquino, the Voodoo Master, is back. Back like Moriarty from the Reichenbach Falls, back like the stench of Hitler on skinheads, back like the invisible push of evil that produces a backshove from The Shadow.

It is fitting and proper.

Just as it is fitting and proper that it is I, Harlan Ellison, who writes this snappy little foreword. You ask why? Well, to deliver the message (and pardonably proud of the content), be it known to you that according to the Great Genealogist of Popular Culture, the brilliant novelist and essayist, Mr. Philip José Farmer, in his recondite, his exhaustive lifeline of the Wold Newton Family that includes such familial links as Natty Bumppo, Doc Savage, The Scarlet Pimpernel, Lord John Roxton, James Bond, Travis McGee, Tarzan himself, and…The Shadow (*Doc Savage: His Apocalyptic Life,* still in print from Bantam Books, last time I checked), there appears the name "Cordwainer Bird." And as all but the palest naïf knows, C. Bird is my long-established, used-primarily-in-television pseudonym; and Bird as avenging juggernaut appears in the fabled novelette "The New York Review of Bird" wherein it is revealed, per Farmer, that Cordwainer Bird is no less a hearty than the actual blood nephew of The Shadow (I believe even constraint permits the use of an exclamation mark at this juncture)!

Credentials abound in my claim. Not only related to The Master of Darkness by purest blood am I, but hark: the last of the three determinedly readable temptations in this volume is a swell radio script of The Shadow written by Alfred Bester, the late author of *The Stars, My Destination* and *The Demolished Man* and more stunning short stories than any of us possessing the rarely-given Grand Master award of the Science Fiction/Fantasy Writers of America could hope to claim in *six* lifetimes of awards. The radio script recycles the immortal criminal originally called Vandal Savage from an earlier comic-book script Alfie wrote for *Green Lantern Comics*. And what has this to do with my bloviating justifications for introducing this volume?

I didn't know Walter Gibson, though we were both working in the trenches of pulp fiction at the same time: Walter had been at it for eons; I was recently booted out of Ohio State University for a quartet of singular offenses, not to mention what may well remain to this day—the lowest point-average in the history of that noble institution. We won't go into the matter of my giving a good one in the chops to the English professor who advised me I had no writing talent. I made my hegira to Manhattan, worked at jobs as odd and diverse as one might require for learning to write while living a life, but I don't think I ever ran across Walter Gibson. No, Maxwell Grant slipped through my skein. I knew Woolrich and Fred Dannay and Ron Hubbard and Heinlein and was, as you know, a very good friend of Isaac Asimov; but of Walter Gibson, sigh, nothing.

That is to say, I'm *pretty* certain I never met him. And yet…

Somewhere on the dark side of the moon that is my memory, there is a vagrant puff of pumice that is the recollection of my once having casually, fleetingly, met the great story-spinner, the progenitor of The Shadow. But I cannot exhume the meteorite that caused the puff, cannot remember if the remembering itself is of a real encounter, or just an unfulfilled desire. And so I will not claim such a meet.

But Tony Tollin had enough such liaisons—and will regale you *without* even a moment's notice, so you don't need my day-late-and-a-dollar-shy. But Bester, ah, that's a different game.

Met Alfie and his brilliant, endearing wife, Rollie, in 1953 or '54. At a meeting of the professional sf writers' klatches, The Hydra Club. Budrys, del Rey, de Camp, Fletcher Pratt, Harry Stine, Judy Merril, Pohl, Asimov, *all* of them. And I, still in my teens. And there was Bester, treated by all the stars and icons in the apartment as if he were a god recently fallen off a pedestal in Thrace. Even the best of them, the most arrogant among them, those who were being published once in a while in *Collier's* or *The Saturday Evening Post*, even they spoke to him with reverence. He was the fount, the source, a jewel existent in the universe in the number of one; and they all knew it.

How we became pals, I have no idea. I was green as grass, more mouth than man, but jackal-hungry to write well; and Alfie treated me as though I mattered, and we became friends, Bester and Rollie and the kid from Ohio.

Years later, as he lay dying, like most freelancers broke and waterlogged, he learned he had won the SFWA Grand Master award. No one can be sure he was cognizant enough to know what was being said to him, attended as he was by only the bartender who had taken care of him in his last days. But that worthy said Alfie *did* smile when he got the news. It was Robert Silverberg and myself who conveyed the news to the nurse, and begged her to go in *now* and tell him. I hope he knew; I hope he smiled.

And so, you get lagniappe this time around. Not just two "novels" with .45s cracking deadly, not just the return of The Voodoo Master, but one of the most fecund creators of marvelous fiction of the latter part of the 20th Century. Like Walter Gibson, Alfred Bester has left us, leaving us on the arid island of Judith Krantz and Tom Clancy and John Grisham. When we say of Gibson and Bester and their staunch workaholic types, that their like will be seen no more, it is a long, drawn-out whisper of sadness.

Bringing us back, of needs, to the concept that all good writers know: every superhero requires a supervillain; for each action there *must* be an equal and opposite reaction.

City of Doom is a prime example.

Rodil Mocquino is sharp. He's no laughable world-craver like most of the nitwits who fight James Bond—multibillionaires with mountain fastness eyries that must've cost more than a hundred big-budget dopey movies, who have rank after rank of crooks and minions working for them (whom they shoot out of pique every so often, so that we ask ourselves "I'll bet they don't even have a good dental plan; so why work for some schmuck who'll aerate your head if he's cranky?") and what's their endgame? What's their great evil plot?

"I want to take over television. I want to set East against West, and out of the radioactive smirch I'll establish a New World Order. I want to make my mommy proud of me via genocide."

No, give me Dr. Mocquino, a Red Blot, a Vandal Savage, a Cain…and I'll feel there is balance in the universe.

The Shadow was for me, as a kid, one of the most important McGuffey's Primers of ethics and morality and How to be a Stand-Up Guy. Kids that age today, well, if I start getting into that, someone a mere fifty or sixty years old will start whispering the dreaded contumely "geezer."

But kids today, as I see them in high schools and colleges where I lecture, simply don't get the simple truth that what they do or don't do has consequences. For every action (and I suppose frozen *in*action) there is a sigh in the skein, an idle rustle of the web. The Shadow knew of such things; he always knew. Today, no idol for the masses named The Shadow, or Steve Canyon, or Doc Savage. Today they have Paris Hilton, George W. Bush, Tom Cruise.

Where is a man with a pair of thundering .45s when you need him? Action…reaction!

HARLAN ELLISON is the multiple-award winning author of more than 1700 stories, non-fiction articles, columns, teleplays, essays and reviews; his oeuvre *currently stands at 76 published volumes including the 50-year-retrospective* The Essential Ellison. *Slated for release later this year is a documentary film about Ellison titled* Dreams with Sharp Teeth. *He is the 2006 SFWA Grand Master, one of only 29 so awarded; and he was on the preliminary list of American authors suggested for the Nobel Prize for Literature last year. He lives in Los Angeles with his wife, Susan.*

The City of Doom

A Complete Book-length Novel from the Private Annals of The Shadow, as told to

Maxwell Grant

CHAPTER I
AT THE STEEL WORKS

THICK night engulfed the valley about the town of Hampstead. One area alone showed brilliance; that was the central district of the little city, where rows of street lamps shone and electric signs added their blinking brightness.

Near the town, a few specks of light showed against the hillsides; but beyond was a blanket of blackness that seemed a shroud of doom. A stranger, viewing the town from some nearby

Back from the grave comes Doctor Mocquino, the Voodoo Master, to battle The Shadow again in a terrific struggle to the death!

slope, could well have pictured the darkness as a monster, about to swallow the city.

Nor would the thought have been too fanciful. Hampstead was a city touched by terror—a town where disaster had already taken toll.

Men who passed upon the streets were melancholy. Smiles were forced when friends exchanged their greetings. Though business was as usual, this was a surface indication only. Secretly, every citizen of Hampstead held a horror of the future.

Out where the railroad line reached the city limits, stood the long, low-roofed buildings of the Hampstead Steel Works. There, quivering light flickered from frosted windows, accompanied by the thrum and clank of machinery. The steel plant was working to capacity. The night shift was on duty.

Two men were standing in a little office, staring through the glass panel of a door that opened into the main furnace room. They were watching a crew of men at work—a score of hardy laborers whose faces showed grimy against the ruddy glare from open-fronted furnaces.

One of the observing men was the foreman of the furnace room. His companion was the general supervisor of the steel plant.

"IT'S been like clockwork tonight, Mr. Harlin," declared the foreman, solemnly. "Not a thing to trouble us. Every man's been right at his job."

Harlin nodded.

"I've been watching them, Steve," he told the foreman. "This department is running as smoothly as every other one. But we can't be sure about anything."

"On account of those other troubles?"

Another nod from Harlin. The supervisor pulled a folded newspaper from his pocket and tapped its headlines.

"This town is jinxed," he stated, seriously. "The people here know it. Our local newspapers have tried to soft-pedal it; but they haven't in other cities. Look at this sheet, Steve."

The foreman took the newspaper, studied it while the supervisor kept steady watch through the window in the door.

"Whew!" Steve's utterance was spontaneous. "They sure made a big *howdy-do* about those two wrecks in the railroad yards!"

"Why shouldn't they?" demanded Harlin. "Both were unexplainable. One would have been bad enough; but a second one, at the same spot, is ten times worse. Read what it says about the quarry company. They're shutting down."

"Afraid to bring in dynamite," nodded Steve. "On account of danger in the yards."

The supervisor continued his watch, while the foreman devoured more news from the out-of-town journal. Steve was mumbling in surprised tone, half to himself, half to the supervisor.

"Eight men killed in those smashes! We thought it was only three. Here are facts on that boiler explosion at the dye plant last week. Two men died along with the engineer! Say, if this gets out—"

The supervisor snapped a query that interrupted the foreman's muttering:

"Who's on the ladle, Steve?"

The foreman laid the newspaper aside and stared through the square window. A huge device shaped like a mammoth cheesebox was moving slowly through the furnace room, suspended from an overhead track. Workmen had ceased their labors while it approached. Harlin was eyeing the advance of the metal monster.

"Old Joe Grandy's handling it," declared the foreman. "Best man in the place. Always holds up when he gets close to the pouring platform, so as to check it for himself."

"Good!" approved the supervisor. "Grandy is reliable. Let's go out, though, and watch while he lets the ladle ride."

THE two men stepped from the office. The mammoth ladle halted as they approached it. They saw a stocky, gray-haired man climb down from a perch where the controls were located. Spryly, he stepped to the pouring platforms, which were at the side of the big room.

Checking those platforms was the foreman's job. It had been done; otherwise, no order would have been given for the ladle to make its trip. But old Joe Grandy took nothing for granted. His job was to tilt that ladle when it reached the pouring platforms; to loose tons of molten steel from the great cauldron that he controlled. Old Joe was making sure that the platforms and their troughs were ready.

"Grandy's the right man," affirmed the supervisor, nodding to Steve, the foreman. "We'll put his system in the regulations: Always stop the ladle short of the pouring platforms; make final inspection, then bring up the ladle."

"That's what Grandy's going to do now," returned Steve. Then, with a laugh: "Look how spry old Joe is! Shoving back those fellows who want to boost him up to the controls! He can make the climb himself."

Workers by the pouring platforms had seen the foreman. They were signaling that the second inspection had shown all in order. Others, beyond the pouring platform were chatting as they stood beneath the bulk of the motionless ladle.

"Steve!" ripped Harlin, suddenly. "What's making old Grandy wait? Why don't he move the ladle up to the platforms? That molten steel can't wait all night."

"He's ready to move it now," snapped back the foreman. "There he goes, handling the controls. Only five feet more and—"

Steve's voice broke with a gasp. Rooted, he stood goggle-eyed; then his new words came with a terrified shriek:

"Grandy's at the wrong lever! Look out—up by the platforms—"

The cry was too late. Old Grandy had swung away from the levers that controlled the forward motion of the ladle. He had placed his hand upon another rod; he was tugging it. The ladle was tilting; a yawning mouth was opening in its side.

Nothing could have halted the deluge that came. Not even old Joe Grandy; for he, least of all, seemed to realize his mistake. That was evidenced by the fact that his back was turned toward the tilting cauldron, giving him no chance to swing away to the safety of his perch.

Out from the mammoth ladle came a cataract of liquid steel, more terrible than the flaming lava of a volcano. With its first gulp, the surge of molten metal overwhelmed the unfortunate man who had released it. Grandy, a shriek upon his lips, was plucked from the forward edge of his control perch. A bobbing shape in a hissing, metallic wave, the gray-haired man was pitched to the floor beside the pouring platforms.

As the wave struck, five other men were caught within its path. Roaring, its own weight adding to the quick tilt of the ladle, the molten steel crashed with the power of a Niagara, engulfing the doomed men below.

Not one of the five could scramble to safety. The cries that they managed to utter were brief— a momentary recognition of the quick death which was coming to them.

Steel scorched flesh, withering its victims before their bodies could sense the pain of the terrific heat. A blast of torrid air swept through the huge room, drowning the fumes of the furnaces. Then molten steel was everywhere, pouring, spreading, seeking lower levels while men found their legs and ran shrieking from the monstrous substance that sought them.

STEVE bolted forward. Harlin grabbed the foreman, hurled him back against the office door. There was no help for the men upon the floor, except the aid that they could give themselves. Harlin, above the level of the flow, held his vantage point and shouted advice to the men.

Some heard the supervisor and heeded. They leaped for iron steps between the furnaces; scrambled upward to levels of safety. Others did not hear. Confused, they lost all sense of direction. Harlin saw three more workers go to doom. Spreading steel caught their ankles, seemed to trip them as they howled. They sprawled, splashing, into the hellish river that had gripped them.

A fourth man, farther away, stumbled at the foot of an iron stairway. He could not follow Harlin's call; but a companion heard the supervisor's shout. From the steps, the other worker snatched the last man to safety. The steel lapped the base of the steps; its heat made the ironwork glow and quiver.

The supervisor sagged, weakened by his ordeal. Nine men had perished including old Joe Grandy, whose slip had loosed the molten horror. The liquid metal had reached its limits; it had lapped the fronts of furnaces, found an emergency doorway. But that would be its farthest mark.

Steadying himself, Harlin managed to reach the office. He was looking for Steve, to tell him that the steel would harden. There would be no more human toll; but other loss would prove tremendous. Harlin found the foreman at the telephone.

"I've called for ambulances!" gulped Steve. "Thanks, Mr. Harlin, for hauling me back! I'd most certainly have jumped in there—"

The foreman buried his head in his hands; the supervisor found a chair.

"No use, those ambulances," he choked. "Not even hearses could find work here, Steve! There'll be no bodies from that mess. They were swallowed alive, Steve, lost in that steel! It happened—worse than I feared."

The clang of ambulances was already sounding. The wail of a huge siren was rising from the steelworks. As Steve arose and pressed open a window to relieve the stifling atmosphere, he and Harlin could see the lights of automobiles stopping on the highway that led into Hampstead.

Once again, stark terror had found this city of doom. The siren's wail; the clang of bells; the shouts of men outside—all were proclaiming the horrendous news.

Rescuers, yanking open a door, saw the seething spread of steel that glistened in the glow of furnaces. They heard the calls of men who were isolated in spots of safety—shouts that warned them to stay back and let the metal cool.

The word passed in terrified tones. It stopped the arriving ambulances. It came to squads of men from other portions of the plant and held them, in awed groups, whispering the news of tragedy.

Those whispers reached the space where cars had pulled in from the highway. Breathless men told others of the terror that had struck; how rescue would be impossible for those who had felt the touch of living, burning steel.

WITHIN the window of a coupe, a silent listener caught those tragic mutters. His eyes turned toward the building where the hellish stream had done its work. The driver of that coupe had chanced to reach the outskirts of Hampstead just as the steel plant's siren had broken loose with its banshee screech of disaster.

A lone watcher among the throngs who

huddled about the steel works—such was the arrival in the coupe. Yet he, more than any other, held regret for the tragedy that had occurred. He had come to Hampstead with a single mission: to prevent disasters such as this. He had reached the town too late to halt the new stroke of unexplainable deaths.

The silent watcher in the coupe was The Shadow. Master of crime detection, he had divined the presence of an evil, unseen hand behind the horrors which had come to Hampstead.

There was determination in the blaze of The Shadow's steady eyes. This tragedy would be the last. No longer would destruction stalk through the city of doom.

CHAPTER II
FROM THE DARK

Two hours had passed since the catastrophe at the steel plant. Lights were glowing in the large furnace room, where workers were present, using electric drills upon chunks of hardened steel. Outside, the glimmer of flashlights told that guards were patrolling the vicinity of the plant.

There were lights in another building. They came from windows on the second floor and marked the offices of the steel company. There was a downstairs door, where a guard stood on duty, chatting with a companion.

"The big guns is upstairs," informed the guard, in an undertone. "They showed up half an hour ago."

"Listening to Harlin and Steve, are they?"

"Sure. The coroner's there with them. Harlin looked pretty shaky when he went up."

"He ought to. Seeing them fellows get swallowed by that steel must have been kind of tough to look at."

With this comment, the guard's friend started away. The guard called after him:

"See if you can find Travers over by the furnace. Tell him it's time I was off the trick. Have him send over some fellow from his own crew."

Three minutes passed, while the guard paced back and forth in front of the dim light that came from the doorway. There was a stir in darkness close by. The guard wheeled, with the query:

"Who's there?"

"Came over to relieve you," responded a gruff voice. "Mr. Travers sent me."

The guard did not see the speaker; but took it for granted that he was the proper man. He grunted a good night and walked away from the door. It was not until he had passed a corner that a figure stepped into the light.

That form was cloaked in black. The arrival was The Shadow. He had heard the conversation; he had taken advantage of it. He had bluffed the guard into believing that he was the man sent as relief watcher.

THE SHADOW did not linger at the doorway. He knew that Travers's man would soon arrive. He wanted the new guard to think that the old one had simply gone off duty because his time was up. The Shadow's own work lay elsewhere.

Entering the doorway, The Shadow took to a darkened flight of stairs. He ascended and reached a hallway that showed a narrow shaft of light from a partly opened door. Edging in from darkness, The Shadow saw the interior of an office.

Officials were gathered about a table. With these company men was another whom The Shadow knew must be the coroner. Harlin was seated at the far end of the table. The supervisor looked pale; his voice came brokenly as he spoke.

"That's the whole story!" declared Harlin. "Just as I saw it, gentlemen. Nothing was wrong mechanically. The mistake was a human one; and those kind are bound to happen."

"We have your full report on Joseph Grandy," returned the coroner, fingering a sheaf of papers. "I regard it as thorough, Mr. Harlin. We can accept the statements of the foreman and three laborers that Grandy was in full possession of his faculties."

"The most reliable man in the plant," stated Harlin. "Always sober and conscientious. A loyal fellow, too, old Joe was. He didn't know the slip he'd made; if he had, he wouldn't have been the first to go."

The coroner drew a penciled diagram from the papers. It was a sketch made by Harlin, showing the position of the levers that controlled the big ladle.

"I think that this explains it," decided the coroner, with a nod. "With all his carefulness, Grandy performed certain actions automatically. He was farther forward than he realized. When he reached for the starting lever, he grasped the tilting device instead."

"That's the way I saw it, coroner," assured the supervisor. "The diagram bears out my explanation."

The coroner arose; he put Harlin's report into a briefcase: then passed carbon sheets across the table to the supervisor. Other men were rising; The Shadow saw them pause. One of the officials had a query.

"Tell us this, coroner," he asked, in troubled tone. "Do you connect this accident with the other disasters that have occurred in Hampstead?"

Emphatically, the coroner shook his head.

"But they look like sabotage," persisted the official. "This is the fourth accident; and every one brought heavy property damage along with its toll of life."

The coroner reached in his briefcase and brought out some sheets of yellow paper. He passed them across the table.

"File those with your own duplicate report," he suggested. "They give the details of the explosion at the dye works, the smashups in the railroad yards. Compare them with the disaster here. You'll see that I am right. In not one instance, was there any outside factor.

"I've had lots of experience, gentlemen. Sometimes accidental deaths are uncanny. Like an epidemic, you might say. A year—two years—no trouble; then they hit in a bunch. That doesn't mean a thing, unless there's proof that someone was culpable or negligent. Not one of these cases shows any such indications."

HARLIN had taken the duplicate sheets. The Shadow saw the supervisor place them in a table drawer. Then it was time to step away; for the men were coming toward the door. The Shadow swung to a darkened corner; when the door opened, it moved outward and covered him completely.

Harlin was the last man from the office. He waited while the others went down the stairs to the lighted entry at the bottom. Then the supervisor clicked off the office light. The top landing was dark when he closed the door and locked it. Harlin had no chance to see The Shadow.

Soon after the supervisor's footsteps had faded, a tiny flashlight shone upon the office door. Its glow was but twice the size of the keyhole; but it was sufficient for The Shadow to work upon the lock. A gloved hand introduced a long thin instrument that resembled a pair of pliers. A *click* came from the lock. The Shadow opened the office door.

Using his flashlight within the office, The Shadow found the drawer that contained the report sheets. He spread the duplicate papers and began a close study of past events in Hampstead. The Shadow soon learned that the coroner's claims were well supported.

The boiler blast at the dye plant had occurred shortly after a routine inspection. The cause had evidently been the failure of a worn safety valve. The engineer had made the inspection himself; he was a man of long service, who would not have omitted an essential detail; nor have been so foolish as to tamper with the machinery.

The first wreck in the railroad yards had occurred when a switchman highballed a shifting locomotive along the main track. The engine had taken the siding instead, mowing down the switchman who stood in its path.

The second wreck had been a brakeman's error. He had been crushed when a string of freight cars crashed into a motionless line of day coaches. In both cases, additional lives had been lost.

Tonight's disaster at the steel plant resembled the others, in two definite ways. First: that no one from outside had tampered with any machinery; second: that old Joe Grandy, like others who had died before him, had been sound mentally and alert in action. Not one of the men who had borne the brunt of disaster could have chosen to make a deliberate mistake.

Behind disasters stood crime, engendered by some master-plotter. A genius of evil was at work in Hampstead. Through some process, this unknown criminal had managed to control the minds of unwitting men. A master of murder and destruction had chosen to work with human tools, of whom old Joe Grandy was the fourth.

The fact that this theory smacked of the incredible was something that gave it strength. There was a reason, however, why The Shadow accepted it immediately. A few days ago, The Shadow had sent a trusted agent to Hampstead to investigate disasters there. That agent's name was Harry Vincent. No word had been received from him since yesterday.

Harry's disappearance had brought The Shadow to Hampstead. The steel plant disaster, at the very time of The Shadow's arrival, had simply added to the supersleuth's belief that crime stood behind every accident that had struck the city of doom.

EXTINGUISHING his flashlight, The Shadow left the company office. He reached the bottom of the stairs to find total darkness. No guard was present; if one had come on duty, he had gone when the officials departed.

The Shadow reached the highway, crossed it and arrived at his coupe, which he had wisely parked in the shelter of a side road before beginning his investigation. The car was just within the town limits of Hampstead. Ten minutes' drive would bring The Shadow to the heart of the little city.

That short journey was to be fraught with danger. Starting his car, The Shadow swung out to the main highway. He headed townward and came immediately to a quarter-mile stretch where buildings were few. Hardly had The Shadow struck this open space before a rakish touring car roared out from the darkness beside a closed filling station.

Instantly, The Shadow knew what was due. Prowlers had spotted his coupe near the steel plant. They had decided that the car belonged to some independent investigator. They had gone into ambush to waylay the coupe when it arrived.

A machine gun rattled. Instantly, The Shadow veered his coupe from the touring car's path. He swung his automobile into a ditch; let it careen and stop with a jolt, tilted far to the left. The men in the touring car thought that they had scored an instant hit. The rakish machine slowed as it swung toward the halted coupe.

An automatic spoke from the darkness of the ditch, just behind the coupe. The Shadow had dived from the wheel, unscathed. He had waited for close range; his first shot was aimed for the rear door of the touring car, where he knew the machine gunners would be.

A howl answered The Shadow's blast. He delivered a second gunshot; another yell was the response. The Shadow had winged a second crook.

The touring car shot forward. Its canny driver gave it a zigzag twist, wheeling over so that the bulk of The Shadow's coupe would make the invisible marksman seek a new vantage point. The lights of the touring car blinked off. Its driver, knowing the road, was chancing darkness.

A mocking laugh sounded in the darkness of the ditch, as The Shadow boarded his tilted coupe. Victor in the short-lived fray, The Shadow had gained the proof he wanted. Crime lay behind the disasters in Hampstead—crime so big that it needed murderous crews to back it in a pinch.

This first encounter would bring others. Battles and opposition could produce clues. The Shadow was satisfied that his stay in Hampstead would lead him to a master-villain's lair.

CHAPTER III
THE DEATH THRUST

IT was half an hour before The Shadow reached the center of Hampstead, for he chose a roundabout course that finally brought him to an obscure garage. His purpose was not to avoid a new encounter; he would have welcomed such a fray. But The Shadow knew that there would be no new ambush.

Spies would be the next enemies. They would be watching for The Shadow's coupe, in hope of identifying its occupants. Hence The Shadow chose to enter Hampstead from another direction; to keep his car away from the main streets. He had, moreover, delayed five minutes during his circuit. In that interval he had changed the license plates on his coupe.

When The Shadow strolled from the obscure garage, he was no longer clad in black. Street lamps showed him dressed in a dark-gray suit. His features were full and bore little of the hawkish aspect which enemies identified with The Shadow's countenance. The Shadow was carrying a large suitcase, which contained his cloak and hat. He looked like a tourist who had stopped off in Hampstead.

The railroad station was near the garage. An approaching whistle told that a passenger train was due. Picking an obscure route, The Shadow neared the depot and stood by an old freight shed until the train arrived. A dozen passengers alighted; half of them had bags. The Shadow stepped up to the station platform and mingled with the small throng. Two arrivals were going toward an old sedan that served as taxi. The Shadow followed them.

The driver announced that his cab took passengers to the Hampstead House. The two men boarded the car and The Shadow joined them. They rode through the main streets and pulled up in front of a pretentious hotel. If spies were about, they took The Shadow merely for another passenger, who had come into town by train.

The Shadow let the two other men register first. He wrote his own name as "Henry Arnaud," with Chicago as his home city. The name and identity of Arnaud were The Shadow's own device. He used them upon occasions such as this.

THERE was a lone clerk at the desk, and only two bell boys available. This meant a delay in room assignments. The Shadow took advantage of it to note the lobby. He saw no potential spies. It was possible that crooks had decided to head for cover, after their fray. That was not surprising, since they had carried away two wounded men.

As he lingered by the hotel desk, secure in his role of Arnaud, The Shadow was rewarded for his courtesy in letting others register ahead of him. The hotel manager came from a little office, spoke to the clerk in an undertone that The Shadow caught.

"This man in 328," queried the manager. "You're sure that his luggage is gone?"

"Positive, sir!" replied the clerk. "He's jumped his bill, all right! Looks like he went out by the window."

"Three floors down?"

"Room 328 is over the kitchen roof, and that's two stories high, sir. The window was open when the maid found the room vacated. I told her to leave everything as it was."

"Humph! Let that room stay empty. I'll go up and look it over myself in the morning. Give me that fellow's full name and a report on what he looks like. He won't beat this hotel and get away with it!"

The Shadow thus learned new facts concerning

his vanished agent. He had already known Harry's room number: 328. He had not known, however, whether Harry had left the hotel openly or been carried away a prisoner. Nor had The Shadow cared to make inquiry. The chance conversation had saved him such a task.

The room to which The Shadow was assigned happened to be on the fourth floor; but at a different side of the hotel than 328. The Shadow spent a short while in his room; then turned out the lights. Any observer would have supposed that he was either going down to the lobby or that he intended to retire. The Shadow did neither.

From his suitcase, he removed black cloak and slouch hat. He tucked a brace of .45 automatics under the folds of his cloak. After donning thin black gloves, he added a tiny flashlight and a set of picks to his equipment. That done, The Shadow opened the door of the room and squeezed out into the corridor, blocking light from the hall.

There was a stairway leading down to the third floor. It was near Room 428, therefore The Shadow knew that it would offer convenient access to Harry's former room, just below. The stairway was but dimly lighted. The Shadow made a fleeting shape as he descended. At this third floor, he peered along the nearest corridor.

Crooks had captured Harry Vincent. There was a strong chance that they suspected their prisoner to be an aide of The Shadow. That, in itself, could have accounted for the ambush on the room. Crooks would also guess that The Shadow knew Harry's room number at the Hampstead House. They would expect him to visit it. This room might prove another ambush.

THE SHADOW eyed every visible door. From gloom, he had the advantage. The slightest motion would have told him that crooks were keeping watch on 328. No indication came. The Shadow deduced that crooks intended to keep clear of the hotel, particularly since they knew there would be a fuss about Harry's sudden departure.

The Shadow moved out into the corridor, reached the door of 328. He worked smoothly, quickly, with the lock. The key of his own room had given him sufficient idea of what the locks were like throughout the hotel. The door yielded.

The room was almost pitch-dark for it was at the back of the hotel, away from any streetlights. The Shadow could feel a breeze from the open window. Approaching, he made out the flat shape of the kitchen roof not far below. There was another building across the street; blank-walled, it appeared to be the hotel garage. Two stories high, the building's roof was on a level with the window where The Shadow stood.

Turning in from the wide-opened window, The Shadow moved about the room, blinking his flashlight in evasive fashion. He was looking for spots that might offer clues. His light dabbed the wall with a small, luminous circle; then touched doors, articles of furniture. Finally, it streaked along the floor.

There, The Shadow spied a clue. Straight across from the opened window was a small table that stood against the inner wall of the room, by the head of the bedstead. That table was slightly oblong. Marks in the carpet showed that it should stand endwise, with a short side against the wall.

The table, however, had been moved, to bring one of its broad sides against the wall. The Shadow saw a reason for the new position. Crosswise, the table could cover a greater stretch of wall. It had been placed thus to hide something on the wall.

The logical step was to remove the table from its position. The Shadow turned out his flashlight. His cloak swished in the darkness; but oddly, there was no sound of motion from the table. Once or twice, the flashlight blinked in guarded fashion, that was all. Then came a pause—an interval of fully a dozen seconds.

That time space was a lull before the surprise that came.

A sudden glare filled the room. It was the beam of a brilliant, straight-focused spotlight, coming from the garage roof across the way. Blazing in from darkness, the bright gleam showed the head of the bed; but not the table beside it. The reason was, that the table stood obscured by a crouched shape clad in black.

It was a sight that some ambushed observer had hoped to see: The Shadow, stooped motionless, in front of that table. Hard upon the blaze of light came another occurrence, so swift that even The Shadow could not have wheeled in time to escape it. A driving object whistled through the window at terrific speed. Like an arrow, it found the cloak between the shoulders; drove to a stop and wavered.

The missile was a knife. It had buried itself full way to the hilt, in the shape beneath the black cloak. Slowly, the stooping form tumbled forward and sprawled in huddled fashion in front of the little table.

As the figure stilled upon the floor, the light from the garage roof was extinguished. Blackness took control along with silence. The death-thrust had been delivered; assassins were departing from the field. Well had they chosen their ambush.

MINUTES passed in the silent hotel room. A flashlight blinked from the corner, following along the floor. It reached the huddled form; a whispered laugh sounded in the darkness. A gloved hand plucked away the knife. It came easily; then the cloak was drawn aside. No knife thrust had found The Shadow. The only victim had been a pillow from the bed.

From the moment that he had noted the turned table, The Shadow had expected a trap—because of the line to the opened window. He had used darkness to prepare a ruse; and his hoax had worked. The Shadow had tilted a chair back against the table, so neatly that only a scant half inch of chair top prevented the whole chair from toppling. Upon the seat of the chair he had placed a pillow; over it, his cloak, draped to form a shape when seen from without the window. The slouch hat had formed the last touch of deception.

The knife had driven through the back of the cloak; it had cleaved the pillow and its point had penetrated the woodwork of the chair. The force of the blow had been sufficient to make the chair back begin a slide from the table. It was the chair, muffled beneath cloak and pillow, that had thudded to the carpet like a huddling human figure.

Listening from a corner near the window, The Shadow had heard enough sounds when the spotlight was extinguished. He knew that his enemies had abandoned their post. This was his opportunity to finish his investigation.

In darkness, The Shadow moved away the table. He glimmered his flashlight upon the wall. There, in penciled letters on the wallpaper, he read:

R-6384

Had Harry Vincent left that clue? It seemed likely to The Shadow. Why had crooks not erased it? The answer was obvious: they had guessed that the penciled marks would interest The Shadow long enough to hold him at the death spot.

Extinguishing his flashlight, The Shadow replaced the pillow on the bed. He put the chair as it belonged; pressed the table against the wall. Donning cloak and hat, he moved from the room, locking the door behind him. The Shadow went to the stairway, ascended halfway to the fourth floor.

Some minutes later, he heard creeping sounds below. Men were coming up to Room 328. They had a double purpose: to remove a dead body; to erase the marks that lay behind the table. They would be nonplused when they discovered that The Shadow was gone.

The Shadow waited; soon he heard the footsteps return, then scurry down the stairs.

Underlings had gone to report the amazing news that they had found no victim. Promptly, The Shadow descended to the third floor, to find the door of 328 unlocked. Quickly, he pulled aside the table and blinked his tiny light. The number R-6384 had been erased. The visitors had not forgotten that detail. The number was an actual clue.

PAUSING, The Shadow stared toward the window and noted the dim edge of the garage roof. On a straight line with the opened window, it told him another story—regarding the knife thrust from the dark. No thrown blade could have followed so straight a path. The uppermost point of its curve would have brought it too high to go through the window. The knife had been dispatched by a powerful, muffled air gun.

With this knowledge of a unique weapon in the arsenal of his foemen, The Shadow made his final departure from Room 328. With gliding tread, he returned to his own room on the fourth floor. From the side window, he surveyed the few streetlights which remained illuminated at this late hour.

A soft laugh in the darkness foretold The Shadow's next adventures. He had foiled his enemies tonight. His own identity concealed, he would be ready on the morrow. Then would he search for the master of crime, who, like The Shadow himself, was hidden.

Whether or not Harry's lone clue would be useless, The Shadow would not cease his efforts until he uncovered the brain who had made Hampstead a city of doom.

CHAPTER IV
THE MAN WHO RETURNED

THE next day found the town of Hampstead in furor. The disaster at the steel plant had shaken the nerves of the hardiest citizens. Those who had feared the future were looked upon as prophets. Anyone who voiced belief in new terror found many listeners.

Hampstead was distinctly an industrial town. It formed the center of a large rural area; and boasted the only factories in the section. It followed that Hampstead was also a railroad center; and the quarries among the neighboring hills gave the city an added importance.

Hence Hampstead depended upon industry; and the threat was therefore the most pressing that the town could possibly encounter.

Today's rumors were unrestricted. The local newspapers had yielded to the strain; they were publishing facts that had hitherto been suppressed. Hampstead realized that a hoodoo lay upon it. That belief was supported by intelligent persons as well as ignorant.

Morning found the dye works closed. Workers had been grumbling ever since the explosion of a week before. The owners had decided to mark time; for they felt that they would be regarded as culpable, if another disaster should occur upon their premises. Already the quarry companies had ceased operations because of the freight yard wrecks. They came out with an announcement that they would bring no explosives into Hampstead until the railroad company could supply a satisfactory answer concerning the freight car smashes.

The steel plant was closed; until the furnace room was put in proper shape, it could not reopen. The officials, when questioned, were unwilling to state when they intended to resume business. Other industries were making a last effort to stem the rising tide of public opposition. Privately, owners met among themselves, to agree that one new disaster would be the last. Should it occur, Hampstead would become a city abandoned by enterprise.

It was known that certain plants had arranged for police protection. Among these were the Century Chemical Company and the Hampstead Knitting Mills, for they represented the most important industries other than the dye works and the steel plant. The chemical company dealt in dangerous materials; the knitting mills employed hundreds of persons. Both concerns knew that they had much at stake.

Nevertheless, to close down would be folly. No threats had been delivered; nothing suspicious had occurred at either plant. The leaders of industry in Hampstead were determined to hold together for a last effort against the strange jinx that had settled upon the enterprising city.

Nevertheless, late afternoon brought a feeling of dread. The main plants in Hampstead were working overtime. Other tragedies had struck during evening hours. Tonight would be the time for new disaster, should it come.

TO The Shadow, this had been a day of futile effort. In his guise of Henry Arnaud, he had hired a sedan in place of the coupe that he had stowed away. He had driven about Hampstead, passing the chemical works and the knitting mills. He had noted other factories; he had located the city's electric powerhouse. The Shadow had seen no signs of threatening danger.

Nor had The Shadow gained any traces of departed crooks. Covering ground close to Hampstead, he failed to discover any houses that could serve as hideouts. When he drove back to the hotel at sunset, The Shadow was forced to admit that his quest had been blank. That very fact disturbed him most; for The Shadow, of all persons in Hampstead, knew how real the threat of doom could be.

Street lamps were aglow when The Shadow entered the dining room of the Hampstead House and took a table by the window. Those lights were early; for the sun had scarcely set. Looking across the street at an angle, The Shadow could plainly observe the fronts of pretentious homes that had been converted into apartment houses.

Just as dinner was being served to the guest who called himself Henry Arnaud, a large gray car, a limousine, pulled up in front of one of the apartments. The chromium-plated radiator caught the glow of a street lamp just above. The same illumination shone on the car's license plate. From a distance of some forty yards, The Shadow read the license number: R-6384.

The number was etched in The Shadow's thoughts. He had been looking constantly for some sign of it. That was the number The Shadow had found inscribed upon the wall of Harry Vincent's room.

A chauffeur was stepping from the big car. The Shadow saw him open a door. A stooped man came from the automobile; he leaned upon the chauffeur's arm, then shifted his weight to a heavy cane. The Shadow caught a view of a muffled face; round, blackened spots indicated dark spectacles that the man was wearing.

The chauffeur preceded his master to the apartment house door, rang a bell and awaited a response. When it came, the chauffeur opened the door and held it while the stooped man entered. After that, the chauffeur returned to the car and drove away.

Watching upstairs windows, The Shadow had only a short wait. A light glimmered suddenly from a room on the second floor.

THE SHADOW lost no time in finishing dinner. He went up to his room, packed garments in a small, pliable briefcase and came downstairs again. Strolling from the hotel, he noticed that the upstairs lights were still burning in the apartment across the way.

Crossing the street, The Shadow calmly approached the door that the bespectacled man had entered. He noted a list of names on the wall mailboxes of the open vestibule. Apartment 2 A bore the name Herbert Prensham; apartment 2 B showed a vacancy.

Both facts were useful. One told the name of the man who had gone up to the front apartment on the second floor. The other indicated an excellent means of entry. The Shadow stepped down to the sidewalk, strolled around the block and came to a narrow alley behind the buildings. He followed it until he reached the house he wanted.

In a darkened space, The Shadow opened his briefcase. He donned cloak and slouch hat; strapped the pliable briefcase under his cloak.

Picking an ornamental ledge in the stone wall of the house, The Shadow began an upward climb.

He gripped a fastened shutter beside a first floor window, used it in ladder fashion and reached the second floor. Another ledge gave him a foothold while he jimmied a window in the rear apartment. Swinging over the ledge, The Shadow entered an empty room.

Through darkness, The Shadow reached the outer hall, to find it unlighted. He picked a path along the wall until he arrived at a door which he knew must be Apartment 2 A. The knob turned noiselessly at The Shadow's touch. The door was unlocked; it yielded inward under pressure.

Silently, The Shadow stepped into a passage. At the front were the lights of a living room. Peering from the passage, The Shadow could see that the shades had been drawn. He knew that they must have been lowered during the time that he had been circling the block.

Approaching closer to the front of the passage, The Shadow spied a bent man seated in a large chair, his feet upon a footstool. The man was Herbert Prensham, whom The Shadow had seen alight from the large automobile.

Prensham's face was tilted forward, his chin buried in the collar of a dressing gown. His dark spectacles still covered his eyes. The stooped man was motionless, apparently dozing. His left hand lay limply upon a table beside his chair.

There, also, The Shadow observed a squatty table lamp, with a large, unfrosted bulb upright in the socket. The lamp shade had fallen from place and was lying on the table. Prensham had apparently not noticed it.

No one else was in the room. Unless Prensham himself had risen to lower the window shades, some intruder must have come and gone before The Shadow's arrival. There was something sinister in that possibility—a connection with the cryptic numerals that The Shadow had found in Harry Vincent's room.

The number R-6384 had signified only the license number of Prensham's car. Had Harry left it as a clue to a man whose life was threatened? Danger lurked here in Hampstead; The Shadow was ready for any startling development. The longer he gazed at the slouched, immobile form of Prensham, the more certain he became that the man's lethargy was not normal.

STILL within the darkness of the passage, The Shadow drew an automatic from beneath his cloak. Swinging into the mellow light of the living room, he glanced keenly toward the inner wall, in search of another doorway. There was none. The Shadow had come in by the only entrance.

In his gaze, The Shadow took in the furnishings. They were luxurious. Oriental rugs adorned the floors; chairs and tables were of fine, dark mahogany. Rich tapestries hung from the walls. In that setting, Herbert Prensham looked pitiful and helpless, as if he—though master of this room—had no ability to appreciate his surroundings.

The Shadow, however, concentrated his gaze upon the man in the chair. Advancing, he studied Prensham, to learn the reason for the man's stupor.

As The Shadow came closer, Prensham stirred. He raised his head, proving that his ears were keen enough to hear the footsteps of the soft-treading visitor. Apparently, Prensham could not see The Shadow through his dark spectacles; for he whined a puzzled query:

"Who's there?"

Motionless, his automatic leveled in his fist, The Shadow gave no response.

"Who's there?" demanded Prensham, his voice testy. "Is it you, Banzarro?"

The Shadow maintained his silence. Prensham's hands came upward. His body straightened as his fingers lifted away the dark spectacles and let them drop into his lap. Simultaneously, the man in the chair delivered a short, musical laugh. His lips produced a gloating smile; his eyes—black in hue—showed an evil sparkle.

With the dropping of the spectacles, the man in the chair had seen The Shadow; but his manner showed that he had expected to view the very visitor whom he saw. His sleep had been feigned; he had waited for this moment to drop away the darkened glasses that amply disguised his face. With the action, the seated man had revealed his identity to The Shadow.

The cloaked visitor recognized the man who called himself Herbert Prensham. Uncannily, The Shadow had suspected danger: that was why he had leveled his automatic toward the man in the chair. The Shadow had anticipated a surprise; yet even he was not prepared for this one. The face revealed to him was one that he had never expected to see alive.

The man in the chair was Doctor Rodil Mocquino, the most insidious foeman whom The Shadow had ever encountered—Doctor Mocquino, the so-called Voodoo Master, whose last reign of crime had been ended by The Shadow. Downed by bullets from The Shadow's guns, Mocquino had last been seen alive when he had plunged, badly wounded, beneath the surface of the Hudson River.*

Even to The Shadow, it was amazing that Doctor Mocquino had returned to life. But with

*Note: See *The Voodoo Master*, Volume #3

the present discovery, The Shadow had gained the end of his first trail. The disasters in the town of Hampstead were explainable, since Doctor Mocquino still remained a living threat.

The Shadow was face to face with the master-villain who had brought terror to this city of doom.

CHAPTER V
THE STALEMATE

"I HAVE awaited you."

Doctor Mocquino spoke the words in musical tone. His manila-hued face was smiling; his dark eyes flashed in friendly fashion. Without moving from his chair, the one-time Voodoo Master gestured with his open right hand.

"Be seated," he invited. "We have much to discuss, you and I."

Mocquino was pointing to a chair between himself and the window. The Shadow kept his eyes toward the Voodoo Master; his gun, in his right hand, was leveled with his gaze. Using his left hand, he drew the chair toward himself, then sat down facing Mocquino.

The Shadow had placed himself at a slight angle to Mocquino's right. The unshaded lamp upon the table was so placed that it stood almost in line with The Shadow's gaze. Mocquino flipped a switch in the base of the lamp, using a single finger.

Instantly, there came a result that showed why the Voodoo Master had lowered the window blinds. The unfrosted bulb delivered a blinding brilliance. Its light was of the most startling sort, a pyrotechnic display within a rounded bowl of glass. Every possible color of light burst loose with dazzling blaze. Like sparks from bursting fireworks, the colors sparkled soundlessly within the bulb. They darted everywhere, those sparks, changing their flashes with kaleidoscopic speed.

The Shadow sat riveted, his eyes upon the startling display. Doctor Mocquino's right hand had come upward; his fingers had promptly replaced his spectacles over his eyes. Thus he escaped those blinding flashes that burned before The Shadow's gaze. Mocquino's laugh was harsh, its musical tone ended. The Voodoo Master deliberately pulled the little switch; the dazzle faded from the blazing bulb. With both hands, Mocquino removed his glasses and spoke to his cloaked visitor.

"You are helpless!" jeered the Voodoo Master. "You, too, have experienced the blinding glare that the others received! You have gone through the ordeal that causes men to see the things that I command! You are in my power! Rise; stand silent; then receive my bidding!"

The Shadow came to his feet while Mocquino chortled. The Voodoo Master's gloat ended a moment later. The Shadow did not stand his ground; instead, he advanced straight forward. The muzzle of his automatic pressed toward Mocquino's eyes. Above the gun, the astonished Voodoo Master saw a blazing gaze, unaltered by the dazzle that The Shadow had faced.

"Speak, Mocquino!" ordered The Shadow. "Tell of the crimes that you committed; of the evil that you intend! I am the one who holds command!"

THE SHADOW had met the Voodoo Master's test. Whatever its effect upon others, the blazing bulb had failed to stagger The Shadow.

Mocquino's face showed huge surprise; his lips were scarcely able to deliver a snarl. It was rage, however, not fear, that had struck the Voodoo Master.

"You command me to speak," mouthed Mocquino. "Listen, then, and hear the facts you came to learn! I brought them here, the men I needed. I let them see the blazing bulb. It left them dazzled, ready for my command.

"While each man sat dazed, I told him how he was to ignore his duty. Each went his way, remembering his experience, like something from a dim past. Each sought to recall what had happened. Memories jogged them at the proper moment; the exact time that I had named."

The Shadow thrust his automatic beneath his cloak; it was a gesture of his contempt for Mocquino's power. He needed no more information regarding the system that the Voodoo Master had employed.

A master of hypnotic influence, Mocquino had applied it to the accomplishment of crime, through men who served as helpless instruments. All hypnotism being dependent upon the full concentration of the person subjected to it, Mocquino had devised the sparkling bulb as a mechanical way of forcing fixed vision. Through the dazzling effect of myriad colored sparks, he had jolted each victim into a state of temporary bewilderment.

That done, he had assigned each a task. The engineer at the dye plant had been told to release the safety valve on the boiler, when he made inspection. Switchman and brakeman both had been instructed to signal locomotives onward; then stand in the engine's path.

Old Joe Grandy had responded to an impulse given him by Mocquino; he had handled the wrong lever at the given moment, when he stood upon his perch beside the ladle of molten steel.

In each case, Mocquino was a murderer. The Voodoo Master had purposely sent his hypnotic victims to their own destruction. He had hoped to do the same with The Shadow. He had failed. His own statement had been forced from Mocquino's reluctant lips.

More was required. Mocquino heard The Shadow's voice, with its commanding tone:

"Proceed! State the crimes that you have planned for the future!"

Mocquino's teeth gritted. His clawish hands clutched the arms of his chair. Despite the steadiness of The Shadow's gaze, Mocquino rallied.

"I have told enough!" he retorted, harshly. "You caught me by surprise, when you met the ordeal that I gave you. I have told of past crimes; I shall not speak of future!"

THE SHADOW'S right hand whipped from beneath the cloak. Again, Mocquino was confronted by the leveled muzzle of an automatic that threatened to burn a message of instant death. The Voodoo Master glared savagely; then managed to deliver an evil smile.

"Why should I speak?" he queried, his voice regaining its smooth, insidious tone. "You cannot afford to kill me when you know the facts that concern your agent, Harry Vincent. He is my prisoner—he and others who tried to block my path! There are five of them in all. My death will mean theirs!

"I took the precaution to place them where escape is impossible. Their time of death has been set every twelve hours. Each time that the execution is due, I postpone it. Should I die, there will be no one to countermand the order.

"Kill me if you choose. By doing so, you will give the death warrant for men whom you have come to save. Moreover, my future crimes are scheduled. They will proceed like clockwork; for my subordinates are men who will not fail in obedience to my given commands."

Mocquino's tone had regained its strength. The Shadow knew that the Voodoo Master spoke the truth. Forced to accept the issue as it stood, The Shadow thrust his automatic out of sight. Calmly, he took the chair that he had left. Mocquino's eyes gleamed with malicious pleasure.

"You have decided wisely," remarked Mocquino. "My threat failed; yours did likewise. That brings a situation that I have long desired; one wherein we can speak freely. I have hoped for such a meeting. My wish has at last been granted."

The Shadow made no comment. He preferred to let Mocquino talk. The Voodoo Master relished the situation. He continued:

"Some time ago, I formed a cult of faithful followers, worshippers of voodoo rites, through whom I sought wealth. You uncovered my headquarters aboard an old ferry boat in the Hudson River. Single-handed you defeated my followers; I plunged overboard, wounded.

"There were police boats all about, and other craft besides. One was a small tug manned by a handful of my reserves, under the command of my most trusted lieutenant, Banzarro. They brought me aboard; they carried me to safety, and recovery."

Smiling, Mocquino began to stroke his chin. He showed no fear of The Shadow; instead, he studied his visitor with a gaze that showed admiration. Mocquino seemed to consider The Shadow as a foe who could put his schemes to future tests. It was plain that the Voodoo Master enjoyed crime and relished opposition.

"I have decided," announced Mocquino, "to attempt a gigantic experiment upon the human race. All people are alike, whether savage or civilized. In tropical countries, a master of voodoo—like myself—can gain a host of followers. The same can be accomplished here in the United States.

"Except for one factor." Mocquino leaned forward and wagged a bony finger as he made the proviso. "The influence of the machine age must be destroyed. To implant the principles of voodoo belief upon a community, that place must be cut off from the world.

"I have chosen this city of Hampstead as my experimental field. Already, I have wreaked destruction; industry is ready to abandon the town. One more catastrophe will produce the final result. Its factories closed, Hampstead will become a city shunned by enterprise!"

MOCQUINO paused, hoping to see the effect of his words. The Shadow gave no visible sign; yet through his brain was flashing the full thought of the future. Outlandish as Mocquino's hopes might seem, the consequences were tremendous.

Steadily, invisibly, Doctor Mocquino would become the absolute ruler of a detached community. Strange cults were not uncommon. Voodoo rites, with their appeal to superstitious minds, could gain strong roots if planted in suitable soil.

The Shadow's thoughts turned to the immediate future. One fact was certain: in his effort to extend his strange scheme, Doctor Mocquino intended to continue with his strokes of crime. Lives were at stake, like those at the steel plant. In addition, Mocquino held prisoners—men whose lives The Shadow must save. If anything could be done to forestall Mocquino's present plans, that course must be learned.

Mocquino was guessing at The Shadow's thoughts. With a smile, the Voodoo Master himself presented new possibilities.

"We are at stalemate," purred Mocquino. "Suppose that we begin our game anew. Banzarro failed twice last night; first, when he sought your life with guns; second, when he missed his knife thrust. I failed tonight, when my color light proved insufficient to overcome you.

"I have no other moves; but I do intend new crime. As I have stated, it will proceed without me; and at the same time, my prisoners will automatically die. Should I be allowed to go my way, I shall proceed with crime; but the prisoners will live. So long as I am free, there is no reason for their death."

Mocquino paused; then added: "I shall find the new game interesting. So much so, that I may become negligent at times, merely to add new zest. That may interest you, particularly since you also enjoy adventure. There will be crime tonight, within the next few hours. You will find it intriguing if you seek to prevent it. Suppose I state my terms."

THE SHADOW remained as motionless as a statue. His attitude was unflinching; but that did not disturb Mocquino.

"You will leave here," proposed Mocquino, "and travel to the city limits, in your coupe. Banzarro will see you before you reach the steel plant. There will be no ambush; I do not care to sacrifice more men in futile effort."

Mocquino's words, dryly uttered, proved that the Voodoo Master was keen enough to recognize The Shadow's prowess. That made him doubly dangerous. Mocquino had dropped all overconfidence. His present plan, though boldly put, was actually a desperate bid for freedom.

It depended entirely upon The Shadow, and Mocquino knew it. If The Shadow himself had a deep plan that would be sufficient to offset Mocquino's threat of automatic crime, there would be no chance for the Voodoo Master. Knowing this, Mocquino added a promise.

"The prisoners will live," he insisted. "They will be the prize at stake. Our new game will begin from the moment that you have again passed the city limits. It will end only when either you or I have won a final conflict."

Leaning forward, Mocquino waited expectantly for The Shadow's answer. It came by action, instead of word. Rising, The Shadow turned toward the door. His cloak swished, as he stepped to the passage. Mocquino heard the closing of the door to the hall.

Slowly, the Voodoo Master approached a window and raised one lowered shade.

Minutes passed before a sudden gleam adorned Mocquino's evil confidence. The sight that produced that evil gloat was the passage of a coupe that rolled along the main street in front of the Hampstead House. The Shadow, like Mocquino, had accepted the fact that the game had reached a stalemate.

The Shadow was driving to the city limits, prepared to begin a new game against the evil plotter.

CHAPTER VI
CRIME TO COME

IN his departure from Mocquino's, The Shadow had accepted the only alternative. Past experience had told him of Mocquino's craftiness; events in Hampstead had proven that the archplotter was more formidable than ever.

Mocquino had proposed a fresh start in his duel with The Shadow. As stakes in the game, Mocquino had promised the lives of Harry Vincent and other prisoners. Mocquino would adhere to his promise, but not because of any mercy in his nature. The insidious Voodoo Master totally lacked that emotion.

Mocquino's purpose was to stir The Shadow to frenzied action; to bring him into the open. Once on the offensive, The Shadow would be forced to discard certain protective measures. Mocquino, always ready to deliver a death thrust, might find an opportunity to end the career of the only living foe whom he feared.

The Shadow had accepted Mocquino's terms for the same reason. He knew that the one way to deal with Mocquino was to thwart him at every turn; to meet his schemes as they came. If foiled, Mocquino would increase his own efforts at evil action. He, too, could become unguarded.

All the while, however, Mocquino would keep his prisoners alive. The Voodoo Master knew that those captives were human bait; that their welfare was essential. As long as The Shadow knew that they lived, he would press his activities without pause. Sooner or later, so Mocquino hoped, The Shadow would be worn down. When that time came, Mocquino could strike.

There was only one choice for The Shadow. That was to keep constantly upon the move; to challenge Mocquino to the utmost.

Driving toward the city limits of Hampstead, The Shadow reviewed these prospects. All the while, he was watching the road with caution. Somewhere along the route, he would pass a hiding place occupied by Mocquino's chief lieutenant—the man whom the Voodoo Master had called Banzarro.

There was a chance that Banzarro would strike from ambush, despite Mocquino's declaration to the contrary. This was one point upon which the

Voodoo Master could not be trusted. The Shadow's impression, however, was that Mocquino would prefer to depend on future strategy, rather than order his underlings to attempt another attack of a type at which they had previously failed.

THE SHADOW'S surmise proved correct. He reached the city limits unchallenged. There, he wheeled his coupe about and started back toward the center of town. Choosing a side road, he swung from the main highway and threaded his way into the city. He reached the obscure garage near the railroad station.

For this journey, The Shadow had used his former license plates. He changed them again, in the garage; there were no employees on duty to observe the action. Wearing his garb of black, The Shadow departed by a side door. He picked his way through darkness, and came again to the converted house where Mocquino's apartment was located.

This time, The Shadow chose another mode of entry. He picked a loose grating at the side of the house, removed it and dropped into the cellar. In his departure from Mocquino's apartment, he had observed the location of stairways; hence he had no difficulty in reaching the ground floor. There was a light in the hall, but The Shadow took a darkened flight of steps at the rear. He went up to the second floor.

All the while, The Shadow exercised full caution. He knew that Mocquino might expect him to return. This house offered many lurking spots for would-be assassins. But The Shadow banked upon one factor that was definitely a part of Mocquino's policy. The Voodoo Master was dealing in hidden, mysterious crime. Therefore, Mocquino would seek to avoid any commotion that would cause the public to guess that crooks were in Hampstead.

Last night's thrusts proved this fact. One had been made upon a lonely stretch of road; the other had been a quick, silent stab from darkness.

The Shadow expected, moreover, to find Mocquino gone; but he was not entirely set for the surprise that he received when he opened the unlocked door of the voodoo doctor's apartment. Lights were glowing from wall brackets in the living room; the illumination showed complete vacancy. Stepping in from the passage, The Shadow stood in the center of complete desertion.

During the scant half hour since The Shadow's departure, Mocquino had accomplished a complete removal. Every item of furniture was gone. including the table lamp and its special bulb. Bare floors sounded hollow beneath The Shadow's tread. Blank walls gaped where gorgeous tapestries had formerly hung. Mocquino had left nothing except the few lights in the wall sockets, to let The Shadow see what had been accomplished.

The Shadow had already decided that Mocquino must have some stronghold outside of Hampstead, but within easy reach of the city. Such a place would be needed as a hideout for thugs who served under Banzarro. That stronghold could also serve as a prison for Harry Vincent and the other captives. It was obvious that Mocquino had chosen the place as his own headquarters for the future campaign.

For the present, The Shadow had no intent to take up Mocquino's trail. He was sure that the search for the stronghold would be a long one. If he made it his immediate objective, he would lose a greater opportunity. Crime was due again in Hampstead. It would come tonight, as part of Mocquino's strategy. The Shadow's immediate purpose was to gain some clue to the next step in Mocquino's campaign.

A BRIEF search through the living room showed nothing of importance. The Shadow went through the little passage and used his flashlight in a darkened rear room. Here, again, was vacancy. The Shadow moved through to another room. His flashlight, glowing on the floor, showed streaky scrapes that had been made when a piece of furniture had been moved. From the marks, The Shadow knew that the object had been either a table or a desk.

The corner baseboard was warped. Its lower edge was fully a quarter inch above the floor. A tiny strip of white showed from the space. Stooping, The Shadow plucked and drew out a small, square piece of paper. It was a page torn from a memorandum pad. Apparently it had been tossed toward a wastebasket, only to flutter to the floor instead. Sliding under the baseboard, the paper had remained unnoticed.

On the square sheet was a penciled scrawl. The Shadow read the notation:

Thursday, 9 p.m. Dynamo room at powerhouse.

This day was Thursday. The Shadow's watch showed half past eight. Thirty minutes until the designated hour. The Shadow had found what seemed to be a promising clue to Doctor Mocquino's next crime: some deed of destruction that concerned the local powerhouse. Yet, in that written notation, The Shadow saw one item that savored of truth; another that bore falsehood.

The Shadow remembered the penciled marks on the wall of Harry Vincent's room. Whether Harry had written that number, R-6384 or whether someone else had scrawled it at Mocquino's order, it had certainly been left with a purpose.

That clue had brought The Shadow to Mocquino's apartment, where the Voodoo Master had sought to overpower him with the brilliant hypnotic bulb.

Similarly, this new clue was a plant. The Shadow knew that Mocquino himself had slipped it beneath the baseboard. Mocquino had expected The Shadow to find it; to take the tip and go to the local powerhouse at nine o'clock.

The true statement on the sheet of paper was the one that concerned the time. Something was due to happen tonight, at nine o'clock. The false item was the mention of a place. When crime struck, it would not occur at the powerhouse. Mocquino's purpose was simply to decoy The Shadow to the wrong spot.

CRIME due at nine. Crumpling the piece of paper, The Shadow stood in darkness, considering the situation. Whatever Mocquino planned, it would certainly be a disaster as great as the catastrophe at the steel plant. There were only two other plants in Hampstead where so huge a tragedy could be duplicated.

One was the Century Chemical Company, with its dangerous type of manufacture; the other, the Hampstead Knitting Mills, where hundreds of workers were employed. On the surface, the choice was equal; The Shadow could reach either place by nine o'clock. But if he covered one, he could not protect the other.

Minutes of silence lingered; then came a whispered laugh amid the darkness. A swish betokened The Shadow's departure. The master investigator had chosen his next destination. The Shadow knew that Mocquino had certainly planned disasters at both the chemical plant and the knitting mills. One would strike tonight; the other would come later.

Mocquino's campaign of horror followed one definite system; to make it most effective, each disaster needed to be greater than the one before. Comparing the chemical plant and the knitting mills, The Shadow chose the one that best fitted the natural progression of Mocquino's evil plans.

Undeceived by the Voodoo Master's fake clue, The Shadow was setting forth to deal with coming crime.

CHAPTER VII
AT THE CHEMICAL PLANT

THE Century Chemical Company occupied a stretch of isolated ground just west of Hampstead. There was good reason for the remote location. The chemical plant produced highly inflammable materials, and the fire hazard was too great for other buildings to be built in the same locality.

The plant consisted of three sections, all housed in the same building. First, the portion where incoming shipments were stored; then the main laboratory where the chemicals were manufactured; last, the storeroom that held the finished products.

Upstairs were offices; most of these were over the storeroom, for it had a low ceiling and there was plenty of space above. Of the sixty employees who worked at the plant, nearly forty were engaged in actual manufacture; most of the others belonged in the upstairs offices.

In their inspection of the plant, officials had marked one danger spot. That lay between the large laboratory and the last storeroom, where the finished chemicals were kept. Fire was always a menace to the laboratory; but the workers were trained to meet it. All inflammable materials were removed as soon as manufactured. The important precaution, therefore, was to keep a fireproof barrier between the laboratory and the storeroom.

This had been effectively arranged. When trucks were wheeled from the laboratory, they followed a slight downward slope and stopped at a steel door. When that barrier was opened, the trucks entered a vestibule, with another steel door ahead. The man in charge of the doors closed the outer one; then opened the inner, so that the trucks could be wheeled through to the storeroom at the end of the downgrade.

Thus there was never an open channel between the laboratory and the storeroom. Fire in the laboratory could not spread; nor could an accident in the storeroom produce disaster in the laboratory.

A FULL shift of workers was in the laboratory on this particular night. A clock by the outer door showed the time as five minutes before nine. Near the door was a small lunch counter; there, a man in overalls was gulping down a cup of coffee before going on duty.

Another worker, wheeling a hand truck in from the inbound shipment room, stopped to nudge the coffee drinker.

"Hello, Danny," greeted the man with the truck. "Whatta you need a cup of Java for? So's you can stay awake on that soft job of yours?"

Danny finished his coffee and grinned.

"Hello, Pete," he returned. "Kiddin' me, eh? Well, it takes brains to handle them control levers when the trucks go through the doors. More brains than shoving a truck."

"I'll be off this trick next week," growled Pete. "They're putting me in the shipping department. Well, Danny, they're waiting for you over in the control room. So long, old scout!"

"Wait a minute, Pete."

Earnestly, Danny gripped Pete's arm and drew

the truck pusher to one side. In an undertone he put a query:

"You're a pal, Pete, ain't you? One guy that I can count on?"

Pete nodded.

"There's something I gotta ask you about," continued Danny. "You remember last Monday night? Were we together anywhere?"

Pete shook his head.

"Tuesday was my night off," he stated. "I was working here, Monday. Only—"

Pete paused suddenly. His eyes were half closed.

"Only what?" queried Danny, anxiously.

Pete opened his eyes and blinked.

"What were you asking about Monday for?" he demanded. "Give me the lowdown, Danny."

"I haven't got time, Pete." Danny shifted as he spoke. "I gotta get over to the control room."

"It wasn't that maybe you'd forgotten something?" insisted Pete. "Like where you'd been at, on Monday night?"

It was Danny's turn to blink. His face showed worriment. Pete had guessed the secret that Danny had been anxious not to let slip. Pete knew it; he was quick to reassure his pal.

"Listen, Danny," confessed Pete; "it hit me funny, you asking about Monday night. I was kinda worried the same way; thinking about where I'd been Tuesday."

"You mean it's kind of hazy, Pete?"

"Yeah. I wouldn't have mentioned it to nobody. Not even to you, Danny, except because of what you just said. Seems like I got a telephone call, asking me to come somewhere; and I went. That was right after dinner, Tuesday. I remember coming home at ten o'clock, telling the folks I'd been to a movie. But I must've sat right through the picture without even looking at it—"

"It's the same with me, Pete! Monday night I was somewhere. Nobody at home asked me about it; but they said something about my hitting the hay at eleven o'clock. I thought I'd turned in around nine. There's a couple of hours, Pete, that I can't account for!"

"That's why you asked me if I'd seen you Monday?"

"Yeah. It makes me feel creepy—like I was trying to remember something I'd dreamed, and couldn't!"

"Same with me, Danny. I keep thinking about it—"

A voice was calling for Pete's truck. The two men ended their confab. Pete shoved his truck off through the laboratory. Danny crossed the floor and reached an inner corner. There he stepped into a small control room, where a man was seated in a chair beside two levers.

Danny took over the controls. The other worker departed by a door that led into a darkened passage. Mumbling to himself, Danny mulled over the event that he had discussed with Pete.

MECHANICALLY, Danny looked toward the big clock at the front of the laboratory. Its hands showed nine o'clock. A shudder came to Danny's shoulders. The man looked about; he had a feeling that eyes were watching him. Vainly, he stared at the darkened passage near the control room. While he gazed, he heard a shriek that made him swing about.

The cry came from the laboratory. From the open front of the control box, Danny saw Pete stumbling beside his truck. Pete was holding a large bottle that he was about to load. Someone had shouted a warning when Pete stumbled. As Danny stared, Pete struck the edge of the hand truck and the bottle shot from his grasp.

It crashed squarely into the contents of the half-loaded truck. As the bottle shattered, chemical solution splashed upon loaded boxes. There was a puff; a flash of flame. The truck was ablaze.

Workers scrambled from their benches. In the excitement, one overturned a large beaker.

New puffs sighed from the workbench. Flames sizzled, while a bell clanged furiously from the end of the room.

Trained to quick response, workers could have met the emergency, had it not been for Pete. On his feet beside the truck, the fellow went berserk. He wanted to get the truck away; he chose the easiest direction. With a shove, Pete propelled the blazing load straight down the ramp that led to the storeroom. The truck jammed to a stop against the steel door that led to the protective corridor.

In a sense, Pete's move had served well. He had at least shoved the truck away from the workbenches, to a place where it could be easily handled. The steel door was a fireproof barrier; the flames could not penetrate it. But Pete's move led to another—one that came from Danny.

Deliberately, the man in the control box grasped the first lever and tugged it. The steel door slid upward. While maddened workers dashed across the laboratory, the blazing truck slid down through the passage to the storeroom. A thump announced its arrival at the second steel door.

Shouting men were leaping to reclaim the truck. Others were staring toward the control room, astounded by Danny's action. None was close enough to stop the next move. With the same slow move that he had used before, Danny gripped the second lever. His hands started its pull, to release the lower door and let the truck roll through to the storeroom, where stacks of inflammable merchandise awaited removal.

Only an instantaneous intervention could forestall Danny's unexplainable move. That intervention came.

A BLACK-GARBED form launched from the darkened passage wherein Danny had suspected watching eyes. A long, cloaked arm sped forward. Gloved, viselike fingers clutched Danny's hand, wrenched the man's grip from the control lever.

Eyes staring straight ahead, Danny emitted a snarl like that of a trapped beast.

Spinning about, Danny saw The Shadow. An expression of fierce rage came over Danny's face as his eyes met the burn of The Shadow's eyes. Like a mechanical figure, a human automaton controlled by a distant brain, Danny sprang upon the cloaked intruder. Clawing furiously, he tried to tear The Shadow away from the control lever. Danny's brain could concentrate upon one purpose only: to gain again the lever and complete his act of destruction.

The Shadow's tall form bobbed backward, yielding to the madman's thrust. Danny shot one hand to the lever; but he was too late to perform the deed he wanted. A gloved fist zoomed through the opening that came when Danny dropped his arm. The Shadow's punch found the workman's jaw.

Danny slumped to his chair; his head tilted forward. His hand lost its clutch upon the lever. Other workers were almost to the control room. The Shadow sidestepped to the outer passage. He was watching when men arrived to find Danny in his chair.

The whole laboratory was filled with fading fumes. Special fire equipment had smothered the flames at the benches. A squad of workmen had headed for the passage leading down to the storeroom. There, they squashed the fire from the blazing truck.

As Danny came groggily to life, he looked from his window to see men hauling the extinguished truck up from the lower door.

The Shadow could view Danny's profile. He saw the awed expression that was flickering on the man's face.

Slowly, dimly, Danny was realizing what he had done. Thought of the averted havoc left the man shaky. Danny looked about hopelessly, as if wondering how to explain matters. Luck was with him. His fellow workers knew him for a man of coolness; they made their own interpretation of Danny's actions.

"Smart work, Danny!" approved one. "You had us guessing when you yanked that upper door. Then we caught the idea. You wanted to let that truck ride down into the passage, to get it away from the laboratory."

Danny nodded weakly.

"Sure!" put in another man. "You knowed that the second door would stop it. It was a cinch, putting out the fire on the truck down there in the passage."

"Some of the fellows got excited," added the first speaker. "Thought maybe you'd gone goofy, Dan; that you was going to pull the second door. I knowed different."

"Sure!" concluded the second man. "Your hand wasn't even on the second lever when we got here, Danny. You looked kind of weak, but I don't blame you. This box was a bad spot to be in, Danny."

A BIG bell was clanging, calling for men to return to work. Danny straightened in his chair. The others left; but after their departure, a lone worker sidled into the control box. It was Pete. The Shadow watched him motion to Danny.

"I—I musta gone bugs, Danny," confided Pete, in a whisper. "Something sort of hit me—like from that dream I had on Tuesday night. When I started to load that big flask on the truck, it was like my feet stumbled over each other. I sorta saw myself pitching the bottle onto the truck—"

"Don't tell me anymore, Pete," put in Danny, his tone awed. "Something clicked back to me when I saw it happen. You shoved the truck against the first door—remember? It was like a picture I was waiting for, out of a dream!

"I yanked that first door open. When the truck slid down, I made a grab to pull the second door. Don't ask me why. All I know is somebody—or something—came crashing in and stopped me. The boys think I did something smart; but I didn't, Pete. I was goofy, that's what!"

Shakily, Danny mopped his brow with a big handkerchief. Pete gave a departing whisper:

"Keep mum, Danny; that's what I'm going to do. Nobody's blaming us. I'm not worried, neither. It seems like my bean has sorta cleared."

"Same here, Pete. I'm just jittery; but it won't stick with me. I'm through bothering my noodle about where I was on Monday night."

Danny steadied in his chair. Pete edged from the control box. The Shadow moved away through the outer passage. His work was completed; he had spoiled Doctor Mocquino's scheme. Wisely had The Shadow picked the chemical plant as the place where crime was due. Here, Mocquino had hoped to send some fifty persons to destruction, reserving the knitting mills for a rarer and greater disaster.

In Pete and Danny, The Shadow had observed two men who had come under the Voodoo Master's evil power. Mocquino had decoyed them to his apartment; there, he had jolted them with his hypnotic light. Upon each man's brain he had impressed a future action, each to make an individual blunder at the hour of nine, on Thursday night.

Like others before them, both Pete and Danny had responded. They had mechanically performed their teamwork in accord with Mocquino's nefarious desire. The Shadow had stopped the menace; Mocquino's influence was ended, so far as those men were concerned.

Still, The Shadow saw more work ahead tonight. Outside the chemical plant his whispered laugh was barely audible in darkness. An unseen traveler in the night, The Shadow was choosing a trail that he knew might lead to Mocquino's new lair.

CHAPTER VIII
AT THE POWERHOUSE

FIFTEEN minutes after his departure from the chemical plant, The Shadow arrived near the Hampstead powerhouse. From the protecting darkness of an old empty house, he surveyed the squarish building that supplied the city with electricity. Motionless, The Shadow watched for signs of prowlers near the powerhouse.

In his past experience with Doctor Mocquino, The Shadow had learned that the Voodoo Master's strokes were double-edged. Any false trail that Mocquino offered would be beset with hazards. The Shadow's knowledge of Mocquino's ways explained the present situation.

Mocquino had planned disaster at the chemical plant; another crime of the sort that would seem accidental. In order to draw The Shadow from the place where scores of workers were slated for doom, Mocquino had planted the memo page with its mention of the local powerhouse.

Another rogue would have been satisfied with the plan of drawing The Shadow to the wrong spot. Not Mocquino, however. He picked nothing at random. Since there was a chance that The Shadow would come to the powerhouse at nine o'clock, it followed that Mocquino would be prepared to trap him at that hour.

Mocquino had henchmen—many of them—with Banzarro to command them. None of these underlings had been near the chemical plant; it was Mocquino's policy to keep them well away from any spot of scheduled disaster. The powerhouse, however, was a blind. It was likely that Banzarro and his crew would be here.

By this time, Banzarro's men would have closed in, on the chance that The Shadow was inside the powerhouse. They would be set to trap him when he emerged. In fact, Banzarro might even have kept the cordon loose in order to let The Shadow enter. Therefore, the present advantage lay with The Shadow. If Banzarro and his crew were close about the powerhouse, he could surprise them by coming inward instead of outward.

ADVANCING from his position, The Shadow began a circuit of the powerhouse. The building was square-walled and compact in construction; the space about it was darkened and offered every opportunity for The Shadow to approach. In his circling, The Shadow chose a course that was somewhat spiral. Always, he was coming closer to the building itself.

At no spot did The Shadow discover any signs of lurkers. During his final circuit, he could almost touch the walls of the building, yet there was no stir to mark the position of hidden enemies. All that The Shadow could detect was the steady *thrum-thrum* of big dynamos within.

There were frosted windows, barred with crisscross gratings. From these came dim light, enough to betray any men who might have chosen the window spaces as hiding places. There was only one door; it, too, had a frosted-glass panel. The Shadow's inspection proved that none of Mocquino's followers was hereabouts.

The Shadow considered another possibility—one that he had hitherto regarded as secondary. Mocquino could have ordered Banzarro to drop the ambush soon after nine o'clock, because of the expected disaster at the chemical plant. Mocquino might have considered it bad policy to have any of his men too close to Hampstead when excitement reigned there.

If such was the case, Banzarro and his men would have left the vicinity of the powerhouse before The Shadow's arrival. The silence about the square-walled building certainly indicated that something of the sort had occurred. Nevertheless, The Shadow did not intend to depart until he had made a through search of the premises. The only area that still remained was the interior of the powerhouse itself.

Stopping at the glass-paneled door, The Shadow performed his evasive move of entering without betrayal. He pressed against the narrow space between the edge of the panel and the door frame. He inched the door inward, so slowly that its appearance scarcely changed. One arm above his slouch hat, he blocked all passage of light. Squeezing through the partly closed door, he let the portal close as slowly as it had opened.

There were other doors inside; all opened from a small central corridor. The Shadow tried each barrier in turn. All were locked, until he came to the last one at the end of the passage. It opened when The Shadow pulled it; light from below showed a short flight of steps that led down into the dynamo room. The rhythm of the powerful machinery was more audible than before.

THE CITY OF DOOM

The Shadow reached the bottom of the steps. There, he observed four huge electric generators set in a row. The two that were closest to The Shadow were in motion. Through the grayish centers of the massive revolving wheels, The Shadow could see a wide space of floor; then the other two dynamos.

The second pair of machines were not in motion; but The Shadow saw that they soon would be. There was an engineer in charge, with an assistant. The two men were preparing to change the dynamo. Apparently, half past nine was the time set for that operation.

WHILE The Shadow waited at the bottom of the stairs, he considered the possibilities that this powerhouse might offer to Mocquino's schemes. It seemed likely that Mocquino had made arrangements to take over the powerhouse, if needed; for by stopping the dynamo, he could deprive Hampstead of electric current. Such action, however, would be of no value in itself. It could serve only as some device to aid another scheme.

Destruction in the powerhouse would not appeal to Mocquino. While the Voodoo Master had declared war on machinery, he wanted to spread terror with his strokes. The sacrifice of human lives was a vital part of Mocquino's campaign of horror. The elimination of a mere two men—the engineer and his assistant—would hardly be worth Mocquino's while, particularly since the size of his disasters had increased.

The time would come when Mocquino would choose to strike without self-concealment; but that time would not be tonight. It would come only when Mocquino had gone the limit in his present campaign. The Shadow had already recognized Mocquino's methods when he ignored the Voodoo Master's invitation to visit the powerhouse at nine o'clock.

The *thrum* of dynamos was increasing. The big wheels had begun to move at the far end of the room. Their massive spokes became blurred, as they advanced to full speed. Then there was a slowing of the generators nearer to The Shadow. Soon those wheels had stopped. The routine changing of the dynamos was accomplished.

The engineer was coming toward the stairs. The Shadow saw a set-in corner close at hand; he stepped quickly toward it and glided from view before the engineer arrived. Listening, The Shadow heard the man's footsteps pound the stone stairs. The engineer was taking a short spell off duty, leaving his assistant in charge.

The Shadow remained in his corner, intending to wait until the engineer returned. Suddenly, there came the sharp ring of a bell, shrill above the humming of the dynamos. The Shadow peered forth and watched the assistant engineer answer a telephone that was fastened to the wall.

Completing a brief call, the assistant looked about and stroked his chin. The man had evidently received a request to meet someone outside the powerhouse. He had a chance to leave for a short while, since the engineer was absent. The assistant was considering what risk there would be if he temporarily neglected his duty. He decided that the dynamos could run smoothly enough without attention. Hurriedly, the man came across the room and ascended the stairs.

THE SHADOW was alone below. This was his opportunity to look about the dynamo room; to find whether or not Mocquino's false message was entirely a hoax. Moving out from his corner, The Shadow passed the first two dynamos, studying the stilled wheels as he came close to them. He reached the center of the dynamo room.

That middle space formed a broad, cement-floored passage between the two sets of generators. Its walls were recessed; and, for the first time, The Shadow saw that each contained a door. The Shadow tried one door; then crossed the space between the dynamos and tested the door opposite. Both barriers were locked. Where they led was a matter that concerned The Shadow; for he saw at once that they offered special exits from the dynamo room.

With one gloved hand, The Shadow produced a set of picks. He paused before attacking the first door; he turned to observe the rear set of dynamos that were whirling at full speed.

As he made the turn, The Shadow suddenly sensed danger. It was amazing that he detected it, for his closeness to the dynamos made it almost impossible for The Shadow to hear other sounds. Nevertheless, his trained ability at sharp hearing was sufficient for the emergency.

Not only did The Shadow catch the sound; he identified it as a footfall. More than that, he detected its exact direction—from the stone stairs that led down from the upper floor. The Shadow's hands swept beneath his cloak; they whipped forth bearing automatics, as The Shadow swung to a position where he could see past the stopped dynamos.

With his quick move, The Shadow had caught a new intruder unaware. Halted at the foot of the stairs was a stocky, evil-visaged man, whose darkish features showed a fang-toothed grin. The Shadow sighted an ugly, pug-nosed face; above it a spread of greasy black hair.

No introduction was necessary. The Shadow knew this intruder for Banzarro. He saw the weapon in the Voodoo Master's lieutenant's square-fingered hands. Banzarro was clutching a gun that looked like a large air rifle; to it was affixed a gleaming knife blade.

AS Banzarro stopped short, his weapon only half raised, other faces bobbed up behind him. Banzarro was backed by a squad of henchmen; these hard-faced servants of Mocquino were brandishing revolvers. They, like Banzarro, were covered by The Shadow's guns. Through his wary shift, The Shadow had caught the foemen in a cluster. Their only hope at that moment was a mad dive back to the cover of the stairs. Had any member of the crew begun to lift a gun, The Shadow would have poured quick bullets into the massed group. He withheld his fire only because his enemies stood motionless.

Even Banzarro was rigid. The pug-nosed lieutenant showed an angry leer; then uttered a harsh cry. Instantly, the situation changed. In that moment, The Shadow realized that he should have shown no quarter to Banzarro and his halted mob. Banzarro's shout was a signal.

Two doors burst inward; they were the doors on each side of the space where The Shadow stood. Each opening revealed a trio of vicious-

No introduction was necessary. The Shadow knew this intruder for Banzarro.

faced henchmen—other minions of Mocquino—who had been hidden within the powerhouse itself.

The trap had closed. The Shadow was faced by foemen from three sides; enemies who covered every exit. Behind him, on the fourth side, were spinning dynamos; beyond them a blank wall that offered no escape.

Doctor Mocquino had returned to his policy of massed attack against The Shadow; but the Voodoo Master had waited until his cloaked opponent had entered a snare that promised death!

As proof of Mocquino's confidence that victory was his, The Shadow heard a burst of jangled laughter from the stairway where Banzarro and his clustered men were boldly springing forward, raising their guns despite The Shadow's coverage, knowing that he could risk no battle with them while he was flanked from both sides.

There, on the steps, stood Doctor Mocquino; he had crept down behind Banzarro's halted group. In his bony hand the Voodoo Master clutched a leveled revolver, ready to fire the first shot at The Shadow.

Death to The Shadow! Mocquino was positive that it would be delivered. The Voodoo Master had come to be present at the kill!

CHAPTER IX
THE LOST TRAIL

THE scene had changed with suddenness. One instant, The Shadow held the bulge. The next second had faced him with a three-way attack. Mocquino's quick appearance at the stairway had supported Banzarro and the others whom The Shadow covered. The Shadow's enemies had staged the unexpected.

In performing their sudden move, those foemen had gained the confidence which The Shadow had so recently held. They had caught the lone fighter in their toils. Had they been dealing with any but The Shadow, Mocquino and his men would have delivered death with ease. But The Shadow also starred in producing the unexpected; even when he had no time to prearrange a plan.

Before Mocquino could fire the opening shot, The Shadow sprang his surprise. It seemed a futile one; on that account, it was the best move he could make. Instead of wild attack; instead of holding ground, The Shadow took to what seemed blind flight. He whirled about, dived wildly for the blank space beyond the two revolving dynamos at the rear of the room.

Mocquino fired; his shot was wide. Though the Voodoo Master was something of a marksman, he had not counted on a fading target. Nor had Mocquino forgotten a previous battle with The Shadow. He knew The Shadow's speed with the trigger, and was taking no chances against it.

Other guns barked hard upon Mocquino's. They, too, were hasty and belated. Had The Shadow kept on to the blank wall, bullets would have reached him. Instead, The Shadow sidestepped just past the first of the two rear dynamos; he dived between the big revolving wheels just as the better-aimed slugs were dispatched in his direction.

Mocquino shouted a harsh order; it was echoed by Banzarro. Underlings closed in; those at the front spread to pass the motionless dynamos; those at the sides crowded in from their doorways. All could see The Shadow. He was behind the first wheel in the set of revolving dynamos. The speed of the wheel was so terrific that its massive spokes were invisible. The Shadow stood framed in a grayish circle.

MOCQUINO'S henchmen paused, seeing their enemy trapped. Banzarro shouted again, from the front of the room. His leering subordinates paused; Mocquino nodded approval while Banzarro stopped at the huge axle of the first dynamo; the nearer of the two wheels that were standing still. His body covered behind an upright spoke, Banzarro leveled his air gun, looking for a chance to pick off The Shadow.

Banzarro preferred this weapon of his. It had failed at the hotel; he saw a chance to use it here. The best marksman in all Mocquino's tribe, Banzarro considered it his privilege to down The Shadow. Through the spokes of the halted wheels, Banzarro saw The Shadow beyond the grayed center of the whirling generator. The Shadow was almost motionless. Banzarro clicked the trigger of his odd gun.

The knife whizzed through space, driving straight for its target. It glimmered in the air; then whirled with a sudden clatter and clashed the ceiling, to rattle finally against the floor.

Above the *purr* of the far dynamos, came a laugh of challenge. Banzarro voiced an oath.

The knife had been stopped by the spokes of the speeding dynamo. That grayish barrier in front of The Shadow had been like a shield of steel against Banzarro's blade.

The reason for Banzarro's failure dawned upon Mocquino and his followers. The Voodoo Master gave a shout. His men aimed their revolvers toward the whirling wheel and fired shots at an angle. Bullets clicked harmlessly. They, too, were deflected by the broad spokes of the speeding wheel. The Shadow's laugh rang out again.

Banzarro started to gesture and shout. Mocquino gripped his lieutenant's arm; talked to him with a bland smile.

The lieutenant then went past the stationary dynamos. He spoke to his subordinates, motioned them to the center space between the two sets of wheels. Formed into a glaring line, the ruffians faced The Shadow. He was less than a dozen feet away, looking straight through the whizzing haze of spokes that separated him from the foes who outnumbered him. Through that almost invisible shield, The Shadow could count ten faces.

Banzarro was by the wall, ready to yank a switch that controlled the dynamo. He stopped as he heard Mocquino call. The Voodoo Master was reminding him to start the front dynamos; then stall the rear ones. These generators supplied all of Hampstead with its electricity, Mocquino did not want the town to know that there had been trouble at the powerhouse.

The front dynamos moved. Banzarro laid his hand upon the switch that controlled the wheel which protected The Shadow. Banzarro grinned as he realized what was coming. The big wheel would slow; his men could open fire as a squad. It would be death to The Shadow.

BEYOND the grayish spoke-barrier, The Shadow was holding leveled guns. His fingers moved suddenly; the big automatics gushed flame, straight through the revolving dynamo. Wild shouts sounded from the men clustered there.

Banzarro stopped, rigid, staring as he saw two henchmen stagger. A third went down; the others began to scatter. In some amazing manner, The Shadow was shooting bullets through the spokes that had stopped every previous shot!

Those automatics had blasted with machine-gun speed. They were gone beneath The Shadow's cloak; he was whipping out another brace of weapons. Two foemen alone had stood their ground, struck with the thought that if The Shadow could fire through the dynamo while it maintained full speed, they could do the same.

They were right. The Shadow had simply seen the weakness of the whirling barrier. It had stopped Banzarro's knife, which had only an air gun's impetus. It had stopped bullets also; but only when they had been fired from an angle. The spokes in the dynamo wheel were broad. That was why they had served against the angled fire.

But The Shadow had pumped bullets straight through, taking advantage of the thinner edges of the spokes. Some of his shots had been deflected; others had not. The bullets that had gone through had served their purpose. Three of Mocquino's ten were down; five were in flight. The two who hoped to copy The Shadow were too late. Each was a target for an automatic. The Shadow was already firing from his second set of guns.

One man sprawled; the other staggered but managed to run for safety. Banzarro was swept back by the wild rush of his own squad. The five who led the flight had not paused to consider facts. They thought The Shadow held a curse over them; that his bullets could ride where theirs could not. Superstitious servitors of Doctor Mocquino, these ruffians had been taught to believe in the incredible. Their training was working against the Voodoo Master this time.

Banzarro wheeled about, alone, clutching his useless air gun. He changed his plan of stopping the rear dynamos. He pulled the switch that controlled the front ones, anxious to leave matters as they were. He saw The Shadow leaping out to the side of the dynamo that protected him. The Shadow was deserting that safety in order to get Banzarro. Wildly, the ugly-faced lieutenant followed the course of his fleeing henchmen.

Mocquino was at the stairway, trying to rally the unscathed five. They were turning about, ready to obey, when Banzarro came hurtling toward them. Wildly, the henchmen forgot Mocquino's order. They sprang in a mad mass for the stairs, carrying the shouting Voodoo Master with them. Banzarro added his weight to the drive. The whole group plunged upward, with Mocquino helpless in his effort to stop their flight to safety.

SHOTS ripped from the dynamo room. The Shadow was delivering final bursts of gunfire to speed the flight. He knew that his cartridges were exhausted; that his plight would be a bad one if the fleeing men returned. Mocquino knew it, also; that was why The Shadow kept to the pursuit. Taking to the stairs, he reached the top just as the surging mass of men went through the outer door. The Shadow had no bullets left; but Banzarro, looking backward, saw him aim. Unarmed except for his knifeless, one-shot air gun, Banzarro dived outside with the others.

Fleeing crooks reached their cars. They started off into the night. Mocquino was in the second of two touring cars, rasping savage orders to Banzarro, who was at the wheel beside him. The Voodoo Master wanted his lieutenant to take a twisting course; to let the car ahead make its getaway.

This time, Banzarro obeyed. He sped the touring car around a corner, swinging in back of a deserted house.

As the machine roared past, lights blinked suddenly from a parked coupe. The second car started forward. Crooks had crossed The Shadow's path; he was again in pursuit.

Cars wheeled wildly toward the outskirts of Hampstead. While Banzarro handled the touring car, taking every twisted route that came, Mocquino leaned from the side, glaring back at the coupe. The Voodoo Master emitted a sudden hiss. He had guessed why The Shadow had not opened fire. The touring car had passed him just as he reached his coupe. The Shadow had not gained a chance to reload his automatics. Mocquino guessed, though, that The Shadow would manage to refill those guns while on the move. That was the reason for Mocquino's hiss.

Banzarro heard the order; he jammed the brakes. Mocquino fired point-blank as the coupe took the corner that the touring car had passed.

The Voodoo Master's shots had accuracy; they cracked the windows of The Shadow's car. The coupe performed a wide skid, ripped through a hedge and halted at a tilt. During the wild maneuver, a popped report betokened a bursting tire.

The touring car was roaring away as The Shadow fired.

Unable to stop the Voodoo Master's escape, The Shadow leaped from the coupe and made a hurried tire change. The trail was temporarily lost; the only course was to get back to the powerhouse and capture some of Mocquino's wounded henchmen.

The coupe limped when The Shadow reversed it through the hedge. It jolted along slowly as he retraced his steps.

NEARING the powerhouse, The Shadow halted. He saw a man entering the building; it was the engineer's assistant. Dropping from the coupe, The Shadow waited until the man was inside; then he followed. At the bottom of the stairs, The Shadow stopped, expecting to see the powerhouse employee gaping at sight of men sprawled on the floor by the dynamos.

Instead, the assistant was back at his post. No one else was in the dynamo room. Mocquino's henchmen had again demonstrated their well-drilled ability. Among the wounded, at least two must have had strength enough left to drag the others out. Perhaps a small crew of reserves had arrived to aid them. Whatever the answer, the work had been done.

The rear dynamos were purring smoothly. The floor was free from bloodstains. Bullet nicks in the wall were meaningless; for the surfaces were already rough and irregular. Time lost by The Shadow had produced another closed trail.

Once again The Shadow, in order to reach the Voodoo Master and rescue the prisoners whom the master-villain held, faced the problem of divining Doctor Mocquino's next move.

CHAPTER X
THE NEW OBJECTIVE

MORNING dawned brightly in Hampstead. It brought good cheer to those who lived in the city of doom. At last, the jinx had lifted. Fear and pessimism were temporarily banished.

A night had passed without new havoc. That fact was a pleasing one in itself; but there was stronger cause for the confidence that the citizens felt. The news was out concerning the brief fire at the chemical plant. Everyone was filled with enthusiasm for the manner in which the blaze had been handled.

There was another side to the wave of confidence that had gripped Hampstead. It showed one thing clearly: that the citizens realized they had need for courage. Persons who had kept their fears to themselves were talking freely at last, for they felt that menace was ended. That, in itself, was a bad sign. It meant that optimism had risen under pressure.

Should new disaster befall in Hampstead, its damage would be double. Not only would it produce its own destruction; it would also drop the present spirit of confidence to a lower level of despair. The jinx was gone; people openly rejoiced in that belief. They did not realize that for the first time it was unanimously agreed that there actually was a mysterious menace over Hampstead.

Only The Shadow could interpret the false hopes of the Hampstead citizens. Only he knew the real menace that existed. Even more than before, The Shadow saw how useless it would be to inform either the public or the law concerning Doctor Rodil Mocquino.

Tales of the Voodoo Master would be ridiculed, particularly since they involved two new heroes such as Pete and Danny. While those two were keeping much to themselves, even they did not recognize Mocquino's existence. The Voodoo Master's hypnotic influence had passed, so far as they were concerned. No matter how hard they taxed their brains, they would never remember the details of their separate visits to Mocquino's abode.

Along with his vanished henchmen, Mocquino had taken the automobile in which The Shadow had first seen him. The Shadow had checked upon the license number R-6384, only to learn that it belonged to an ancient roadster that had been consigned to a junkyard more than a month ago. Obviously, Mocquino had obtained a pair of discarded license plates and had put them on the big car which he himself used.

The Shadow remembered that car well. It was a long, gray limousine, as fine a machine as any in Hampstead. The Shadow had noted every detail of the car when he had seen it from the window of the hotel dining room. He had made casual inquires at local garages; no one knew of the limousine. Some had remembered seeing it about town; but none could name the owner.

AFTERNOON found The Shadow seated in the lobby of the Hampstead House. He had spent the morning in and out of town, looking for any trails that might lead him along Mocquino's path. The Shadow was sure that the voodoo doctor was not far distant; but the hill district about Hampstead was too extensive to be covered by a quick search.

One possible method had occurred to The Shadow; that was to use an airplane as he had done on previous occasions. In this case, however, it was unwise. Hampstead, though otherwise progressive, was lacking in an airport. Planes were seldom seen near the town; there were no through air routes. Any plane that The Shadow might use would be noted at once by some of Mocquino's spies.

So far, The Shadow had managed to protect completely his guise of Henry Arnaud. That was a vital point in his campaign. It enabled him to keep as completely hidden as Mocquino. Only by using the Voodoo Master's own methods could The Shadow hope for success.

The Shadow had come to a definite conclusion regarding Mocquino's future plans. He was sure that the Voodoo Master would forget last night's failure. To offset the disaster that missed, Mocquino would simply proceed with the next one that he planned. Such a stroke would hit Hampstead harder than ever.

Mocquino would also use his previous system. For every disaster, he had coached a hypnotized victim in advance. He would have one for tonight; and The Shadow knew where destruction would be due to strike. The marked place would be the Hampstead Knitting Mills, largest of all the local industries.

Crime could be averted only by an inspection at the mills, plus a search for the man whom Mocquino had chosen as a tool. Both of these steps were difficult ones. Unlike the steel works and the chemical plant, the knitting mills had no danger spot; it was impossible, therefore, to recognize immediately the sort of stroke that Mocquino might intend. Moreover, the knitting mills had hundreds of employees. To find the one Mocquino had swayed was a long task.

Soon after three o'clock, The Shadow strolled from the lobby of the Hampstead House. Passing as Arnaud, he hailed one of Hampstead's improvised taxis and gave the driver a destination. The car started on its route. After several blocks, The Shadow inquired about the location of the knitting mills. The driver gave it, stating that the mills were in a direction almost opposite the one they had taken.

"Drive me out to the mills," ordered The Shadow. "I want to handle some business there, before it is too late."

They reached the mills at half past three. The plant was a large one, sprawled over a few acres of ground. The Shadow alighted at the office entrance; he noted several salesmen going in and out. Visitors were frequent at this busy plant. An extra one would not attract suspicion, even if Mocquino did have spies present.

Entering, The Shadow wrote a message on the back of a card that bore the name of Henry Arnaud. He asked for James Chadron, the president of the plant, and learned that Mr. Chadron had just returned from a vacation. The Shadow's card was sent into the president's office. Very soon, word came through to usher Mr. Arnaud into the office.

The explanation was simply that The Shadow had mentioned the name of a prominent woolen manufacturer in the note that he had written. He had worded the message so that James Chadron would believe him a close friend of the man whom he had named. The Shadow found a warm reception awaiting him in consequence.

CHADRON, a puffy, portly man, was inside the door, waiting with extended hand. He wheezed an immediate greeting:

"Glad to meet you, Mr. Arnaud! So you're a friend of Louis Gathrop! That means you're my friend, Mr. Arnaud! Sit down—have a cigar! Plenty of time for a chat with you!"

The Shadow accepted an expensive perfecto. As soon as he and Chadron had lighted their cigars, The Shadow spoke in a slow, steady tone:

"I have something important to discuss with you, Mr. Chadron."

"Word from Gathrop?" queried Chadron. "He had a message for me? Odd that he didn't wire me—"

"He could not have done that. Nor did he think it wise to write. He wanted me to convey this matter personally."

"No trouble has come to Gathrop, I hope—"

"None at all. He is concerned about you, Mr. Chadron."

"About me? Why business is at top! Working overtime—"

The Shadow shook his head.

"I refer to recent disasters here in Hampstead," he declared in an undertone. "They must not be discounted, Mr. Chadron. They are a real threat! Louis Gathrop recognizes it; so does everyone outside of Hampstead."

Chadron shifted in his chair. His face became troubled.

"I know it," he admitted. "The matter has been worrying me all day. I have just returned from my vacation, to run right into the middle of this business. You are right, Mr. Arnaud; it may be serious.

JAMES CHADRON—president of the Hampstead Knitting Mills.

Yet I cannot see how this plant can suffer. We do not have the dangers that were present at the others."

"You have checked on everything?"

"Absolutely! I could show you through the plant, Mr. Arnaud, only that might be unwise. Suppose"—Chadron paused to glance at his watch—"suppose that you leave here with me. Come out to my house for dinner. I live a dozen miles away from Hampstead. My car will be here shortly. We can go then. At home, I have diagrams, blueprints, everything that pertains to the plant and its machinery."

Chadron had accepted The Shadow without question. The Shadow's best course was to accept the invitation. He did so; and the mill president seemed pleased. Beaming, Chadron changed the subject; he began to ask questions about his old friend Gathrop. The Shadow was well provided with facts that concerned Gathrop. As they talked, Chadron became more and more pleased. Four o'clock had arrived when a secretary entered and interrupted with the statement:

"Your car is here, Mr. Chadron. It is at the rear door."

Chadron arose. "Let us go, Arnaud," he suggested. "On the way out, we can glimpse a few floors of the plant."

THE route that they took led past the doorway of long rooms, where scores of workers were busy at looms and other machines. The Shadow noted lines of steadily moving belts connected to overhead rollers. Each room was cramped; filled with masses of machinery and workers who were almost elbow to elbow.

At one door The Shadow saw a locked transformer box, that served the room within. He observed the same arrangement at each succeeding workroom. Then Chadron reached the last stairway; he and The Shadow descended to step outdoors where a large car was waiting in a narrow driveway.

A chauffeur was standing, holding the rear door open. For a moment, The Shadow's eyes shone with a brilliance that seldom showed with the guise of Arnaud. The light faded almost instantly. The Shadow boarded the car with Chadron and settled leisurely back into the cushions as the chauffeur took the wheel.

In one quick flash, The Shadow had recognized the unexpected. Singularly, he had come across a clue at the time when he had least been likely to find it. A clue to Doctor Mocquino; an unmistakable one.

This car that The Shadow had entered was gray. It was a limousine. The chauffeur's face—his uniform—were instant reminders. This automobile that belonged to James Chadron was the very machine from which Doctor Mocquino had alighted outside the apartment house across from the hotel in Hampstead!

CHAPTER XI
THE SHADOW AT DUSK

JAMES CHADRON was silent as the limousine rolled toward his country home. The knitting mill owner had exhausted all questions concerning Louis Gathrop, the man whom he supposed to be a friend of Henry Arnaud's. As for matters at the mill, Chadron preferred to discuss them after they reached his home.

The Shadow, too, was silent. His eyes were straight ahead, as if looking toward the road that the car was following. Actually, The Shadow was studying the rear-vision mirror, catching frequent glimpses of the chauffeur's face. Five minutes of this convinced him of one important point: whatever the connection between this car and Doctor Mocquino, it concerned Chadron's chauffeur alone; not the mill owner.

The shiftiness of the chauffeur's eyes, the occasional twitches of his lips were visible in the mirror. The Shadow knew that the man was burdened with some secret. Whether or not the chauffeur would discuss the subject was something that The Shadow intended to find out later.

The car was swinging along a rough road, heading toward a valley between two hills. As they turned to the right, the car jolted. Chadron emitted a grunt; then spoke testily to the chauffeur.

"Why did you bring this car, Wishart?"

demanded the mill owner. "It does not ride as well as the sedan."

"The mechanic had finished with it, sir," returned the chauffeur, half turning his head toward the rear seat. "I thought that it would be in good condition. What is more, sir, I had some packages to deliver in Hampstead—ones that Mrs. Chadron sent. This car was roomier than the sedan, sir—"

"That's enough, Wishart. The packages were large ones, I suppose?"

"Yes, sir."

"Then they explain why you brought the limousine."

There were a few minutes of silence; then Chadron turned to The Shadow.

"This limousine is a white elephant," declared the mill owner. "I purchased it a year ago and brought it out to my estate from New York. The car is too large and unwieldy for the roads in this section of the country. It broke a spring the first day we started into Hampstead.

"Then there was trouble with the generator. I scarcely used the car for six months. Soon after Wishart became my chauffeur, the car broke a rear axle. That was being repaired when I went away on my vacation."

"The car was repaired in Hampstead?"

The Shadow spoke the question casually. Watching Wishart, he saw that the query had no effect on the chauffeur.

"No," replied Chadron; "we sent the car over to Newburg, some miles from here. There is a better mechanic there. By the way, Wishart, when was the job completed?"

"Only this morning, Mr. Chadron," replied the chauffeur. "The car was brought over from Newburg."

The Shadow knew that the chauffeur's statement was incorrect. Yesterday, the limousine had been used by Doctor Mocquino in Hampstead. In fact, The Shadow had reason to believe that it was in this very car that the Voodoo Master had made his rapid departure from the city of doom.

The repair job had certainly been completed some time ago; early enough for Harry Vincent to spot the limousine while it was in Mocquino's service. At that time, the car had been bearing the false license plates, as it had last night. Moreover, The Shadow was positive that Wishart had been Mocquino's chauffeur.

Wishart had lied. The question was whether or not the chauffeur's falsehood was intentional. There was a chance that Wishart—like other persons—had been a victim of Mocquino's hypnotic influence. Yet the odds were equal that the chauffeur might be a paid underling in the employ of the Voodoo Master.

THE big car took to a side road, curved beneath the looming bulk of a high hill and entered a broad gate. It followed a driveway and pulled up in front of a large mansion. The Shadow alighted with Chadron, who dismissed the chauffeur. The Shadow watched the limousine swing past the house and roll into a four-car garage.

Chadron's house seemed gloomy when they entered it. The sun had settled beneath the huge hill that flanked the large estate. There was a servant in the darkened hall; Chadron told him that there would be a guest for dinner. Then the mill owner led The Shadow to a secluded room at the side of the house. Turning on the lights, Chadron displayed a desk and file cabinets.

"We have everything here, Mr. Arnaud," he declared. "Even to models of the latest machinery in use at the plant. These blueprints"—he brought an envelope from a cabinet—"show the complete arrangements of our electric installations. Here are plans of the entire plant; also lists of the employees, with their full records."

The Shadow had seated himself at the desk. He took the envelopes as Chadron extended them. As The Shadow spread papers on the desk, Chadron smiled wisely.

"I have assumed, Mr. Arnaud," he stated, "that you are an expert in these matters. Though you have not declared yourself to be a special investigator, the circumstances of your visit have caused me to believe that you are one."

The Shadow delivered a slight smile. Looking up, he nodded; then went back to work. Chadron took a chair beside the desk. As The Shadow made quiet queries, Chadron answered them.

The Shadow looked up from a set of diagrams. He had completed a thorough survey; he noted that darkness had settled meanwhile. Pointing to the diagram before him, The Shadow made comment.

"All of your machinery," he stated, "is geared to a low current. I observe that each circuit is controlled by a separate transformer."

"That is correct, Mr. Arnaud."

"Your current, of course, comes from the local powerhouse—"

"Yes. That is why the transformers are necessary."

The Shadow nodded. He had seen the transformer boxes outside the large rooms with their long rows of steadily humming machines.

"Suppose," suggested The Shadow, "that there were no transformers to reduce the current. The effect, as I see it, would be chaos. Machines would speed up; flywheels would be loosened; belts would snap. The damage would be instantaneous and tremendous! Hundreds of workers would be trapped at their looms!"

CHADRON'S pudgy face showed horror; then the expression faded. The mill owner tapped the diagrams and smiled.

"For a moment, Mr. Arnaud," he declared, "I was so frightened that I was ready to call that plant and order it to shut down before the night shift. But you have overlooked the one point that provides against such disaster. There is no possible way to remove the transformers. Should they burn out, the current would cease. There would be no disaster."

"Someone could cut off the transformers."

"Not without deliberate intent. The boxes are locked; there are twenty of them altogether. That would require twenty men, all provided with keys for the boxes. Only one man has those keys; he is the plant supervisor."

"Richard Lassman," read The Shadow, referring to the lists. "He is scheduled to act as supervisor tonight."

"Lassman is one of our oldest and most trusted employees," declared Chadron. "But granting that he did, by some quirk, pull the switch of a transformer, even then there would be no damage. Other men are close at hand, inspecting each room at the time when the supervisor examines the transformer box for that particular unit of machinery.

"They would notice the speeding of the machines. They would immediately offset Lassman's action. The machinery would be shut down; any excitement would be confined to one room alone. No, Mr. Arnaud, such disaster could not occur. I can assure you of one thing: half past nine—the time of the inspection—is the safest moment during the entire evening."

STUDYING Lassman's record card, The Shadow considered Chadron's statement. The mill owner was right; yet The Shadow still saw the transformers as the only danger. He noted that Lassman's duty ended at ten o'clock. Rising from the desk, The Shadow spoke to Chadron.

"I shall not stay for dinner," he remarked quietly. "Instead, I should like to be present at the plant. If you will give me a personal pass, Mr. Chadron, it will serve me."

For a moment, Chadron hesitated. He had gained his only moment of suspicion. If danger existed, it seemed unwise to allow a stranger to visit the knitting mills. Thinking over The Shadow's visit, Chadron realized that he had accepted him on his own word alone.

Then came an afterthought. The Shadow had pointed out the only possible danger. Certainly he would not have done so had he held any interests other than those of preventing crime. Chadron sat down at the desk and wrote out the required pass.

"It is half past six," he remarked. "I shall have Wishart take you to the knitting mills in my coupe."

"To Hampstead would be better," stated The Shadow, quietly. "I can go out to the mills later."

"Of course," agreed Chadron. "That would be preferable. One moment, Mr. Arnaud, while I call up the garage."

Chadron reached for a telephone on his desk. The Shadow stopped him.

"A quiet departure would be best," he told the mill owner. "I noticed a side door as we came through the hall. Suppose that I go to the garage, instead of waiting for the car to come to the front."

"But Wishart will want to hear the order direct from me."

"You can give it over the telephone while I am on my way to the garage. I should like to reach Hampstead as soon as possible. That will save time."

"Of course. Very well, Mr. Arnaud."

CHADRON shook hands at the door of the room. Crossing the darkened, deserted hall, The Shadow reached the outer door. He saw the lights of the garage, less than fifty feet away. With quick stride, he followed the grassy edge of a gravel walk.

The door of the garage was drawn slightly back. The Shadow entered the lighted space where the big limousine was parked alongside a coupe and a sedan. He saw a small door at the back of the garage; half opened, it showed a lighted room. The Shadow heard Wishart's voice; the chauffeur was talking over the telephone.

"Certainly, Mr. Chadron..." Approaching, The Shadow heard Wishart's half of the conversation. "Yes. I can have the coupe ready in a few minutes... Very well, sir. I shall look for Mr. Arnaud..."

Wishart hung up the receiver. He turned about, his lips twitching. Evidently the chauffeur was troubled by this new development. First there had been the questions about the limousine; now a dinner guest was going back to town. Wishart mumbled to himself as he stepped toward the door that led out to the main room of the garage.

Then the chauffeur stopped with a blurted gasp. On the threshold of the doorway was the man whose arrival he had not yet expected. Keen eyes burned in the chauffeur's direction—optics that shone from the face of Henry Arnaud. Those blazing eyes transformed The Shadow's visage.

Had Wishart encountered The Shadow cloaked in black he could not have been more terror-stricken. The Shadow's fierce gaze made up for his drab attire. His eyes carried the accusation that made men of evil quail. Wishart stood rigid.

That instant told its story. Wishart was no mere victim of Mocquino's hypnosis. Chance had served The Shadow well. He had trapped one of the Voodoo Master's own henchmen.

The Shadow was prepared to gain the facts he wanted. From Wishart's lips, he would learn the location of Doctor Mocquino's lair.

CHAPTER XII
DEATH'S TRAIL

THE room where The Shadow had confronted Wishart was the workshop of Chadron's garage. The room was equipped with benches and tables; tools lay strewn about, except in the nearest corner which was bare only for a battered table that supported the telephone.

The Shadow had entered by the only door. The opposite wall was blank; but far to one side was a wide, opened window, which might have served Wishart as an emergency exit had the chauffeur expected this encounter.

The room was illuminated by a single brilliant light bulb that hung from the ceiling. The glare upon Wishart's face showed the man's features more plainly than had daylight. Previously, The Shadow had noted a certain shrewdness in the chauffeur's expression. That glossy look had changed.

Eyes beady, lips drawn, Wishart resembled a human rat. Cornered, he squirmed; his hands seemed itchy for action, yet all the while he showed a preference for flight. Once his tenseness had ended, Wishart snarled. He made a sudden shift in the direction of the window. As The Shadow blocked him with a quick stride, Wishart darted a look toward the door.

The Shadow had picked a midway position. He was ready to seize the chauffeur, no matter which way the fellow turned. Wishart backed toward the corner where the telephone stood. Almost there, he sprang to a workbench and snatched up a huge monkey wrench. With livid face, he swung his arms blindly in The Shadow's direction.

A gripping hand caught the chauffeur's arm, stopping the drive of the heavy monkey wrench. An elbow jabbed a back-arm stroke, upward to Wishart's chin. Catching the man just above the neck, that short blow crippled him.

Wishart gurgled; staggered backward against the table in the corner. He lost his hold on the wrench; a twist of The Shadow's hand dropped Wishart to his hands and knees.

The rat-faced chauffeur turned yellow.

"I'll—I'll talk!" he gulped. "Don't sock me! I'll spill it all—about the dirty business! All about—"

Wishart stopped short, trying to hold back a name.

"Doctor Mocquino!"

It was The Shadow who supplied the name of the Voodoo Master. Wishart stared; his eyes blinked. He did not recognize the name. The Shadow gave another:

"Herbert Prensham!"

Wishart nodded. In gulping tones, he talked.

"THAT'S him!" asserted the chauffeur. "The guy that had the apartment down in Hampstead. Herbert Prensham—but it's not his own moniker. I don't know him by any other, though. I'm giving that straight!"

The Shadow's eyes were steady upon the kneeling chauffeur. Wishart recognized that further talk might help him. In hurried phrases, the chauffeur gave his confession.

"He called me up, Prensham did. About a week ago." Nervously, Wishart tried to tell his whole story at once. "Said he knew Mr. Chadron. Wanted to see me. I went down there. Prensham let it out that he was a big shot. Knew a lot about me, he

On the threshold of the little doorway was the man whose arrival was not yet expected.

did. About my doing time once, in a State penitentiary. Something that Mr. Chadron didn't know.

"Prensham wanted me to get a car for him. That's why I used the big limousine. I dug up some auto tags off an old junker. Put them on instead of the regular plates. Prensham told me to do it. I was scared—honest—"

"By his offer of money?"

Wishart winced at The Shadow's sharp query. Knowing the ways of Doctor Mocquino, the wealth of the evil Voodoo Master, The Shadow was confident that more than mere threats had urged Wishart to become Mocquino's tool.

"How'd you get wise to that?" gasped Wishart. "About the dough that Prensham slipped me?"

"Name the amount," returned The Shadow.

Wishart hesitated; then saw it was no use to lie.

"Two grand," confessed the chauffeur. "Half of it when I saw him the first time. The rest after—"

Again, Wishart broke. The Shadow supplied the finish of the statement.

"After you learned the sort of crime in which your new friend specialized."

Wishart nodded feebly. The Shadow's knowledge was uncanny. Wishart did not realize that The Shadow had penetrated deeply into the schemes of Doctor Mocquino, alias Herbert Prensham. Considering Mocquino's dealings with Wishart, The Shadow had naturally assumed that the Voodoo Master would require the chauffeur's silence. Mocquino was the sort who would pay well for such service.

More than that, The Shadow saw another use to which Mocquino had put Wishart. Not only had the Voodoo Master known about the chauffeur's past; he had probably recognized that Wishart was still a crook at heart. As Chadron's chauffeur, Wishart would know facts about the town of Hampstead. It was likely that Mocquino had found him a valuable source of information.

The steadiness of The Shadow's gaze made Wishart guess that his inquisitor had divined the truth. Wildly, Wishart began a protestation of innocence.

"I—I didn't know what was due!" he claimed. "The trouble at the steel works—the terrible accident at the chemical plant—"

QUICKLY the chauffeur tried to check himself. He had made a slip. There had been no actual disaster at the chemical plant. Wishart's reference showed that he had known that crime was scheduled there.

Steadily, The Shadow's eyes focused closer to those of the cowering traitor. The Shadow was pressing Wishart's fears. He knew that the man had more to blab; but statement of that fact was unnecessary. Through action, alone, The Shadow was forcing Wishart to a point of final confession.

"I'll tell you where the big shot is," promised Wishart hoarsely. "I took him out to the place where he keeps his crew. They've got prisoners there—in the old house where they are. It's two miles north of the Denbury road—first turn to the right after the forks. Maybe you've heard of the house. It's an old joint that looks like a castle. They called it 'Myram's Folly'—after the guy who built it."

The Shadow had not heard of Myram's Folly. But he had long since come to the conclusion that Mocquino's hideout must be some isolated house, reached only by a back road. The wooded slopes and valleys near Hampstead had many such buildings, relics of the days when there had been no through highways in this region.

The Shadow was ready to proceed with a simple plan. He would have Wishart drive him to Hampstead and lead the way from there. Wishart could drive Chadron's car, while The Shadow followed in his own. Knowing that he was trailed by a master of vengeance, Wishart would be too yellow to attempt any deed of treachery.

Slowly, The Shadow stepped back and motioned for Wishart to rise. The chauffeur came to his feet; lips twitching, he faced The Shadow. Standing between Wishart and the window, The Shadow motioned toward the door. His gesture indicated that the chauffeur was to precede him out into the garage proper.

Wishart began to nod; then stopped. With hoarse outcry, he began a sudden protest as he faced The Shadow.

"I won't talk!" voiced Wishart. "I don't know nothing, I tell you! You can't make me talk! I never met this doctor guy—never even heard tell of him—"

Instantly, The Shadow spun about. He had caught the reason for Wishart's change of front. Staring past The Shadow, Wishart had seen someone at the window of the little workshop.

The chauffeur had recognized a peering face. The Shadow knew that a menace had arrived.

AS he swung, The Shadow grabbed Wishart and sent the chauffeur sprawling to the cover of a workbench. Still spinning, The Shadow continued toward the door, reaching it at the end of his rapid whirl. His entire move was one continuous action. As he reached the doorway, The Shadow was facing toward the window.

There he saw vacancy, backed by darkness. The outside watcher had dropped away. Quickly, The Shadow snapped an order to Wishart—to stay in his spot of safety. The chauffeur, however, had other hopes. He saw an open path to the window; he believed that he could take it and elude The Shadow. He was a double-crosser, this yellow crook, ready to forget any promise.

Leaping from the cover of the workbench, Wishart took two long strides toward the window. As he sprang in that direction, a muffled, sighing sound came from the outer darkness. There was a whistle through the window, accompanied by a glimmer from an arrowlike missile.

Wishart jolted upward as he took his third long stride. A gasped cry broke from the chauffeur's lips; clutching air, Wishart staggered backward, lost his balance and flattened, face up, upon the floor.

From the darkness, The Shadow heard a quick scramble; then the thud of an automobile door, accompanied by the *purr* of a motor. The car was starting from an obscure lane beyond a hedge that ran parallel with the garage.

Wishart lay motionless, dead. His assassin was gone; but The Shadow knew the murderer's identity. The killer was Banzarro; the proof was the handle of a knife that projected from Wishart's breast. Amid the outside darkness, Banzarro had been ready with his powerful air gun. Again, Mocquino's lieutenant had lost his chance to down The Shadow with that weapon.

Thwarted by The Shadow's quick twist for cover, Banzarro had reserved his single shot for another victim. Wishart had leaped squarely into the path of Banzarro's aim; the murderer had fired a knife thrust straight to the chauffeur's heart. Banzarro had decided to eliminate the one man who could serve as an informer. Mocquino needed Wishart no longer; Banzarro had seen to it that The Shadow would learn no future facts from the chauffeur.

Wishart's lips were rigid. They had ended their twitches forever. Those lips, however, had spoken in response to The Shadow's urge. They had named the location of Doctor Mocquino's headquarters. Though death had ended the chauffeur's confessions, The Shadow had gained the final trail.

CHAPTER XIII
MYRAM'S FOLLY

STANDING in the doorway between the workshop and the garage, The Shadow listened to the trailing fade-out of Banzarro's motor. After that sound had ended, silence reigned complete. Neither Wishart's last cry nor the departure of Banzarro's car had attracted attention in Chadron's house.

Alone on the scene where death had struck, The Shadow was confronted with a problem. That concerned Wishart's body. Once found, it would cause inquiry. James Chadron, when questioned, would remember that Henry Arnaud had been the last person to see the chauffeur alive.

That was a fact that could not well be eradicated. The simplest way to handle it would be to erase the character of Arnaud altogether. By such procedure, The Shadow would have full leeway to move against Doctor Rodil Mocquino. Since there would be no trail to Arnaud, it would not matter if the law blamed him for Wishart's death. The character of Henry Arnaud was purely a fictitious one that offered no lead to The Shadow himself.

The Shadow chose the simplest and most effective course. He left Wishart's body where it was. He turned out the light in the workshop; he went into the garage and did the same. Sliding the outer door open, The Shadow boarded the coupe and drove from the garage. He rolled slowly past Chadron's mansion.

To all appearances, Wishart was setting out for Hampstead with Henry Arnaud as his passenger. It would take half an hour for the coupe to reach the little city; another half hour for Wishart's return. It was obvious, therefore, that no one would wonder about Wishart until an hour had passed. The Shadow had all the time that he required.

All the way into Hampstead, The Shadow was alert. There was always a possibility of ambush, where Doctor Mocquino was concerned. Though The Shadow believed that Banzarro had headed back to the headquarters at Myram's Folly, he was not certain on that point. His vigilance did not lessen until he had actually arrived in Hampstead.

There, The Shadow parked Chadron's coupe on a side street. Leaving the car, he strolled to the Hampstead House and went up to his room. Using the guise of Arnaud for the last time, The Shadow packed; came down to the lobby and checked out. Carrying his suitcase, he walked to the garage where he had stored his own car. A few minutes later, he was driving along the main street of Hampstead, bound toward the Denbury road.

THE main street was ablaze with lights; long lines of blinking bulbs had been strung from lamp posts. People were plentiful; storefronts were lighted. The Shadow saw large banners and sparkling lights that advertised a double feature at Hampstead's largest motion picture theater. Already crowds had formed a line in front of the box office.

Pulling into a corner gasoline station. The Shadow ordered the attendant to fill the tank. That done, the man began to wipe the windshield. In the fashion of a chance visitor, The Shadow inquired:

"What is all the celebration tonight?"

There was a whistle through the window, accompanied by a glimmer from an arrowlike missile.

"Sort of general enthusiasm," chuckled the attendant. "People hereabouts have been feeling kind of glum lately. On account of some pretty bad accidents that have hit Hampstead. They sort of think the jinx is through. That's why everybody's turned out tonight."

The Shadow dropped the subject of the celebration. He inquired if he happened to be headed toward Denbury; the attendant told him he was. The Shadow then made guarded inquiries concerning Myram's Folly, found it had been built by an old judge, who had died thirty years ago. The place hadn't been lived in since, and was watched over by a caretaker.

The Shadow thanked the attendant in the casual tone of Arnaud. He paid for the gasoline and drove from the filling station. Soon The Shadow was riding along the Denbury road.

Near the forks, The Shadow stopped. He donned cloak and hat of black. This was the attire that he intended to wear until his work was completed. He had finished with the role of Arnaud; even at the filling station, The Shadow had kept his disguised features from view.

With two sets of automatics beneath his cloak, The Shadow drove past the forks. He found the road to the right; took it and continued with dimmed lights until he reached a clearing in the woods. He was one and seven-tenths miles from the beginning of the road; here was a suitable spot to leave his car. Driving over the chunky ground of the clearing, The Shadow parked beneath the shelter of silent trees.

Extinguishing the lights, The Shadow stepped from the coupe. He groped to the road, followed it farther inward. There was light enough to pick the path, for an early moon had risen and the whitish rays filtered through the upper boughs of trees. Only the road showed splotches of moonlight. The woods themselves were like looming walls, waiting to engulf any unwary person who might step into their blanketed area.

To The Shadow, those woods were welcome. They offered a vantage spot anytime that he might choose to seek it.

FOLLOWING the old road, The Shadow reached a spot where moonlight revealed a pair of huge stone gateposts. Each was surrounded by a battered, crouching lion. One of the stone beasts was tilted on its pedestal. The moonlight showed a name chiseled in old English letters, upon one gate. The Shadow read the dim name of "Myram."

Moonlight showed that the stone gates were flanked by a wall, also of stone. This barrier probably girded the entire estate. The posts, themselves, were barred by a rusted iron gate. Half off its hinges, the barrier offered no obstacle.

The Shadow approached; he managed to wedge the big gate inward, although the task was more than a one-man job. Stepping through the opening, The Shadow forced the gate back to its former position.

Trees still shrouded the stony road that now served as a driveway to a house somewhere in the woods. From Wishart's confession, from the filling station attendant's talk in Hampstead, The Shadow was confident that he had reached the actual headquarters of Doctor Rodil Mocquino.

It was after eight o'clock; but there was time for the campaign that The Shadow intended. As he glided along the curving stretch of driveway, the cloaked investigator summarized his findings and his plans.

Danger threatened at the Hampstead Knitting Mills. Although The Shadow had found no weakness in the management of that plant, he felt sure that Doctor Mocquino had discovered one. Granting that point, The Shadow had decided that trouble might come at half past nine, when Richard Lassman, the night supervisor, began his tour of inspection.

Therefore, The Shadow had planned to be at the knitting mills at that time, coming there openly, if necessary, in the guise of Henry Arnaud. Circumstances had caused The Shadow to alter that intention. Banzarro's murder of Wishart had forced The Shadow to abandon his role of Arnaud.

Coming here to Myram's Folly, The Shadow saw a better opportunity. By a meeting with Doctor Mocquino, he would have a chance to block off disaster at its source. If he could deal with Mocquino within the next hour, The Shadow would still have time to drive back to the Hampstead Knitting Mills and be there at half past nine. A road that skirted Hampstead offered a shortcut to the mills.

The Shadow believed that Mocquino would expect him to concentrate upon the knitting mills; then seek the Voodoo Master's hideout afterward. By learning of Mocquino's presence at Myram's Folly; by coming here first, The Shadow saw opportunity to take Mocquino by surprise.

Though deep in these thoughts, The Shadow was watching the curving driveway ahead. He saw trickles of moonlight; he edged closer to the trees at the side of the old driveway. Stealthily, invisibly, The Shadow came to the inner fringe of the woods. He stopped upon the edge of a large, irregular clearing. There, beneath the dull glow of moonlight, The Shadow viewed a most remarkable old mansion.

THE building was in the center of the clearing. It was constructed in sections—some of stone, other portions of wood. The front of the edifice looked like a colonial mansion. It had pillars; but they were small ones. Once white, the pillars were weather-beaten and looked tawdry, even in the moonlight.

The driveway went past the front of the mansion and anyone approaching the home from that direction might have accepted it as an old colonial homestead. But The Shadow's view, from the side, enabled him to see the many styles of mongrel architecture that had been added to the original portion of the house.

Directly in back of the colonial section was a mid-Victorian annex that was built in garish style. It had a square-shaped room that formed a fourth floor above the three-story building. The square room had windows in every wall; all of these were heavily shuttered. Above the square room was a broad roof, the size of the room itself. This was girded by a solid wooden railing, four feet in height.

There were other extensions of the house, all unsightly. They had been connected to form an almost solid building. In one rear corner was the most curious part of all. Old Judge Myram had not stopped with a mid-Victorian addition to a colonial mansion. He had finished with walls of gray stone; above these he had added a roundish tower that looked like the turret of a castle. It rose two floors above the house roof and was topped with odd-shaped battlements that were considerably higher than the mid-Victorian tower in the center of the building.

The Shadow could picture but one reason for this unsightly pile. The builder had probably intended to study the completed effect of each section; then rid himself of the composite eyesore by tearing down the portion that he liked least. After that, new wings could have been raised to conform with the section of the house that remained.

Apparently the castlelike portion of the house had been prompted by the fact that a small pond stretched from the rear of the building and continued as a moat on one side. The Shadow could see the stretch of water that shimmered in the moonlight, just behind the rear wall of the massive house.

Such speculations, however, did not concern The Shadow long. One feature of the building was all that interested him: that was some mode of entry that could be accomplished without observation. To The Shadow, Myram's Folly was important only as the lair of Doctor Rodil Mocquino.

CHAPTER XIV
THE PURPLE LAIR

UNTIL his arrival at Myram's Folly, The Shadow had followed the simple process of performing the most direct action that offered. Through that policy, he had arrived quickly at Doctor Mocquino's headquarters. The most obvious step would be to choose the shortest route into the house itself—with the exception of the front door, which would naturally be guarded.

The Shadow, however, decided against quick entry. He knew that Mocquino's henchmen were many. He could picture patrolling groups, keeping constant eye on spots where intruders might try to enter. The Shadow's choice was the most difficult one; for that would mark an unguarded place.

One portion of the building filled the bill. That was the high, castellated turret at the rear. It could not be reached directly without crossing a stretch of water. Therefore, The Shadow chose a roundabout course.

He circled along the edge of the clearing, swinging past the extent of pond behind the house. Following almost to the front of Myram's Folly, The Shadow paused on the far side. The house stood between him and the moonlight. The bulk of the building shaded a direct approach.

Like a ghost come to haunt the monstrous building, The Shadow approached the front corner. He could see a portico beneath the pillars; the space was flooded with moonlight. The Shadow observed three automobiles parked in a cluster. He recognized the rakish touring car in which he had last seen Doctor Mocquino.

Edging to the side wall, The Shadow glided toward the rear of the house. He came to the forward end of the moat, which was nothing more than a slimy ditch dug frontward from the pond. There was space between the moat and the wall. Clinging to that precarious fringe, The Shadow continued his rearward course.

He came to the stone-walled extension that was topped by the castellated turret. The stone was dark, untouched by moonlight. It was rough; it offered projection for gripping hands, space for toeholds. Clutching the wall, The Shadow began an upward course. Black against the wall, he remained invisible as he climbed like a human beetle.

The Shadow's climb was comparatively easy until he reached the tower. He encountered difficulties, but slits in the stone of the tower aided him. Climbing farther, he found the crenelles of the battlement. Hunching himself up from the darkness, The Shadow rolled over the edge and lay flat upon a rounded roof.

THE moonlight showed The Shadow's cloaked form clearly; but no observers could have seen him. Not only was The Shadow above the level of the square room that topped the center of the house; he was also hidden by the irregular wall that girded the small turret.

Here, as he had hoped, The Shadow discovered a trapdoor. Lying flat, he produced a compact jimmy. Prying in expert fashion, he loosened the fastenings that held the trapdoor from beneath.

Once inside, The Shadow lowered the trapdoor above him. He risked a flashlight's blink, keeping the rays almost covered by folds of his cloak. The beam showed the top step of a spiral stairway.

Descending, The Shadow found no further use for his light. The stairs were revealed at intervals by streaks of moonlight that came through slits in the wall. There were eight of these slits; two for each quadrant of the rounded tower.

At the bottom of the steps, The Shadow expected a door. Instead, he saw an unclosed exit that formed a dull frame against the dim lights of an inner, third-floor hall. Stepping into the corridor, The Shadow noted shuttered windows at the ends.

Obviously, wherever rooms or halls were lighted, windows were kept covered so that Myram's Folly would retain its abandoned appearance. Visualizing the composite house as he had seen it from the outside, The Shadow remembered a stretch of blocked windows on the second floor, directly beneath the square, mid-Victorian tower.

The Shadow wanted to reach that portion of the house; for there he believed that he would find Mocquino's own sanctum. To arrive at his destination. The Shadow chose darkness instead of the lighted hallway. From that moment on, he began one of the most fantastic trails that he had ever undertaken.

THE various portions of the house had been built upon different levels, probably from separate plans supplied by different architects. There were short flights of steps in every hallway; rickety doors offered access to deserted rooms. Moving from one apartment to another, The Shadow followed a maze-like course through the side of the house that was toward the rising moon.

The whitened gleam, coming through grimy windows, was sufficient for The Shadow to trace the route he wanted. At intervals, however, he paused to step behind open, badly hinged doors or to linger in some cobwebbed corner. Each halt came when The Shadow heard the shuffle of footsteps or caught the sweeping flicker of an approaching flashlight upon the floor.

Soon after a shuffling guard had passed a room where The Shadow lingered, the cloaked invader emerged into a hallway. There, the moonlight from an end window showed a stairway down to the second floor. The Shadow descended; he was greeted by a lighted hall below. Stopping in the gloom of the stairs, he looked along the passage.

It was deserted; there were rows of doors on both sides. One door attracted The Shadow's immediate notice. It was new, and made a strong barrier. It had evidently been put in place since Mocquino had occupied this strange house.

Advancing, The Shadow reached the door. Edging close against the portal, he tried the knob. It yielded. The Shadow inched the door inward and peered into a tiny anteroom that was dimly lighted and backed by purple curtains.

For a moment, The Shadow paused; then, from a turn in the hallway, he caught the sound of footsteps. The Shadow's only course was to glide from view. He opened the door farther, stepped silently into the anteroom and closed the door behind him.

Gripping an automatic, The Shadow listened just within the door. He was ready to slide behind the barrier if the arriving man opened it; should he encounter the guard, quick fray would be necessary. As The Shadow listened, the footsteps went past the door and faded in the hallway. Need of battle was ended. The Shadow still had opportunity to continue his stealthy search. He had need of speed as well. The Shadow had used up valuable time in his foray into the heart of Mocquino's own domain. The purple curtains promised new discovery. Still gripping his automatic, The Shadow approached the curtains and spread them far enough to peer through.

Beyond the curtains was mellow light that displayed a room of barbaric magnificence. The walls were draped with hangings of a royal purple hue, broken only by grotesque designs in gold. Depicted on the walls were hideous figures, all in golden pattern. Some were dwarf-like shapes, lifesize, with glaring faces, fanglike teeth, claws that served for hands. Others were tigerish beasts that gaped with yawning jaws so lifelike that no observer would have been astonished if they had emitted snarls.

There were snakes upon those purple drapes—golden serpents with venomous fangs and twisted coils. They were as lifelike as the beasts; they looked ready to writhe and raise their heads to hiss.

The room was a fiend's nightmare. No sane man could have stood long, imprisonment within its walls. The Shadow could remember another such room that Doctor Mocquino had owned in the past. That had been a room hung with crimson, where captives lost all time sense under the glare of ruddy lights. But this purple room, with its walls that seemed alive, was a greater and more vivid threat than any that Mocquino had formerly owned.

AT the far end of the room was a dais; that platform was carpeted in purple. Upon it stood a thronelike chair of ebony black, with gold designs on the arms. The chair was upholstered in purple that matched the velvet of the walls. Each arm formed a miniature lion's head in gold. Beside the throne was a high pedestal, also of ebony. Its top was square and deep.

Upon the pedestal stood an object that The Shadow had seen before. This was Mocquino's hypnotic light. The unfrosted bulb was mounted in a squatty lamp base that formed a coiled figure of a lizard. With spread jaws and extended tongue, the golden lizard was as lifelike as the other ornamentations in the room.

Behind the throne were golden curtains, that formed a relief against the purple walls. Viewing them, The Shadow understood the purpose of the apartment. It was Doctor Mocquino's throne room. The Shadow recalled the Voodoo Master's boasts of grandeur; the promise that someday he would rule over hordes of superstitious followers.

A whispered laugh crept weirdly through the curtained throne room. That subdued taunt foretold The Shadow's purpose. The Shadow had found Mocquino's purple lair. The room had become The Shadow's own base of operations.

Within this hideous room, The Shadow planned to learn Mocquino's schemes; then seek the Voodoo Master in person, to finish his present career of crime and evil.

CHAPTER XV
THE PATH BELOW

FROM the moment when he had reached the center of Doctor Mocquino's throne room, The Shadow had taken definite interest in one particular object that stood in the purple lair. That was the ebony pedestal beside Mocquino's throne.

The pedestal was the size of a low table. Its single leg was large and square-shaped. The top of the pedestal resembled a box, its depth almost as great as its other dimensions. That fact indicated that the top was some sort of a receptacle.

Approaching the pedestal, The Shadow discovered that the lizard lamp base was not a permanent fixture. A cord ran from it to the floor. Lifting the lamp, The Shadow rested it upon Mocquino's throne and began an inspection of the pedestal. Fingering the under edge, he discovered a slight separation in the woodwork.

Carefully, The Shadow probed for a hidden spring. The pedestal was like a Chinese puzzle box, dependent upon a secret catch. The Shadow found a section of wood that gave under pressure. There was a muffled *click;* the top of the pedestal slid to one side. Pulling it farther, The Shadow saw the space within.

Indirect lights that shone from corners of the curtained room supplied sufficient glow for The Shadow to discern the contents of the pedestal box. There was a folded sheet of heavy paper that lay beside a thin, leatherbound book. The Shadow unfolded the heavy paper; standing beside the purple throne, he studied diagrams that were inked upon the sheet. They represented plans of this mansion. Shaded portions represented the parts of the house that Mocquino had occupied for his headquarters.

On each floor, The Shadow noted stairways. He discovered—as he had supposed—that the mid-Victorian square tower in the center of the building served as an observation post. In addition, he learned a fact that interested him even more. One diagram showed the basement of the building. The cellar space was marked off into little rooms.

Those could be Mocquino's dungeons, where Harry Vincent and others lay prisoners. The Shadow had not forgotten the men whom he had come to rescue, the human stakes whose lives depended upon the outcome of his duel with Mocquino. Studying stairways and halls, as depicted in the diagrams, The Shadow chose a definite route to the cellar. That done, he folded the paper and replaced it in the pedestal.

OPENING the leatherbound book, The Shadow scanned written statements that pertained to the Voodoo Master's recent crimes. Moving through the pages, he came to one that bore the entry he wished to see. In bold hand, Mocquino had written these cryptic statements:

> Knitting Mills
> Richard Lassman
> Control switch C
> 10:15 P. M.

The first two items were obvious. Mocquino actually intended destruction at the knitting mills; and Lassman was the hypnotized dupe who had become the Voodoo Master's tool. The reference to "Control Switch C" was something, however, that did not conform with facts that The Shadow already knew. In going over papers with Chadron, The Shadow had studied every phase of mechanical methods that concerned the knitting mills and their operation. He had seen no reference to any control switch that bore the letter "C." Turning farther in the book, The Shadow discovered listings that gave an answer to the riddle. They read as follows:

> Control Switch A—Outer door.
> Control Switch B—Alarm lights.
> Control Switch C—Power transformer.
> Control Switch D—Hampstead Theater.
> Control Switch E—Hampstead House.
> Control Switch F—Powerhouse.
> Control Switch G—Time fuse.

As he studied these items, The Shadow grasped the full significance. A and B meant apparatus that operated here in the old mansion. Control Switch C, however, referred to an outside matter. Mocquino had found some way to tap the power line leading into the Hampstead Knitting Mills.

The "power transformer" must mean one of Mocquino's own. It explained how the Voodoo Master intended crime tonight. His transformer had been placed to intercept the current to the mills. It was cutting down the flow of electricity, taking the burden from the regular transformers in the mills.

When Lassman made his nine-thirty inspection, he would simply switch off the transformers at the mills. The action would cause no havoc; therefore, it would pass unnoticed by others who were inspecting the looms and other mechanism. Lassman would lock the transformer boxes and go his way. The simple reason why no trouble would occur was because Mocquino's outside transformer would still be in operation.

At quarter past ten, *after* Lassman had gone off duty and would be back in his own home, Mocquino would swing Control Switch C. The outside transformer would quit. Full current would travel through to the mills, producing a simultaneous effect in every machine room. Looms would speed; flywheels would ride free; belts would snap. Complete chaos would engulf the hundreds of night employees.

The disaster would prove the greatest that had yet struck Hampstead. Its cause would never be discovered. Lassman could not be blamed; for all would happen after he was elsewhere, with a complete alibi. Everyone would concede that the supervisor could not be responsible for a sudden failure of transformers forty-five minutes after inspection time. As Chadron had told The Shadow, those transformers could do no worse than burn out, and thus cut off all current.

Chadron, however, had never dreamed that a master transformer had been implanted outside the mills to take over the work of the inside equipment. The Shadow had not divined the existence of such a device; although he had gained the conviction that Mocquino somehow intended to nullify the regular transformers. At last, The Shadow had the answer.

THE discovery simplified The Shadow's task. It meant that he could handle everything here in Mocquino's own domain, without returning to the mills. It also gave him three quarters of an hour longer in which to work. At present, it was nearly nine o'clock. The Shadow would have until quarter past ten.

In items D, E, and F, The Shadow saw new evidence of Mocquino's machinations. There was only one sort of damage that the Voodoo Master could hope to deliver at the theater, the hotel, and the powerhouse. That would be destruction through explosion. It was apparent that Mocquino had mined the three structures named; that when he pulled the switches, he would blast the buildings sky-high. Tapped wiring; dynamite planted in basements; high-speed fuses attached to the hidden bombs—those items could have been arranged long ago.

When would this destruction come?

The Shadow could give the answer. The explosions would follow the disaster at the knitting mills, probably within a half hour. Mocquino would destroy the theater while it still had a capacity audience. The hotel would go up soon afterward. Last of all the powerhouse, to cut off lights and leave the wrecked town in darkness.

The last on the list—Control Switch G—unquestionably referred to this very mansion. The time fuse was an emergency device. Through its use, Mocquino could dynamite Myram's Folly. Such would be his course if he discovered that his lair was known. The purpose of a time fuse was important: it would allow Mocquino and his henchmen time to pack up and leave before the house was wrecked. The blasting of Myram's Folly would cover Mocquino's trail; the Voodoo Master, ever elusive, could move to a new hideout.

AS he began to turn farther in the book. The Shadow heard a slight sound that indicated an opening door. It came from beyond the curtains on the other side of the room: those drapes through which The Shadow had entered.

Instantly, The Shadow replaced the book in the pedestal, along with the folded diagrams that he had already put there. With his right hand, he slid the pedestal top shut; with his left, he swung the lizard lamp base and its dazzle bulb from the throne to the tabletop.

With the same motion, The Shadow faded behind Mocquino's purple throne. His cloaked form dropped, merging with the darkness of the floor. The golden curtains behind the throne parted at the bottom. Their upper borders scarcely rustled as The Shadow moved into a darkened space behind them.

The cloaked investigator was just in time. Rising behind the golden curtains, The Shadow peered between them to view a man who had entered the room from the other side. It was Banzarro; the ugly-faced lieutenant was carrying his powerful air gun in the crook of one arm. He looked straight toward the throne as he entered.

Pausing as if he expected to see Mocquino, Banzarro waited a few moments; then shrugged his shoulders and turned about. As he went back to the purple curtains, his weapon swung into clearer view. The Shadow saw a long-bladed knife projecting from the end of Banzarro's gun.

The fact that the lieutenant had come inside, bringing his gun with him, was proof that he had merely arrived to deliver a routine report. Not finding Mocquino, Banzarro was going back on outside duty.

Another fact was evident. Banzarro had access to the purple throne room. That explained the reason for the diagrams and the book that were hidden in the pedestal. Banzarro was schooled to carry on with Mocquino's schemes, in case the Voodoo Master should be absent. So, perhaps, were others. Mocquino had spoken facts, when he had announced that his evil would continue whether he lived or died.

A SLIGHT thud told that Banzarro had departed beyond the anteroom door. The Shadow remained behind the golden curtains; but he risked a flashlight, knowing that he was free from observation. The rays showed that he was in a small space between the curtains and a wall. It had a door of its own—one that probably served Mocquino when he wished to enter.

That was not all. Against the wall The Shadow saw an insulated board. Upon it shone a row of glittering switches, each marked with a different letter. Beside the last switch—G—was a clock dial marked off in minutes. It was designed to set the time fuse.

Hinged above the switches was a metal panel, with overlapping edges. It was held upright by a catch. Once lowered, it would cover the switchboard. The Shadow saw three spring locks attached to the panel, each with a keyhole. If Mocquino chose to cover the switches, he could do so by simply swinging the metal panel downward. It would lock automatically; only Mocquino could open it afterward, unless Banzarro or others were also provided with keys.

A few moments ago, The Shadow had held the opportunity to drop Banzarro with a single pistol shot. He had spared the evil ruffian simply because he had not wanted to start action too soon. Similarly, The Shadow had a present chance to put Mocquino's switchboard out of commission, from A to G. Again, he refrained from action. The Shadow wanted to leave no evidence that he was present in Myram's Folly.

With more than an hour ahead of him, The Shadow could let such deeds wait. There were prisoners below, including his own agent, Harry Vincent. The first task was to release those captives; to gain them as allies in the work that was to come. For The Shadow could foresee hard conflict before he settled scores with Doctor Mocquino.

Stepping through the golden curtains, The Shadow crossed the throne room. He put away his flashlight; moved through the purple exit and reached the outer door of the anteroom. With hand on the knob, The Shadow paused. He was sure that he had heard a sound from the depths of the throne room. Stepping back, The Shadow peered between the drapes.

Across the room, he saw the golden curtains part. Into view stepped Doctor Mocquino, clad in a purple robe with sleeves and borders of golden braid. The Voodoo Master had come through the doorway that The Shadow had seen beside the switchboard.

CALMLY, Mocquino seated himself upon the throne. His hand rested upon the ebony pedestal, fondling the golden lizard that served as lamp base. Upon the Voodoo Master's countenance appeared a benign smile, that The Shadow knew to be more dangerous than a leer.

To Doctor Mocquino, human lives were trifles. He relished the part that he played in their destruction. He was looking forward to the deeds that were scheduled for tonight, patiently awaiting the time when his plans would mature.

Hand beneath his cloak, The Shadow gripped an automatic. Again he paused, to let the .45 slide back into the deep pocket that served as its holster. As he had spared Banzarro, so did he decide to let Mocquino live. Even the death of the insidious Voodoo Master could not serve The Shadow at this moment.

Henchmen would respond if they heard a single shot. Mocquino's death would madden them. Some would battle The Shadow, while others would reach the helpless prisoners in the dungeons. The captives would die before The Shadow could reach them. Therefore, Mocquino must wait.

Leaving the Voodoo Master to his thoughts of crime, The Shadow glided noiselessly across the anteroom. He reached the outer door, opened it so silently that even Mocquino's keen ears could not detect the sound. Edging out into the hallway, The Shadow found it clear. He closed the door as softly as he had opened it; then glided to the nearest stairway.

The Shadow was taking the path that led below. Venturing alone through this stronghold peopled with Mocquino's minions, he was choosing a swift but dangerous task: the release of the prisoners to whom Doctor Mocquino had allowed life only while he still sought to balk The Shadow.

All depended upon this present mission. If it succeeded, The Shadow would hold power equal to Mocquino's, within the Voodoo Master's own fortress!

CHAPTER XVI
MONSTERS OF DOOM

THE SHADOW'S course was clear until he reached the ground floor. There, he found immediate need for caution. At the foot of the stairs, he heard the pacing that indicated one of Mocquino's patrolling henchmen. Swiftly, The Shadow drew back to semidarkness; clung close to a wall while the man passed.

The patroller was a squatty, dark-faced rogue, who looked ugly enough to be a cousin of Banzarro. He was clad in rough clothes; from his belt extended the heavy blade of a knife, which The Shadow recognized as a machete. Squinty eyes glanced toward the stairs; they failed to detect The Shadow. The patrolling henchman continued on his way.

Following the hall, The Shadow chose a path through a darkened room. He found a closed door; he opened it and peered into another corridor. There he saw another of Mocquino's minions standing by a doorway. This fellow was taller than the rogue who had passed The Shadow; but he was of similar appearance. He was wearing a dirk at his hip; but The Shadow also saw the handle of a revolver projecting from the man's jacket pocket.

Like the first patroller, this henchman failed to detect The Shadow's approach. After a few moments, the man went along his route. The path was clear to the last flight of stairs.

From his close-up view of Mocquino's watchmen, The Shadow had observed that they were the sort of servitors upon whom the Voodoo Master had always depended. They were imported killers, brought from tropical lands. Their presence here explained, in part, why Mocquino had chosen so isolated a hideout. The Voodoo Master knew that his dark-visaged followers would excite attention, unless kept undercover.

Such men served as the inside guards. There were other rogues outside, under Banzarro's lead. Among them, The Shadow was positive, were thugs recruited from American cities. Such crooks could move about more freely; they would also prefer guns to knives. They had proven that fact in their combats with The Shadow.

Though the inside guards, with their knives, would prove more dangerous in hand-to-hand combat, The Shadow preferred them on the present occasion. He knew that a forced encounter could be made a silent one. Confident on that point, he proceeded more rapidly. He found the stairway that he wanted; he made a swift, but silent descent.

NEAR the bottom of the steps, The Shadow paused. Directly ahead was a door; in front of it stood another of Mocquino's men. A ceiling light showed the rogue's sallow face, his shocky, jet-black hair. Short, but wiry of build, the guard was also one who preferred a knife. His dirk rested in a leather sheath that hung at his right hip.

The sallow guard did not note The Shadow's approach. He was busy, for the moment, rolling a cigarette. The Shadow watched the process; saw the sallow man fish in his pocket for a match. Finding none, the guard grumbled under his breath; then turned to the door and gave four quick raps.

The door opened inward, cautiously. The guard thrust his face through the aperture; spoke a few words. Finally he emerged, bringing a few matches in his hand. The Shadow heard him speak to someone on the other side of the door.

"Bah, Toussant!" snarled the guard. "Why is it not important that I should call you when I need a match? You have nothing to do in that cave of yours! When I give the signal, it is for you to answer!"

Slamming the door himself, the guard stepped away from it. He struck a match to light his handmade cigarette. As the flame flickered beneath the sallow face, The Shadow glided forward.

The guard was alert. He sensed The Shadow's approach. He flicked the match away, gave a sudden snarl as he looked toward the stairs. The Shadow lunged. The guard saw the sudden surge of blackness and made a quick grab for his knife. He managed to wrench the dirk from its sheath.

Then The Shadow was upon him. Bare-handed, the cloaked battler smashed down the guard's raised left arm. With a quick grab, The Shadow caught the hand that was beginning a knife thrust. For a moment, he grappled with the guard; then gained a jujitsu hold.

The guard struck a match to light his handmade cigarette.

The next effect was terrific. The light form of the wiry guard buckled upward. The Shadow spun the man in midair; then released him. Flat on his back, the rogue struck the floor. He lay stunned, almost paralyzed by the jolt that he had received.

Looking about for a place to stow his prisoner, The Shadow saw a space beneath the stairs. He carried the man there; bound his arms with the belt that the fellow wore. Ripping lining from the prisoner's jacket, The Shadow used it for a gag. There was a broken barrel in the corner. The Shadow wrenched away a wire hoop, used it to bind the sallow guard's ankles.

RETURNING to the door at the foot of the stairs, The Shadow gave four quick taps. A few moments passed; the door moved inward. Shoulder first, The Shadow bashed the door wide open. He flung himself into the space beyond and swung quickly about to meet the man whom he knew must be behind the door.

Here was a dingy, stone-walled passage, lighted by dim bulbs set in the wall. The glow showed Toussant. The Shadow had staggered the inner guard by the quick smash against the door. Nevertheless, in Toussant, The Shadow was due to meet a most formidable antagonist.

Floundered against the wall, Toussant formed a

gigantic figure. He was fully six feet eight in height; his physique was proportionate. Though dull-faced, Toussant showed himself quick of action. He rallied as The Shadow spied him. With a terrific spring, the giant came leaping forward.

Huge arms flayed forward. Hamlike hands gripped for The Shadow's throat. In a trice, the cloaked battler was confronted with a situation that he had scarcely foreseen. The Shadow had expected fight from Toussant; but he had not guessed that the man would possess such formidable proportions. By choosing hand-to-hand conflict, The Shadow had gained chance for a silent struggle; but such advantage was offset by the size and power of the combatant who loomed upon him.

Had The Shadow tried to elude Toussant's grip, he would have failed. The giant's drive was too quick; his arms and hands were too long and powerful to escape. Instead of wresting away, The Shadow let Toussant's clutch take hold. Then within the gripping circle of the giant's arms, The Shadow drove forward.

A cloaked shoulder pounded the pit of the giant's stomach. Toussant doubled backward; The Shadow's surge thrust the huge man against the door. The barrier swung shut. His back against it, Toussant recovered. His fingers had slipped from The Shadow's throat; but he had gripped the cloaked arms below. With a mammoth heave, Toussant sent The Shadow rolling to the floor.

Grimly, The Shadow had gripped Toussant's arms. In sprawling, he took the giant with him. They rolled across the stone floor. As The Shadow tried to twist away, Toussant at last gained a throat grip with one mammoth hand. His other arm girding The Shadow's body, Toussant steadied to drive his opponent's head against the wall.

One such smash would have been The Shadow's finish. Toussant had the strength to crack a skull with such a stroke. His own arms trapped in Toussant's girding grip, The Shadow's plight seemed hopeless, at least to Toussant. One of The Shadow's hands was jammed beneath his cloak—a fact that made his cause look even worse. But The Shadow's hand was busy. Upon it rested his salvation in this fray.

As Toussant shouted a fiendish laugh, he started his forward thrust. Simultaneously, there was a muffled report from within the folds of The Shadow's cloak. Toussant's laugh changed to a high-pitched shriek. The giant's arm quivered. It did not complete its thrust. Huge fingers loosened; slow, like an overbalanced tower, Toussant swayed and sprawled headlong to the floor.

His collapse revealed a curl of smoke wreathing at the spot where he had been. That coil of smoke came from The Shadow's cloak.

The Shadow had managed to twist a .45 toward Toussant's body. With a jab of the trigger, he had dispatched a bullet to the giant's heart; Toussant was dead. The Shadow had passed the last of the guards who blocked the path to Mocquino's dungeons.

THE SHADOW was panting; wavering, he slowly recovered from the effects of the clutching fingers that had temporarily choked his throat. Stepping past Toussant's prone form, The Shadow followed the passage toward its inner end. There he found a vaulted opening that led down a short flight of steps to a corridor that ran at right angles to the passage that Toussant had guarded.

The Shadow remembered the diagrams in Mocquino's throne room. All the small rooms opened from that inner, lower corridor. There, The Shadow would find the prisoners behind their bars. With Toussant dead, there would be no one to interfere with the rescue that The Shadow intended.

There was a glow from the lower corridor; dim, like the lights in the passage where The Shadow stood. About to descend the steps, The Shadow noted a sudden blink ahead. He stopped short; turned about.

The lights in his own passage were blinking also. Instantly, The Shadow remembered the instructions in Mocquino's book. Control Switch B: the alarm lights. Someone had learned of trouble here below. Either The Shadow's fight with Toussant had been heard; or the bound outside guard had been found beneath the stairs.

Whichever the case, the result was the same. Word had been carried to Mocquino's purple lair. The Voodoo Master had pressed Control Switch B. Everywhere, lights were blinking the emergency signal. Soon Mocquino's minions would converge upon this spot.

Gripping a pair of automatics, The Shadow started for the outer door of the passage. He had wanted to avoid this conflict until later; but his only course was to begin battle. At least, The Shadow had gained a vantage point that would help his plans. By holding this passage, he could also protect the prisoners, for he would be between them and all incoming invaders.

By reaching the door, The Shadow could first offer resistance on the stairs; then withdraw, if necessary, to the passage. Since the door was his immediate objective, he headed for it rapidly. Before he reached it, the door burst inward.

STOPPING short, The Shadow stood face to face with six blocking enemies—men whose faces and attire were as strange as any that he had ever seen. Each antagonist was brawny; all bore a marked resemblance. Dark of features, glaring of eyes, they faced The Shadow with fixed expressions.

Each foeman wore a helmet with raised visor. Each was equipped with a steel breastplate that resembled Roman armor. For weapons, the six held upraised sabers. They stood like waxen figures, as if awaiting a command that would bring them to life.

Instantly, The Shadow recognized the nature of these foemen. They were zombis—human machines who lacked will of their own. Well did The Shadow know that the zombi lore of Haiti was pure superstition; that the belief that dead bodies could be brought to life had never become a proven fact.

But The Shadow knew the ways of Doctor Mocquino. He knew how the Voodoo Master could take living victims and make them appear as zombis. These were former henchmen who had incurred Mocquino's displeasure. The Voodoo Master had forced them to face his brilliant, dazzling light of many colors; not once, but often. Through such regular treatment they had become the equivalent of zombis. They were shock troops, entirely at Mocquino's call; fighters who would battle like machines, never stopping, even though threatened by instant death.

Their visored helmets; their heavy breastplates, were thick enough to stop pistol bullets. Equipped with such armor, each fighting zombi would come forward, flaying with his saber until too crippled to proceed. Unless they could be stopped before Mocquino arrived, these monsters of doom would become a hideous menace.

The Shadow leveled his automatics straight for the rows of glaring eyes. His move was too late. From the stairway beyond the zombis came the sound of a fierce hiss. Arms raised mechanically, at the very instant when The Shadow aimed his automatics. Hands slapped the sides of helmets; visors clicked down, covering the faces of the six foemen.

A musical laugh sounded from the stairs; the melodious tone was tinged with an insidious note. Beyond the zombis, The Shadow sighted a figure in a purple robe. Doctor Mocquino had arrived in time to give his order. The Voodoo Master was ready to launch his steel-clad monsters of doom against The Shadow!

CHAPTER XVII
THE SNARE BELOW

BRIEF moments would have sufficed The Shadow in his attempt to down Mocquino's inhuman warriors; but those moments were denied. The zombis had heard the Voodoo Master's *hiss*. They had obeyed the order to prepare. All that they needed was another signal to advance.

Mocquino alone could give that command. Knowing it, The Shadow tilted an automatic farther upward; he jabbed quick shots at the stairs. Again, Mocquino was too quick. With his *hiss*, the Voodoo Master had leaped forward. His purple clad figure dropped from view just as The Shadow fired.

At the bottom of the stairs Mocquino was protected by the massed bodies of his zombis. Clustered in the doorway, those six saber-armed fighters formed a solid phalanx. There was no space through which The Shadow could stab new bullets.

A fierce cry from Mocquino; a harsh order in some unknown tongue. The zombis heard it; they recognized their master's wish. With martial stride, the six stepped forward, spreading to form a fanlike rank in the wider space of the passage. Sabers lifted, they closed upon The Shadow.

As the zombis closed upon him, The Shadow did not retreat; nor did he open fire. Instead, he sprang directly into the closing circle, under the very weapons that gleamed from upraised arms.

Instantly, the zombis halted. Mocquino had trained them to strike when they closed with a foe. Arms began their saber strokes.

Those arms were met by hands that carried steel. Swifter than the mechanized warriors, The Shadow had begun strokes of his own. His arms flayed above his head; his fists drove his heavy automatics straight for the sabers and the hands that gripped them.

Clanging one automatic at the guard, The Shadow knocked the weapon from the zombi's grasp. With backhand upswing, he struck a descending forearm to ward off another fighter's blow. Twisting, dropping back, The Shadow dropped his hand to the floor. Coming up with his other arm, he used the barrel of his second automatic to meet the sharp blade of a saber that was cleaving straight for his head.

The zombis were breaking rank. Twisting about, The Shadow threw his back against the wall. He clamped one foot upon the saber which the first zombi had dropped. Beating back two attackers, The Shadow made a side swing with his arm and sent his right-hand automatic scaling along the passage, clear to the arched opening that led to the dungeons.

That gun would be safe there—ready, later when The Shadow needed it. For the present, The Shadow wanted another weapon; one that he had a chance to gain. Dropping to the floor, he grabbed the saber which he held beneath his foot. Swishing away, he grasped the handle with his right hand. The zombi who owned the weapon had already clutched the blade. The Shadow's tug took the saber from the zombi's grasp.

THE CITY OF DOOM 47

A ZOMBI—one of the armored bodyguards of the Voodoo Master.

Hands streaming with blood, the zombi lurched forward. Though weaponless, though wounded by the slither of the blade, he intended to fight until death.

THROUGH his lunge, the zombi served The Shadow.

One swinging saber had just slashed The Shadow's sleeve. Another was driving downward with a truer stroke, when the weaponless zombi jostled the one who sought to cleave The Shadow's skull. The stroke was diverted as The Shadow whirled away. Retreating a few paces along the passage, The Shadow was ready for his attackers. He had only five saber bearers with whom to deal.

Moreover, The Shadow had a saber of his own; and with that weapon, he held an unexpected advantage. The zombis were cluttering forward, swinging their sword arms. The Shadow, slowly retreating, had assumed a fencer's pose. His right arm was extended; his hand used its saber like a fencing foil. His left was ready with its automatic. The time would come when he could use that weapon.

Framed in the outer doorway, Doctor Mocquino leered with rage. He had not anticipated this situation. He foresaw that his zombis would fail to reach The Shadow with their blades. In mechanizing these henchmen, Mocquino had deprived them of all human emotions. They lacked cunning, just as they had no fear. They were trained for close-range battle; they would advance until they gained it. That type of fight would be impossible while The Shadow parried with his saber. Not one of the five zombis could get within arm's length.

Only the sixth zombi, weaponless and bloody-handed, could manage an approach. Having no saber, he kept marching forward, clutching at The Shadow. Each time he came close, The Shadow shifted to deliver a left-hand, backswing stroke with his automatic. Each crash found the visor of the zombi's helmet, jolted the stupid monster and stopped his brief advance.

With clenched fists, Doctor Mocquino snarled from his doorway. Clashing with the zombis, The Shadow heard and saw the Voodoo Master; he took quick aim and fired with his .45. A side-stepping zombi blundered into The Shadow's path and took the bullet against his breastplate. Saved from The Shadow's quick shot, Mocquino took to cover outside the doorway.

DESPITE his superhuman efforts, The Shadow was losing the advantage. He had backed far along the passage. His limit would soon be reached. Though tireless, The Shadow knew that his enemies were the same.

Death to the zombis was The Shadow's only course. Such death, when delivered, would be merciful. Long under Mocquino's hypnotic sway, these creatures could never be brought back to a state of individual intelligence. They were no longer human; nor could they ever be again.

In his parries, The Shadow had discovered the system of the strokes delivered by the zombis. Their mechanical motions were uniform. In meeting the strokes, The Shadow was making a regular round, always ahead of each expected blow. Mocquino has seen that from his doorway; on that account, the Voodoo Master had delivered his snarl.

Twisting his position, The Shadow found that the zombis followed. He shifted; two enemies ran afoul and their saber blades clashed. The Shadow dodged both strokes; drove straight in on a zombi who had completed a swing. With a thrust of his own saber, The Shadow stabbed the point between the close bars of the zombi's helmet visor.

Jamming his shoulder against the mechanical fighter's breastplate, The Shadow gave a forceful pry. His thrust ripped the helmet upward, clear of the zombi's head. Twisting away from the glaring face, The Shadow warded off a pair of saber strokes; pressing back against the wall, he thrust his saber point into another visor and served the second zombi as he had the first.

The first of the two unhelmeted zombis was again upon The Shadow, coming from an angle which cut off retreat. The saber arm was swinging from above the glaring face. Another fighter, this one with a helmet, was beginning a saber stroke.

Lunging from the wall, The Shadow jabbed his automatic straight at the zombi who wore no helmet. As he pressed the trigger, The Shadow swung his saber to ward off the other zombi's blow.

Both moves sufficed. The Shadow's gun blast dispatched a bullet through the unprotected zombi's brain. The killer sagged, a glare still on his face. His body clattered to the floor; his arm never completed its saber stroke. Simultaneously, The Shadow had blocked the other slash.

Swinging back toward the steps to the dungeon, The Shadow turned suddenly to meet the second zombi whom he had deprived of a helmet. He fired another straight shot to stretch this adversary on the stone floor.

Passing the guard of the nearest zombi, The Shadow made another of his expert visor thrusts. Off bobbed a helmet; even before it clattered upon the floor, The Shadow delivered a close-range bullet that destroyed this adversary.

MOCQUINO had heard the shots. Venturing a quick look from the doorway, the Voodoo Master saw the climax. Three of his zombis were flattened upon the floor. Above the motionless, steel-breasted forms, The Shadow was handling the last two saber bearers.

A helmet popped off as Mocquino stared. An automatic thundered. Clanging, a zombi hit the floor, his steel breastplate adding new echoes to the clatter of his helmet.

Sabers flashed as The Shadow parried with the last of the pair. Then came a thrust; a helmet jounced upward and an automatic tongued its doom. Clear at the rear of the passage stood The Shadow, triumphant.

Suddenly, a darkish form lurched up from the floor. It was the sixth zombi; following in the wake of those whom The Shadow had dropped, this forgotten battler had stumbled upon a saber. He still wore a helmet, this zombi; swinging his fresh blade, he was blindly charging upon The Shadow, undeterred by the fate that had overcome five battlers before him.

The Shadow met the lunge; parried and stepped back to gain a position from which he could stab the zombi's visor. The backward pace was one too many.

It brought The Shadow over the top sill of the steps that led down to the dungeon corridor. The cloaked fighter lost his footing; before he could regain it, the zombi was upon him. Clutching the monster's bloody hand, The Shadow went sprawling to the stone floor below, carrying the zombi with him.

Mocquino heard the clatter and dashed madly through the passage. He reached the steps, to see The Shadow rising from beside the zombi's body. Twisting away, The Shadow had let the steel-weighted monster strike head foremost. The crash against the stone below had broken the zombi's neck. The Shadow, however, was only halfway to his feet when Mocquino reached the steps.

Grabbing at an iron ring that projected from a stone wall, the Voodoo Master tugged. There was a clatter from above; with a terrific clash, a steel gate dropped within the archway, at the very top of the steps. Never pausing, Mocquino wheeled about, to dash for the safety outside the front door of the passage, where The Shadow's bullets could not reach him.

Doctor Mocquino had offset The Shadow's victory. The cloaked warrior had slain the Voodoo Master's zombis, only to be snared in the trap that lay below.

CHAPTER XVIII
THE NEW MENACE

IT was six feet to the top of the stone steps. Jarred by the fall, The Shadow was slow to gain a position behind the barred gate. He had plucked up the automatic that he had tossed down the steps; he was ready to add Mocquino to the list of casualties. He arrived too late, however, to find the Voodoo Master.

Stopped by the steel gate, The Shadow found it a most formidable obstacle. Not only was the gate a heavy one; it had dropped between two portions of the archway. There was no way to attack the barrier; its bars were too close to do more than wedge a hand through.

The dim passage showed the sprawled bodies of the zombis. Mocquino had picked a route between them and had gained the cover of the outside door. He had pulled the door shut after him; but it was not quite closed. As The Shadow stared, with automatic leveled, the tones of the Voodoo Master echoed to his ears.

"Seek the prisoners!" issued Mocquino's snarled challenge. "Rescue them! Bring them past the barred gate! Do so, if you can!"

A pause; then a gangly sneer that betold Mocquino's belief in the strength of his snare. Then, in harsher tone, Mocquino added:

"You have slain Toussant and my zombis—but you can thank them for your plight. It took their full strength to raise that gate to its position. To lift it, you will require the power of seven men.

"When you are free, you will find me in my throne room. Perhaps you may arrive in time to witness the completion of my schemes. But I warn you, unless you reach me before the appointed moment, you shall never again interfere in my plans!"

The sixth zombi ... swinging his fresh blade, was blindly charging upon The Shadow.

The outer door slammed shut. Mocquino was gone from beyond it.

THE SHADOW lowered his automatic. Eyeing the gate, he recognized that Mocquino had spoken actual facts concerning it. Its weight was certainly sufficient to tax the strength of Toussant and the six zombis.

Plainly, The Shadow saw what Mocquino's course would be. It would not be long until quarter past ten. At that time, the Voodoo Master would operate his control switches. First would come the havoc at the knitting mills; then destruction of theater, hotel and powerhouse. Finally, Mocquino's tone had told The Shadow, this fortress would also be destroyed.

Mocquino would have no further use for Myram's Folly. His move would be to pack his belongings; set the time fuse and depart with his henchmen. Knowing Mocquino's speed at such transfers, The Shadow could foresee that the time interval would be short. Its exact duration was unimportant, however. The Shadow, even in his present plight, was determined to be free of this pit before Mocquino began his first operations.

Hundreds of lives were at stake. Actual massacre was scheduled for the town of Hampstead. The Shadow alone could avert the slaughter that threatened the city of doom.

To avert it, The Shadow must leave this trap. He must bring a band of followers with him. Therefore, the first step was the rescue of the prisoners. The Shadow knew that they would be comparatively few in number; certainly less than half a dozen. Otherwise Mocquino would fear that they could lift the steel gate, copying the former example of Toussant and the zombis.

Mocquino certainly felt no fears. As proof of his surety, he had removed all guards from below. That was good policy on his part. Having witnessed the slaughter of his zombis, Mocquino was too wise to put other henchmen within range of The Shadow's guns. The steel gate might bar progress; but it offered loopholes for The Shadow's weapons.

Knowing that the outer passage would be clear, The Shadow moved down to the bottom of the steps. The corridor below was lighted; The Shadow looked for the dungeon doorways. He still saw a chance to free himself and the prisoners—to escape the fate of living entombment that Mocquino hoped to bring by blasting the walls of Myram's Folly.

Four doorways greeted The Shadow's gaze. Each was fronted with steel bars. Each dungeon was dark; but as The Shadow gave a commanding whisper, a face appeared at the one gate. The Shadow recognized Harry Vincent. Approaching, he spoke to his agent.

"How many are here?" queried The Shadow. "Who are the other prisoners?"

"Five," replied Harry. "Two are caretakers who belonged here. Another is a man who had some trouble with Mocquino. There are two others who landed here in their car, taking the wrong road by mistake. They are in the last cell—"

Harry's voice broke off. A sudden, gushing sound had started in the darkness of his dungeon. Harry pointed downward, indicating steps upon which he stood. His eyes were wild.

"The sluices have opened!" he exclaimed. "Mocquino promised us that such would be our death! The water pipes are large; one in every cell."

THE SHADOW understood. The dungeons were below the level of the broad pond in back of the large house. So was the corridor wherein The Shadow stood. Cells would be flooded first; then the corridor. Mocquino was not waiting until his departure to destroy the prisoners.

The Shadow looked for the lock on Harry's cell. The agent shook his head; Harry's well-molded features looked weary and hopeless.

"These bars are not doors," stated Harry. "They are solid gratings. Mocquino's men fixed them in place with stone and mortar."

Stepping back, The Shadow studied the bars. Harry was right; Mocquino had placed these prisoners in cells where he intended them to stay forever. Though they had been fed and well-treated, they had known that doom would be their lot.

Yet, in permanently sealing the cells, Mocquino had not gone to great labor. The stone walls of these cellar archways were old and crumbly. Holes had been driven into one side of Harry's door; bars had been inserted there. The other side of the doorway had been torn down, so that the bars could be swung inward. After that, new stone had been mortared into place.

There was no use to attack the new masonry; it was too solid. The old stones, however, told their own story. Since one side of the doorway had been broken down, the other side could be similarly handled. The Shadow saw spaces where cracked mortar had fallen loose.

"I've worked on the stones," began Harry. "But without tools, I couldn't move—"

Harry stopped as The Shadow swung away. Over by the spot where the dead zombi lay, The Shadow stooped and picked up two sabers. One was the weapon that he had used; the other was the sword that the last zombi had carried on his fall.

Coming back to the cell, The Shadow thrust one weapon through to Harry. Keeping the other, he rammed its sharp point between two stones. Jabbing, prying, The Shadow began to loosen the masonry that held one end of the bars.

Harry cooperated from his side. One stone fell under The Shadow's efforts; it struck the steps by Harry's feet, bounced down into the dungeon and splashed into a six-inch depth of water. The gushing pipes were still at work, steadily flooding the dungeons.

There were clangs at the doors of other cells. Prisoners, excited by the inpouring torrents, had roused to hear the noise of rescue. They were shouting for aid. It was due to come.

The Shadow pried away another stone; Harry chiseled one loose, higher up. Finding a deep cavity for his saber, The Shadow gained a powerful leverage and broke away the intervening chunk.

Shoulder against the bars, The Shadow shoved back and forth. Harry supplied added effort. The barrier swayed; its own weight served to crack other sections of the decayed masonry. At last, as The Shadow tugged, Harry fought frantically outward. The bars ripped away; Harry sprawled to the stone of the corridor.

HARRY splashed water as he came free. The tide had risen to the top of the inner steps upon which he had stood.

The Shadow passed the sabers to his agent. In response to a quick command, Harry hurried the weapons to the next cells and passed them through to eager prisoners within. Coming back to the cell that he had left, Harry found The Shadow wrenching one of the loosened bars. It came free from its cross-fastenings; The Shadow passed it along to Harry, who carried it to another prisoner. This new implement was better than the sabers.

Within the next four minutes, every prisoner had a tool with which to smash at the weak side of his cell door. The Shadow had a bar of his own; so did Harry. The water had reached the corridor; its torrent seemed swifter than before. But The Shadow had found the way to defeat disaster.

Stones were clattering; barriers were yielding. One row of bars came down from the doorway where two prisoners were confined within. Eagerly, these rescued men joined in the outside work. Stones cracked; bars twisted. The third door fell. With the water knee-deep, the fourth barrier crashed, releasing the two last men.

Wearied prisoners stood gasping, until one saw the steps up from the corridor, with the formidable gate beyond. That upper archway was new, it had been specially installed by Mocquino. There was no way of smashing the masonry that surrounded the big gate.

The other prisoners stared. They recognized that their combined strength would be insufficient to hoist the gate that had taxed the gigantic Toussant and the six inhuman zombis. Not including Harry, these prisoners were but five in number; and they were wearied. Even if The Shadow could exert the strength of two Toussants, his crew could not perform its part.

Not by mere brawn alone—but The Shadow saw opportunity for an added measure. It was one that Mocquino had not considered; for the Voodoo Master had not supposed that his dungeon doors could be shattered and their bars transformed to implements of labor.

To Harry and the other rescued prisoners, The Shadow issued this command:

"Gather the largest stones. Take these to the gate."

THE ex-prisoners obeyed. Each groped in the water that surged about his knees and found solid stones from the shattered doorways. Harry remembered one that had rolled down into his dungeon. He ducked below the surface of the water to get it. Others copied Harry's example.

Dripping as they brought the last large stones, the eager men found The Shadow on the topmost step by the big gate. He was holding the steel bars battered from the prison cells. As the men laid the stones beside him, he supplied each with a rod. Taking a bar of his own, The Shadow wedged it under the space formed by the lowest crossbar of the gate. The others did the same.

Standing on the dry step just below the top, The Shadow brought his bar down upon one of the raised stones. The bar became a lever; the stone served as the fulcrum. All were ready; The Shadow called for downward pressure. Together, the prisoners leaned upon the bars.

The long leverage brought an instantaneous result. Groaning, the steel gate went a full foot upward. The strength of the combined crew had gained double its normal lifting power.

Strongest of all, The Shadow held his weight upon his lever while he ordered a weaker man to wedge stones beneath the gate. That done, The Shadow piled smaller stones on larger, to gain a closer, higher fulcrum. The aiding men worked quickly, performing the same action. Again, the leverage was applied in unison. New stones were stacked upon the ones that already held the gate.

The water was almost to the top step. Further leverage was impossible with the slippery footing; but no more was necessary. The two-foot space beneath the gate was sufficient. Shoulders first, The Shadow wriggled through between the two pairs of supporting stones. He was on his feet, an automatic in his hand, watching the far door of the passage as the rest came through.

Meeting no challenge, The Shadow ordered his followers to arm themselves with sabers that lay scattered beside the dead zombis. He had his extra automatics ready to pass to others, if they encountered groups of Mocquino's henchmen; but for the present, The Shadow held his own weapons. He had reason to believe that he would need them later. Hence he preferred, if possible, to keep his

The Shadow ... was on his feet, an automatic in his hand, watching the far door of the passage as the rest came through.

own men armed with swords instead of guns.

For The Shadow planned more than mere escape. In his release of the prisoners, he had accomplished his first objective in less than the time required, thanks to the stout cooperation that the men themselves had given.

There was still an interval wherein The Shadow could accept Doctor Mocquino's ironical invitation to meet him in the purple throne room. Within that space of time, The Shadow hoped to save the city of Hampstead from the doom that Mocquino intended to deliver.

CHAPTER XIX
DISASTER'S HOUR

THE SHADOW expected encounter with Mocquino's henchmen. It came soon after he and the prisoners had escaped the Voodoo Master's snare. Hastening through the passage where five dead zombis lay, The Shadow wrenched open the outer door. He stopped short, blocking the six men who were behind him.

Harry Vincent, at the head of the former prisoners, saw why The Shadow had halted. Coming down the stairs from the first floor were two of Mocquino's inside guards, probably bound for a last inspection of the cellar.

Both were armed with two weapons: revolver and knife. Each chose differently, when they sought to deal with The Shadow. One man raised his gun; the other whipped the knife from his belt. The Shadow, one hand still on the doorknob, jabbed two quick shots.

He dropped the man with the revolver before the ruffian could fire. The other hurled his knife just as he received The Shadow's bullet. Staggering as he finished his throw, the knife hurler never found his mark. Dropping back, The Shadow flipped the door half closed and stopped the blade in flight. The knife stopped in the woodwork.

The blade had traveled too high to strike The Shadow; he made his quick move with the door to protect the men behind him, for the arching knife was curving downward as it struck.

The Shadow started for the stairs while his enemies were still tumbling toward him. Harry, close behind his chief, grabbed up the revolver which the first sprawled man had dropped. One of the caretakers snatched the gun from the second foeman's belt. Two of The Shadow's followers were supplied with revolvers, instead of sabers.

In the first-floor hallway, The Shadow encountered four more of Mocquino's men, who had converged there when one had called out the news of shots below. The Shadow opened with quick fire; Harry and the caretaker joined immediately. This skirmish was a short one. Three of Mocquino's minions flattened; the other dashed away to give the alarm.

This produced two more guns for The Shadow's followers. The Shadow passed one of his own automatics to Harry; ordered him to give his revolver to the fifth member of the band. All were now armed. In quick tones, The Shadow gave a final command. Even as he spoke it, lights began to blink. The alarm had reached Mocquino's lair.

LEADING the way, The Shadow cut through to the front of the house, following a route that he knew from Mocquino's diagrams. His purpose was twofold: first, to beat back Banzarro's outside band; second, to make Mocquino think that the fight was confined below.

His order to his followers was a simple one. They were to drive outward, with Harry Vincent at their head, while The Shadow remained within the house.

None was to return to Myram's Folly, once they had left it.

The Shadow was the first to reach the massive front door. None of Mocquino's men had arrived to block the path. Opening the door, The Shadow swung halfway through; then dropped back. His action was perfectly timed for the stroke that he expected.

A missile whistled through the air; it struck the door frame by The Shadow's shoulder and quivered there. The object was a knife, fired from Banzarro's air gun. Mocquino's lieutenant had seen The Shadow, had started to fire, then altered his aim as the cloaked target disappeared. He had pressed the trigger too late.

Banzarro had fired from some spot of darkness. There was no gun flash to betray his position. The Shadow, however, had a better line on where Banzarro lay. The instant after the knife struck, The Shadow clamped his hand beside it, let the muzzle of his automatic lie straight along the handle of the knife. With that, The Shadow pressed the trigger.

The big .45 ripped its return message to Banzarro. A howl from the darkness marked The Shadow's hit of an unseen target. The Shadow had remembered the knife that Banzarro had fired into the room of the hotel in Hampstead. He knew the dead line on which these blades could ride. Deliberately, The Shadow had made himself a target for Banzarro, that the assassin might dispatch an indicator to mark his position. The knife had served The Shadow; not Banzarro. The Shadow's aim was sure, the moment that he chose the line of the knife handle.

SWINGING back into the hallway, The Shadow pulled the door wide. Harry Vincent was awaiting the move; he dashed outside, with five followers behind him. Wild shots began as Harry and the former prisoners passed the portico. Banzarro's men were opening up with their revolvers.

From the doorway, The Shadow opened a short barrage, picking the spots where guns spurted.

Harry and his men were opening quick fire. Spurred by the advantage that The Shadow had given them, they were pursuing the outside horde. Though outnumbered two to one, Harry's stout band had the edge; for their opponents were in flight. Inspired by The Shadow; anxious to serve the superman who had saved them, the released prisoners were not to be stopped.

Within the house, The Shadow closed the door. A strange lull had fallen. The front stairs—short route to Mocquino's lair—remained deserted. Wisely, The Shadow chose another course. He hurried through the ground floor, found an obscure stairway and ascended to the second floor. He reached the hallway that boasted one new door: the entrance to Mocquino's lair, by way of the anteroom.

Only for a moment did The Shadow slow his progress; that was while he opened the door. He made that action silent so as not to warn Mocquino, should the Voodoo Master be within. The door opened, The Shadow did not stop to close it after he had entered. He surged through the anteroom, past the purple curtains, into Mocquino's royal-hued throne room.

The golden curtains at the far wall had been drawn apart. There, by the mellow light, The Shadow saw Mocquino. The Voodoo Master was at his switchboard; the gloat upon his face showed that the time for disaster had arrived.

BOTH of Mocquino's clawlike hands were ready. His left grasped Control Switch C, prepared to cut off the transformer that intercepted the power line between the powerhouse and the knitting mills. His right hand, as eager as his left, clutched two switches at once. They were D and E; if pulled, they would produce instantaneous explosions at the theater and the hotel, in the very heart of Hampstead.

The Shadow had arrived at precisely quarter past ten. Stopping short in the center of Mocquino's throne room, he delivered a burst of sinister laughter that halted the motion of the Voodoo Master's hands. The Shadow's challenge was a wise one. He had seen the clutch of Mocquino's claws. Bullets could not stop the Voodoo Master's intended deed. Mocquino could pull the switches as he fell.

Turning as he heard the laugh, Mocquino saw The Shadow. His glaring eyes spotted an aimed automatic; keenly, Mocquino saw the mark to which the gun pointed. It was his own right hand—the one that was ready to deliver an electric current to the distant dynamite charges.

Quickly, Mocquino yanked his hand away. His action was instinctive. The Shadow fired; Mocquino snarled triumphantly and yanked the lone switch that his left hand held. In the same move, the Voodoo Master dived for the exit from the space behind his throne.

The Shadow sped forward. He had tricked Mocquino, without giving the Voodoo Master time to pause and realize it. Had The Shadow aimed for Mocquino's heart, the fiend would have tugged all the switches. By picking Mocquino's right hand, The Shadow had given his enemy an option.

Letting the explosions wait until later, Mocquino had managed to complete his first objective. He had pulled the switch that would wreck the knitting mills, at the precise time that he had prophesied. Pressed by The Shadow, Mocquino had taken to flight, forgetting that his one deed could be offset.

At the switchboard, The Shadow seized Control Switch C and pressed it upward. Through his own knowledge of Mocquino's device, he was quick enough to avert the disaster that had been started. The Shadow's move restored the operation of the transformer outside the mills.

MILES away, the effect of those moves was felt. At the knitting mills, a sudden roar had greeted workers at their looms. Machinery had begun to speed. Employees had leaped from their benches, shouting in terror as huge wheels wabbled; while belts began to snap. For a moment, destruction had been on its way. Then, only brief seconds later, chaos ended. Machines had speeded up, threatening horror, at Mocquino's tug of the switch. They had slowed, found stability, when The Shadow had thrown off the extra load of power.

Had Mocquino pressed the other switches that he had first handled, his move could not have been rectified. By outguessing the Voodoo Master, The Shadow had prevented even greater destruction than that which threatened the knitting mills.

Crowds in the theater and hotel at Hampstead would have perished without a warning, had Mocquino had his way. As it was, The Shadow's action had saved those threatened hundreds without giving them a single inkling of their danger.

The Shadow's next duty was to prevent any possibility of Mocquino again operating the switchboard. Reaching above the control switches, The Shadow released the metal panel that was hinged to cover the switchboard. He paused as he noticed Control Switch G and the clock dial beside it. Quickly, The Shadow set the dial for ten minutes; then pulled the switch. He was allowing time for his own departure; also relying on the probability that Mocquino would remain longer in Myram's Folly.

That done, The Shadow pulled down the panel.

BANZARRO—chief aide to Doctor Rodil Mocquino, the Voodoo Master.

As soon as the latches clicked, he bashed the locks with a gun handle. No key could open those locks; if Mocquino should return, he would try vainly to raise the panel. Given half an hour, Mocquino might manage to jimmy the locks. But Mocquino would not have a half hour. Ten minutes would be his greatest limit.

At the end of that period, Myram's Folly would go up in thunder. The Shadow had set Mocquino's own time fuse to destroy this useless structure. There was no need to follow Mocquino, to rout him from some hiding place. The Shadow's own course had become departure; to join Harry and the rescued men before the blast went off.

The surest course was back through the throne room, out by the hall. Combat en route did not seem a great threat to The Shadow. He had already quelled Mocquino's scattered henchmen whenever he had met them.

With surety that he could clear the way, The Shadow started through the throne room. He stopped as he reached the throne itself.

Purple curtains ripped away from the doorway at the anteroom. Revolvers bristled, glimmering, from the hands of a dozen foemen. Mocquino's henchmen were here in greater number than The Shadow had known. Summoned to one duty, they had arrived en masse to block The Shadow. Glaring faces, leering lips; these told of the confidence that inspired Mocquino's horde.

No lone fighter could hope to survive a battle with that throng. The Shadow had nullified Mocquino's hour of disaster; he had averted doom that threatened hundreds of helpless victims. Mocquino would never have a chance again to deal the destruction that he wanted.

Probably, the Voodoo Master had realized it. Therefore, he had chosen a course which pleased him equally. He had hurled his henchmen to a final thrust. The Shadow, himself, was the victim whom Mocquino sought.

This was Mocquino's challenge. The Shadow, though he had saved the lives of hundreds, was faced by death from a firing squad. The Shadow was trapped within Mocquino's purple lair.

CHAPTER XX
DEATH'S HARVEST

HALTED between Mocquino's purple throne and the ebony pedestal beside it, The Shadow stood half crouched. He was at bay; his foemen recognized his plight. The Shadow was too far forward to escape through the golden curtains. The throne could not serve him as a shield. Bullets from revolvers would rip through woodwork and plush, if The Shadow chose such a refuge.

Mocquino's henchmen had spread in the same fashion as the zombis. The Shadow faced them with a lone automatic; his weapon was not even raised. Beneath his cloak he had another brace of guns; but he would never have time to draw them. For he was faced by vengeful marksmen, who would fire as one. Unlike the blundering zombis, these henchmen were not mechanical in action.

Individually, they feared The Shadow. In a horde, they lost their dread because of numbers. Once a single trigger finger tugged, all would follow. The only factor that stayed the assassins was the motionless position of The Shadow.

They knew the fallacy of quick aim, did these killers. They welcomed the pause that gave them a chance to steady and level their revolvers. They were ready to fire before The Shadow could move his gun hand.

They saw The Shadow's gun fist loosened; clad in a thin black glove, it seemed helpless. They spied a tremble of the gun hand; it was matched by a twitch of the other gloved fist. His fingers shaking as if seized by a palsy, The Shadow let his free hand steady upon the ebony pedestal.

Suddenly, the tremble ceased. Free fingers moved; a sharp *click* sounded. With it, the purple-walled room was filled with spontaneous light. The Shadow was gone, hidden in a protecting glare. In his place was a dazzle of tremendous light that came in vivid colors from a rounded cage of glass.

The Shadow had pressed the switch at the base of the lizard lamp stand. He had snapped the current into Mocquino's high-powered bulb. The Voodoo Master's own device was loosened, shooting the instantaneous flashes of brilliance that could overpower all who faced it—excepting The Shadow and Mocquino himself.

WITH wild shouts, Mocquino's henchmen dived for the cover of the purple curtains. They knew the power of that light; how Mocquino used it to turn sane men into zombis. With one mad surge, the entire dozen took to the anteroom not waiting to fire a single shot.

Nor did The Shadow wait. The instant that he clicked the switch, he made for the golden curtains—on the chance that some adversary might sizzle a potshot in his direction. Though he could resist the glare himself, The Shadow—like others—was unable to discern objects beyond it. He did not care to waste wild shots. His plans were already made; there were less then ten minutes for his departure from Myram's Folly.

Cutting out through Mocquino's own exit, The Shadow was confronted by a trio of Mocquino's reserves. They were at the end of a hallway; they opened fire suddenly, but not in time. The Shadow was swinging for cover as they attacked. Springing to a doorway, he heard a sharp snarl from beyond the marksmen. Mocquino, himself, was stationed with that protective trio.

Jamming a door inward, The Shadow cut through a darkened room. He came out into another hall; made for a stairway, only to reverse his course. Four more enemies had bobbed in view; they were from the crew that had invaded the purple lair. Safely away from the sparkling light, they had again become maddened, desperate fighters.

The Shadow delivered quick shots from a doorway. One enemy sprawled; the others took to the stairway that The Shadow wanted. Knowing that attack upon that ambush would be futile, The Shadow took to the other end of the hall. More of Mocquino's men appeared. Quickly, The Shadow cut through another room.

The next few minutes produced quick surprises. Weaving in and out from unexpected doorways, The Shadow encountered Mocquino's henchmen at every turn. The house was alive with the murderous rogues. The dozen who had grouped against The Shadow were but half of the total that Mocquino controlled. Needing one hand to yank at doorknobs, The Shadow was restricted to use of a single gun. He employed it at every turn, switching his emptied weapon for a fresh one. Halts were useless; they would only bring a massed throng to the spot.

The Shadow's one objective was the front door; to gain it, he needed to reach a stairway.

The Voodoo Master's own device overpower all who

was loosened, shooting the instantaneous flashes of brilliance that could faced it ... excepting The Shadow and Mocquino himself.

Each flight of steps proved to be a nest for Mocquino's minions. All that The Shadow could accomplish in four minutes of hectic fray was the elimination of three enemies, each a member of a different group that he encountered.

WITH sudden change of tactics, The Shadow chose a stairway that led upward to the third floor; and hence proved unguarded. At the top, The Shadow came upon a group that he had not seen since his first encounter with them on the floor below. There were four in the cluster: Doctor Mocquino and the three underlings who served as his own bodyguard.

As The Shadow opened fire, Mocquino leaped for a doorway. The Shadow saw him spring upward, taking the stairway that led to the central lookout tower of the building, that square-walled room that loomed above the roof. Two of the bodyguards succumbed before The Shadow's rapid shots. The third followed Mocquino, slamming the stairway door as he passed it.

There was no chance to follow. The Shadow's gun was emptied. As he reached for his last automatic, he heard thuds of footsteps everywhere. Bands of enemies had located the sound of the fray. They were coming to surround The Shadow, to block off his escape. This time, he would be ambushed if he tried to reach the second floor.

Few minutes remained. Departure by the ground floor would be impossible. Any delay would bring the moment of destruction. The Shadow took the one course that remained—a route that he had reserved in case of final emergency. Speeding toward a darkened hall, he dashed through the rear portion of the third floor, just as the first of the arriving squads sighted him.

Shouting fighters followed, thinking their enemy in flight. They fired wildly, uselessly, in the darkness. They could not see The Shadow; but they heard his footsteps, for he was making no attempt to cover his route.

Suddenly, The Shadow's course led upward. Mocquino's minions stopped at the entrance to the old castle tower that adorned the back corner of Myram's Folly.

The Shadow had gone above, following the circular stairway, keeping to the wall, away from the open center. With shouts to their fellows, half a dozen of The Shadow's enemies dashed upward in pursuit.

The Shadow reached the rounded roof; slamming the old trapdoor, he pounded its surface with the handle of an emptied automatic. Wood splintered and jammed the trap in place. It would take minutes for the men below to crack it. Swinging to the rough-hewn parapet, The Shadow looked beyond the stone bulwark, toward the center of the building.

There, in the clear glow of moonlight, he saw a figure above the solid wooden rail of the mid-Victorian tower, a dozen feet lower than The Shadow's own vantage point. It was Doctor Mocquino, his purple robe blackish, its gold trimmings dull against the moonlight.

The Voodoo Master had guessed The Shadow's objective, for he had heard shots from within the rounded tower that The Shadow had ascended.

AS he saw The Shadow, Mocquino rasped a command. Mocquino's last bodyguard bobbed up beside him. Both opened fire with revolvers. Bullets chipped the stone beside The Shadow; he dropped below the level of the bulwark.

Jabbing his automatic through a stone crenelle, The Shadow used that space to return the fire. His bullets splintered the wooden rail; one found Mocquino's henchman. The Shadow heard a cry. He fired for the rail, knowing that Mocquino would be behind it.

Men were pounding at the trapdoor close by The Shadow. That sound did not trouble him. Mocquino was the only enemy who could battle him during the scant moments that remained. The Shadow halted his fire, reserving last shots for the Voodoo Master, should he reappear.

The moonlight revealed a grisly sight. Up from the rail of the square roof moved a death-stilled figure. It was Mocquino's last bodyguard, his corpse as mechanical as one of the Voodoo Master's zombis. From beneath the dead man's right arm there came a living hand, aiming the bodyguard's own revolver.

The hand was Mocquino's. The Voodoo Master had taken his dead henchman for a shield. Ready with the gun, Mocquino awaited The Shadow's reappearance. Through ghastly artifice, Mocquino hoped to win a last combat with his superfoe.

The Shadow delivered a triumphant laugh. From his parapet, the mirth rose in sardonic mockery. The trapdoor was breaking below him; Mocquino was prepared to stop him with a deadly aim; nevertheless, The Shadow knew that victory was close. He sprang into view, wheeled across the rounded roof and neared the rear parapet.

MOCQUINO fired. His bullets sizzled wide of the moving target. The Shadow was too swift for Mocquino's hand to follow him, for the Voodoo Master's arm was burdened with the weight of the dead man whom he held as shield.

The Shadow fired return shots; weaved one direction, then the other. Suddenly, he sprang to the rear parapet itself, just when Mocquino expected him to drop to cover.

Again, Mocquino fired wide.

The Shadow sped a bullet that came a scant inch from Mocquino's projecting arm. It was his last shot; but it made Mocquino shift, swinging the dead body with him.

At that moment, the trapdoor splintered open; a head poked through; with it a fist and a revolver.

The Shadow hurled his emptied automatic straight for the glaring, grimy face. The heavy weapon crashed the upthrust jaw; Mocquino's henchman dropped back through the trapdoor.

Mocquino saw the action; observed that The Shadow was weaponless. Dropping the corpse that served him as shield, the Voodoo Master aimed. Simultaneously, The Shadow spun upon the parapet. With a long, sweeping dive, he went head foremost over the rear edge, taking a forty-foot plunge for the pond below.

The Shadow had held out to the last possible

moment, knowing that he would be a target when he reached the moonlit pond. He was gone from Mocquino's range; but there would be others, on the rounded roof. Last moments had seemed slow to The Shadow. He had lingered in hope of a quake which he knew would come. That was the sign he wanted before he made the dive.

The token came while The Shadow was speeding downward through the air. From the depths of Myram's Folly came a muffled blast. The building quaked; the depths delivered another burst. Then came the third explosion one that seemed to rip the countryside with a searing volcano of flame.

The Shadow had hit the water; arms tilted upward, he shot to the surface at the end of a shallow dive. Nearly ten feet deep, the pond had given him ample leeway.

As his face came above the water, The Shadow swung his head toward the tower that he had left. He was met by a sweeping tidal wave, as if the whole pond had lifted.

SWIMMING away with the sweeping wave, The Shadow saw the end of Myram's Folly. The gray stone tower had buckled inward. Pygmy men who had reached its top were tilted from it, down into the crumbling ruin of the building below. Foundations had been shattered by the buried mines that Mocquino had installed. Old, decaying, the building added to its own collapse.

Outer walls had fallen to ruin. The stone tower was gone, to give weight to the debris. Cracking stone and splintering wood were scourged by the thrusts of flames. The men on the stone tower had met their doom; those within were buried in the crash. Others, lower in the house, were lost in the destruction.

Oddly, amid that tremendous smash, one portion of the building resisted. Swaying, it seemed to fight against the fall. That was the square room above the center roof—the mid-Victorian tower.

Upon it, his clenched fist high above his head, stood Doctor Mocquino. With his other hand, the Voodoo Master was clutching the wavering wooden rail—like the captain of a sinking vessel, stationed on the bridge.

From the shore of the pond, The Shadow saw the finish. Others, too, observed it: Harry and the rescued men, back from the chase in which they had downed the last of Banzarro's ruffians. They watched Mocquino sway as the square tower lurched; they saw the lookout room collapse and take its final plunge.

Down into the ruins of Myram's Folly went Mocquino, still clinging to the wooden rail. The woodwork splintered as the Voodoo Master went from view, into the very center of the shattered mass that no longer resembled a building.

Last sections of wall tumbled. Flames crackled high amid the dust of crumbled stone. The last sign of life had disappeared from the ruin.

ABOVE the roar of the rising fire came a grim, sardonic laugh. Mirthless, it told of deserved triumph. It marked the doom of evil men who had engaged in schemes of murder and destruction. It foretold that facts would be made public, when revealed by Harry Vincent and the others who had been prisoners in Mocquino's dungeons.

Crime would be laid where it belonged—to Doctor Rodil Mocquino and his chief assassin, Banzarro. Some past deeds would be understood, such as Banzarro's murder of Wishart, the chauffeur. Others would be guessed at, yet their true facts never learned.

For the full tale of Mocquino's mad reign of crime had been grasped by The Shadow alone. He, the master of right, would preserve those details in his hidden archives. The Shadow, alone, had conquered Doctor Rodil Mocquino.

THE END

The smoldering ruins of Myram's Folly.

RISE OF THE SUPERVILLAIN by Will Murray

This Nostalgia Ventures Shadow volume is a sequel to our recent Batman theme wherein we delved into the Shadowesque origins of the Caped Crusader. Without the first Knight of Darkness, there would be no Dark Knight today.

Here we examine the influence of The Shadow on the infamous villains of Batman.

Supervillains in *The Shadow* go back to the 1932 novel *Dead Men Live,* wherein Walter Gibson introduced the concept of "supercrime." These were criminal acts so devious that law enforcement authorities either didn't suspect they were crimes, or were so spectacular they could not effectively deal with them.

Of course supercrimes could only be committed by super-criminals. Gibson sometimes called them that. He coined other terms: supercrook was his favorite. There were variations. Superfoe. Superhand of crime. And superspy. Strangely the term supervillain was one he seldom evoked.

Gibson once recounted the rise of the Shadow supervillain:

"Avid readers of *The Shadow Magazine* began listing villains from the very start, but very few of them were worthy—or unworthy—of more than passing notice. Mostly, they simply crossed paths with The Shadow to their own deserved misfortune, although there were some whose schemes were so fiendish that they demanded rapid counteraction on The Shadow's part. But by the time the magazine was entering its third year, it was evident that crimedom would be on the way out unless a new breed of supercrooks arose to match The Shadow's might with machinations of their own."

Early Shadow supervillains included Gray Fist, The Crime Master, The Scarlet Macaw and The Red Blot. Readers loved them, and demanded more.

This culminated in *The Voodoo Master* in 1936. That story was sitting in the Street & Smith office safe awaiting publication when *The Shadow Magazine* entered the throes of turmoil. To meet rising competition from other pulp avengers Gibson was asked to modify his plot formulas. He did, and one of the innovations that came out of this period was *The City of Doom,* in which the first recurring superfoe was resurrected.

Neither Gibson nor his editors imagined when *The Voodoo Master* was completed that it would spark a sequel. Street & Smith shied away from such things. But in searching for new angles, a question was probably asked: "Do we have any villains who could be brought back?"

The short answer was "No." The Shadow invariably saw to their just and final demise. Someone must have remembered the villain of a story still awaiting publication, Dr. Rodil Mocquino.

Resurrecting Dr. Mocquino was easy enough. The final passage of his introductory story was revised to allow him to survive his first brush with the Dark Avenger.*

So *The Voodoo Master* was fast-tracked into production and Gibson went to work on a sizzling sequel, which he called "Dr. Mocquino's Return" and his editor retitled *The City of Doom.* They were published two months apart in the spring of 1936.

Bad guys returning from the dead were nothing new. Sax Rohmer periodically resurrected Dr. Fu Manchu. Professor Moriarity plagued Sherlock Holmes. And there were others, going back to Nick Carter's dime-novel archnemesis, Dr. Quartz, believed to be the first recurring villain in all of mystery fiction.

DOCTOR RODIL MOCQUINO—the Voodoo Master

So it was probably inevitable that when Bob Kane and Bill Finger moved through their first year or two of Batman, they were forced to turn to The Shadow for villainous inspiration. After all, they were facing the same story problem Walter Gibson had back in 1931-32.

Pitting Batman against typical machine-gun wielding hoods and gangsters quickly became boring for creator and reader both. More powerful adversaries were needed if the series was to last.

The first was Dr. Death, an evil scientist and extortionist who appeared in the third and fourth Batman stories in 1939. With his fiery finish and subsequent resurrection, he might well have been modeled after the Voodoo Master, who had returned for a third time in the 1938 Shadow novel *Voodoo Trail.* Like Dr. Death, Dr. Moquino did not reemerge unscathed from his punishing defeat at the hands of the Master of Darkness. Both were horribly disfigured by fire. Another clue to Dr. Death's Shadowy origins was his Indian assistant, Jabah. Walter Gibson often gave his master villains

---

*Note: See *The Shadow* Volume #3.

hulking henchmen of East Indian or Afghan extraction. Usually they went by single names. Finger once said, "The villains were patterned after those in the pulps, kind of bizarre and wild."

The most famous recurring Batman adversary was of course The Joker. He first appeared in *Batman* #1, in two stories, and was slated to die of a self-inflicted knife wound in the concluding tale. Recognizing the crime clown's potential, editor Whit Ellsworth brought Bill Finger up short, saying, "Bill, are you crazy? We have a great character here." The ending was hastily redrawn to allow the Joker to live. He's tormented Batman ever since.

Having grown up on pulp-magazine conventions, it never occured to Bill Finger that The Joker could return again and again and again.

As revealed in our previous volume, Shadow ghostwriter Theodore Tinsley had created a white-faced villain for his Bulldog Black series in 1937, who was known as The Joker. He was not so much a direct inspiration of the Batman villain as was Tinsley's 1939 superspy, Number One, who tangled with The Shadow in *Death's Harlequin.*

Tinsley had a knack for master villains modeled after playing cards. The villain of one 1933 pulp series was known as the Scarlet Ace. He wore a red hood to conceal his true identity, and in that way bore a startling resemblance to the Joker in his pre-crime clown incarnation as the Red Hood. Coincidence might explain this uncanny parallel.

One 1938 Shadow foe could easily have inspired Two-Face, who had been District Attorney Harvey Kent until half his face was scared by acid. The Face used glowing green makeup and special lighting to distort his true visage. On the cover of *Face of Doom,* he's depicted with the classic split Two-Face look. Kane's Two-Face was half-purple, not green, however.

"Two-Face was inspired by Robert Louis Stevenson's classic story of the good and evil sides of human nature, *The Strange Case of Dr. Jekyll and Mr. Hyde,"* Kane explained. "I saw the Fredric March movie when I was a kid; I hadn't read the novel when I created Two-Face."

Undoubtedly Dr. Jekyll and Mr. Hyde provided the core conceit for Two-Face, but his depiction seems straight out of *Face of Doom.* His origin, however, seemingly stemmed from another source.

"Ironically," Kane noted, "Bill Finger may have been inspired by the origin of our competitor, the Black Bat, in writing the first Two-Face story. Like Harvey Kent, the Black Bat was a handsome district attorney whose face was splashed with acid by the criminals he was prosecuting. Aside from this, the two characters were quite different. The Black Bat's real name was Tony Quinn...To disguise his identity as the Black Bat, Quinn pretended that the acid had blinded him. However, Quinn's disfigurement was confined to the scars around his eyes and he never became a hideous-looking monster like Two-Face."

A Shadow imitation, the Black Bat debuted only a month after Batman. His scarred features inspired him to don an ebony hood and black batwing cloak in order to fight crime secretly. As he explained to his confederate, Silk Kirby, in *Brand of the Black Bat:*

"But there must be some means of identification," Quinn pursed his lips. "Something by which men can recognize me. An insignia—a name, Silk—I have it! I've been blind—as blind as a bat. I still am so far as anyone knows. I shall prowl during the night. Bats are blind and fly by night also. I'll be the bat, Silk. *The Black Bat!"*

"His costume was reminiscent of Batman's," Kane pointed out. "He wore a cowl, gauntlets with fins, and a batlike cape, but his cowl was rounded, didn't cover his nose, and had no ears. He also lacked a bat emblem on his chest."

Other Shadow imitators also influenced Batman. One was the Phantom Detective. Some of Batman's more nefarious villains were lifted from colorful supercriminals like the Green God and the Crimson Clown that the Phantom battled. Take the Keyboard Killer from Charles Greenberg's 1940 novel, *The Phantom and the Melody Murders.* Like the Joker, the Riddler and so many others, his M.O. was to leave clues to future crimes via taunting lyrics, challenging the police to catch him first.

Greenberg graduated from The Phantom to scripting Batman. His *Phantom* editor, Jack Schiff, went on to edit *Batman* for 20 years, inspiring further parallels.

"It's funny," Schiff once mused. "Not until it was brought out so sharply, that Batman was a combination of the Bat and the Phantom Detective, did it really hit me. There's no question in my mind that [those characters] must have influenced Bill and Bob. And then the whole business of the Bat and the origin is so similar. Bill was honest and if I had cornered Bill with that—I don't know why I didn't—he would have admitted it."

Schiff seemed unaware of the Shadow influence. But then The Shadow inspired that entire generation of pulp and comics writers and artists and editors. His intense shadow fell over them all.

The villain of our second story is nothing like The Face or Two-Face but his name, Five-face, might well have inspired the latter's name. It's also one of the most ingenious Shadow puzzles of the 1940s, which is why we've chosen *The Fifth Face* to round out this villainous volume. •

A Complete Book-length Novel from the Private Annals of The Shadow, as told to **MAXWELL GRANT**

Was it the face of death? Only The Shadow knew!

CHAPTER I
THE FIRST FACE

THREE men were gathered in a garish apartment that had an appearance of past glory. Gold-braided curtains were frayed at the edges; mahogany chairs were scratched and battered. Even the fancy wallpaper looked ready to peel itself.

As for the men, they had a shabby touch. They were playing cards around a table, and each had a stack of bills along with his chips. But they were harboring their cash, and the sharp looks that they exchanged marked them as a trio of leeches, each intent to bleed the others.

Three big shots who hadn't made the grade. The term defined the trio to perfection. All were men of evil ambitions, but with balked careers. They had been in the money once, but never to the extent they wanted.

The man at the left was Grease Rickel. His nickname, Grease, was a shortened term for Greaseball. His fattish face was oily, ugly, and his slicked hair, black like his eyes, merely added to his unlovely appearance.

In his palmy days, Grease had specialized in the hat-check racket, gaining "concessions" from restaurants. Smiling girls had coaxed sizeable tips from patrons, and Grease, as owner of the concession, had collected ninety cents on the dollar. But the racket was all over. Restaurants weren't letting out concessions to Grease Rickel any longer.

Opposite Grease was Banker Dreeb. He was long-faced, solemn, and looked something like a banker, which, in a sense, he had been. A few years ago, when certain people wanted money they borrowed it from Banker. The certain people were crooks who were in trouble, and Banker supplied them bail money, along with special services.

In brief, Banker had operated as a professional "springer" who could get friends out of jail. But the law had become very suspicious of Banker's money and would no longer take it. The old-line politicians who had formerly smoothed Banker's path were no longer connected with civic affairs.

Third in the group, the man who faced the door, was Clip Zelber. He was sharp-faced, shrewd of eye, but quite as seedy as his two companions. Clip had once been a very crafty fence who disposed of stolen goods, but had lately found such merchandise too hot to handle.

The three were snarly as they talked. From their very manner, they recognized that their card game was futile. They wanted better prey than themselves, and when a cautious rap came at the door, the trio came to their feet, exchanging eager looks.

"It's Jake Smarley," chuckled Grease. "You guys know Smarley, the bookie. I told him to come around."

"So you said," nodded Banker. "Smarley is hitting it tough, too. He had to close his horse parlor. He's doing his own legwork, coming around to collect bets from guys like us."

"Yeah," agreed Clip, in a short tone. "Let Smarley in. It makes me happy to see that old sourpuss. He'll probably put on a crying act before he leaves here."

Grease went to the door and opened it. He was right; the visitor was Smarley. No one could mistake the decrepit bookie, who was living on the small bets that he collected on a flimsy percentage basis.

Smarley was shambly and stoop-shouldered. His face was dryish, gaunt, with deep furrows stretching downward from his eyes, like waiting channels for the "crying act" that Clip had mentioned.

From a pocket of his shabby overcoat, Smarley produced a newspaper and placed it on the table. His dryish lips were straight, as his beady eyes looked from man to man. Grease picked up the newspaper and started to thumb through the pages.

"We'll take a look at the races, Smarley," Grease began, in an indulgent tone. "Maybe we can spare some dough for the ponies, if you give us the right break—"

"Wait!" Smarley's tone was a cackle. "Take a look at the front page first, Grease. It's got something extra special."

Flattening the paper, Grease scanned the front-page headlines. Banker and Dreeb peered over his shoulders, fascinated by what they saw there. It was Grease who voiced:

"One hundred grand!"

"Better read about it," crackled Smarley. "Maybe it will give you fellows an idea."

ANYTHING involving a hundred thousand dollars could give ideas to the ugly three. Their faces showed elation as they read the preliminary details. The hundred thousand was the present property of Arnold Melbrun, head of the United Import Co., and the sum was entirely in cash.

It had to deal with the steamship *Anitoga*, which, along with its valuable cargo, had run into war-zone troubles. For weeks, the ship had been tied up in a belligerent port, its fate a matter of doubt. Finally, it had been released, and the owners of the cargo had agreed to pay the crew members a substantial bonus as soon as the *Anitoga* docked in New York.

They had turned the money over to Melbrun; he had put it into cash, which was guarded in his office. The *Anitoga* was due this evening, and the money was going to the pier by armored truck.

There, police would be on hand while the crew members received their cash awards. The sum total came to approximately one hundred thousand dollars.

"Say, Clip," began Grease, turning to Zelber, "if you could round up those rats who used to work for you, they'd make a slick mob. They could pile onto that ship and take the dough off the sailors—"

"With the coppers on the job?" demanded Clip. "Not a chance! Banker, here"—he nudged toward Dreeb—"is the guy to handle it. Those smoothies that work for him could grab off the dough while it's going to the dock."

As he finished, Clip gave Banker a sharp-eyed glance, which the solemn-faced man returned in a cold fashion.

"My bunch couldn't knock off an armored truck," declared Banker. Swinging to Rickel, he continued: "I'm passing the buck to you, Grease. Send some of your strong-arm boys over to Melbrun's office and grab the dough before it even starts."

Grease appeared to be considering the proposition; then his oily lips formed a smile, as he shook his head. His smile, however, was not a pleased one. With Grease, a smile usually indicated the opposite of pleasure.

"It would be a giveaway," declared Grease. "It says here that the dough is being watched. Melbrun has some private dicks on the job. I'll agree that the office is the best place to stage the grab, but we can't get anybody who will do it. They'd be marked as soon as they stuck their noses in the place."

There was a glum silence, which ended when Grease crumpled the newspaper and flung it on the floor.

"This town has gone to pot!" snarled Grease. "There used to be a chance to get away with anything. Plenty of soft pickings, until one guy put the crimp in it. The Shadow!"

Banker and Clip acknowledged the name with scowls; nevertheless, they gave reluctant nods.

"It was The Shadow who swung things the wrong way," continued Grease. "He kept busting into everything, and that got the coppers on their toes. He's still in it, too, The Shadow is. That's why nobody will take chances, unless they've got a perfect setup.

"Suppose we three did the job ourselves. We couldn't go to Melbrun's office wearing masks, or we wouldn't get inside. So we go as ourselves, and then what? We get the dough and lam with it, before the bulls can nail us. But we're marked, and there's one guy that will never forget us."

Pausing, Grease stared from Banker to Clip, then snarled the name that both of his pals had in mind:

"The Shadow!"

IN the following silence, the three forgot Jake Smarley. They didn't remember the sad-faced bookie until he broke the spell with one of his crazy cackles.

"Three big shots!" jeered Smarley. "Three big guys, chopped down to midgets! Maybe you'd be useful, though"—his dryish lips took on a grin—"if a real big shot let you work for him. Suppose a real brain came along. Would you play ball?"

Puzzlement, then interest, showed on the faces of the three listeners. It was Grease who gruffed:

"On what kind of terms?"

"Forty percent for the big shot," proposed Smarley. "You three divide the other sixty. The big guy walks in and gets the hundred grand, and you three have your outfits outside, to cover his getaway. And this"—Smarley was crouched forward on the table—"won't be the only job."

No vote was needed. Grease, Banker, Clip, all voiced their instant agreement. They were willing to serve as lieutenants under such a chief, if Smarley could produce him. When they inquired who the bigshot was, Smarley gave them a dryish grin.

"Call him Five-face," suggested the bookie. "Because he's got five faces—get it? He gets spotted when he grabs the mazuma, sure, but even The Shadow won't find him. Because Five-face will wipe off his map, like this"—Smarley started to spread his hands across his face—"and be another guy!"

An instant later, the lieutenants were gawking in amazement. They weren't looking at Jake Smarley any longer. His face had changed; it was shrewd, rather than drab. As the three men squinted, Smarley's hands made another sweep.

★ ★

THE SHADOW KNOWS!

Crime-fighter—master of darkness—elusive as the night from which he comes—such is The Shadow. The knowledge of all pending crime is his, and thus does he thwart the master crooks of crime. From the depths of San Francisco's Chinatown to the underworld of New York; from the dark dives of New Orleans to the Boston waterfront; wherever crime brews—crooks quail at the name of The Shadow.

To The Shadow, with news of crime and criminals, come his agents; men who, under the guise of professions, have been trained by the master of darkness to see crime in the making and report such immediately. None know The Shadow's identity, but faithful are they in serving him, to the end that crime must be nipped in the bud. For, agents all, they owe their lives to The Shadow.

There is Moe Shrevnitz, taxi driver without peer, who carries The Shadow on many of his dangerous missions; Clyde Burke, star reporter of the Classic, *who,*

His face seemed to enlarge, to become fuller and more genial. Then, as his hands performed another swing, he turned his head and gave them a brief view of a set profile that wore an expression of disdain.

One more quick change came, as the face turned toward them, but before the three lieutenants could gain more than a vague impression, a sweep of the swift-moving hands restored the drab features of Jake Smarley.

"That's just the general idea," cackled Smarley. "From now on, you'd better call me Five-face. Because, after tonight, you won't see Jake Smarley again. I'll need some makeup, and a reasonable amount of time, to make each face look permanent."

Thoroughly amazed, Banker and Clip finally turned to Grease, expecting him to be their spokesman. With a glance at his companions, Grease took the assignment.

"Listen, Five-face," said Grease. "You mean you'll pull this job as Smarley, get the dough, and come back here as another guy?"

The man who looked like Smarley was nodding as Grease spoke. With a half gulp, Grease continued:

"And then you'll pull another job, in the open, and show up different. You'll keep on—"

"Until I've done four jobs," inserted Five-face, in Smarley's wheezy style. "I'll get rid of four faces and show up with the fifth. That's when we'll make the final settlement. But, meanwhile, you three have got to cover for me. The kind of jobs I pick"—the crackly tone was sharp—"will mean some swift getaways. I'll need guns and plenty of them."

Grease shoved his hand across the table. The man called Smarley received it with a scrawny grip that suited the bookie's style. Banker and Clip proffered their hands to seal the bargain. Each was conscious that Five-face was giving them a shake that went with his present role of Smarley.

Then, with a final chortle, Five-face stepped to the door. He looked like Smarley, he acted like the bookie, but the lieutenants accepted him as a master hand of crime, a brain that they were ready to serve. Their new leader, the man of marvels, gave them a final admonition.

"Get posted at six," ordered Five-face, "outside of Melbrun's building. I'll be Smarley when I go in, and Smarley when I come out. Tell your crews to cover for Smarley; nothing more. Let them think they're working for Smarley; they can spill that to the coppers, if any of them are ever asked."

The door half opened, Five-face paused. Still wearing the withery look of Jake Smarley, he added:

"Because it won't matter in the future. After tonight, no one will ever see Jake Smarley again—not even The Shadow!"

CHAPTER II
CRIME TO COME

IT was midafternoon when the incredible Five-face changed the ambitions of three lesser crooks and made them glad to be lieutenants, instead of

★ ★

because of his newspaper contacts, furnishes many unknown facts; Burbank, through whom all agents make their reports to The Shadow; Rutledge Mann, quiet-spoken investment broker, who is invaluable to the master-fighter; Cliff Marsland, known to mobland as a killer, but to The Shadow as his underworld contact man; Jericho, giant African, whose strength is equaled only by his devotion to The Shadow; Hawkeye, insignificant in appearance, but who can follow a trail like an Indian; Harry Vincent, youthful and with a keenness that makes him The Shadow's most valuable and trusted agent.

These and others are the agents on whom The Shadow relies, and never do they fail him. The Shadow himself, at times, assumes the role of a globe-trotting millionaire—Lamont Cranston by name—at such times when the real Cranston is on his many travels, and in this guise meets crooks face to face. In this manner he also makes his many social contacts, particularly being friendly with Ralph Weston, New York's police commissioner.

The Shadow's real identity is that of Kent Allard, internationally known aviator. As such he sometimes appears in public; but only to two Xinca Indian servants is Allard known as The Shadow.

Such are the methods of The Shadow. The Shadow knows!

big shots, on their own. The plan that Five-face proposed—that of crime at six o'clock—was quite in keeping with the situation, and therefore satisfactory to all.

By six, darkness would arrive, offering suitable surroundings for the lieutenants and their followers. But there was also a chance that other things could happen prior to the hour that Five-face had set. Crime's new brain had not fully calculated the effect of the newspaper report that told of cash in the office of the United Import Co.

Shortly before five o'clock, a car pulled up in front of the building where the importing company was located. Two private detectives, stationed near the building entrance, gave the car a wary eye, until they recognized its occupant. The man who alighted was Arnold Melbrun, head of the United Import Co.

Melbrun was middle-aged, but he had the buoyancy of youth. Tall, broad-shouldered and erect, he displayed the true manner of a business executive. His face was broad and strong-chinned, marking him as a man of action. But his gray eyes, quick and restless, were those of a deep thinker and matched the tapering shape of his features.

From the people thronging from the building, Melbrun promptly picked out the private detectives and drew them to one side. From beneath his arm, he brought a newspaper, showed them the headlines. The detectives began to understand Melbrun's worried air.

"I don't like it," declared Melbrun, in a crisp tone. "The newspapers were not to know about this matter until the *Anitoga* docked. I'm going up to the office, to learn who let the news out. Meanwhile, I expect the utmost vigilance from both of you."

The detectives assured Melbrun that they would be on their toes. Entering the building, Melbrun waited while an elevator disgorged a load of workers who were going home. Riding up, he reached his own suite of offices, to find another pair of detectives on guard. He showed them the newspaper account, and repeated the admonition that he had given to the men below.

The employees of the United Import Co. were still at their desks. They often worked late, and Melbrun had insisted that they stay on the job this evening, without telling them why. As he glanced from desk to desk, the half dozen men busied themselves, as they always did when Melbrun was about.

Near an office marked "Private" was a single desk, with a sallow man behind it. The fellow was Melbrun's secretary, Kelson. His eyes shifted when Melbrun's met them.

Without a word Melbrun opened the door of the private office and beckoned for Kelson to follow. When Kelson entered, Melbrun spread the newspaper and ordered the secretary to read it.

"I'm sorry, Mr. Melbrun," pleaded Kelson, in a weak tone. "The newspapers called up this afternoon and asked me—"

"About the money!" snapped Melbrun. "And like an idiot, you told them!"

"But they knew about it," insisted Kelson. "They mentioned the armored truck that was coming here, and the fact that the *Anitoga* was due to dock."

Melbrun stroked his chin, reflectively. Anger faded from his eyes; still, his tone was brusque.

"I can't hold you to blame," he told Kelson. "Still, I wish that you had used better sense. It isn't wise to let a whole city know when you have a hundred thousand dollars in your custody."

Turning to a large safe behind his massive desk, Melbrun turned the combination. Kelson watched, his face quite worried, while the importer opened a metal box that contained stacks of currency.

Melbrun was thumbing through the cash, nodding because he found it quite intact, when he noticed Kelson watching him.

"Don't stand there stupidly!" snapped Melbrun. "Go to the outside office, Kelson, and tell the rest of the employees about the money. Show them the newspaper, and admit that it was partly your mistake. Explain that I kept the matter secret so they would not worry. But since all New York knows that I have the money here, the office staff should be informed."

BY the time Kelson had given the news to the interested office force, Melbrun appeared. He was carrying a suitcase that he always took on business trips. He laid it aside, while he assembled the employees and took up the story where Kelson had left off.

"The truck will be here at eight," announced Melbrun. "It will take the money directly to the pier, because the *Anitoga* will be docked by then. I shall be at the pier, and afterward, I intend to leave on a business trip to Boston.

"Meanwhile, I am depending upon all of you to be watchful. I have placed detectives on duty, and the job is really theirs; but, since you know the facts, I expect your cooperation. Remember to keep at your work, as usual; receive any visitors cordially and in the accustomed fashion.

"But watch them! If you have any suspicions of anyone, report promptly to Kelson. This newspaper story means that we must adopt additional precautions. I shall tell the detectives that they can depend on all of you, if needed."

Before leaving, Melbrun called police headquarters and talked to an inspector named Joe Cardona. From Melbrun's conversation, the office workers learned that Inspector Cardona was the official in charge of arrangements at the pier; that everything was satisfactory there.

However, Cardona had seen the newspaper account and agreed with Melbrun that there might be an earlier danger.

Over the phone, they concluded new arrangements, which were satisfactory to Melbrun. His call finished, the exporter sat at Kelson's desk, stroking his firm jaw and nodding in a musing fashion. Finally, Melbrun arose and picked up his suitcase.

"Inspector Cardona is detailing two men to watch the building," he explained. "That will give us added protection outside, as well as in here. Later, the inspector will arrive in person, and he has promised to have a full squad on duty by the time the armored truck appears.

"I am depending upon you, Kelson." Melbrun turned to the sallow secretary. "You have the combination to my safe. But do not open it until Inspector Cardona gives the word. Turn over the cashbox to him, for delivery at the pier."

As he concluded, Melbrun dangled a ring of keys, and Kelson nodded at sight of one he recognized. It was the key to the cashbox in the safe, a special key that had no duplicate. The contents of the cashbox would certainly be intact, when the box itself was delivered to Melbrun at the pier.

Methodical to the last degree, Arnold Melbrun contacted the private detectives as he left the office, and told them of the amplified arrangements. As he entered his waiting car, Melbrun glanced at his watch and noted that the time was five twenty.

His suitcase on the seat beside him, he glanced back at the office building as he rode away. Despite his new precautions, Melbrun's face looked troubled.

The day was cloudy. Early dusk was already gathering about the building, where only a few lights remained, those of the exporting offices. Though the building was not large, it had taken on a vast appearance against the darkening sky, and other buildings looked like crouching creatures, ready to devour it.

Melbrun could picture certain loopholes in his plans, and he wondered just how well he had provided against them. Nevertheless, his final expression was a smile, which he delivered as his car neared a hotel not far from his office building.

The custody of one hundred thousand dollars was no longer weighing heavily on Arnold Melbrun, as he strolled into the hotel and left his suitcase at the checkroom.

If crime should come, Melbrun was quite sure that crooks would be disappointed as a result of his precautions, plus those provided by the law.

In fact, there seemed but little reason why anyone should be worried about crime in Manhattan. It had been spiked very effectively during recent months, and New York City, criminally speaking, was much like a millpond. Such calmness, however, necessarily had an answer.

THE answer, at that moment, was riding in a large limousine that was coming across the New Jersey Skyway, en route to the Holland Tunnel entrance to New York City.

His name was Lamont Cranston and he was a gentleman of leisurely manner, who seemed quite at home in his elegant surroundings.

Cranston's face was hawkish, and had a mask-like appearance. When he was alone, and therefore unobserved, Cranston's eyes often took on a burning glint; their gaze became a piercing sort that seemed capable of penetrating darkness.

Had certain persons seen him at such moments, they would have realized that this person who posed as Lamont Cranston was actually The Shadow.

His was the hand that banished crime. The Shadow was the reason why the law prevailed. He had weighed the balance in justice's favor, and was keeping it there. This present trip, at dusk, was another evidence of his foresight.

The Shadow had learned of the cash that was in Melbrun's custody. He recognized its importance. Not only was it the very sort of loot that crooks would most prefer; the theft of that cash would mean something more. It would mark crime's comeback. A criminal thrust, involving sure, quick profit, would embolden hordes of skulking mobsters throughout Manhattan.

Long had human rats been waiting, hoping for the call of some Pied Piper who would lead them anew along a route of crime. They would be willing, ready, to follow such a leader blindly, once he proved himself a master of crime.

To start a new reign of crime, a supercrook would first have to score a success despite The Shadow. Melbrun's money would prove a great inducement for anyone who sought to be an overlord of crime.

Leaning forward a bit, Cranston thumbed a dial. A voice came across the air, tuned in by shortwave radio. It was the quiet tone of Burbank, The Shadow's contact man, giving reports from various of The Shadow's secret agents. They had checked the news account in the afternoon paper and had not determined the source of the leak.

There were many channels through which it could have come. It might have drifted from some shipping office, or been given out by someone with the steamship company. The banks which supplied the cash knew all about it, as did the trucking company which was to furnish the armored car.

Any one of several dozen persons could have been responsible, but that did not explain why the facts had been released in the first place. Behind that point, The Shadow could see intended crime as a motive.

More reports came by shortwave. Agents had checked on Melbrun's building. The exporter's office was on the sixth floor. Next door was a building that had a roof on the same level, and also offered a view of a fire tower that showed a rear exit from Melbrun's building. The adjacent roof was the very sort of post that The Shadow wanted.

The limousine was entering the Holland Tunnel. Turning off the radio, Cranston leaned forward and noted the clock on the dashboard in front of the chauffeur.

Reaching lazily for the speaking tube, he instructed the chauffeur to take him to an address near Melbrun's building. The clock said quarter of six; ten minutes would bring the big car to its destination.

Cranston's leisurely pose ended as the car sped from the tunnel. His hands slid open a drawer beneath the rear seat, whipped out a black cloak, which he whisked across his shoulders. Opening a flattened slouch hat, Cranston clamped it on his head. Drawing thin black gloves over his hands, this man of sudden action reached for a brace of .45-caliber automatics and slid them beneath his cloak.

A whispered laugh stirred the darkened interior of the car. Darkness had settled over the city, too, and it furnished the very element that this black-cloaked master wanted. Should crime be scheduled for this evening, it would find trouble in the gloom.

The Shadow, master of the night, was on his way to combat crime!

CHAPTER III
TWISTED BATTLE

AS The Shadow's car was nearing the vicinity of Melbrun's building, a shambling figure sidled in from the darkness and paused before the lighted entrance. He was promptly recognized by men already on the ground: the private detectives stationed by Melbrun. The arrival was Jake Smarley, the bookie.

One of the dicks acted as if he owned the building. Accosting Smarley, he asked him what he wanted. The stooped bookie whined that he was going up to Melbrun's office to see Mr. Kelson. He argued that Kelson would be there, because he always stayed until six o'clock.

From across the street, two plainclothes men shifted into sight. They recognized Smarley, too, and gave the private dicks a nod. Smarley, the bookie, wasn't the type who could start trouble. It was better to pass him through and find out what he really wanted.

Upstairs, Smarley encountered another pair of watchers, who gruffly demanded what he wanted. When they learned that he was going to the offices of the United Import Co., they pointed out the door to him. As soon as Smarley entered, the dicks moved to the door, opened it a trifle and looked in on what followed.

The employees recognized Smarley and exchanged grins, with the exception of Kelson. The secretary was seated at his desk, wiping a pair of spectacles. He squinted as he saw Smarley; putting on his glasses, he recognized the bookie. A squeamish expression promptly decorated Kelson's sallow face.

"Hello, Kelson," wheezed Smarley, in an almost fatherly fashion. "All through your work? We can have a little chat."

"Not today, Smarley," pleaded Kelson. "I've got a lot of things to do for Mr. Melbrun."

Smarley gave a sharp look toward the door of Melbrun's office, then inquired in a low voice:

"Is Mr. Melbrun still in there?"

Kelson nodded. He figured that it would support his argument. On previous visits, Smarley had always called up first, to make sure that Melbrun wasn't in. Since his business with Kelson was a personal matter, involving unpaid racing bets, he had not wanted Melbrun to know about it. But on this occasion Smarley went against form.

With an ugly, dryish grin, Smarley arose from the desk and turned toward Melbrun's door, saying, loud enough for the rest of the office force to hear:

"This has gone far enough, Kelson. You haven't paid me what you owe me, so I'm going to take it up with your boss."

"No, no!" Kelson rose, excited. "I forgot, Smarley. Mr. Melbrun went out—"

By then, Smarley had opened the private door. He peered into Melbrun's office, saw that it was empty. His face showed reproval, as he turned to Kelson.

"So you lied to me," whined Smarley. "Tried to trick a poor old man who trusted you. Look at me"—he tugged his pockets, turning them inside out; then extended his hands, palms upward, letting them tremble—"a poor old man who hasn't a cent of his own! Yet you owe me money and—"

"I'll pay it, Smarley," inserted Kelson, anxiously. "I'll let you have some cash, right now. Here!"

He pulled two ten-dollar bills from his pocket. Smarley eyed the cash as though he wanted to cry, much to the amusement of the other men in the office, who enjoyed Kelson's plight. In the hallway, the detectives closed the door and went back to the elevators, laughing at the situation.

It was really funny, to learn that Kelson had played the races and lost to a bookie like Smarley. Kelson was the sort who tried to act like a human machine, as though he didn't have a single fault or weakness. Having found out what Smarley's business was, the private dicks were quite willing to let him thrash it out with Kelson.

As for the office force, they were quite delighted. They disliked Kelson, and were finding out, to their great glee, why Smarley had come to the office other times when Melbrun was out, to hold conferences with the private secretary.

To their enjoyment, Smarley shook his head at sight of Kelson's twenty dollars.

"It won't do, Kelson," whined Smarley. "I want the full amount, two hundred and fifty dollars."

"But I don't have it, Smarley—"

"Then you can give me a note for it," inserted the bookie, loudly. "A promissory note, for thirty days. You ought to have some of those in your desk—the blanks, I mean."

Kelson shook his head; then, deciding that a signed note would certainly end the frequency of Smarley's visits, the secretary changed his gesture to a nod.

"I'll sign the note," he decided. "Wait here, Smarley, while I get a blank from Mr. Melbrun's desk."

PUSHING past Smarley, Kelson entered the private office. Solemnly, Smarley eyed the other office workers, and received their approving grins. Reverting to his suspicious attitude, the bookie looked into Melbrun's office again; then, entering, he closed the door behind him.

It was done neatly, so naturally that the men in the outer office did not link Smarley's action to anything more sinister than a desire to collect money that was really owed to him.

Nor did Kelson guess Smarley's purpose. At Melbrun's desk, Kelson was writing out a promissory note; he scarcely noted Smarley, as the withery bookie stepped past him.

There was a strong door in the rear corner of Melbrun's office; a barrier that was heavily bolted. Smoothly, Smarley pulled back the bolts. Despite his care, the last one grated, bringing Kelson around. Anxiously, Kelson gasped:

"What are you doing, Smarley?"

Whipping from his crouch, Smarley sprang for Kelson with a speed that left the sallow secretary breathless. As he came, the bookie pulled a revolver from his hip. Reaching the desk, he planted the gun muzzle squarely against Kelson's ribs.

"Get busy on that safe!" hissed Smarley. "Open it up! Hand me over the *Anitoga* cash!"

Kelson gulped loudly, then:

"But I don't know the combination!" he panted. "Honest, Smarley, I don't. Mr. Melbrun was coming back."

With all of Kelson's pretense at sincerity, Smarley was not deceived.

"No stalling," he prompted. "Get busy, I tell you! If you don't, I'll shoot!"

Quivering, Kelson approached the safe. He fumbled at the dial, as though trying to get the combination by guesswork. Smarley nudged harder with the gun.

"Start over." The bookie's tone was low and harsh. "No fake stuff, Kelson. I want results in a hurry!"

Light from a floor lamp showed the tenseness of both faces. Kelson's sallow features were twitching; Smarley's visage was hard. It looked like a devil's mask, that first face belonging to the man who boasted that he had five.

The tense pair were between the floor lamp and the rear window of the private office. The window shade was drawn; Melbrun had lowered it earlier, when he turned on the office lights. But the shade, thanks to the position of the floor lamp, did not hide the scene in Melbrun's office.

The Shadow had arrived upon the adjacent roof. He was viewing a drama silhouetted against the yellow shade. Enlarged, the shadows of Smarley and Kelson looked grotesque, but their actions were portrayed in excellent detail.

Kelson's moving hands told what they were doing. At moments, The Shadow could see the shading from the safe dial, a lump of black against a smooth, upright block. Smarley's hand was plain, too, and as it shifted, the outline of his revolver was quite visible.

A move at this moment would be fatal for Kelson. Awaiting the proper time, The Shadow gauged the distance from his roof to Melbrun's window. It wasn't far; a spring would carry The Shadow to the window ledge, which was fairly broad and below the level of the roof where The Shadow crouched.

The problem was to remain on the ledge, and The Shadow had a simple plan. Drawing an automatic, he reversed it, clutching the barrel and raising the handle of the gun as though it were the head of a hammer.

As The Shadow watched, a big shape of enlarging blackness blotted out the silhouettes of Smarley and Kelson. It was the safe door, swinging open.

With a lunge, The Shadow left the roof. He swished through the darkness, at a downward angle toward the window ledge. His arm was swinging as he came; his gun struck glass an instant before his feet landed on the window ledge.

That sledging blow shattered the glass in the upper window sash; the descending gun caught the woodwork like a grappling hook. The Shadow's cloaked form gave a backward sway, that would have pitched an ordinary jumper to the depths.

But this strange venturer did not fall. He still gripped the gun barrel, and its handle served him as a brace, hooked to the stout woodwork where the window sections joined.

The Shadow's recoil served merely to give him impetus for another lunge. His free hand whipping his cloak across his face, he drove in shoulder first. His new momentum carried him right through the window.

Amid a terrific crash of woodwork and a clatter of glass, the shade rattled upward. Continuing his lunge, The Shadow struck the floor and made a rapid roll for the shelter of Melbrun's big desk.

THINGS were happening as The Shadow wanted. In opening the safe door, Kelson had gained its partial shelter. Smarley's gun was no longer pressing the secretary's back, because the bookie was grabbing the metal cashbox. Matters were just right for Kelson to make a break, if he had nerve to try it.

By his sudden entry, his dive in the opposite direction, The Shadow added to the opportunity. Smarley saw the black-clad shape come crashing through the window and recognized The Shadow, even before he heard the cloaked fighter's defiant laugh from beyond the desk.

Forgetting Kelson, Smarley began to shoot, wildly, as he shifted for the rear door that he had opened.

Another gun gave immediate answer. The Shadow was juggling his automatic as he rolled, catching it deftly with the muzzle frontward, his finger on the trigger. He stabbed a shot above the level of the desk; one that came surprisingly close to clipping Smarley, considering the guesswork behind The Shadow's aim.

The Shadow wasn't counting on that first jab to stop the mobster. He simply wanted to get into rapid action, to keep things safer for Kelson.

Unfortunately, the secretary grew surprisingly bold, when he saw the spurt from The Shadow's gun and its result on Smarley. The bookie went frantic, as he snatched at the knob of the rear door. His gun in one hand, the box under his other arm, Smarley was in a fumbling mood.

Leaving the safe, Kelson drove across the path of The Shadow's fire, to grapple with Smarley.

As the two locked, The Shadow vaulted the desk, to drive into the fray. Kelson had Smarley's gun wrist; the crook made a downward swing. Poking his own gun in between, The Shadow stopped the forceful blow; but Kelson, ducking in the wrong direction, received a glancing stroke.

Madly depending upon luck instead of common sense, Smarley shouldered Kelson toward The Shadow and made for the front door of the office, instead of the rear exit. His reversal of direction gave him a temporary leeway, and during the interval Kelson became the crook's unwitting ally.

Half groggy, Kelson grappled with the first person at hand, who happened to be The Shadow.

There were shouts from the outer office that seemed to blend with The Shadow's mocking laughter. Smarley was heading straight for a trap. Men had heard the fray and were coming in to learn the trouble. Dragging Kelson with him, The Shadow made for Smarley as the bookie fumbled with the doorknob.

It was then that Smarley made his smartest move, his one clever stroke amid the twisted battle. Almost under the muzzle of The Shadow's looming gun, the bookie yanked the door open and sprang away from it, still clutching his revolver with one hand and catching the slipping cashbox with the other.

With a mere shift, The Shadow had the thug covered, but his own move came too late. Smarley's tug at the door had released a flood of office workers, followed by a pair of detectives. They saw only Kelson and The Shadow, engaged in what seemed a grapple.

As The Shadow whirled Kelson away with one hand and aimed for Smarley with the other, he was flattened by a human avalanche of misguided attackers who mistook him for a foe intent on crime!

CHAPTER IV
MURDER WITHOUT PROFIT

FROM the moment that they sprawled The Shadow beneath them, eight attackers found that they had taken on an unruly bargain. They were unarmed, for even the detectives had shoved away their own guns at sight of a lone fighter going floorward.

The Shadow did not drop his gun, nor did he put it away; he needed it for Smarley, later. Nevertheless, he handled his present adversaries in a gunless style.

Doubling his knees, The Shadow drove his legs between a pair of plunging men and found two others. His feet met them so hard that they were hurled back into the mass behind them.

With a sideward roll, The Shadow took care of the two who were already upon him. Grabbing one, he flung the fellow against the other, so suddenly and vehemently that both were sprawled.

Out of the human tangle, The Shadow extricated himself, like a living knife slashing its way to freedom. He had not reached his feet yet, but it did not matter. He was able to deal with his quarry: Jake Smarley.

Profiting by the brawl at the doorway, the bookie cut across the room, past Melbrun's desk, timing his flight well. The crook had escaped the

The Shadow was juggling his automatic....
He stabbed a shot above the level of the desk.

notice of the new invaders; Kelson saw him, but the secretary's shouts went unheard.

Smarley was counting on a clean getaway, through the rear door that he had previously unlocked. But The Shadow still could reach him.

This time, Kelson wasn't in the path of the black-cloaked marksman's aim. Nor did others interfere with The Shadow's thrust. The private detectives saw him, but the point of his automatic indicated Smarley. Seeing the metal money box beneath the bookie's arm, the dicks realized that they had grabbed the wrong invader.

They had heard of The Shadow, master avenger who battled crime. They expected him to drop Smarley with a single blast. He would have accomplished the worthwhile deed, if the dicks hadn't yelled encouragement.

Hearing the shout, Smarley wheeled about just short of the rear exit. The Shadow's gun blasted just as the bookie turned. With the spurt of the .45, Smarley staggered backward. His stumble was accompanied by a resounding clang.

Luck was still with Smarley. His twist had put the metal cashbox between his body and The Shadow's gun. Already a trophy of crime, the box served Smarley as a shield that stopped the bullet inches short of his heart.

Smarley's stagger carried him part way through the door. Instead of pursuing him, The Shadow took a long, upward spring toward the center of the room, ending with a vault across the desk. He was choosing the open door of the safe as a new barricade from which to reopen fire.

The Shadow wasn't thinking of his own protection. His gun was enough defense against Smarley's fire. He was considering the men behind him, those invaders from the outer office. Wild shots from Smarley's revolver might clip them. The only course was to draw the crook's fire to another quarter.

Smarley fell for the game. He was wasting bullets, when The Shadow cleared the desk. His last shots pinged the safe door after The Shadow was beyond it. Smarley was yanking at a useless trigger, when he heard The Shadow's laugh, sinister and sibilant, a promise of coming doom. Frantically, Smarley turned and ran.

One shot was all The Shadow needed; he took deliberate aim, hoping to bring Smarley down. As yet, he did not regard Smarley as a master crook, but simply as a fugitive who had accomplished a crude, though somewhat daring, theft.

Straight through the doorway lay the fire tower, a dim background against Smarley's approaching figure. The mobster's back made a perfect target; as he ran, he was clutching the box in front of him, and therefore no longer had a shield.

It seemed that Smarley's new career of crime was due for a sudden finish, considering The Shadow's skill as a marksman.

Then intervention came, from a new source— the fire tower itself.

TWO thuggish figures leaped forward as Smarley neared them. Passing the running crook, they converged, opening fire as they came. They had spotted The Shadow's head and shoulders, rising above the top of the open safe door.

Their target was gone before they fired. Dropping instantly to the floor, The Shadow was out of sight as bullets whined above the huge safe door, which was ample enough for shelter. The gunners aimed lower, but their slugs merely pommeled the metal barrier. Again, they heard The Shadow's taunting laugh.

Then, almost from the floor, a gun fired upward. By a dipping twist, The Shadow had poked from cover below the level of the opposing fire. He was putting in quick jabs, with double purpose. Not only were the gunning thugs blocking his path to Smarley; their presence had become dangerous.

The two private detectives were hustling across the room, guns in hand, making for the rear exit. They thought that they could handle the opponents who had failed to nick The Shadow. But the dicks didn't stand a chance against such opposition; they were blundering right into serious trouble. The Shadow had to take a risk to save them.

Trained in all varieties of trick marksmanship, The Shadow's quick hand performed in a superhuman style. There were yells from the hallway, as crooks sprawled. Beyond the floundering thugs, The Shadow saw Smarley on the top step of the fire tower. The stoopy crook was turned about, a smirk on his face, watching to see The Shadow's finish.

When he saw his own gunners sprawl, Smarley did not wait for a further climax. He took an agile dive down the stairway, dropping from sight like a figure in a puppet show.

Smarley was quick enough to escape the shots that The Shadow delivered a few moments later. Immediately, the cloaked marksman halted fire. The private dicks were at the rear door and were dashing through, in pursuit of Smarley.

With them went another man, who scooped up a revolver that a wounded crook had dropped. The third man was Kelson; the sallow secretary was anxious to redeem himself.

The Shadow followed. He trailed the chase to the street, stopping briefly at floors along the way. The Shadow foresaw a difficulty that the others did not anticipate: the prospect of other marksmen, down below. At one floor, through a window, he saw huddling men edging forward from a parked car across the way. The Shadow fired two quick shots that scattered them.

Still lower, The Shadow spied a rakish automobile wheeling in from a corner. He jabbed shots that caused the driver to whip the car across the sidewalk, so that occupants could leap out the other side and take to shelter.

Then, as The Shadow neared the ground, he heard a volley of shots, accompanied by the whining sirens of police cars.

Inspector Cardona was on the job. From out front, he had heard the sounds of battle high up in the building. He and his men knew what it meant and had smartly made for the rear of the building. More police were coming up to aid them, in what promised to be a major battle against hordes of crimeland.

Smarley had reached the street and was jumping into a waiting car. He was yelling something about The Shadow, and thugs in other cars could hear his shouts. Among those listeners were Smarley's three lieutenants: Grease, Banker, and Clip. In their turn, they were bawling orders to the various thugs and snipers they had supplied for the present enterprise.

Things weren't panning out as Five-face had promised. This wasn't a mere cover-up job. It was the type of fray that might disclose the identities of the lieutenants, along with that of Smarley.

Naturally, Five-face did not worry over his dilemma, for he intended to drop the guise of Smarley, anyway. But discovery could prove disastrous to the three lieutenants.

They hit upon a compromise. While yelling for men to cover Smarley, they put their own cars in motion. Opening fire upon police cars, they made it look as though they were trying to clear a path for others to follow. Actually, they were trying to save their own hides and faces.

Of course, they wanted Smarley to get clear, too, and he had a chance to make his getaway at the expense of the thugs who were out of their cars and spread along the street.

But Smarley hesitated. Thrusting his face from the window of his car, he waved his empty gun, pointing it toward the ground floor of the fire tower. At Smarley's yell, shooting thugs quit aiming at police cars.

They heard his shout:

"Get the guy with the specs!"

THE "guy with the specs" was Kelson, who had reached the street along with the private dicks. Smarley's shout was followed by a quick-hissed order that came from the steps of the fire tower. The dicks heard it—The Shadow's command—and grabbed Kelson, to haul him back to safety. But the maddened secretary showed a sudden savagery.

Spinning about, he slashed his gun at his friends; as the dicks ducked, he lurched from their grasp. Taking the last half dozen steps in a long leap, The Shadow made a grab for Kelson but lost him, as a stumbling detective blundered in between.

What happened in the next half second was something that even The Shadow could not prevent.

Springing wildly for Smarley's car, Kelson was met by a concerted fusillade from half a dozen directions. Flayed by bullets, the sallow man jolted; twisting, he stumbled across the curb and sprawled in the gutter, to the tune of triumphant howls from the outspread firing squad.

Smarley's car was in motion; the master crook had dropped below the window. Maybe others still thought of him as Smarley, the fugitive, but The Shadow had him classed as a criminal of a fiendish caliber. Though others had fired the shots that killed Kelson, the real murderer was Smarley. He was the man that The Shadow wanted.

Springing from the fire tower, The Shadow reached the moving car. He was on its running board before the outspread snipers spied him. At sight of their archfoe, thugs wheeled to aim. The Shadow gave them no attention; he knew that, by this time, the stings were gone from that crew of murderers.

The Shadow was right. Other guns were talking as he boarded Smarley's car. The police had spotted the killers who put the blast on Kelson. Aiming thugs were hitting the asphalt and the sidewalks before they could tug their gun triggers.

Cardona and his amplified squad were performing double service: avenging Kelson's death and giving The Shadow a clear path to Smarley.

Yanking open the car door, The Shadow lunged for Smarley. In the front seat, a cowering mobster clung to the wheel, trying to get the car around the corner.

Smarley, in his turn, yanked open the door on the other side. When he saw The Shadow's big gun loom for him, he hurled the metal cashbox at the weapon's muzzle.

The Shadow's bullet plunked the dented box and dropped it to the floor of the car. Leaping for Smarley, who was diving to the street, The Shadow hooked the box with his foot and brought it along. It clattered to the curb and lay there. Ignoring Smarley's lost trophy, The Shadow continued his pursuit.

Smarley was just past the corner when The Shadow fired. This time, a slug nicked chunks of brick from a building edge. Again, Smarley had managed to keep a mere jump ahead of The Shadow, and the crook's luck held up.

Reaching the corner, The Shadow was greeted with shots from across the street; he dropped back to cover before foemen could find the range.

Those shots came from two cars: Grease commanded one, and Banker the other. There was a third car, even closer, with Clip in charge. As Smarley reached that car, all three vehicles sped away. They had doubled their tracks, escaping the police cars, and were off again before The Shadow could halt them.

A few unwise snipers were still about, which was why The Shadow could not follow. Arriving police spied the crooks shooting at an imaginary target. Somehow, somewhere, The Shadow had whisked to cover like a wraith of evaporating smoke.

There were shots from somewhere in the darkness; yells, as ugly-faced gunners came tumbling into sight from doorways where they lurked.

Then a strange, mocking laugh—a promise of vengeance upon other men of crime, who had escaped along with Smarley. Listening police heard the trail of The Shadow's eerie taunt; it seemed to blend with the distant sirens of patrol cars that were hunting for a trail.

INSPECTOR CARDONA reached the corner. He was a stocky, swarthy man, his expression a poker face. He listened while the private detectives told him about Smarley's raid, The Shadow's intervention, and Kelson's death.

By then, an officer was approaching with the much-battered cashbox. The private detectives promptly identified it as the box containing Melbrun's hundred thousand dollars.

"The money is safe, anyway," decided Cardona. "It doesn't make up for losing Kelson; he was a game guy. Still, he wanted us to get this box back, and we did, thanks to The Shadow."

Eyeing the lid of the cashbox, Cardona saw that it was loose on its hinges. As a mere matter of routine, to certify before witnesses that the money had been saved for Melbrun, Cardona inserted a revolver muzzle under the lid and gave a wrench.

Then Cardona's poker-faced expression was gone. He was staring with eyes as wide in amazement as those of the men about him. If ever Cardona had seen proof that crime did not pay, this was it. Crime couldn't have paid Smarley, even if he had taken the cashbox along with him.

Instead of crisp green currency, the box was stuffed with blank checks and old receipts. Tilting the box, Cardona let the worthless paper flutter to the sidewalk.

Except for the valueless contents, the box was entirely empty. Robbery had been forestalled even before it was perpetrated, producing a mystery that the ace police inspector could not fathom!

From somewhere—perhaps in his own fancy—Cardona thought that he heard the whispered laugh of The Shadow!

CHAPTER V
CRIME'S RIDDLES

THE exclusive Cobalt Club, to which Lamont Cranston belonged, was noted as a gathering place for limousines.

Sometimes the fancy line-up was jarred by the presence of a big official car which belonged to Police Commissioner Ralph Weston, who was also a member. However, the commissioner's car was tolerated. It looked enough like a limousine to pass muster.

This evening, when Cranston arrived at the club, the commissioner's car was present. However, the doorman had a pained look on his face and was glowering at the commissioner's car. The Shadow understood the reason when he glanced across the street.

Parked on the other side, between two limousines, was an armored truck that had evidently come here at the commissioner's order.

In Cranston's strolling style, The Shadow entered the club. He knew that he would learn the reason for the armored truck as soon as he met Commissioner Weston.

Not only did Weston esteem Cranston's acquaintance, the commissioner was constantly trying to interest his wealthy friend in facts concerning crime.

Such matters seldom intrigued Cranston, which was why Weston pressed them all the more. By playing the indifferent role of Cranston, The Shadow therewith received much information concerning police investigations.

Commissioner Weston, long impressed by The Shadow's uncanny knowledge, would have been amazed to learn that he made personal contributions to it.

Though he had not expected to see the armored truck, The Shadow had struck upon a simple explanation for its presence by the time he reached the grillroom, where the commissioner held important conferences.

Commissioner Weston was at his usual table. Seated opposite him was a dignified gentleman, whose keen, broad face and strong chin marked him as a man of action. Though he had never met the visitor, The Shadow could have named him.

Weston's companion was Arnold Melbrun.

As The Shadow joined the pair at the table, Weston hastened to introduce Melbrun to his friend Cranston. Melbrun gave a smile as he shook hands, but his face immediately saddened. His hand, too, lacked the strong grip that should have come from a man of such commanding presence.

Melbrun's sorrowful expression was explainable. He had just heard the details of Kelson's death and was taking it as a severe blow.

"Poor Kelson!" he said sadly. "If I could only have foreseen the fate to which his loyalty would bring him—"

"You are not to blame," interrupted Weston. "You did the best thing under the circumstances, Melbrun. Thanks to your foresight, Smarley not only showed his hand but was doomed to failure. If others had only done their part—"

"Which they did not do," inserted Melbrun. "As a result, Kelson is dead."

Melbrun's voice was choky. It took an effort for him to recover his composure. Meanwhile, Weston was explaining matters to The Shadow, recounting the details from the start.

He told of the crew-money story that had appeared in the afternoon newspapers; how it had induced a crook named Jake Smarley to raid Melbrun's office, with gunners waiting to aid his getaway.

Coming to the climax of his tale, the commissioner announced:

"Yet the box which Smarley took was worthless, Cranston. When Inspector Cardona recovered it, he found the money missing—"

"Because Mr. Melbrun had previously removed it," interposed The Shadow, in a casual tone. "Fearing that criminals might make a thrust, he wisely took the funds with him when he left the office."

The commissioner stared, astonished. Such knowledge on the part of Cranston amazed him. Slowly, Weston began to nod; then, finding his voice, he demanded brusquely:

"Who gave you those details, Cranston?"

"I saw an armored truck outside the club," returned The Shadow, "and I find Mr. Melbrun inside. As for that suitcase"—he gestured, as he lighted a cigarette—"it isn't yours, commissioner. It happens to have Mr. Melbrun's initials on it."

THE suitcase was standing beside Weston's chair. With a cross between a grimace and a smile, the commissioner lifted it to the table. Opening the bag, he showed stacks of money, all in neat bundles.

"Your guess was right, Cranston," conceded Weston, in a depreciating tone. "Melbrun took the cash before the robbery and checked his bag at a hotel. When he called my office, asking for an escort to take him to the pier, I told him of the robbery."

"If I had only called sooner," groaned Melbrun. "But I dined first. I knew there might be trouble at the office, but not the serious sort that occurred there."

"You left enough men to handle matters," insisted Weston, "and the dummy cashbox was excellent bait. It made Smarley show his hand, and your whole office staff, as well as the private detectives, made an earnest effort to save the box, thinking it was really valuable."

Weston's argument did not help Melbrun. He felt that his strategy had been a mistake; that it was the direct cause of Kelson's death. Naturally, Kelson's ardent pursuit of Smarley was based upon his lack of facts; but had the secretary used good judgment, he would still be alive. So Weston argued, and Melbrun finally began to believe him.

"Take the money to the pier," ordered the commissioner, pushing the suitcase to Melbrun. "You will be quite safe in the armored truck, and the pier is thoroughly guarded. Proceed with the distribution of the bonus money to the crew of the Anitoga, and stop worrying about Kelson. The chap is dead, Melbrun, and it can't be helped."

Soon after Melbrun's departure, Inspector Cardona arrived. Cardona had been quizzing wounded crooks, and doing a rapid job of it. Riddled with police bullets, in addition to the slugs that The Shadow delivered, the thugs had been dying off while Cardona questioned them.

"All they could say was 'Smarley,'" growled Cardona. "It was Smarley who hired them; Smarley, who was out to grab the dough; Smarley who made the getaway."

"Quite correct," nodded Weston. "What else could the hoodlums say?"

"They could have told me how Smarley got hold of them," snapped Cardona. "They never worked for him before. You can't build a mob up overnight, commissioner."

"I never intend to do so."

"Sorry, commissioner. I was referring to Smarley. We know what he was—a bookie, running a small-time horse parlor. All of a sudden, he sprouts out like a big-shot. Where did he get all of those mobbies?"

The commissioner had an answer. Crime had been quiet over a long period. It would have been easy for Jake Smarley, or anyone else, to enlist a thuggish horde. The fact that the gunners were of varied types, merely supported Weston's theory. Apparently, Smarley had approached any who were on the loose.

"They were men who placed bets through Smarley," analyzed Weston. "That is how he learned about them, inspector. If he paid them in advance, which is probable, he naturally would not have told them where he intended to go.

"Your job is to find Smarley. Use every means to do so. Treat him as a public enemy, a lone wolf bent on murder. But from all descriptions of the fellow"—the commissioner's tone became contemptuous—"he is an amateur at crime. You will probably find him cowering in some hideaway that your stool pigeons will uncover."

WESTON and his ace inspector were still discussing matters, and getting closer in accord, when The Shadow left the Cobalt Club. He was Cranston when he stepped into his limousine; but after a ride of a few blocks, he became a figure cloaked in black.

The Shadow had not forgotten the armored truck, with its hundred-thousand-dollar load. Though the police commissioner had taken full precautions to insure its arrival at the pier, The Shadow did not regard the delivery of the cash as a certainty.

In The Shadow's opinion, Jake Smarley was more than a small-fry criminal who had attempted a robbery through sheer bravado.

Smarley's quick-witted work in Melbrun's office, his coolness under fire, and his disposal of Kelson showed how dangerous the man could be. His getaway, accompanied by at least a dozen followers, proved Smarley a skillful organizer.

In short, The Shadow, while in the thick of battle, had recognized something that had entirely escaped the police.

The Shadow knew that lesser crooks had been left to take the brunt; that the cream of Smarley's forces had gone with him. He sensed, too, that the repeated name of "Smarley!" that dying hoodlums had squawked in parrot fashion could be a cover-up for certain lieutenants who had provided Smarley with his mob.

As the core of a compact criminal organization, Smarley could attempt new crime despite the law. He still had plenty of shock troops at his command, and The Shadow could conceive of Smarley ordering another, and more daring, thrust to get Melbrun's funds this very night.

Near the North River, The Shadow left the limousine. He became a gliding, fleeing shape that followed an untraceable course to a darkened pier, where a skeleton force of guards kept watch over a huge liner that had been interned because of war.

Slipping through the thin cordon of guards, The Shadow boarded the great ship. Reaching the liner's superstructure, he had a perfect view of an adjoining pier.

There, The Shadow saw the steamship *Anitoga*, dwarfed beside the great vessel which he used as his observation post. The decks of the *Anitoga* were brilliant with light. More than a hundred men were clustered there, like figures on a stage.

Among one tiny batch, The Shadow spied Melbrun, together with the shippers who had provided the bonus money for the crew of the *Anitoga*. Sailors were stepping forward, one by one, while Melbrun, as spokesman for the shippers, gave them their awards.

While the hundred thousand dollars was being pieced out to the men who deserved it, The Shadow's eyes roved the pier from the land end to the river.

Police were on hand, a score of them, ready for any emergency. The pier, however, provided a long stretch to patrol. Should crooks choose some salient point and make a concerted attack, they would have a chance of driving upon the unarmed ship crew before the officers could halt them.

Thus The Shadow held real command of the situation, from his shrouded lookout post. His laugh, and a few well-directed shots, could frustrate any invasion and bring the police to the vital spot before crooks might gain a foothold. The Shadow was ready, vigilant, awaiting such attack.

The moment did not come. Nothing disturbed the scene upon the pier. The money was distributed; some crew members went to their quarters, while others came ashore, where police escorted them away from the treacherous waterfront.

Arnold Melbrun and the shipping men drove away in their cars. Lights were extinguished on board the *Anitoga*. Deep quiet lay along the river.

Guards about the interned liner were puzzled by a whispery laugh that came from the ship's bridge, like a ghostly echo. They made a search, but found no one. By then, The Shadow was gone. His parting laugh had a significance which the men who heard it did not understand.

It was a tone of prophecy. The Shadow foresaw that crime would strike again. Melbrun's cash was a thing of the past, so far as crooks were concerned. Their next effort would involve larger game. Meanwhile, it would be The Shadow's business to locate the missing man who managed crime, Jake Smarley.

The law had chosen the same quest, and regarded it a simple one. The Shadow felt that it might prove more complex than the police supposed, for he credited Smarley with foresight in choosing a suitable hideaway. Nevertheless, The Shadow's whispered laugh denoted confidence.

As yet, The Shadow had not struck upon the crux of the whole case. He did not know that in searching for Jake Smarley, he would be hunting a man who no longer existed!

CHAPTER VI
THE SECOND FACE

THREE glum men sat in their customary meeting place, glowering at one another. They were the lieutenants who had taken orders from the mysterious crook who called himself Five-face, and they were beginning to regret their new alliance. Their apartment looked shabbier than ever; they had less money in their card game.

It was Grease Rickel who broke the monotony, by slapping a fistful of cards upon the table. Rising with a growl, the slimy-faced racketeer stalked the room, then began a verbal outburst.

"Jake Smarley!" sneered Grease. "A flash in the pan! A guy who couldn't deliver. We were boobs to join up with him!"

Banker Dreeb did not fully agree. His solemn face was thoughtful. At last, he spoke dryly:

"Why blame Smarley? He worked the game as well as he could. It just happened that Melbrun outfoxed him."

"Yeah?" Clip Zelber put the sharp query. "Smarley didn't know the cashbox was a dummy, did he?"

"No," admitted Banker, "I guess he didn't."

"Then what did he drop it for?" snapped Clip. "I'll tell you why. Because he was yellow! He met up with The Shadow, and he couldn't stand the gaff. Smarley, the big shot! We were lugs to waste a bunch of good trigger men helping that guy."

Outvoted two to one, Banker became silent. Both Grease and Clip continued to gripe. Three days had passed since the raid at Melbrun's. The whole thing had been a fluke. The only luck lay in the fact that their own parts in the crime lay undiscovered. At least, they had managed to cover their tracks, but that was small comfort.

They needed cash, and said so. The argument was one that Banker could not dispute. Plucking a newspaper from a table, Grease shoved it under Banker's nose and pointed out two photographs on the front page.

"There's the guy that claimed he had brains," sneered Grease, pointing to Smarley's picture. "Look at that dried-up map of his. Five grand reward for Jake Smarley. Say—if he comes crawling in here, the best thing we could do would be grab him and collect the dough.

"When it comes to brains, here's the fellow that really has them." Grease tapped the other picture. "Arnold Melbrun, who is putting up the reward. You know why he's offering it—because Smarley was dumb enough to put the blast on that secretary, Kelson. That was the biggest boner of all."

Banker was seated at the table, shuffling the pack of cards. He invited Grease and Clip to join him, but they saw no reason for the game. As Clip put it, they were tired of passing money around the triangle and borrowing it back from each other. Banker smiled at Clip's remark.

"We'll get some new money into the game," he said dryly. "I just heard that Flush Tygert is back in town."

Mention of the name brought eager looks from Grease and Clip. They remembered their last game with Flush, a few months before. It had proven profitable to everyone except Flush Tygert.

"A funny gazebo, Flush," chuckled Banker. "Card hustling is his racket. He used to trim the chumps every time he took a boat trip. But he never could make dough playing poker straight. It kind of annoyed him."

"I remember," nodded Grease. "He said he liked to join a game with guys like us, just to see how it felt being on the losing end. There's one thing I never could figure out. If Flush was so smart, why couldn't he trim us?"

"Because he didn't have a shill," explained Clip. "He always signed up a stooge when he rode the packets to Europe. I guess you weren't here, Grease, the day he showed us the flush trick. That's the one that gave Flush his moniker."

Grease showed new interest.

"I heard it different," he said. "I thought they called him Flush because he always looked flush. You know, with diamonds sticking all over him and wads of dough bulging from his pockets."

"That's the story he tells the chumps," explained Banker. "Flush had to have some alibi for his moniker, after the other hustlers pinned it on him. When Flush gets here, Grease, we'll have him show you that pet trick of his, just to put him in the right mood."

THE three lieutenants were deep in a new card game, when a knock at the door announced the arrival of Flush Tygert. They were due for a disappointment, as soon as the gambler entered.

Flush looked the same as ever: tall, thin-haired, with a long, sallow face that wore a perpetual gold-toothed smile. But his blue serge suit was shiny; its glitter took the place of diamonds. As for his pockets, they hadn't the slightest sign of a bulge.

It was quite plain that Flush Tygert had fallen on bad times. His roving eyes were actually greedy, as they studied the few hundred dollars of cash that lay on the card table.

Grease Rickel gave a snarling welcome, which brought him a shin kick from Clip Zelber. Meanwhile, Banker Dreeb covered the incident by extending a glad hand to the visitor.

In this instance, Banker and Clip were outvoting Grease. They considered it good policy to give Flush a welcome, even if he did look broke. Flush had quick ways of getting into the money. He might come back within a week quite as flush as ever.

"Sit down and play a few hands, Flush," suggested Banker. "Your credit is good, if you need any. By the way, before we start, show Grease the flush trick. He was asking how you trimmed the chumps so easy."

A pleased gleam showed on Flush's face, as apparent as the glitter of his gold teeth. He took a chair and invited Clip to sit opposite, to assist him in the stunt. Then, gesturing toward Clip, Flush stated in a smooth but drawly tone:

"The stooge wins, see? But I do the dirty work. Here's how. In a poker game, a guy often gets a four flush but finds it hard to fill when he draws the extra card. I take care of that problem."

He gave Clip four hearts and a spade, and took a five-card hand for himself. He tossed a few cards on the table, to represent a discard.

"There's four signals," continued Flush. "Hold those cards square; that's it, Clip. Left thumb, right thumb, both thumbs, no thumbs. Those mean clubs, diamonds, hearts or spades."

Clip promptly poked both thumbs above the top edge of his cards. Flush gave an approving nod.

"That means you need a heart," he said, "and I've got one. I cop it, here in my right duke, the face of the card against the palm. Meanwhile, you've got to slide off that odd spade of yours and slip it face down with the discards."

Clip managed the maneuver; as Flush explained, the process was easy, because people wouldn't be expecting a player to get rid of one card from a legitimate hand of five. As it now stood, Clip had an incomplete hand of four hearts.

"Plank them face up on the board," ordered Flush. "Tell everybody you've got a flush. Say it like you meant it."

When Clip gestured at the four cards that he laid on the table, the only objector was Flush himself. In his smooth drawl, the gambler said:

"Spread 'em out, fella! Always spread 'em out, so everybody can see 'em. Maybe there's a wrong card in that mess."

Before Clip could move, Flush spread the cards himself. His right hand snaked forward, gave the four hearts a wide sweep. With the movement, Flush added the extra heart from his own palm, so deftly that the onlookers blinked. He didn't simply drop it on the other cards; he sliced it right in among them, so that it formed the center of the five.

"All hearts," admitted Flush, in a grieved tone. "The pot is yours, old man. Worse luck next time."

Such skill won immediate approval for Flush Tygert. He had shown the stunt to Banker and Clip once before, and they agreed that he had repeated it in the same slick style. The compliment produced another gleaming grin from Flush.

"You can't always win, you know," drawled the gambler, "even with the best of setups. I ought to be in the money right at present, but I'm not. I played what looked like a sure shot, but it didn't work out."

The listeners looked interested.

"I was out to get a hundred thousand bucks," added Flush. "But the dough was gone before I could grab it. Besides—"

Flush went no further. It wasn't necessary. He had changed his tone from a drawl to a half whine. The men who heard it recognized that voice.

It was the voice of Jake Smarley!

THE missing bookie had returned in the guise of the slick gambler. Jake Smarley and Flush Tygert were the same. But neither of those names sprang to the lips of the three amazed men who viewed the smiling visitor before them. In concert, they exclaimed a bigger, more important name:

"Five-face!"

"I told you I'd be back," drawled the master crook, in the style of Flush Tygert. "You can

MOE SHREVNITZ

forget Jake Smarley. He's the same as dead and buried. I'm only sorry that he didn't grab off Melbrun's cash and split it with you fellows.

"Anyway, he made his getaway. That's why I'm here. And remember"—the speaker raised his left hand and bent his forefinger inward—"the Melbrun job was only the first one. There are four more to come"—he was counting his fingers, one by one—"and I'll use a different face for each."

Eagerly, the lieutenants gathered close. Lowering his drawl to an undertone, Five-face began the details of the crime next on the list. As they listened, Grease Rickel and Clip Zelber exchanged approving glances that pleased Banker Dreeb, the lieutenant who had been confident that Five-face could come through.

New crime was in the making—crime that would require the mobbies that the lieutenants could supply. Crime without mercy toward anyone who might oppose it. Five-face, at present known as Flush Tygert, was including all factors in his plans.

There would be a surprise for all foemen who crossed crime's coming path; even for The Shadow!

CHAPTER VII
CROOKS ON THE MOVE

THE black-walled room was thick with darkness, except for a corner, where a bluish light gleamed upon the polished surface of a table.

Deflected downward, the bluish rays made little impression on the deep gloom; in fact, the whole room seemed a mammoth shroud encroaching upon the spotted light. A figure stood beside the table; yet it was invisible against the darkness.

Living things came into the light: a pair of hands that moved like detached creatures. They were slender hands, yet sinewy, showing power beneath the velvety surface of the long, tapering fingers. Upon the third finger of the left hand shone a strange gem, with ever-changing hues that ran the gamut of the spectrum.

The stone was a girasol, a magnificent fire opal, unmatched in all the world. The iridescent gem proclaimed the identity of its owner, but only to the privileged few, who knew the significance of the gleaming token. The girasol was The Shadow's token.

This room was The Shadow's sanctum, a hidden headquarters where darkness always persisted. Buried in the heart of Manhattan, its very location a deep-guarded secret, the sanctum was the place wherein the master avenger formed his plans to frustrate men of crime.

Newspaper clippings moved about under the touch of The Shadow's fingers. He was arranging them along with report sheets from his agents: stacks of data, that often proved important.

Tonight, they meant nothing.

The quest for Jake Smarley had been fruitless. The missing bookie had completely vanished. The Shadow's competent agents had scoured hideout after hideout ahead of the police, and had found no trace of crime's new overlord.

Nevertheless, a whispered laugh stirred the sanctum's blackness. The Shadow had probed crime's depths, and understood. He was no longer thinking in terms of Jake Smarley; he was considering the possible moves of a supercrook who had discarded the bookie's guise.

Negative results had told The Shadow that he was seeking a criminal who had more faces than one. He had therewith instructed his agents to drop the search for Smarley. Instead, they were watching for massed moves on the part of lesser crooks, as sure proof that crime's master hand would again be conniving evil.

A tiny light twinkled on the sanctum's wall. Lifting a pair of earphones, The Shadow clamped them to his head. As the light extinguished itself, a methodical voice came over the wire:

"Burbank speaking—"

"Report!"

At The Shadow's command, Burbank, the contact man, gave long-awaited news. Crooks were on the move; their destination had been discovered. The Shadow's agents were covering the scene, awaiting the arrival of their chief.

A long hand lifted itself from the table, vanished into darkness. There was a *click* as the bluish light went off. A low, weird laugh stirred the sanctum, fading with The Shadow's departure.

WITHIN the next quarter hour, a taxicab swung from a side street and followed the Bowery, moving slowly along that famous thoroughfare.

There was a double reason for the cab's slow progress. An elevated railway ran above the Bowery, impeding speed. In addition, the street was a favorite haunt for shambling bums, who crossed the thoroughfare with little regard for traffic.

Besides those reasons, there was a third cause for the cab's reduced speed.

There was a passenger in the cab, though it looked quite empty. Seated deep in the rear seat, The Shadow, fully cloaked, was enveloped in darkness as he gazed from the window. His keen eyes were studying lights along the street. For the most part, the Bowery was gloomy, but one building showed a stretch of brilliance.

It was the Diamond Mart. Oddly situated in this doubtful section of Manhattan, the Mart formed an exchange where huge deals in gems were transacted daily. Its ground floor teemed with booths, the headquarters of merchants who displayed their diamonds and serenely made sales totaling many thousands of dollars, as if dealing in mere trifles.

The evening being early, the Mart was still open. Its doorway was wide; the portals seemed to welcome visitors. But the Diamond Mart was as closely guarded as the United States Mint. To start trouble within its walls would be akin to suicide.

Along the Bowery, The Shadow saw policemen, who were regularly assigned to guard the Diamond Mart. They were like figures in a guessing puzzle; there were about twice as many as the eye would ordinarily suppose. In addition to the bluecoats, plainclothes men were on duty. Patrol cars were also in the neighborhood.

It happened that The Shadow's present destination was a block south of the Diamond Mart. Knowing that crooks were about, he wisely gave the Mart a careful inspection as he passed. Had anything disturbed the calmness of the scene, The Shadow would have paused for further study; but it happened that the building was as serene as he had ever seen it.

Inside the Mart were special watchmen, who spotted suspicious customers at sight. Knowing their capability, The Shadow spoke a low-toned order to his driver and the cab proceeded onward. The next place that needed observation was The Shadow's special goal, an arcade that ran from the Bowery to another street.

The arcade formed a contrast to the Mart. Long, low-roofed, it offered shelter to the riffraff of the neighborhood, and such characters were plentiful.

At this hour, the arcade was rather dark, and as he passed it The Shadow noted that it held more than its usual quota of human drifters. He observed, too, that many shamblers were circulating about, always keeping within close range of the arcade.

Among these, The Shadow recognized his own secret agents, four in number. Two of them frequently patrolled the badlands, and were therefore quite at home. The other pair were posing as panhandlers and were doing a good job of it, but they were careful to remain in the offing so as not to be too conspicuous.

Reports were correct: crooks were assembling at the arcade. They were passing themselves as the lowest of human scum, which wasn't difficult, for they were rats by trade. But the arcade, itself, offered no target for crime.

Having covered the Diamond Mart, The Shadow decided to take a look at Chinatown, only a few blocks away.

The cab in which The Shadow rode was his own. Its driver, Moe Shrevnitz, was one of The Shadow's agents and a very capable hackie. At his chief's order, Moe weaved the cab into Chinatown, where a slow rate of speed was natural.

Chinatown proved as quiet as the Diamond Mart. Along the curve of Doyers Street, The Shadow saw patrolmen on their regular rounds. All was quiet near the corner of Mott and Pell, the real center of the district. Moe continued his roundabout course, finally making another trip past the Diamond Mart.

The cab halted there, abruptly, to let another cab stop. The Shadow saw the man who alighted, watched him wave an affable greeting to a detective who shifted into sight. The dick recognized the arrival; so did The Shadow. The man from the cab was Flush Tygert.

HE was a different Flush Tygert from that afternoon. He was more prosperous in appearance. Flush was wearing a natty-looking suit; the lights from the Mart brought a gleam from a diamond on his finger, and his cuff links showed the same sparkle. Moreover, Flush had cash. He showed a bundle of it when he paid the cab driver.

Flush peeled his bankroll like a head of lettuce. He had thumbed through ten-dollar bills and twenties before he found a stray five among the fifties. He used the smaller bill to pay the driver. While the cabby was finding difficulty in making the change, Flush stuffed the big roll back into his pocket.

Chance played its hand right then.

A scrawny bum was slouching past the Diamond Mart. The shambler showed interest at sight of the cash. He shoved himself toward Flush, mouthing something about "sparing a dime." Flush gave a glance at the fellow's pasty face, then told him to be on his way.

The detective stepped forward; the bum made a quick scramble. A little farther along, he stopped to tell another panhandler what had happened. Both threw quick glances back at Flush.

This episode had all the markings of a well-timed act. It looked as though the two bums were on hand to spot how much cash Flush had with him. The gambler's bankroll certainly ran into thousands of dollars, big enough game to account for the assemblage down in the old arcade.

Diamond cut diamond; crook rob crook. The setup impressed The Shadow, as his cab wheeled away. Flush Tygert was certainly flush tonight, and the news had been passed along.

As for Flush's presence at the Diamond Mart, it

was natural enough. The Shadow had listed Flush and his habits, long ago. Records showed him to be a gambler who played the ocean liners, varying his trips, traveling to Europe and South America. When he came back with big winnings, Flush always invested them in diamonds.

Not having seen Flush that afternoon, The Shadow naturally assumed that the gambler had been lucky on his last South American excursion, since European voyages were no longer popular. Therefore, his trip to the Diamond Mart was logical.

Flush might rate as a crook on boats beyond the twelve-mile limit; on shore, he passed muster. The Shadow classed him as a normal customer at the Diamond Mart.

Elsewhere, Flush might be prey, either for his cash or his diamonds, particularly if he passed the old arcade after he left the Mart.

On the chance that such might be the case, The Shadow decided to drop in on the meeting place where he had seen too many mobsters. At his order, Moe swung the cab past the next corner.

Flush Tygert had not seen The Shadow. It was unfortunate, therefore, that the unseen cab rider had not waited a little longer. For Flush performed his next action in a fashion that was a trifle too dramatic. Pausing in the doorway of the Diamond Mart, the crook tried to light a cigarette with a lighter that worked too well.

Several times, Flush's flicking thumb produced a flame, which he promptly suppressed. He didn't want his light as soon as he was getting it. An elevated train was approaching, high above. As it came by, Flush finally let the cigarette lighter work, and held the flame steadily until the train had roared beyond him.

Then, with a gleaming smile, the man who called himself Five-face stepped into the welcoming portals of the Diamond Mart. Flush Tygert had used his cigarette lighter to touch off crime of a most unusual sort.

Things about to come would reveal the planning of a master plotter whose tricky schemes were to convince The Shadow that a real brain had designed them.

Crime was due, in the very presence of The Shadow, before he could reach the main scene of its action!

CHAPTER VIII
CRIME IN REVERSE

IT took The Shadow just three minutes to reach the vantage point he wanted: the rear street in back of the old arcade. During that interim, the elevated train stopped at a station and an oily faced man stepped off.

The passenger was Grease Rickel; he had caught the signal given by Flush Tygert with his cigarette lighter.

In his turn, Grease was spied by crooks below. He didn't have to leave the elevated platform. He merely stepped to the rail and gave a quick gesture. It started the real fireworks. Flush had supplied the flame; Grease was the fuse.

Instantly, a brawl broke loose outside the old arcade. It looked as though two bums had started to grab for a loose dime that they saw in the gutter and their scramble brought a flood of others, like sparrows flocking for a crust of bread.

The sudden strife brought shouts from policemen, followed by the pound of footbeats. Then, as the brawl increased, a whistle sounded.

Fighters accepted the police signal as their own. Not only did they break apart; there was a flash of revolvers, followed by quick-stabbed shots in the direction of the officers. Diving for shelter of doorways and elevated pillars, the police pulled their own guns, to return the fire.

Like a thing rehearsed, the swirl of shabby men went into the entrance of the arcade. Thinking the opposition poorly armed and in retreat, the officers followed, their own fire bringing up reserves, who were prompt to aid them.

No outside aid could have stopped the coming slaughter. The charging police were thrusting themselves into the ugliest ambush ever designed in the badlands.

Seldom did crime's success depend upon such wholesale killing. Few big brains of crime, no matter how fiendish or desperate, cared to stir the vengeance of the law by a massacre of policemen. But tonight's crime had a reverse twist which slaughter would aid, and it was being managed by a supercrook who could laugh at the law after the deed was done.

The police would never find Five-face, no matter how far they looked for him. He had wiped out one personality, that of Jake Smarley. He could as easily dispose of his present guise. With crime done, Flush Tygert would no longer exist.

Five-face had given the word for slaughter in the name of Flush Tygert, and gleeful mobsters were eager to deliver death. Banked within the entrance of the old arcade were two squads of marksmen, four to a side, waiting for the decoys to bring the police into the fatal mesh.

No longer posing as bums, the killers held big revolvers of .45 caliber. They had chosen the "smoke wagons" as weapons in order that their bullets would produce a fuller share of carnage. As the last batch of decoys came diving into shelter, a harsh voice gave the word:

"Give it!"

Crooks were met by blazing guns, a brace of .45 automatics that The Shadow handled with utter ease.

With the signal, assistance came to the officers, who were already in full sight. It didn't come from outside the arcade; that was impossible. The men who sprang the surprise were in the very midst of the crooks.

Four in number, The Shadow's agents. One pair had entered the arcade earlier; the other two had hurried in with the decoys. But all four had the same objective.

Whipping out guns of their own, they flung themselves upon the firing squads, slashing hard at heads and arms, determined to prevent the reception that the crooks intended for the police.

Guns blasted, wildly. The whole arcade roared, its confines magnifying the fusillade to the tumult of a cannonade. Stabs of flame issued in all directions, except the one that crooks intended.

Bullets were digging the low roof and walls of the arcade; slugs were whistling over the heads of the police and ricocheting from the sidewalk. But the charging police were still coming, unscathed by the fire!

They saw what had happened; how a few valiant men had hurled themselves on twice their number. The officers weren't shooting any longer; they didn't want to harm their friends. But the

police were blocked when they tried to return the rescue.

A veritable flood of howling hoodlums gushed from the arcade, pouring down upon the forces of the law. Guns were everywhere, slugging at close quarters. In a trice, the officers were fighting for their own lives against a formidable horde. It looked like sure death for the four unknown valiants who had spoiled the ambush.

Then, supreme amid the tumult, came a battle challenge that drowned all cries and shots. It broke from the very heart of the arcade, signifying an attack that was coming from the rear.

It stood for a lone fighter; a champion of justice who cared nothing about odds, a warrior whom crime had never conquered. Alone, he was more formidable than an entire squad; his very strength lay in his solitary ability to be everywhere, yet nowhere, when he hurled himself against a mass of foemen.

The battle laugh of The Shadow!

IN answer to that taunt, crooks forgot all else. The Shadow's agents were hurled aside by men who wanted to get at crime's archfoe. Fighting police suddenly found that they were struggling only with thugs who couldn't get loose to return into the arcade. Like a massive tide, the pour of killers had reversed itself.

Mobsters couldn't see The Shadow. They knew only that he was somewhere in the darkened arcade, and they wanted to smother him en masse before he could escape. They had turned themselves into a living juggernaut, numbering more than a score. No one, not even The Shadow, could stand against such a surge. So crooks thought, but they were wrong.

They were met by blasting guns, a brace of .45 automatics that The Shadow handled with utter ease. His shots were directed at the very center of the overwhelming wave, while thugs were clumsily trying to get their big revolvers into play.

The tide broke as men stumbled, and The Shadow lunged into its very vortex, like a diver going beneath a sweep of surf.

Snarling crooks wheeled from the flanks. The thing had happened at what seemed the very start of battle. The Shadow had gone almost before they realized it, but they knew where to find him: somewhere in their own midst.

A clever trick on The Shadow's part, but only a temporary stopgap. A suicidal move, if ever a fighter had made such.

Crooks had forgotten the cops out in the street. Outnumbering the few thugs who had remained to battle them, the police were free for another charge. They made it, at the very moment when the billow of crooks reversed itself to trap The Shadow. Under the unexpected drive, the maddened thugs were caught entirely off guard.

They were surging again toward the rear of the arcade, but not at their own desire. They were being propelled by a storming mass of blue-coated warriors, whose guns were stabbing devastating close-range shots that thinned the swirl of hoodlums.

Given a foothold by The Shadow, the police were turning the fight into a rout. Mobsters, not officers, were taking the brunt of bullets before they could reply with their own guns.

Along with the blast of guns, staggering crooks heard The Shadow's laugh, mocking in its triumph, from somewhere near the front of the arcade. The police had literally bowled the enemy clear of their black-clad prey!

WITHIN the Diamond Mart, sounds of battle were quite audible, but by no means ominous. Most of the shooting was muffled within the arcade; the guns that the diamond merchants heard seemed sporadic in their fire.

Behind a little counter that barely gave him room to spread his portly elbows, one fat-faced jeweler turned his head and smiled blandly at his neighbors. He was old Breddle, who had been in business at the Diamond Mart almost since its opening day. Rioting in this neighborhood did not disturb him.

In Breddle's opinion, a fight a block away was as remote as the European war zone. His bland smile widened as he heard the gunfire dwindle. The fray was bearing off in another direction, probably toward the twisty streets of Chinatown, where rioters could find holes and scurry into them.

Breddle gave a wise nod that calmed the neighboring merchants. They passed the word along the booths. No need to worry any longer; old Breddle had given the nod. Glancing in Breddle's direction, other diamond sellers saw that the old-timer was talking with a customer as ardently as if the noise outside had been nothing more than a few firecrackers.

It chanced that Breddle's customer was Flush Tygert. The gambler was interested in buying diamonds in a big way. Practically all of Breddle's best gems were on the counter, but Flush wasn't satisfied.

Glancing at the adjoining booths, Flush quietly asked if Breddle could make deals with his nearest neighbors, provided that they had what Flush wanted. Figuring that his own stock would stand up in comparison, Breddle nodded. Beckoning to the other two merchants, he invited them to show the best they had.

None of the diamond sellers observed the thing that Flush took in with a casual glance out toward the street. Only Flush knew the size of the arcade battle; he was looking to see if it had produced the required result.

It had. The fray had drawn all available police from their usual posts, plainclothes men as well as bluecoats. For once, the street in front of the Diamond Mart was totally unprotected.

Trays of diamonds came across the sides of Breddle's booth, thrust there by the adjoining merchants. They wanted Flush to compare their wares with those that Breddle offered. With a grin that lacked gleam because of the glittering diamonds, Flush drawled:

"Thank you, gentlemen. I think that I can take all your gems!"

Had Breddle and the other merchants stared Flush in the eye, they might have guessed a most important secret. His features were undergoing a series of changes. He was Five-face, rather than Flush Tygert, though the gambler's countenance predominated during his facial betrayals.

But none of the three merchants was meeting the gaze of Five-face. They were staring at a gun muzzle that poked from the edge of Flush's coat. Snakelike, the revolver wangled back and forth under its owner's skillful hand. The gun point carried the hypnotic threat of a cobra's eye.

"Bring out the old valise," Flush told Breddle. "The one you always keep handy. Open it and put it on the floor below the counter."

BREDDLE followed instructions without a murmur. As he glanced at his fellow merchants, his eyes warned them not to make an unwise move. No one could get away with wholesale robbery, here at the Diamond Mart. Flush Tygert would be stopped before he could leave the building. Placing the valise as Flush ordered, Breddle politely awaited the crook's next order.

"Start to put your trays away," said Flush. "When you get them below the counter, dump them into the bag. Don't let any of the gems splash over. I might miss out on one I particularly want. In that case, Breddle, I'd have to give you a bullet as a reminder to be more careful."

Tray by tray, the old merchant poured diamonds into the waiting bag. Even at Breddle's prices, which were low, the gems he had displayed ran close to two hundred thousand dollars in total value. When Breddle had finished with his trays, Flush told him to take those that the other merchants held handy.

More diamonds went into the bag, and Breddle left the empty trays beneath his own counter. With the natural smile of Flush Tygert, Five-face told the other merchants to relax and looked unconcerned while Breddle handed over the valise, which now contained a quarter of a million in loot, at rock-bottom prices.

Straightening up from the counter, where he had leaned as though inspecting diamonds, Flush let his gun slide from sight. His last words were a warning that he would hold Breddle responsible, should any alarm be given. The threat meant nothing by the time Flush had carried the bag halfway to the big doorway.

With a gesture, Breddle ducked beneath his counter, and his neighbors followed his example. Breddle pulled a switch that gave an automatic alarm. Customers at the Diamond Mart were instantly treated to a demonstration of how rapidly things could happen in those preserves.

To the strident *clang* of alarm bells, merchants scooped up trays and loose diamonds, to shove them into safety. Guards appeared as if from nowhere—a few from behind counters, others among the customers, additional men through doors that bobbed open along the walls.

They almost blocked the outer door before Flush could reach it. Only by a rapid dash did the lone crook get there first.

By his spurt, Flush gave himself away as the thief they wanted; but he was smart enough to yank out his revolver and brandish it with one hand, while he swung the jewel bag across his body, exactly as he had done with Melbrun's cashbox when passing as Jake Smarley.

Flush fired, aiming for counters, not for the guards. It was a cute trick, for it threatened the lives of merchants and customers. On that account, the guards gave him leeway. They wanted him outside, where he could do no damage.

To a man, they thought that the foolhardy gem thief would run right into the arms of the police. But when they reached the door themselves, they saw Flush leaping into a taxicab parked a short way up the street.

The guards aimed; before they could fire, guns roared from two low-built sedans that wheeled in from a side street. Before they could drop back, the guards saw the muzzle of a machine gun thrust out from one car, ready to rake them.

Down the street, police were piling from the old arcade, too far away to give rescue. The aid that came was from a different quarter.

A CLOAKED figure sprang into sight from the gloom of an elevated pillar only a dozen yards away. A fierce laugh, taunting, defiant, made the machine gunners swing their formidable weapon toward the attacker in black. Automatics spurted, in tandem style, from the gloved hands of The Shadow.

The men at the machine gun were withered. Their car kept on, following the cab that Flush Tygert had taken. The other sedan also sped along, to cover the getaway. A third automobile was cutting in from another street. Mobsters had literally whisked themselves away from The Shadow's range.

But they couldn't escape this master foe who had arrived to take up the duty that the police had dropped. With the law triumphant in the arcade, The Shadow had sensed what was due at the Diamond Mart. Not quite in time to prevent the actual robbery, he was prepared, nevertheless, for the chase.

A cab lurched into view, arriving in almost as surprising a fashion as The Shadow. Moe Shrevnitz was at the wheel; he had been cruising, looking for his chief. The rear door slashed open; the cab seemed to swallow The Shadow as it passed him. Momentarily jabbing the brakes, Moe let the swinging door slam shut.

Again, a strange, weird laugh quivered the

A cloaked figure sprang into sight from the gloom of an elevated pillar.

gloom beneath the elevated, as gloved hands poked from the cab window, gripping a brace of automatics that still showed wreaths of smoke coiling from their muzzles.

The Shadow was on the trail of Five-face, the crook of many parts, who had staged crime as Flush Tygert. How long the man of crime could retain his quarter-million-dollar loot was a question soon to be decided!

CHAPTER IX
VANISHED BATTLERS

VEERING westward from the Bowery, the chase covered a few dozen blocks in uneventful style, while The Shadow kept close tabs on the speeding cars ahead. Ironically enough, the pursuit passed very close to police headquarters, on Centre Street, without producing a ripple.

Five-face had planned well. The battle in the old arcade, staged by riffraff acquired through the master crook's lieutenants, had drawn patrol cars in the wrong direction. If The Shadow hadn't come along to take up the pursuit, the getaway would have been perfect.

News was just reaching police headquarters when the caravan went by. In the radio room, dispatches were going out to patrol cars to pick up a fleeing taxicab and three convoying sedans. Perhaps crooks realized it, for they were increasing their pace, to get as far away as possible.

Unquestionably, they hoped to find a hiding place before the law was in full cry. The Shadow was preventing it, by his policy of dogging their trail. Thus crooks were caught between two problems: that of being spotted by their speed, as soon as the full alarm went out; and the alternative of letting The Shadow overtake them.

They feared the first proposition less. The Shadow's victory at the arcade seemed a superhuman accomplishment. People who stopped to get The Shadow usually stayed too long. The Shadow would certainly draw patrol cars with his gunfire; after that, the crooks would be trapped.

So the speeding cars kept right ahead, and while Moe clung to the chase, The Shadow leaned through the front window and inquired how his other agents had fared.

They were all right, Moe reported. He had contacted them, somewhat battered and bewildered, outside the arcade, but on their way to safety.

Rescued by The Shadow, the agents had survived the police onrush by the simple expedient of lying low at the sides of the arcade and letting the surge travel past them. So many thugs had been fighting the police hand to hand that the agents had easily escaped notice.

Sirens were wailing as Moe finished his report. Patrol cars were on the job, searching for the fleeing caravan. Leaning from his window, The Shadow tried long-range fire at the wheels of a crook-manned car.

The vehicle was too far ahead, but the shots counted. Sounding loud in the narrow side street, they were sure to be reported to the police when they cut in along this route.

Results came sooner than The Shadow hoped. As his cab passed a corner, patrol cars appeared. Fortunately, they recognized that The Shadow's cab held a pursuer, not a fugitive. Soon, they were actually gaining on The Shadow, a fact which was quite important.

It meant that the last car in the caravan must have slowed somewhat, since Moe was guiding by its pace. Thus, when that car swerved a corner, The Shadow ordered Moe to keep ahead.

Crooks fired a volley as The Shadow's cab whizzed by, and he returned the fire. The lone car fled by the side street, its occupants unrecognized.

Grease Rickel was in command of that car. He had found it waiting for him near the Bowery elevated station. Grease snarled curses as he took to flight. It had been his job to decoy The Shadow and the police cars, getting them away from Five-face and the swag. The Shadow had seen through the ruse.

Only a few blocks along the straight route, Moe was picking up the real trail again. He had spurted the cab, drawing away from the police cars, but they were again beginning to gain. The fact told The Shadow that another trick was coming. When he saw the last car of the caravan keep straight ahead at a street crossing, The Shadow ordered Moe to turn.

How The Shadow guessed the correct direction was a mystery, even to Moe; nevertheless, the black-cloaked observer picked it. This time, it happened to be Banker Dreeb who staged the dodge. Like Grease, Banker was angry because he managed to get clear so easily.

Only one car still clung to the cab that carried Flush Tygert. The man in charge was the third lieutenant, Clip Zelber, and he was in a dilemma. He didn't know whether to stay along with Five-face and protect him or to make another effort to divert the trail.

Clip hadn't expected the chase to reach its present state. While he was puzzling over the situation, The Shadow solved it for him.

Knowing that only one car lay between him and the fugitive cab, The Shadow ordered Moe to overtake it. As Moe made a marked gain by a swift turn at a corner, The Shadow opened a bombardment.

Had Clip allowed it to continue, he and his companions would have found themselves in a wrecked car, for The Shadow had neat ways of puncturing tires and crippling drivers at the steering wheels.

Frantically, Clip ordered his driver to take the next corner. The sedan scudded for safety, leaving The Shadow a clear route to the cab ahead.

IN that cab, Five-face rode alone. The term suited him better than his recent identity of Flush Tygert, because Five-face no longer looked like Flush. He had started to change his personality with the aid of materials from a makeup box.

He was using a fake chin and a molding substance that looked like putty. He spoke in the tone of Flush, however, as he ordered his driver to start dodging corners.

Oddly, the driver of the fugitive cab was not a thug. He was simply a scared cabby, who had been drawn into this mess by chance. Choice of the cab was another tribute to the mastery of Five-face. The chameleon crook had foreseen that a threatened driver would show more speed than any other, and the cabby was proving it under the present strain.

He took corners on two wheels, whizzed right through traffic lights, jounced the curb in order to escape blocking traffic. In the course of a dozen blocks, the fellow actually gained a few on Moe Shrevnitz, which was a very remarkable feat.

The numbers on the street corners were clicking past like those on a roulette wheel. Almost finished with his makeup, Five-face glanced from the window. He couldn't spot the street numbers, but he recognized the district. He was very close to the destination that he wanted.

With one hand, Five-face gripped the jewel bag beside him; then, in the tone of Flush Tygert, he ordered:

"Take it easy, jockey. We're getting too near Times Square to raise hob with the traffic. You know where Lody's Cafe is?"

The cabby gulped that he did. The fellow's tone brought one of Flush's typical laughs. Lody's was noted as a hangout for mobsters of a deluxe sort, but patronized only by those against whom the law had no definite complaints. Despite its glitter, Lody's was a joint, and recognized as such.

"We're going to Lody's," came the assuring tone of Flush. "Nice and properlike, understand? Pull up in front and drop me like I was any ordinary customer."

The cabby began to stammer that they were east of Lody's, and that it happened to be on an eastbound street. It wouldn't do for an ordinary cab to be bucking traffic. Flush's tone cut the driver short.

"Don't you think I know it?" drawled the big shot. "Take the first westbound street before you get to Lody's, then swing around to the place."

As he finished, Five-face threw a glance to the rear. He could see The Shadow's cab and hear the sirens of the police cars behind it. Nevertheless, he laughed and leaned forward to the front seat.

"Remember that gat I showed you?" he inquired. "Here it is again, where you'll remember it. Take it easy, jockey, in case I want to jump out in a hurry."

The cabby quivered as he felt the cold ring of steel that pressed against the back of his neck. The gun had worried him enough; the pressure of a muzzle completely cowed him. Still, he found strength enough to follow orders. He idled the cab the moment that he swung the corner, reducing it almost to a crawl.

By the time the cab had turned the next corner, The Shadow's taxi swung the first one. The next block was very short, along an avenue; the cab navigated it and took the turn that brought it in front of Lody's. By then, Moe had overtaken it, and sirens could be heard from the avenue.

Hurling a door open, The Shadow reached the other cab just as it stopped. He saw the driver sitting stiff, his hands upraised. Hearing his own door clatter open, the fellow pleaded:

"Don't start nothing! He's got me covered; he'll croak me! He's poking my neck with a gun—"

The Shadow's laugh intervened; it came as a reassuring whisper. Glancing in the mirror, the cabby saw to his amazement that his recent passenger was gone. In place of Flush Tygert was a black-clad rescuer, who was calmly telling the cabby to pull ahead.

As he spoke, The Shadow placed his gloved fingers against the back of the driver's neck and plucked away an object that was stuck there.

It was a dime that Five-face had pressed against the cabby's neck, instead of a gun muzzle. Pushed slightly upward, it had adhered to the fellow's perspiring skin. The cabby felt it each time his neck tilted back against his collar.

By so placing the coin, Five-face had kept the driver on his way after the master crook had found a chance to drop off from the cab.

WHILE the cabby was staring at the dime that The Shadow dropped into his hand, the police cars swerved into the side street. Springing to the curb, The Shadow waved arms to flag them.

He didn't want them to open fire on the empty cab, which no longer contained the crook they wanted. The wanted man must be somewhere in the vicinity, the bag of diamonds with him.

The next step was to block his escape from the neighborhood.

Five-face had foreseen that prospect.

As the white-topped police cars were halting at sight of The Shadow, a hard-faced waiter in Lody's was answering a telephone call. Hanging up, the fellow stepped to a table where three men were dining. Their tuxedos did not disguise the fact that they were mobsters of the first water.

These three did not belong to Five-face nor any of his lieutenants. They were ex-racketeers, still living on ill-gotten cash, like most of the patrons in Lody's.

"Just got a tip-off, gents," informed the waiter. "The Shadow is outside. Thought you'd like to know it."

They *did* like to know it. Nowhere was the name of The Shadow voiced more venomously than at Lody's. These has-beens of crime belonged to the same ilk as Grease, Banker, and Clip. They happened to be dining at Lody's because they still were prosperous. With each day, they had been looking forward to the time when someone would settle The Shadow once for all.

They didn't regard the waiter's tip-off as a hoax. It wasn't healthy to play practical jokes on the crowd that dined at Lody's. These crooks deluxe saw their opportunity to deal with The Shadow personally. Instead of mobbies, they could depend upon a score more of their own kind, who were also in the restaurant.

The word passed instantly from table to table; with one accord, tuxedoed rats came to their feet and started out to the street. Undaunted by the arriving police, they whipped revolvers from their pockets the instant that they saw the cloaked figure outlined in the lights of the patrol cars.

The first member of the throng gave the cry to which all responded:

"The Shadow!"

With the cry, the cloaked figure wheeled. The Shadow knew instantly that Flush Tygert had phoned the word to Lody's after dropping off from his cab. He recognized, too, that these attackers were not part of the big shot's horde. Again, the touch of the master hand; he was playing it safe, turning a crowd of volunteers upon The Shadow.

The shout gave the attack away, but not well enough to save The Shadow. Too many guns were on the draw for him to remain as a target. As for blackness, there wasn't any close enough for The Shadow to make a quick fade. His only system was to provide darkness by beating the crooks to the shot, and he did.

Whipping both guns from his cloak, The Shadow blasted the lights of the nearest police car, producing a swath of blackness into which he dived. The instant that the gloom swallowed him, he reversed his course. He was speeding out again, into the light, as the tuxedoed marksmen dented the hood of the car into junk.

Another shout; the crooks wheeled; too late. The Shadow reached the cover that he needed—the cab that Flush had used. Its driver was gone, running along the street. Springing into the cab, The Shadow turned it into an improvised pillbox.

It had a slide-back top, which enabled the cloaked sharpshooter to fire as if from a turret. When crooks blazed bullets for the cab top, The Shadow's hands jabbed from one window, then the other, poking quick shots from ever-ready guns.

By then, the police were in it. At first, they thought that shots were meant for them. They had mistaken The Shadow's strategy for an attack. But when the cloaked fighter had diverted the fire, the officers knew how matters stood.

They were out of their cars, charging the frenzied men in tuxedos exactly as they had gone after the pretended bums in the arcade.

Crooks surged for the cab, hoping to get The Shadow at any cost, while others were fighting off the police. When they reached the cab, The Shadow was gone again. He had chosen the moment of the police surge to spring to the sidewalk and take a new vantage point in a narrow alleyway. He was sniping off his foemen in a fashion that promised them sure defeat.

Then came a quick end to the battle, through aid from a unique and unexpected source.

NEXT door to Lody's was an upstairs gymnasium, rather well known in the vicinity. It was a boxing stable managed by a fight promoter named Barney Kelm, a familiar figure on Broadway, whenever he was in New York. Barney happened to be on hand tonight, and shooting didn't bother him any more than the boos of a prize-fight audience.

Portly, wide-shouldered, with a broad, bluff face beneath his derby hat, Barney Kelm stepped to a little balcony that fronted the gym. He scanned the street and saw what was going on—a frenzied, slugging battle between uniformed police and men that he knew as hoodlums.

There was no sign of The Shadow. From his balcony, Barney could not observe the telling shots that the hidden marksman delivered. Turning back to the gymnasium, Barney gave an ardent bellow, along with graphic gestures. A dozen boxers quit skipping rope and punching away at bags. With Barney among them, they dashed downstairs to the street.

They were pulling off their gloves, to get in

punches that would hurt. Grabbing men in tuxedos, the pugs gave them expert treatment. Hard uppercuts counted more than the wide swings of police guns. With Barney cheering them on and waving his own pudgy fists, the boxers made short work of the mob from Lody's.

Soon, the police were carrying away the wounded, while the pugilists were dragging slap-happy crooks from gutters. More patrol cars were arriving, to give the law full control. His guns stowed away, The Shadow saw Inspector Cardona step from a car and start shaking hands with Barney Kelm.

The fat-faced fight promoter was taking credit for having quelled the fray. As far as The Shadow was concerned, Barney Kelm was welcome to it. The Shadow was more interested in learning what had become of Flush Tygert. With that purpose in mind, he glided away into blackness.

Two battlers had vanished: one, The Shadow, a figure in black, his real identity unknown; the other, Five-face, who changed his personality after every deed of crime.

When, where, and how they would meet again, neither could foretell; but the fact that there would be such a meeting was something that both knew!

CHAPTER X
THE PUBLIC HERO

SEATED in the library of the Cobalt Club, Lamont Cranston was scanning two newspapers. One was several days old, telling of the foiled robbery at the United Import Co. It showed the photo of Jake Smarley, the missing bookie, beside the picture of Arnold Melbrun, the man who had outguessed the vanished crook.

The other newspaper was recent. It had two front-page photographs. One portrayed Flush Tygert, his long face displaying its habitual smile; the other, the fat, serious features of Barney Kelm, who rated as a public hero.

Like Smarley, Tygert was wanted, but to a greater degree. Where Smarley had missed out on a robbery, Flush had succeeded. It would go hard with both, however, if they were found, for there were manslaughter charges against them, too.

Folding one newspaper, Cranston placed it on the other, so that only the two pictures showed, those of Smarley and Flush. Side by side, they made an interesting contrast. Facially, there was nothing in common between Jake Smarley and Flush Tygert; the remarkable thing was that both had disappeared.

Very remarkable, considering that they had not been highly rated in the underworld until their recent exploits. Neither Smarley nor Flush should be the sort to have an airtight hideaway; yet, apparently, each had one. Not a trace of either criminal had been found by the police.

Placing the newspapers aside, Cranston drew a notebook from his pocket. With a fountain pen, he wrote the two names in a vivid blue ink:

Jake Smarley
Flush Tygert

Alone in the library, Cranston phrased a whispered laugh. Its low, uncanny tone identified him as The Shadow. So did the ink with which he had inscribed the names. As it dried, it faded, obliterating itself completely.

It was the special ink that The Shadow used for important messages. He employed it, too, when he transcribed his impressions into written words.

The names linked. The Shadow had divined that Smarley and Flush were one and the same. His keen brain was visualizing the next step in the process; namely, that by this time, neither Smarley nor Flush existed; that the master criminal must have adopted another identity.

In tracing this vital fact, The Shadow had pictured two events from the past.

He remembered how Smarley had cleverly used Melbrun's cashbox as a shield to deflect bullets. Flush had done the same thing with the bag of gems when he fled from the Diamond Mart.

In flight, Five-face had been off guard, and each time, The Shadow had spied him. Though The Shadow did not know the title used by the master crook and therefore could not tell how many faces the criminal had, he was certainly on the correct track in the detection of crime's greatest secret.

An attendant entered the library, carrying an envelope. He saw The Shadow and approached on tiptoe, carefully trying not to disturb the quiet of the room. The Shadow was rising, in the leisurely style of Cranston, before the attendant arrived. Cranston's lips showed a smile as he scanned the note.

It said that Commissioner Weston was in the grillroom and would like Cranston to join him. Apparently, the commissioner had something to tell regarding the police investigation of the recent robberies.

IN the grillroom, Weston had a pile of police reports, stacked six inches high. Cardona was with him, and the two were thumbing through the papers.

Again, there was a resemblance between the raid at Melbrun's and the robbery in the Diamond Mart. Small-fry crooks had been quizzed, with only one answer.

First it had been Jake Smarley; now it was Flush Tygert. In each instance, thugs blamed all crime on men whose identity the police already knew.

"Perhaps the two are working in cahoots," said Weston, suddenly. "They might even be sharing the same hideout. An excellent theory." Weston nodded, proudly, as he turned to Cardona and added: "Make a note of it, inspector."

While Cardona was making the note, two men entered. One was Arnold Melbrun; the other, old Breddle. The commissioner introduced the importer to the diamond merchant.

"Sorry about your misfortune, Mr. Breddle," condoled Melbrun. "I was lucky to save the money that had been entrusted to me. I wish that you had experienced the same good fortune."

"You took the right precautions, Mr. Melbrun," returned Breddle. "I was just unfortunate, considering how well the Diamond Mart was guarded."

Weston was laying out photographs on the table. He was anxious to link Jake Smarley with Flush Tygert, though he did not realize how closely the two could actually be identified.

Looking at Smarley's pictures, Melbrun gave a slow nod. From descriptions given by the office workers, the pictures showed Smarley, well enough. But when he saw photographs of Flush Tygert, Melbrun shook his head emphatically. He declared that he knew nothing at all concerning Flush.

In his turn, old Breddle looked blank when he saw the Smarley pictures, but became quite voluble at sight of those portraying Flush. Unfortunately, Breddle had never seen Flush, except when the gambler came into the Diamond Mart; therefore, he could offer no worthwhile information concerning the mobster.

Both Melbrun and Breddle were rising, when Weston stopped them with a gesture.

"Another man will be here, soon," announced the commissioner. "Barney Kelm, our public hero. He and his boys gave us some very valuable assistance. I would like you both to meet him."

Melbrun happened to have an appointment and could not stay. He regretted, however, that he could not meet the famous Barney Kelm.

"Give the chap my congratulations," said Melbrun, "and say that my door is always open to all fine citizens like himself. I know that our friend Breddle"—he turned to the jeweler—"will give Kelm proper thanks. Kelm came close to catching Tygert for you, Breddle. I wish he had been around when Smarley tried to rob my office."

With Melbrun gone, Breddle was anxious to learn what progress the police had made toward reclaiming the stolen diamonds. Weston went over the police reports in methodical style, but he wasn't halfway through the batch before Breddle's face showed absolute gloom.

The jeweler recognized that the commissioner was simply trying to show that the law had done its utmost, though no real progress had been made. Patiently, Breddle let Weston continue.

It was half an hour before the process was completed; all that while, The Shadow sat silently by, his mind engaged in other matters.

Thinking in terms of a disguised master crook, The Shadow was wondering how many faces the man could display and what identity he might be using at present. Even more important was the question of coming crime: whether the unknown could risk another daring robbery, and, if so, what it would involve.

A BIG-TONED voice brought The Shadow from his reverie. Barney Kelm had arrived; the bluff-faced fight promoter was receiving a welcome. When Breddle shook hands, Barney clapped a broad hand on the jeweler's shoulder.

"Sorry my boys weren't down at your place," declared Barney. "They'd have stopped Flush Tygert in a hurry. They've been talking about him all afternoon. Say—if we could only locate Flush, I'd like to let them loose on him. They're like a pack of wolves, those boys, when I let them loose!"

Weston was introducing his friend Cranston. Barney gave The Shadow a powerful grip. Seating himself at the table, Barney tilted his derby hat back over his head and began to look at the police reports. Mention of his own name pleased him.

"So I'm a public hero," he chortled. "That's swell! They'll be pointing me out when I walk along Broadway. You know, I was thinking of moving that gymnasium of mine. I didn't like it, because my boys were so close to Lody's.

"A bad influence, that place, but I'm glad I stayed. A good thing that I was there. Good, too, that I keep an eye on whatever is happening. When I heard that shooting, I knew that something big was up. I took a look outside and saw Lody's door bust open. When those rats tried to put the cops on the spot, I knew it was up to me to stop them."

Barney's bluster was rather painful to old Breddle, who was still thinking in terms of his lost diamonds. Cranston, too, seemed bored by all the palaver. When Breddle decided to leave, the commissioner's friend went along. In the foyer, Cranston paused to make a phone call, then went out to his limousine.

Inside the big car, he slid open the drawer

beneath the rear seat and rapidly cloaked himself in black garments. Watching from the window, he saw old Breddle turn the corner, walking toward the subway. Opening a door with one hand, The Shadow reached for the speaking tube with the other. He spoke to the chauffeur, using Cranston's tone.

"I think I shall remain at the Club, Stanley," said The Shadow. "See if you can overtake Mr. Breddle before he reaches the subway. Tell him that this is my car, and that I instructed you to take him wherever he wants to go."

Stanley heard the slight slam of the rear door and started the limousine forward. It happened that the closing door was on the street side of the car. The figure that left the limousine wasn't Cranston's. It was The Shadow who whisked himself away toward the darkness across the street.

While Stanley thought that Cranston had actually gone back to the club, the doorman and others on the sidewalk supposed that he had left in his limousine. Instead, The Shadow had taken up an unsuspected vigil. Obscured in the opposite darkness, he was watching the entrance of the Cobalt Club!

A taxicab coasted into sight. It stopped when the driver saw a tiny red gleam from a special three-colored flashlight. Moe Shrevnitz was the driver of that cab; The Shadow had summoned him through a call to Burbank.

But even Moe was rather amazed to learn that The Shadow was spying on the Cobalt Club, the place to which he had access as Cranston anytime he wanted it.

The reason was explained when a burly man with a tired derby hat stalked from the club and strode manfully along the street. Instantly, The Shadow's light flashed green, but followed with a cautioning blink of yellow.

It meant that The Shadow was taking up a trail on foot, but wanted Moe to be close, ready if needed. The Shadow had used that system frequently; hence the process offered no surprise. The astounding thing was the nature of The Shadow's trail.

The master of darkness was playing a long hunch. He was picking up the trail of Barney Kelm, the public hero who rated as a champion of law and order, not as a man who dealt in crime!

CHAPTER XI
THE THIRD FACE

GREASE RICKEL was in an impatient mood. The living room wasn't large enough to hold him. Pacing back and forth, he slashed aside the curtain of the wide doorway that led into a dinette. He kept on pacing through to the kitchen.

Looking at Clip Zelber, Banker Dreeb gave a shrug. They could hear Grease yank open the door of the electric icebox; they heard the rattle of ice cubes, the gurgle of liquid from a bottle. Grease was fixing himself another gin buck, the sixth that he had sampled in the last hour.

"Don't blame the guy," said Banker. "Why should he keep sober? There's not much chance that Five-face will be needing us."

"I don't think Five-face has lammed," returned Clip. "He's got a schedule, like he told us."

"Like he told us, yeah," repeated Banker, with a snort. "But that may have been the old baloney, sliced nice and thin. Maybe he was just counting on one big job, instead of four."

"And playing us for suckers," said Clip, with a slow nod. "That's what Grease thinks, although he hasn't said so."

The two silenced, as Grease came storming back. Slashing the curtain shut with one hand, Grease gestured a half-filled glass with the other. Turning, he took a gulp of liquor, then wagged a forefinger in emphatic fashion.

"Flush Tygert has pulled a runout," voiced Grease, thickly. "He'll clean up a couple of hundred grand out of those rocks he grabbed from old Breddle. He won't ever show his face around here; his own, or any other—"

A heavy thump interrupted. It came from the apartment door. Clip was the first man to reach it; as he opened the door, he heard a snarl from Grease.

Flinging his glass aside, Grease started forward with a drunken lunge, trying to tug a revolver from his pocket. Banker jumped in front to intercept him. Unable to guess what it was all about, Clip pulled a gun to cover the man who had entered. Seeing the fellow's face, Clip mouthed:

"Barney Kelm!"

Banker had Grease under control and was shoving him to a battered sofa. Nudging the door shut, Clip concentrated on Barney. Ordinarily, such a situation would have called for smart bluff work, but it was useless, now that Grease had given things away. Clip came to the real point in a hurry.

"Hello, public hero!" he snapped. "Think you're a copper, too, don't you? Figured we were working with Flush Tygert. Well, that means it's your own idea, or the bulls would have come here ahead of you."

Barney's big lips spread in a wide grin.

"Suppose I told you that this joint was covered," he said, "with coppers all around, outside. What would you guys do about it?"

"We'd put the blast on you," informed Clip, "and then shoot it out with them. Only, you haven't got those coppers with you, Barney. You thought you could bluff us better alone."

Barney said nothing. He simply stepped to the table and picked up a greasy pack of cards. He picked out four spades, showed them in his left hand, then dropped them faces upward.

"Spread 'em out," said Barney. His voice had lost its boom and was taking on a drawl. "Show all of 'em, fella."

His other paw showed sudden skill, as he made a deft sweep across the four cards. There they lay, spread wide, before the astonished eyes of Clip and the other lieutenants.

Not four spades, but five!

Only one other man could perform that gambler's trick to such perfection: Flush Tygert. To see it duplicated by the seemingly clumsy hand of Barney Kelm was proof of the visitor's real identity.

Flush Tygert and Barney Kelm were the same. Like Jake Smarley, they were Five-face. Crime's new overlord was again with his lieutenants, displaying the third face in his collection.

"QUITE a surprise, eh?" chortled Five-face, reverting to the boastful tone of Barney. "Maybe some of it needs explaining, so here goes. First I was Smarley, then I was Flush. The next step was to be Barney Kelm.

"That's why I headed for the gym. But I couldn't shake The Shadow off the trail. It didn't worry me a lot, though. I had my boxing stable close to Lody's just in case that joint would come in handy, someday."

The lieutenants began to understand. They realized how well the part of Barney Kelm fitted Five-face. It wasn't so much the matter of his disguise, though that detail was perfect. The important thing was that Barney Kelm was a rover, like Jake Smarley and Flush Tygert.

As a bookie, Smarley had kept his office in his hat most of the time, and was often hard to find. Flush, the gambler, was in New York only between boat trips. Barney also traveled frequently, promoting fights throughout the country, and his friends heard from him only at intervals. All such factors were a tribute to the ingenuity of Five-face.

It was plain, too, that Five-face had considered the welfare of his lieutenants, after he had robbed old Breddle. First Grease, then Banker, finally Clip, had left the caravan, like tail men in a game of crack the whip.

Simply carrying the burden himself was not enough for Five-face. He had kept two thoughts in mind: to eliminate The Shadow, and to pin the blame on persons who knew nothing about him or his lieutenants.

HAWKEYE

The crowd at Lody's were made to order for that little game. With another laugh, Five-face described the final touch that he had provided.

"I was Barney when I ducked out of the cab," he boasted. "I bluffed the hackie into keeping on around the block. He thought I was still with him when he pulled up at Lody's. Meanwhile, I'd gone into the gym, by the back door.

"I wish that Lody crowd had croaked The Shadow. I phoned the tip-off that started them in the right direction. When I saw that The Shadow had ducked out on them, I figured I might as well make myself a public hero.

"So I gave the word to the boys, and they did the rest. I took the credit"—Barney dug his thumb against his chest—"and I'm going to play it to the limit! Say—if there's anybody that people will trust, it's Barney Kelm. What a setup the next job will be!"

Both Banker and Clip agreed. Their doubts of Five-face were completely dispelled. Eagerly, they looked forward to further service with this crime master who had covered their part in such skillful fashion. The only dissenting voice came from Grease.

Rising unsteadily from the sofa, the oily faced lieutenant approached his chief.

"Listen, Five-face," said Grease, thickly. "You're talking about the next job. What about the last one?"

"You mean down at the Diamond Mart?"

"That's it." Grease shook his glass, which he had reclaimed. The glass clinked, and Grease eyed the ice cubes that were in it. "I'm thinking about ice," he said. "Not ice cubes"—he pointed to the glass—"but another kind of ice. Diamonds!"

Grease looked at Barney as though he expected the big shot to disgorge a glittering shower. Barney shook his head and gave a bland smile.

"I've just been with the police commissioner," he said. "I met a stuffed-shirt friend of his, a guy named Cranston. Old Breddle was there, too, and our pal Joe Cardona. I couldn't have lugged any sparklers along with me.

"Suppose I'd pulled a handkerchief out of my pocket"—Barney illustrated the statement—"and spilled a lot of Breddle's rocks on the table. Don't worry about the diamonds. You'll get your split on them, when the time comes. Meanwhile—"

Pausing, Barney produced a roll of bills. He began to peel off currency of high denomination, but soon he came to a thick batch of one-dollar bills.

"There's a lot of leaves in this cabbage," said Barney, ruefully, "but they're mostly small. This is the wad I used to bluff Breddle. I can let you fellows have a grand or so—say twelve hundred bucks—to pay off your hired help.

"The next job will be for cash. Real mazuma, and plenty of it! You'll hear from me when I'm ready, and it will be soon. This dough"—Barney distributed four hundred dollars each among the lieutenants—"will hold you over until then."

GREASE RICKEL was standing stock-still as he received his share. The oily racketeer was staring at the curtain that blocked off the dinette. Grease thought that the curtain bulged; he remembered that there was another entrance to the apartment, by way of the kitchen.

Lowering his gaze, Grease blinked at a patch of blackness on the floor. He thought that it formed a silhouette.

Actually, Grease's imagination was at work, but his guess happened to be correct. The Shadow was behind that very curtain; he had entered by the rear route.

The Shadow had overheard every word between the master crook and the lieutenants, and he had learned the name under which crime's overlord traveled.

Five-face!

Jake Smarley, Flush Tygert, Barney Kelm—those were three of the identities. A third crime was due, to be maneuvered by Barney Kelm. Afterward, a fourth crime, by some new personality. Then the fifth face—

Forgetting the future, The Shadow concentrated on the present. Barney Kelm was leaving; it was just as well to let him go. Having found the three lieutenants, The Shadow could keep tabs on Barney Kelm.

Easing back from the curtain, The Shadow was turning away, toward the kitchen, when he noted that Grease was going along with Barney, apparently to hold a conference in the hall.

The Shadow waited; then, listening intently, he stirred the curtain. His lips gave a low whisper.

Banker and Clip were counting their money. It was Banker who lifted his head.

"Hear that, Clip?"

"Out in the hall?" queried Clip. "It's only Grease talking to Barney."

"What I heard came from the dinette—"

Both thugs looked toward the curtain. They heard creeping sounds beyond. Banker made a quick leap, grabbed the heavy drapery, wrenching it from its hooks. As Banker sent the curtain to the floor in a tangle, Clip charged in with a drawn gun.

Figures were lunging through the dinette, to meet the drive. Fortunately for them, Clip tripped across the curtain; otherwise he would have drilled his opposers. Losing his gun as he hit the floor, Clip was flattened by two adversaries, who grabbed Banker as he joined the pileup.

Men were rolling across the dinette, while a big voice boomed for them to quit the fight. Coming to hands and knees, Banker and Clip saw Barney Kelm facing them, with Grease seated on the floor beside the big shot.

Barney and Grease had come around through the kitchen, to see if anyone was hiding behind the curtain. The Shadow, hearing them, had lured Banker and Clip to an attack. The result had been a floundering fray involving Five-face and his lieutenants, which had almost ended in disaster.

CLIFF MARSLAND

Grease was blaming Clip and Banker for the mix-up; they argued that the thing was his fault. Barney put an end to the altercation.

"There's nobody here," growled Five-face. "Grease had too many drinks; that's all. But you fellows"—he swung to Clip and Banker—"didn't use your brains any too well. Lay off the dumb stuff in the future!"

Five-face stalked out, the lieutenants following, all eager to curry favor with the big shot and have him forget the misguided combat. The dinette looked quite empty; in fact, it was well lighted, because the glow from the living room now came through the wide doorway.

A singular thing occurred. Silently, the crumpled curtain uncoiled itself. Out of the fallen drape emerged a figure clad in black: The Shadow. His ruse had deceived the crooks entirely. Caught between them, The Shadow had wrapped himself in the curtain and tumbled with it when Banker snatched it loose.

His black cloak had not shown amid the snarl of dark velvet, which formed a sizeable shroud when he had lain on the floor. Fixing the curtain to resemble its former crumple, The Shadow glided to the kitchen just as the lieutenants came back into the living room, from the hall.

Five-face was gone; so was The Shadow. Their next meeting would come when crime was again on the move. Then would be the time when The Shadow could trap the supercrook in deeds that would lay bare the past and expose the methods that the evil master used.

For the first time, the advantage would lie with The Shadow; but he did not regard victory as assured. Uncovering Five-face had been no simple matter; trapping him in crime might prove even more difficult.

The Shadow knew!

CHAPTER XII
THE SUDDEN STROKE

THREE faces were staring at The Shadow from the table in his sanctum. They were photographs, all different, yet they represented one man: Five-face.

Jake Smarley, Flush Tygert, Barney Kelm—

There would be two more, and that fact made The Shadow ponder. Nothing had been heard of Barney Kelm during the past week. Barney was still a public hero, yet he had vanished like Smarley and Flush.

People acquainted with Barney said that he had gone on the road to promote some prize fights. Despite his bluster, Barney was a very modest and self-effacing chap, his friends claimed. He didn't like to be in the public eye. Too many people had pointed him out, so Barney had just dropped out of sight.

The rumor did not please The Shadow.

He knew how self-effacing Barney Kelm could be; that the man was able to obliterate his identity entirely. It was possible that Barney had dropped out of sight altogether. If so, The Shadow's plans for trapping a master criminal called Five-face would probably fade away to nothing.

Reports from agents. The Shadow studied them beneath the blue glow. They were encouraging in one respect. Plans for future crime were being made by Five-face's lieutenants.

The Shadow's agents were keeping close tally on Grease, Banker, and Clip. The lieutenants had spent nearly all the money that Five-face had given them, lining up thugs to be ready on call.

Checking on such activities was an easy matter for certain of The Shadow's agents. One agent, Cliff Marsland, had quite a reputation in the underworld.

For a long while, Cliff had been gunning for The Shadow and boasting about it to mobsters. Anyone who could get away with such talk in the badlands necessarily had to be tough. Naturally, Cliff's immunity existed because he was in The Shadow's service; but no one suspected the fact.

Working on The Shadow's information, Cliff had met up with hoodlums who worked for Grease and Clip and had learned enough to give regular reports to The Shadow.

Aiding Cliff was Hawkeye, a clever spotter who could follow a snake's trail through the grass. Hawkeye roved the toughest districts, spotting snipers who worked for Banker. His reports, though less frequent than Cliff's, were quite as reliable.

Nevertheless, there was one question.

Did the activity of the spendthrift lieutenants mean that Five-face actually intended new crime?

At their last meeting, the lieutenants themselves had expressed doubts about Five-face. They had been ready to brand him a double-crosser, until he had appeared as Barney Kelm.

They trusted him again, this time implicitly. Yet there was a chance that Five-face, playing the Barney role, had bluffed his lieutenants, after all— and had, at the same time, deceived The Shadow!

Grim, sinister, The Shadow's laugh throbbed through the sanctum. The bluish light went off with a sharp *click*.

The Shadow was not pleased by the idle week that he had spent. Unless this night developed something new in crime, he would have to change his policy and carry through a search for Five-face, rather than await the reappearance of Barney Kelm.

Meanwhile, the evening promised one slight possibility. Perhaps a chat with Commissioner Weston would produce a trifling result. So far, the law had been going around in circles looking for Jake Smarley and Flush Tygert, always regarding them as separate individuals. Yet out of such a whirligig might come a flash of something worthwhile to The Shadow.

REACHING the Cobalt Club in the guise of Cranston, The Shadow found the police commissioner poring over some recent reports, that might as well have been blank papers. Inspector Cardona was sitting by, poker-faced and taciturn.

Weston finished his review of the reports and was about to say something, when an attendant entered bringing a note.

"It's from Arnold Melbrun," stated Weston, after reading the message. "He wants me to meet him at his office. He will be there in half an hour. He says that the matter is urgent. Perhaps Melbrun has learned some new facts regarding Smarley."

Concluding, the commissioner invited his friend Cranston to go along to Melbrun's office. The Shadow delayed long enough to telephone Burbank and learn that the agents had reported nothing new.

Arriving at the offices of the United Import Co., the visitors were received by Melbrun's new secretary, Boland. He told them that he had heard from Melbrun, but knew nothing about the matter that was to be discussed. However, after the visitors had seated themselves in the private office, Boland remarked:

"Mr. Melbrun received a special-delivery letter just after he returned from Norfolk, this afternoon. It was from that man they call the public hero."

"Barney Kelm?" inquired Weston.

"Yes," nodded the secretary. "Mr. Melbrun put the letter with some other correspondence from Kelm. I suppose that I could show it to you, commissioner."

Before Weston could reply, the telephone bell rang. It was Melbrun, calling from his home; he had not been able to leave there as soon as he expected. He wanted to talk to Weston, if the commissioner had arrived. When Weston took the telephone, the first thing that Melbrun mentioned was the Kelm correspondence.

"Get those letters, Boland," ordered Weston. "Mr. Melbrun wants to talk about them over the telephone."

Soon, the letters were spread on the desk. In Cranston's casual style, The Shadow glanced over Weston's shoulder and noted what the letters said. It was apparent that Barney Kelm had taken advantage of his position as a public hero, as well as pushing his brief acquaintance with Melbrun.

In the letters, Barney proposed that Melbrun and five other wealthy men contribute fifty thousand dollars each, toward the promotion of a championship prize fight to be held in the Middle West. Barney could guarantee them a high return upon their money, so he said. A guarantee was needed to make the championship bout possible; after that, all would be plain sailing.

Considering Barney's status, the commissioner saw nothing wrong with the proposal, and so stated to Melbrun. Listening, with quite different thoughts, The Shadow learned that Melbrun agreed with Weston. The thing that bothered Melbrun was another phase of the matter.

Melbrun's voice was audible through the receiver; The Shadow caught every word, along with Weston.

"Look at the last letter, commissioner," insisted Melbrun. "The one that came this afternoon. Kelm wanted us all to bring our money in cash. I arrived too late to go to the bank, so I decided to wait until I heard from Kelm again.

"It seemed dangerous, having all that money loose. I wanted to tell Kelm so. If such men as Jake Smarley or Flush Tygert should hear of it, they would attempt another of their daring crimes. Then it occurred to me that you should be the person to warn Kelm."

There was a pause. Weston inserted the words:

"Quite so, Melbrun."

"I was just about to leave the house," continued Melbrun, "when I received a call from Kelm. He tells me that he is at the Hotel Clairmont; that the other five financiers are with him. They have all brought their money, and are simply waiting for me."

"Did you tell Kelm you would come?"

"Yes," returned Melbrun. "I told him to wait; to do nothing until I arrived. It will take me at least twenty minutes to reach the hotel, commissioner. But you are nearer; you could get there in a quarter hour."

"I'll see you there, Melbrun."

HANGING up, Weston turned to Cardona. The commissioner expostulated on the importance of the news.

Meanwhile The Shadow, glancing toward the window, saw a blink of lights below. Moe's cab had parked in the side street; the driver was flashing a signal. Unnoticed, The Shadow strolled from the office.

"Suppose that crooks have been watching Barney Kelm," Weston was saying. "They might be watching him, too, hoping for revenge because of what he did to them at Lody's. If so, they have learned of tonight's transaction. Call headquarters, inspector, and order some picked men to meet us at the Clairmont. We must start there, at once."

While Cardona was phoning, Weston looked about, then questioned Boland:

"Where did Cranston go?"

Boland replied that the commissioner's friend had gone back to the Cobalt Club; that he would meet Weston there later. The commissioner gave a contemptuous snort; then, as Cardona finished the headquarters call, Weston dismissed thoughts of Cranston and told the inspector to come along.

Before Weston and Cardona had reached the street, a cab was pulling away. Its passenger was Cranston, but Weston would not have recognized his friend. Already, Cranston had become The Shadow. Garbed in black, he was tuning in his shortwave radio, to get Burbank's latest word.

Reports from agents. The lieutenants who served Five-face had suddenly begun to move. Driving separate cars, the three were picking up thugs as passengers. As The Shadow listened, Burbank relayed a report from Hawkeye. The spotter had learned where the crooks were heading—to the Hotel Clairmont.

According to Arnold Melbrun, the Clairmont could be reached in fifteen minutes from his office. In Moe's cab, with the speedy driver at the wheel, The Shadow expected to cut the trip to ten. Those minutes would be precious.

Barney Kelm was already at the Hotel Clairmont, chatting with the five financiers who had brought fifty thousand dollars apiece. Barney Kelm wasn't the public hero that the law supposed. He was Five-face: Jake Smarley, Flush Tygert and Barney himself, all rolled into one, the most dangerous master crook in all America!

Would Barney wait for Melbrun to appear? If he did, all would be well. If not, even The Shadow, with all his speed, might be too late to prevent the theft of another quarter million by the public enemy who basked in a hero's guise.

CHAPTER XIII
CASH IN ADVANCE

FIVE men were seated in a little room on the mezzanine floor of the Hotel Clairmont, bundles of cash piled in front of them. They had brought their money; they were waiting for Barney Kelm to finally sell them on his proposition. A few details, certain guarantees, were all that had to be settled.

The financiers felt quite secure. This conference had been kept strictly private; it seemed impossible that news of it could have leaked out. The doors of the room were bolted and the windows had grilled gratings, for this room was specially designed for conferences.

Besides, the very presence of Barney Kelm was a guarantee of safety. These financiers did not share the qualms of Commissioner Weston. They did not think of Barney as a man hounded by criminals. They regarded him as a man who could settle crooks; for he had proven his ability in that line.

Down in the lobby were half a dozen of Barney's "boys," tough-fisted pugs who would rally the moment that their boss called them. The financiers had looked those young chaps over when they entered, and felt quite happy because such guards were on hand to protect them.

There was a heavy knock at the door, repeated in the fashion of the signal. A gray-haired man opened the door and admitted Barney. Wearing his derby hat, the smiling promoter strolled cockily to the table.

"I just called Melbrun," said Barney. "He was at his house, and he says he'll be coming down here. But he came in late from Norfolk, and from the way he talked, I don't think he'll have his cash with him."

Sharp looks passed among the financiers. This was to be a strictly cash transaction; one man mentioned it, and Barney nodded his approval.

"We don't need Melbrun," he decided. "This is a quarter-million-dollar deal, and we've got that much right now. Here are the papers, gentlemen. Look them over."

Barney placed an old valise on the conference table. Oddly, it was the same valise that Flush Tygert had carried away from the Diamond Mart. Old Breddle hadn't given a good description of that bag, so it excited no suspicion. Still, it was curious that Barney should be using an item that might link him with Flush.

There was a reason. Like nearly every big time criminal, Five-face was superstitious. As Flush, he had lugged that valise through a very tough tangle of circumstances, and had wound up with a successful getaway. As Barney, he wanted his luck to hold, and the valise was a good token.

In addition, Barney knew of only one person outside of Breddle who would recognize the valise. Barney was thinking of The Shadow. He was positive that on this occasion the cloaked fighter would not cross his path.

From the valise, Barney took stacks of papers that looked like contracts and handed them around the circle. Strolling across the room, he stopped near a side door and took a cigar from a box that lay on a table. Lighting the perfecto,

Barney leaned against the door and let one hand steal behind him.

He was sliding back the bolt, leaving the door unlocked. Thus, he was opening a route by which others might enter, when he called them. The room, therewith, would have two exits, for the front door was merely latched, not bolted.

Surprised exclamations came from the men about the table. The documents that Barney had given them were merely blank contracts, specifying nothing regarding the promoter's proposition. Hearing queries, Barney responded in booming tone:

"It's all right, gentlemen! Just a trifling mistake! I can explain everything—"

He was stepping forward, reaching in his pocket. From behind him, Barney heard a slight creak of the door. The thing that he drew from his pocket wasn't a contract, but it was quite the thing to seal a bargain. It was a .45 revolver, that Barney flourished under the noses of the astonished financiers.

BEFORE the group could come to their feet, two other men entered the room. They were thuggish men, ill-clad, who wore handkerchief masks across their faces. Like Barney, they carried revolvers, but of a lesser caliber.

Though Five-face still preferred a big smoke wagon, for the show it made, he had instructed his lieutenants to let their trigger men bring whatever weapons they chose. Big guns hadn't proven their worth during the battle in the old arcade, wherein The Shadow, almost single-handed, had routed fighters who carried oversized revolvers.

The two men who now flanked Barney were ordinary thugs, delegated to this duty. Clip Zelber had provided them, but with instructions that, whatever happened, they were to blame the mess on Barney Kelm.

Their eyes, peering through the masks, showed surprise when they saw that they were actually siding with Barney. They had taken Clip's instructions to mean that they were framing Barney, not helping him.

But when they glanced at Barney, they understood. His face didn't wear the smile that went with his pose of a public hero. Bearing down upon the cowed financiers, Barney was showing an ugly leer that was quite out of character. With his present manner, Barney could have kept the financiers under full control without any assistance.

However, Barney had other work to do. He told the masked men to herd the victims into a corner. Quaking, the financiers retreated, leaving their money on the table. Stacking the piles of currency into the valise, Barney strolled to the front door of the room and laid his hand upon the knob.

"Stay just as you are, gentlemen," he sneered, "but put your hands in back of you. My men are going to tie you up. Don't try to make a break, because"—he gestured toward the side door—"we have a few more on hand, to keep you covered."

At Barney's back, the door swung open to admit another pair of gunmen. The first two put their guns away; brought out coils of wire and rolls of adhesive tape from their pockets. Bundling the victims together, they began to bind and gag them.

Barney opened the front door of the room and sidled through, pushing the valise ahead of him. He poked his head back into the room, to take a last look.

Then, as an afterthought, Barney again addressed the helpless prisoners.

"Blame me for this," he chuckled. "Anybody would turn crook, if the stakes were big enough. That's the whole story. My boys downstairs are going to be as surprised as you fellows—"

Barney halted, staring at a window straight across the room. Outside the pane, he could see the dull gleam of the bronze grille. It seemed to blacken as Barney watched it. He didn't like the looks of the thing; it reminded him too much of The Shadow. Then Barney chuckled.

The Shadow wouldn't be at that window. There was a little balcony outside; one that extended away from the window's edges, and therefore offered a good lurking spot. But the bars weren't the sort that could be filed or pried loose. Such a process would take a long time and make a lot of noise.

It would be funny, Barney thought, if The Shadow really happened to be out there. When Barney reached the street, he would signal his lieutenants and point out the balcony. The Shadow would be a fine target, on that unprotected ledge.

Unwittingly, Barney pushed the door a trifle wider, exposing the valise that he carried, though he didn't know it. Then, stepping out into the hall, he slammed the door behind him.

Chuckling, Barney visualized the room just as he had left it: Five prisoners in the corner, being bound by two thugs; another pair of armed guards, at the side door across the room.

The window did not matter; not in Barney's calculations. Nevertheless, the window was to prove important.

HARDLY had Barney stepped from sight before darkness shifted away from the bronze grille. Something still remained near the bottom bars—a roundish object, that gave a slight sputter.

Barney would have noticed that tiny squidge of light. But the thugs who had taken over for him were not in positions to observe it. Something was about to happen very suddenly.

Five-face was wrong, when he supposed that it would take a long while to crash through the heavily barred window. He was right, however, in his guess that noise was necessary.

A huge flare of light blazed beyond the darkened pane, lighting the room vividly, along with the outdoor scene. The gush of brilliance was accompanied by a huge roar—the explosion of a powerful bomb that twisted metal bars into hanging strands. Smashing inward, the blast blew the window into fragments, turning the glass pane into powder.

Like the men who were binding them, the prisoners in the corner were flattened by the powerful concussion. The masked guards at the side door were staggered. They clawed at the handkerchief masks that slipped across their eyes. They didn't see the figure that came from the outer shelter of the balcony, leaping through the gap that had once been a window.

They heard him, that challenger who had blasted his way into the scene of crime. They recognized him by the laugh that quivered, a fierce, challenging crescendo amid the echoes of the bomb's explosion.

Only one fighter could deliver such strident mockery, the taunt that all men of evil dreaded.

The Shadow!

CHAPTER XIV
CROOKS IN THE DARK

A SWEEP of blackness in a room where lights seemed dim. Such was The Shadow, as he wheeled beneath the tilted chandelier in the center of the conference room.

Though half shaken from its moorings, the chandelier still had lighted bulbs; but their glow was feeble to the thugs who were yanking away their masks.

The brilliance of the blast had dazzled everyone, except The Shadow. He had held his cloak across his eyes, out on the balcony, while the short fuse was completing its brief fizz. He had counted upon dazzling the crooks; otherwise, he would not have made his tremendous entry, with the lives of five prisoners at stake.

Some of the financiers were bound, and the rest were practically helpless. So The Shadow went to their rescue, first, completing it in rapid style. The thugs who were doing the binding had put their guns away; they had barely managed to get the weapons from their pockets, when The Shadow was upon them.

He settled that pair with hard blows from his guns. Shots would have betrayed his position, and he wanted no firing in this direction. Thugs at the door across the room were still wondering where The Shadow was. Half blindly, they turned toward the ruined window, supposing that he was keeping to its shelter.

Instead, The Shadow was skirting wide along the front of the room. Again, crooks heard his laugh, almost at their elbows. They turned, tugging their gun triggers, trying to aim point-blank at swirly blackness.

The Shadow was on them before they fired. He sledged the pair out through the door, driving them as human blockades against reserves who were lunging in from a stairway.

Guns roared at close range. New gunmen, who could see to fire, drove their bullets home. But it wasn't The Shadow who received those deadly slugs. The shots found the thugs that he had shoved ahead of him. His guns, blasting in reply, sent sizzling bullets past the human shields and clipped the marksmen beyond them.

There was the sound of bodies tumbling down the stairs; shrieks that turned into groans.

Wheeling full about, The Shadow saw the room again. He hadn't heard the front door rip open, but he guessed that it would be wide. On the threshold stood Five-face, still in the guise of Barney Kelm, aiming his big revolver, hoping to find The Shadow. He heard the tumble of bodies, saw the swirl of returning blackness.

Five-face dodged as he fired. The shot from his .45 went wide. Like the mobbies who had perished in his service, crime's overlord was learning that a heavy gun couldn't be handled quickly enough in combat with The Shadow. With a smaller weapon, he might have been able to jab in a telling shot as he made his dive.

He was smart enough, however, to yank the door with him as he went. Otherwise, The Shadow would have clipped him. The heavy door took the bullets that The Shadow meant for Barney and splintered big chunks from the woodwork. Racing across the room, The Shadow yanked the door open.

Five-face had reached a stairway, leading down from the mezzanine. He had left the valise at the top, and was scooping it up as he went. He disappeared as The Shadow aimed.

Pausing, the cloaked pursuer motioned for the rescued prisoners to follow, which they did, some tugging themselves from the half-twisted wires that partially bound them.

Dashing down the stairs, The Shadow saw Barney darting across the lobby, still lugging the valise. Barney was shouting something, and as The Shadow aimed, a flood of punching men flung themselves in the way. They were Barney's "boys," who still thought that their boss was honest.

They were sluggers, those boys from Barney's stable, but they couldn't reach The Shadow with their punches. Weaving among them, The Shadow made long sweeps with his arms, and his guns gave him a much longer reach than his opponents. Barney's boys were bouncing all around the floor, and Five-face did not wait to see how they fared.

He was gone, with his valise out through the rear exit, just as Commissioner Weston and Inspector Cardona came in through the front of the lobby, followed by a squad of headquarters men.

IT was a puzzling sight: The Shadow scattering a crowd of earnest boxers, who had so recently proven their ability to aid the law. One of those cases wherein The Shadow might have been mistaken for a crook; for there had been times when men of crime had donned black cloaks and hats, solely to confuse the police.

But The Shadow had foreseen a circumstance such as this, and had provided for it.

Hearing wild shouts from the mezzanine, Cardona looked up and saw five frantic men, who could only be the financiers that Melbrun had mentioned in his phone call to Weston. They were yelling something about Barney Kelm and a bag of missing cash.

As The Shadow turned toward the rear of the lobby, Cardona beckoned to his men and gave the word:

"Come on!"

The police followed The Shadow through the exit, spilling rising boxers who tried to stop them. Reaching the rear street, they were greeted by a hurried fire from cover-up cars.

There wasn't a sign of Barney, nor of The Shadow. But the cloaked fighter suddenly denoted his presence, by opening fire from across the way. The Shadow had made for the opposite darkness, to wait until crooks showed their hands.

Again, the lieutenants who served Five-face were trying to spring a surprise on the police, and The Shadow was turning the game on them. The crooks didn't wait around, when they recognized the laugh that came with The Shadow's gunfire. They spurted their cars for corners, glad to get away.

Only a handful still remained on the scene; the usual brand of small fry who could be sacrificed to save the others.

Police were spreading, to deal with those scattered foemen. Picking spurts of thuggish guns, The Shadow supplied timely shots that picked off the nearest snipers. The rest took to flight, with Cardona's men in full cry. Alone, The Shadow began to scour alleyways in search of Five-face.

This time, Five-face had made a rapid getaway, probably to a car parked in another block. In his hunt, The Shadow was joined by Cliff Marsland and Hawkeye, who had been on the outer fringes of the mob and had filtered through when the cars sped away. Cliff only remembered the lieutenants and their cars, but Hawkeye recalled another automobile in the offing.

It had sped away during the brief fray in back of the hotel, and while Hawkeye hadn't seen Barney Kelm, he had heard someone running toward the car in question. Hawkeye's testimony settled the problem of Five-face. The master crook had completed escape, along with robbery, despite The Shadow.

Hearing spasmodic firing from the street that fronted the hotel, The Shadow started in that direction to take a final hand. He arrived in time to witness a near tragedy.

Arnold Melbrun had just reached the hotel, and was stepping out of his car. Melbrun wasn't alarmed by the excitement, until a pair of thugs bobbed into sight and flung themselves upon him.

They wanted Melbrun's coupe and were trying to slug him, to get the keys he carried. Melbrun had a heavy cane with him and tried to ward off the attack. People from the hotel were jumping in to help him, and with figures intervening, The Shadow was unable to aim at Melbrun's attackers.

It was Joe Cardona who brought the real rescue. He had been chasing the thugs, and he was close enough to grab one who was shoving a revolver against Melbrun's ribs. Hotel attendants captured the other hoodlum, but Melbrun was shaky when people hauled him to his feet.

He asked what had happened, and Cardona told him. All the while, the captured thugs were snarling at detectives who had taken charge of them. All that the thugs would mention was the name of Barney Kelm.

"Sure, we was working for Barney," voiced one. "So what? He got away, didn't he? He was lucky and we wasn't. It wasn't Barney's fault we didn't get away."

THE financiers were crowding about Melbrun, bewailing their ill luck. Commissioner Weston joined them and explained that if they had shown the same judgment as Melbrun, their money would be safe. But Melbrun shook his head, when he heard the truth about Barney Kelm.

"I suspected trouble," he said, "but not from Kelm. I would have trusted him fully. I still have my money, commissioner, but only because the bank was closed when I arrived from Norfolk."

Blood was trickling from Melbrun's forehead, where one of the thugs had given a glancing blow with a gun. When Weston offered to have a detective drive him home, Melbrun gratefully accepted the offer.

The coupe pulled away, with Melbrun leaning back beside the driver's seat. Turning matters over to Cardona, the commissioner summoned his official car.

By then, The Shadow had glided away toward a solitary taxicab parked down the street. His next destination was the Cobalt Club, where, as Cranston, he would hear Weston's version of new crime.

But The Shadow was looking beyond this night, to a time when Five-face, no longer Barney Kelm, would reappear in another guise, intent on further crime.

Despite handicaps, The Shadow had nearly ruined the robbery at the Hotel Clairmont; but he knew that Five-face, overconfident because of success, would not admit the fact. The Shadow was sure that the master crook would strike again, as boldly as ever before.

One move more could be one too many for the intrepid criminal who had dared The Shadow's might!

CHAPTER XV
CRIME ON THE SIDE

THE evanishment of Barney Kelm was no more singular than the disappearances of Jake Smarley and Flush Tygert. By this time, the public was getting used to crooks who staged one big thrust and then evaporated. Such things, criminologists said, always came in cycles.

It was all very plausible. Nobody in the underworld had ever rated Smarley high. Though he fluked his robbery at Melbrun's, he had managed to hide himself completely away; therefore, a smarter crook, like Flush, had thought it easy to follow Smarley's example, with better success.

Barney Kelm was a different sort of case. A professor was writing a book about him, using long words, like egocentrism and megalomania, to show that acclaim had gone to Barney's head and twisted his brain. Public hero or public enemy, only a hairbreadth separated them, according to the professor.

All this was a tribute to Five-face, though neither the public nor the professor knew it. The master criminal had done far more than disguise himself facially. He had established and effaced three different personalities as widely separated as the points of a triangle.

In fact, Five-face had his lieutenants guessing. Gathered in their shabby apartment, the three were speculating heavily as to what had become of their chief.

"It's been three days, now," argued Grease, "and we haven't heard a thing from the guy. It's giving me the jitters!"

"It was a week last time," reminded Banker. "So why should we worry?"

"Because we need dough," put in Clip. "Five-face knows it. He's got dough, too, from the last job. Two hundred and fifty grand of it."

Banker shook his head. Reaching for a newspaper, he pointed to a paragraph.

"The cash is hot," he stated. "Those Wall Street guys gave Barney big bills right out of their banks. They didn't expect Barney to grab the mazuma, but they had the numbers listed, just the same."

Clip was still in an argumentative mood.

"We need dough," he insisted. "We've had to hire some new torpedoes, to be ready for the next job. What are we going to pay them with?"

"They'll wait," returned Banker. "Take that guy Cliff Marsland, for example. We were smart, hiring him. He wants to get in a lick at The Shadow, and knows we're the fellows who can put him in line for it.

"The little guy, Hawkeye, is another good bet. Dough doesn't worry him. He gets lonely unless he's trailing somebody, and we've promised him a lot of work, which is what he wants. Say—I'll bet Hawkeye could even pick up The Shadow's trail and keep it!"

"You'd better put him on the trail of some hamburgers," snapped Clip. "We won't be eating after tonight, unless we hear from Five-face."

"Hamburgers sound good," spoke up Grease, "with onions on the side."

Banker was looking at the newspaper. His eyes, narrowing, showed a gleam, as he heard what Grease said.

"Something on the side," remarked Banker. "Say—that isn't a bad idea. While Five-face is going after hamburgers, we can try onions."

The others thought that Banker was trying to be funny, but he wasn't. He showed the newspaper and said:

"Take a gander at that guy, Clip."

"Which one?"

Clip chuckled as he put the question. He was looking at a row of three photographs, showing Smarley, Flush and Barney, with the caption: "Three Wanted Men."

"I don't mean those photos of Five-face," said Banker. "Over here, Clip, on the other page. This glamour boy with the fancy moniker: Count Raoul Fondelac."

THE picture showed a man with a foreign face, high aristocratic nose, thin lips that had a bored droop at the corners. Count Fondelac fitted his name; he looked like a nobleman. His age was problematical. He could have been called a young man who looked oldish, or an old man who looked youngish.

"His nibs is stopping at the Hotel Bayonne," declared Banker, "a very exclusive place. You couldn't walk through the lobby without a dress suit, but I'll bet it would be easy to sneak in the back way."

"To rob the guy?" demanded Clip. "Counts and such don't have a dime; not the sort that hang around New York. They're big-time panhandlers, that's all they are!"

"Count Fondelac is engaged to Albertina Adquin," continued Banker, referring to the newspaper. "You've heard of that dame, Clip. She's had three husbands, worth about ten million bucks apiece. Now she's buying a fourth one."

"Yeah. So what?"

"I'm just wondering," said Banker, "why she shouldn't buy him from us."

Clip brightened instantly, and Grease showed sudden interest. It was Clip who queried:

"You mean, why don't we snatch the guy?"

"That's it!"

The three men scanned the newspaper eagerly. They learned that Count Fondelac was to be the guest at a reception in the Adquin mansion at ten o'clock in the evening. It was only half past seven, which gave them plenty of time to operate.

Leaving the apartment, they contacted men across the street, told them to follow in another car. Among the small group of hirelings were Cliff and Hawkeye, who had worked themselves into the service of the gang lieutenants, at The Shadow's suggestion.

It wasn't until they stopped near the Hotel Bayonne that The Shadow's agents learned what the game was to be. Banker Dreeb had taken charge; he posted Cliff and others near the rear of the hotel, and sent Hawkeye ahead to reconnoiter a route to Fondelac's hotel suite. During that trip, Hawkeye performed a double job.

Not only did he find a service entrance that connected with a rear stairway; he crawled out through a window and took a passage to the front street, where he sneaked up to a taxicab that had parked in the hack stand.

Moe Shrevnitz was the driver of that cab; he had trailed the cars after they left the old apartment.

Small, hunch-shouldered in manner, Hawkeye poked a wizened face in through the cab window and gave the facts to Moe. By the time Hawkeye was sneaking back to join Banker and his companions, Moe was driving away to put in a call to Burbank. The way matters were fixed at present, such a call would bring The Shadow in rapid order.

Hawkeye made a lengthy report that stalled the expedition for several minutes. Having finally impressed the details on Banker, Hawkeye joined the cordon, taking the next post to Cliff's. Both agents watched Banker enter the service door of the hotel, followed by Grease and Clip.

The waiting period seemed long, though it was a very few minutes. There came a whisper from the darkness, one that drew Cliff and Hawkeye close together. They couldn't see The Shadow in the gloom, but they could sense his presence. Hawkeye gave the necessary details; a cloaked figure glided forward.

There was dim light near the service entrance. It had shown the gang lieutenants plainly when they entered. But The Shadow passed that hazard, observed only by his own agents. To others, posted by Banker, the blackness that glided beneath the light was nothing more than a flicker of the light itself.

THE SHADOW quickly made up the few minutes that he had lost. When he reached Fondelac's floor, he saw a valet come out from the suite, and knew from the man's manner that nothing could have happened yet.

Choosing the next door, The Shadow picked its lock with a tool that resembled a tiny pair of tweezers. He stepped into a bedroom of Fondelac's suite.

From there, The Shadow looked into a lavish living room. He saw the count standing in front of a mirror, admiring his evening clothes. From a vase of flowers, Fondelac tried to choose one which suited his present mood. Had he continued to look into the mirror, he would have noticed something that The Shadow saw.

The window in another room was opening. Into the darkness of the room came three men, one by one. Despite the gloom, The Shadow could see the glitter of their drawn revolvers.

Coolly, The Shadow drew an automatic from beneath his cloak. His doorway had a perfect background of almost solid blackness. Since crime was in the wind, The Shadow was quite willing to abolish a few of Five-face's lieutenants, if occasion demanded.

Still, he was hoping that things might work out. These crooks would be satisfied with carry-over money; perhaps a robbery would suit them, instead of a kidnapping.

Provided that Fondelac had any money. That was the real problem.

As the crooks moved in on the unsuspecting count, The Shadow's hopes were dwindling, for he could see eagerness in the eyes of the men who planned the abduction. As Fondelac happened to glance into the mirror, The Shadow's hand was tightening on its gun.

Then, with a sweep, The Shadow slid the weapon beneath his cloak and eased back into the darkness!

Whatever happened, The Shadow was willing to be a mere witness to the affair. Count Fondelac had seen the mobsters in the mirror, and his face had registered an expression that was sufficient for The Shadow.

This was to be crime with a most curious twist, that promised the very results The Shadow wanted!

CHAPTER XVI
THE FOURTH FACE

HIS fingers placing a flower in his buttonhole, Count Fondelac let his sleek hands turn palm forward. They were not only empty, they were practically raised, when he happened to turn in the direction of the invaders.

Seeing the three crooks, Fondelac gave a gasp to denote surprise and let his hands move slowly apart. He stood quite helpless, and made no effort to change his predicament. Except for the trifling gasp, the count remained silent.

Banker moved forward, as spokesman for the three.

"Just take it easy, Count," he said. "We want you to come along with us."

"Why so, *m'sieu'?*" queried Fondelac, in a rather mild tone. "I already have an engagement."

"Yes, and you can keep it," declared Banker, "provided that you can make the future countess listen, when you call her on the phone. We're going to hold you until she coughs over some big dough, pretty boy!"

"Dough?" Fondelac looked puzzled. "Ah, *oui.*" He nodded. "You mean money. What is it we shall do—play that game with the cards, that you call poker?"

"That's it," put in Clip, giving Banker a nudge. "We want to deal you in on a poker game, over at our place. If you lose, you can call up your girl friend and tell her to send over what you owe us."

Grease was grinning from the background. He was beginning to see how this kidnapping job could be managed without Fondelac ever realizing what it was. Apparently, the count thought that poker parties were something like a fraternity initiation.

"I shall go," decided Fondelac. "But there is one thing which I must remind you. I have played this game of poker"—he gestured toward a table and a pack of cards upon it—"and I have found one thing strange."

Fondelac was reaching for the cards. Guns nudged close to him, in case he reached for one of his own. But the visiting crooks weren't expecting trouble from the count. They simply thought it best to humor him, to help their own game along.

"There is a hand like this," said Fondelac. He counted four clubs face upward on the table. "But it is not enough. You must have five, I am told. So—"

Laying the pack aside with his left hand, he swept his right over the four clubs. The bunched cards spread apart; in their midst was a fifth club. In perfect fashion, Count Fondelac had executed the stunt that Flush Tygert had made famous!

Guns lowered in the hands that gripped them, as though the sheer weight of the weapons had carried them down. Three astounded thugs had lost their muscular control, though one of them, Grease Rickel, still had vocal cords that functioned. He blurted:

"Five-face!"

COUNT FONDELAC gave a grin that was anything but aristocratic. It was the grin that belonged to Barney Kelm. When he spoke again, he used a drawl that was reminiscent of Flush Tygert, though there was something of Jake Smarley in his voice, as well.

"I was going to call you tonight," said Five-face, "after I got away from this shindig that Albertina Adquin is throwing for me. It's kind of tough, being Count Fondelac. I have to stick around Park Avenue. It would look funny if I barged into your place."

He gestured for his lieutenants to sit down. Then, stroking his chin, Five-face remarked slowly:

"A cute idea, trying to kidnap me. Only, it wouldn't work. That fool Albertina would call up all the lawyers in town, and hire a special train to bring the F.B.I. in from Washington. No, I'd better go through with the next job the way I planned it."

"What's that to be?" asked Clip. "Are you going to marry the dame?"

"Not a chance," returned Five-face. "All she'd ever hand me would be allowance money. I started this Fondelac racket one time when I was abroad. There was a real Count Fondelac, and he faked it for me to be his successor.

"I paid him, of course, and he did what I expected. Finished himself off by drinking absinthe as fast as he could buy it. So I became Fondelac—when I wanted to be—and it was worth the price. You see"—he gave a broad smile—"Fondelac and Flush often traveled on the same boat. A good out, in case of trouble."

Banker put a query:

"How did the Adquin dame get hold of you?"

"By accident," replied the fake count. "I thought it was a good break, but it didn't turn out that way. I've got to get rid of her, and the only way is to get rid of Fondelac."

"Like you did the other faces," nodded Banker.

"What's the next job—to trim the dame out of a lot of dough?"

"It won't work," replied Five-face. "No, the racket is this: I rate high as Fondelac, and a lot of people think I already have nicked the dame for plenty. Tonight, I'm going to put the clamps on some guy with plenty of dough, and hook him. I'll sell him fake bonds, telling him that Albertina gave them to me."

"Good enough," agreed Banker, "but how do we come into it?"

"The same as usual. If the guy gets wise, I'll have to lam like I did before. It means a cover-up, because if the victim won't hand over the cash, I'll take it from him."

Lieutenants showed their approval of the scheme. While they were nodding, Fondelac drew some money from a wallet and distributed a few hundred dollars to each man.

"That will carry you over until tomorrow night," he said. "I don't know who the dub is going to be yet, but I'll pick one out at the reception. I'll add the take to the rest of the loot, and we'll split afterward.

"I couldn't keep the stuff around here, not with the snoopy valet that I hired. Don't worry, though. I've got it stowed away, and I know how to freeze the hot stuff. So let's have a drink before I start to the reception."

Five-face folded back a screen, to display a miniature barroom, with an array of bottles and glasses on shelves behind the mahogany counter.

WHILE Count Fondelac was mixing drinks for his uninvited friends, The Shadow left the suite by his own route. Descending the stairway, he reached the ground floor.

There, instead of leaving through the service entrance, The Shadow peered into the hotel lobby. He saw the porter's room, empty and dark as he expected. In hotels like the Bayonne, the porter was seldom in his quarters. Usually, the clerk summoned a porter when guests called for one.

Crossing the dim lobby of the Bayonne was easy for anyone inside the place, since only the doorman kept tabs on unlikely strangers.

Reaching the porter's room, The Shadow used his tiny flashlight and found exactly what he wanted: a cardboard box of the size used by florists. Removing his cloak, hat, and other accouterments, he packed them in the box and wrapped it.

He was Lamont Cranston when he stepped from the porter's room, the box beneath his arm; but the clerk did not notice his arrival until he was almost at the desk. Seeing a gentleman in evening clothes, the clerk supposed that he had entered by the main door.

Giving Cranston's name, The Shadow asked for Count Fondelac. The clerk called the suite where Five-face was entertaining his lieutenants, and soon announced that Mr. Cranston could go upstairs. Before turning to the elevators, The Shadow laid his package on the desk.

"Kindly call the Cobalt Club," he requested, in Cranston's style. "Ask them to send my limousine over here. And by the way, will you turn this package over to your doorman and ask him to deliver it to my chauffeur?"

Upstairs, Five-face was stepping out from behind the bar, which filled an alcove in his living room. He was urging his lieutenants to finish up their drinks. Gesturing to the alcove, he added:

"Get in here, all three of you, and keep quiet. I know this fellow Cranston; he's worth a few million bucks, and he's been invited to the reception. That's why he's stopping by. Watch me handle him."

The lieutenants moved behind the bar. Five-face pulled the screen in place, completely hiding them, though they were able to see through the cracks and watch what happened in the living room.

There was a buzz from the door. Five-face answered it. Immediately, he was Count Fondelac, sophisticated of face, bowing in manner, as he shook hands with the gentleman whom he addressed as *"M'sieu'* Cranston."

Behind the screen, the lieutenants watched in admiration. It was impossible to guess that Fondelac was anyone other than himself. The same applied to Cranston, though they did not guess it.

Here was a historical meeting: The Shadow, foe of evil, shaking hands with Five-face, master of crime, under the gaze of the super-crook's own lieutenants!

Fortunately, only The Shadow knew the full details of the situation. Neither Five-face nor the others guessed his real identity.

Posing as Cranston, The Shadow invited Fondelac to ride with him to the reception, and the count agreed to go. But behind the mask of Fondelac, a keen brain was at work, and The Shadow knew it. He had expected that it would be. Five-face was taking The Shadow's bait.

"Ah, *M'sieu'* Cranston"—Fondelac's tone had a pleasant *purr*—"this is one excellent meeting. You are the man who can tell me what I wish to know. I have some French government bonds, which Albertina gave me, of which I must dispose, since Albertina insists that I never return to *la belle France.*

"Perhaps they would be a good exchange for some American securities. But I know nothing"—

he shrugged—"of your investments here. I may lose money, but—*pouf!*" He snapped his fingers. "What is money to me, when I have my Albertina?"

The question was logical enough, and provided its own answer. No one ever thought of Albertina Adquin except in terms of money, and that in big figures. As Fondelac expected, Cranston showed immediate interest.

He asked more about the bonds. Fondelac recalled their year of issue, and finally set a price on them, which was about two thirds their actual value. What he did not mention was the fact that he had already told his lieutenants; that the bonds in question were counterfeits.

"Suppose we meet tomorrow night," suggested Cranston. "We can get together at the Cobalt Club, say about eight. Bring the bonds along, Count, and I shall have some American securities to show you."

THE two were talking in hundred-thousand-dollar terms, as they left the suite together. It was Fondelac who closed the door; his face dropped its suavity, as he grinned back toward the screen and gestured to the hidden lieutenants.

Cranston had set the place, even the hour, which was all the lieutenants had to know. As soon as the door went shut, they came from hiding. Pushing back the screen, Banker suggested that they have another drink before they cleared out.

"We'll do a sneak from here," declared Banker, "and get the mob away. This Fondelac stunt is the best bet that Five-face has staged yet. He can count on us at the right time tomorrow."

Outside the hotel, two members of the picked mob had sneaked away from the rest. Cliff and Hawkeye were conferring in an alleyway, wondering why they hadn't heard from The Shadow. The lapse of time made them think that Fondelac had been abducted, and that The Shadow had run into grief trying to save him.

Suddenly, Hawkeye gripped Cliff's arm, pointed from the mouth of the alley to the front of the hotel. The Shadow's agents stared in utter amazement at two men who came from the main door and entered a waiting limousine.

One was Lamont Cranston, otherwise The Shadow. He was arm in arm with a suave-looking friend, who could only be Count Raoul Fondelac. Rescuer and victim were leaving the Hotel Bayonne as if nothing at all had happened!

There was added mystery when the agents rejoined the mobbies and found that the lieutenants had returned. It was Banker who simply said that the job was off and that the crew could have the cash that had been promised them.

That Fondelac was Five-face did not occur to Cliff and Hawkeye. The fact would have puzzled them even more, considering Cranston's friendly departure with the pretended count. It would have told them, however, that tonight's strange events would bode even stranger consequences.

With The Shadow and Five-face matching wits in each other's company, anything might happen!

CHAPTER XVII
BEFORE EIGHT

IT was late afternoon and Commissioner Weston was leaving his office, accompanied by Lamont Cranston. All afternoon, Weston had been talking to the financiers who had been robbed by Barney Kelm, trying to get any sort of clues regarding the missing fight promoter.

With the Barney matter a total blank, Weston decided to check on previous cases, as a matter of routine, even though he had no expectations of results.

"We'll go to Breddle first," said the commissioner, "and see if anyone at the Diamond Mart can remember anything about Flush Tygert. After that, we can drop in at Melbrun's office and thrash over the case of Jake Smarley."

The Shadow smiled at the commissioner's use of the word "thrash." The term "hash" would have been better. Nevertheless, The Shadow was willing to encourage Weston. He wanted the commissioner to be in the proper mood for the coming evening, when The Shadow intended to introduce the law to Count Fondelac and surprise the pretended nobleman in a fashion that would end his career as Five-face.

THE trip to the Diamond Mart took more than half an hour. It was nearly six when the commissioner and Cranston arrived at Melbrun's office, to find the importer hard at work.

Melbrun was planning a trip to Buenos Aires, to open up new channels in South American trade. He had practically forgotten the matter of Smarley.

"I'll be tied up here for the next couple of hours," said Melbrun. "Suppose I see you tomorrow, Commissioner. Of course, if the matter is important, I could stop by at the club this evening."

"It is not important," returned Weston. "Besides, I shall not be at the Cobalt Club tonight. I have been invited to a banquet, and will have to go there."

"Why not stop off anyway, Melbrun?" inquired The Shadow, in Cranston's fashion. "I happen to have something urgent on my mind, and you are the very man to help me with it."

"What can that be, Cranston?"

"Some French government bonds," replied The Shadow. "I intend to exchange some American securities for them. I would like the opinion of a man versed in international exchange. You are the very person, Melbrun."

Melbrun agreed to be at the club soon after eight o'clock. The visitors left, and Weston promptly inquired why Cranston happened to be buying foreign bonds. The Shadow mentioned that he was purchasing them from Count Fondelac.

"I might suggest that you slip away from the banquet shortly before eight," added The Shadow. "I would like you to be present, too, Commissioner."

"Just why?"

"Because I don't trust Fondelac," was the reply. "It would also be an excellent idea to have Inspector Cardona outside, with a picked squad. But impress upon him that he is to restrain himself. Fondelac is very clever; he might have friends on hand to warn him if police were about. The fellow strikes me as being an experienced swindler."

The thing intrigued Weston. Watching the commissioner, The Shadow noticed his flickers of expression and read them correctly. Weston did not, in any wise, class Count Fondelac with such crooks as Smarley, Flush and Barney. Therefore, the commissioner could be depended upon to handle his part of the job in smooth style.

Weston could be smooth enough under proper circumstances; and that applied to a chance meeting at the Cobalt Club, where the commissioner was a member and therefore likely to drop in at any time.

Dropping off at the club, The Shadow strolled about, looking over strategic spots. He knew that tonight's task would be no setup. It wasn't just a case of dealing with a smart swindler, as The Shadow had led Weston to believe. Five-face would have his usual quota of reserves, headed by his three lieutenants.

The master crook was anxious to dispose of the Fondelac personality; to efface it forever, as he had three others. He wouldn't care if he identified himself with mobbies in a spectacular style. The law had not guessed that three previous crimes had been staged by one master crook.

Fondelac, of all people, would never be linked with Smarley, Flush or Barney, no matter how he staged the coming crime.

In looking over the setting, The Shadow remembered that his agents would be present, as actual members of a crooked horde. He saw ways in which they could play a part. When he called Burbank, The Shadow included special instructions that were to go to Cliff and Hawkeye.

Others, too, were given orders. Harry Vincent, long in The Shadow's service, was an agent who could come to the Cobalt Club at Cranston's invitation. Clyde Burke, a reporter on the New York *Classic,* was another who could logically be in this neighborhood. As for Moe, he and his cab would certainly be on hand.

Down the street was a small apartment house where a uniformed doorman could take a post without exciting suspicion. Tenants in the building would merely think that the management had decided to make the place fashionable. So The Shadow ordered Burbank to contact Jericho, a big African, and tell him to put on a fancy uniform for this evening.

Five-face would be walking into a double mesh when he came to the Cobalt Club as Count Fondelac. The police formed one net; The Shadow's agents, the other.

DINING as Cranston, The Shadow forgot the clock. Fondelac was to arrive at eight, the hour that The Shadow had set for Melbrun. If anything, the count would probably be late, in keeping with his rather indifferent character.

Hence it was a mild surprise, even for The Shadow, when an attendant entered the grillroom, at quarter of eight, to announce that Count Fondelac had arrived to see Mr. Cranston.

The grillroom was the proper meeting place. Telling the waiter to clear the table, The Shadow gave word to show Count Fondelac downstairs. When Fondelac arrived, he saw Cranston rising from the table, holding a leather portfolio beneath his arm.

"Sorry to be early," purred Fondelac. "But it is on account of Albertina. She insists that she must go to the theater this evening. So instead of coming at eight o'clock, I find that I must leave by then."

There wasn't a slip in Fondelac's manner to indicate that he had obtained any knowledge of The Shadow's preparations. It might be that his mention of Albertina was the truth, and not an alibi. In his turn, The Shadow was very careful to give no indication that he wanted to hold Fondelac past the hour stated.

Five-face produced the French bonds. They were very clever counterfeits, but they did not deceive The Shadow. He had been to his bank that afternoon and had examined French bonds thoroughly. Glaring from Fondelac's bonds were various errors, tiny to the ordinary eye but magnified to The Shadow's gaze.

In the detection of false securities, The Shadow had no equal. At Cranston's home in New Jersey he kept a collection of counterfeit stocks and bonds, trophies of his battles against crime. He had gone over them thoroughly, this very morning, looking for samples of French forgeries.

There had been none in The Shadow's collection,

though he had many varieties of worthless paper. At least, Five-face was using judgment in peddling a new brand of counterfeit, which had never before been foisted in America. But The Shadow's inspection of genuine French bonds enabled him to know that Five-face was going through with the swindle.

Five-face was supremely clever. Smart enough, in fact, to change his game at the last minute. The Shadow had foreseen that the crooked count might even walk in with genuine bonds, if he suspected Cranston's bait. To make this transaction complete, The Shadow had to be sure that the bonds were counterfeit, before he took them. That part of the game was certain.

Fondelac rated the bonds at two hundred thousand dollars, a third less than their face value. They were an issue that was soon to mature, and the French government would surely meet its obligation, Fondelac insisted, despite wartime conditions. Apparently convinced that the deal was a good one, The Shadow opened his portfolio.

He spread various issues in front of Fondelac: stocks in copper mines and established oil companies; bonds guaranteed by large, thriving concerns. He even helped Fondelac pick out the ones that seemed best. Then, in Cranston's style, The Shadow remarked:

"But this is only my opinion, Count. For your benefit, I have invited a gentleman named Arnold Melbrun to join us. I think that he will render an impartial judgment."

There wasn't the slightest change on the face of Fondelac. His expression indicated that he had never heard of Melbrun. In fact, The Shadow did not expect such mention to bother Five-face. But there was another reason for Fondelac's indifference.

"I must keep my engagement," the crook insisted. "I am sorry, but I cannot remain to meet your friend—What was his name, *m'sieu'*? It has slipped me."

"Arnold Melbrun," repeated The Shadow. "He should be here at any moment. Wait, Count—here he is!"

IT wasn't Melbrun who stepped into the grillroom. The arrival was Commissioner Weston. Again, The Shadow was watching the features of Fondelac; they were not at all perturbed. In fact, Five-face simply gave a pleased nod when Cranston introduced Weston as the police commissioner.

"It is one honor, *M'sieu'* Commissioner," said Fondelac, with a profound bow. Then, turning to The Shadow: "I shall take these that you offer."

This time, The Shadow caught a sudden gleam from the eyes of Fondelac. Five-face was watching Cranston put away the French bonds. On the table lay Cranston's securities, double the amount that the trade required.

To give Fondelac his choice, Cranston had brought negotiable stocks and bonds that totaled considerably more than half a million dollars!

Would Five-face walk out with only half of those, letting the transaction appear bona fide until the fraud of the French bonds was discovered?

Or would he show his hand in full, by seizing all of them and taking to headlong flight, as he had done on other occasions?

The Shadow already knew the answer. Five-face would swallow the full bait. Nevertheless, he knew the risk and sensed that this might prove a trap. To some degree, he had to play the role of Fondelac; even more, he wanted to know that flight would prove sure.

It was Weston who paved the way for Five-face. Turning to The Shadow, the commissioner remarked in a brisk tone:

"Inspector Cardona is coming here, Cranston. I told him that I wanted him to wait outside for Melbrun. I've been worried about Melbrun lately."

Weston meant what he said. Rather than crimp the Fondelac matter, he had actually told Cardona to look out for Melbrun. The commissioner did not realize that such instructions could nullify the trap, so far as the law was concerned. But Five-face recognized it.

Like a flash, the slow-moving Fondelac became a human dynamo. With a sweep of his left hand, he scooped all of Cranston's bonds from the table and jammed them underneath his coat. Spinning toward the stairway, he whipped his right hand from his coattail, bringing out a revolver.

There was a murderous glint in the eyes of Five-face, as the supercrook began his sensational departure. He was ready to kill if either Commissioner Weston or Lamont Cranston made a single gesture to halt him!

CHAPTER XVIII
THE BANISHED TRAIL

UNTIL that instant, Five-face could not have known that Cranston was The Shadow. If he had, he would have shown his hand before. In all his guises, Five-face had encountered stern opposition from The Shadow, and could have asked nothing better than to slay his mortal foe in combat.

Had Cranston's hand gone for a gun, Five-face would have known what it meant. His own revolver already drawn, the master crook would have been prompt with the blast. It was impossible, under present conditions, for The Shadow to stop the pretended Count Fondelac.

Such a move, however, was possible for Cranston. He showed just what could be done, in a very surprising style.

Cranston was seated; his hands, having laid aside the portfolio, were on the table edge. They clamped, as he made an upward, forward lunge. The light table came with him, launched in a powerful fling for the darting figure of Fondelac.

Completing that upward hurl, The Shadow ended it with a dive to the floor, tripping Weston with a side-swinging foot.

Five-face didn't see that clever finish, which might have told him that Cranston was The Shadow. Half dodging, Five-face opened fire, splintering the cloth-covered table that was flying toward him. He thought that those bullets would reach the men beyond, not knowing that they had flattened beneath the level of his fire.

The bullet-ripped table struck the crook's shoulder. It wasn't heavy enough to floor him. It was merely a portable table, of very light construction. But the tablecloth flapped forward, covering the head and shoulders of Fondelac.

It was like a living shroud that had flopped in from space, to play its part in ruining crime. As Five-face tried to snatch the cloth away, he merely wrapped it tighter. He was blundering toward the stairway, mouthing muffled yells. In a way, the thing was ludicrous.

The Shadow had counted on the table; not the cloth. His purpose had been simply to spoil an enemy's aim. Instead, he had entangled Five-face in a mesh that rendered the criminal physically helpless. In trying to reach the stairs, Five-face stumbled, and lost his gun as he struggled against the tangle.

With a shove, The Shadow thrust Commissioner Weston to his feet, sending him after the master crook, It was the simplest possible job for Weston. All that he had to do was tighten the cloth that already held Five-face half smothered.

Having propelled Weston in the right direction, The Shadow came full about and drove for the kitchen door. He knew that Five-face had yelled with purpose; that the tangled crook expected prompt aid. Such assistance could be coming only from the kitchen.

The door came flinging inward. Catching it with a side step, The Shadow slashed it shut again, ramming it against the faces of two thugs who were driving through. Then, pulling the door wide, he hurled himself upon the staggered pair, slugging them with a gun that he yanked into play.

Other invaders were in the kitchen, lunging toward The Shadow. He met them with bullets, and new guns echoed the blasts. Cliff and Hawkeye were with the mob, nicking crooks in expert style.

The surge became a sprawl of bewildered, wounded thugs. The way trouble overtook them, they thought that The Shadow must have started it; yet they couldn't see a sign of any cloaked opponent!

Leaving the crippled crooks to Cliff and Hawkeye, The Shadow wheeled back to the grill-room, still Cranston to all who saw him. As he shoved through the door, a hurtling figure met him and began to grapple. Twisting his foe about, The Shadow met him eye to eye.

The face of Lamont Cranston was thrust squarely against the countenance of his friend, Commissioner Weston!

They broke apart. Showing Fondelac's gun, which he had picked up from the floor, the commissioner tried to explain things.

"I thought they had trapped you, Cranston!" he panted. "I saw them yank you into the kitchen. In my excitement, I forgot Fondelac—"

THRUSTING Weston aside, The Shadow started for the stairway. Snapping from his stupor, the Commissioner followed. The tablecloth was lying on the steps, but there was no sign of Fondelac. He had dashed up to the foyer, carrying Cranston's stocks and bonds with him.

Things hadn't happened as Five-face wanted. He had expected to be well away before the commotion started below; more than that, he had counted upon his gun, which he no longer had.

He crossed the foyer at a lope, clutching the bonds beneath his coat. As he reached the outer door, a squatty man shoved in to block him.

Inspector Cardona had heard the shooting within the Cobalt Club and was on hand, with a squad behind him.

"Quickly, inspector!" exclaimed Five-face. "I'm Count Fondelac. The commissioner sent me up to find you. He said to rush your men downstairs and"—faltering, the crook gave a wince—"and to help me out of here. I'm wounded."

Cardona pointed his men through the doorway. Turning, Joe rushed Fondelac out into a waiting squad car. He knew who Fondelac was, and he didn't want the Count to die on his hands.

Joe Cardona believed that Fondelac was really wounded, because he had noticed how the man was clutching his hands tight against his side. Joe didn't guess that the count was really hanging on to a bundle of stolen securities that he had pilfered from Lamont Cranston.

Once in the car, Fondelac relaxed and sat back with a long sigh. Cardona told the driver to get them to the nearest hospital in a hurry. He didn't hear the shouts that came from back at the Cobalt Club, where the inrushing squad had met Cranston and Weston coming out.

The squad car was around the corner, halfway along the block, when Fondelac pointed to a cab parked in front of a small hotel. He gestured for Cardona to stop the squad car.

"I am better now, inspector," informed Fondelac. "I can go to my apartment in the taxicab. The commissioner wants you to return. He said that you are to wait for *M'sieu'* Melbrun."

"Forget Melbrun," snapped Cardona. "You've got to get to a hospital, Count, because of that bullet."

"Bullet?" Fondelac looked puzzled; then he laughed lightly. *"Non,* inspector. The ruffian did not have a gun. He used his fist, this way"—he clenched his hand—"and gave me one big punch."

The car had stopped. Count Fondelac stepped to the street; Cardona saw him wince and tighten his hands, as though the punch still hurt him. Cardona was still staring, when Fondelac entered the cab and rode away.

Joe turned to the driver of the squad car.

"A punch in the belly!" growled Cardona. "I ought to have handed that sissy another on the jaw! Say, if Fondelac didn't get hit, I wonder what all the shooting was about."

Abruptly, Cardona quit speculating about the past. He had the present to think about. More shooting was in evidence, from the direction of the Cobalt Club.

Remembering that the commissioner had ordered him to cover Melbrun's arrival, Cardona promptly forgot Fondelac, except to congratulate himself that he had sent the softy from harm's way. Joe ordered the driver to speed around the block and get back to the Cobalt Club.

THINGS were happening very rapidly outside the club. Two groups had witnessed Fondelac's departure with Cardona and had been puzzled because of it.

One group consisted of the lieutenants who served Five-face. They were afraid to take pot shots at Cardona, because of Fondelac. The fact that Five-face had not called upon them to open fire was sufficient to keep them quiet.

The other watchers were The Shadow's agents. Farther away, they supposed that Cardona had taken Fondelac into custody. Thus, everything had remained latent, until a surge of men appeared on the sidewalk. Commissioner Weston was with Cardona's squad, yelling for cars in which to begin pursuit.

Guns talked promptly from across the street.

The commissioner dived for shelter and the detectives scattered. They were saved only by the intervention of a friend who had followed them from the club: Lamont Cranston.

From the doorway, which offered satisfactory cover, The Shadow picked out the source of the first wild shots and responded with a prompt fire.

Though The Shadow's bullets took effect, he was unable to get the result he wanted; namely, a prompt pursuit of Five-face. Grease, Banker, and Clip were at least giving their chief the support that he needed for a getaway.

Moreover, the lieutenants were unusually bold tonight. They and their henchmen were ready to dare the shots offered by the lone marksman in the doorway of the club.

Piling in from many angles, they made for Weston and the diving detectives. The attackers were too many, too widespread, even for The Shadow to stop them, particularly as snipers had begun a fire toward the doorway, to hold back the lone sharpshooter.

Perhaps The Shadow's laugh would have diverted the surge, but he preferred to count on other assistance, while he adhered to the part of Cranston.

In came the aid The Shadow wanted, provided in prompt and efficient style. Harry Vincent and Clyde Burke popped out from doorways and opened a flanking fire on the charging crooks. Around the corner came Cliff Marsland and Hawkeye, finished with the thugs back in the kitchen. They added telling shots.

All the while, The Shadow was shooting from the doorway. The lighted space in front of the Cobalt Club might well have been marked with a gigantic X, for it indicated a spot where bodies would be found if any crooks came that far.

The few who reached the fringes of the light were staggered by The Shadow's direct fire, while his agents were working the flanks.

Leaders of the scattering mob were shouting for reserves. A car came roaring up the street, but it never reached the Cobalt Club. Moe's cab whipped in from a corner and diverted the car across the street.

A batch of thugs leaped out, intent upon many things; primarily, they wanted to obliterate the cabby who had stopped their course.

That was just the time for Jericho. He was pacing in front of the apartment house, just beyond the corner. With a gleaming grin that matched the glitter of his goldbraided uniform, the giant African reached the batch of crooks and went to work with bare hands.

Jericho cracked two heads together like a pair of eggshells. He grabbed a third mobbie, used him to bludgeon a fourth. There was a fifth man among the reserves, but he didn't wait around. He scudded for an alleyway, leaving Jericho in full possession of a sedan equipped with a pair of machine guns.

Other cars were starting away. Cardona met them with the squad car, around the next corner. Brakes shrieked as the squad car drove one automobile into a wall. The Shadow and his agents riddled another car with bullets.

But the third car managed a getaway, for the squad car offered a barrier between it and the marksmen, who now included the intrenched detectives who had come out from the Cobalt Club.

In the fleeing car were the three lieutenants who served Five-face. Banker was at the wheel, Clip on the seat beside him. Grease was lucky enough to reach the running board just as the car sped away.

RETURNING to the club, Commissioner Weston found Cranston standing idly in the doorway. The commissioner knew that his friend had joined in the fire, but had no idea that Cranston had been the mainspring of the whole affray.

While Weston was offering congratulations for what he considered a rather trifling service, a coupe pulled up in front of the Cobalt Club.

Arnold Melbrun was in the car; he was amazed when he learned the full details of the battle. He wanted to know who had returned: Smarley, Tygert, or Barney Kelm.

When Melbrun learned that a new king of crime had taken over the scene, he stood bewildered. Like nearly everyone else, he had heard of Count Raoul Fondelac, and the fact that such a celebrity had gone crooked merely added to Melbrun's daze.

The size of the robbery was also something to talk about. At least, Lamont Cranston could congratulate himself upon having kept Fondelac's bonds, in place of his own, although their value totaled less. But when Melbrun saw the French bonds, he shook his head. In his opinion, they were fraudulent.

It was curious how lightly Cranston took the news. He turned the bonds over to Weston, requesting the commissioner to look into the matter. Then, tired by the evening's excitement, Cranston decided to go home.

Riding away in his limousine. Cranston gave a regretful laugh. It wasn't the sort of laugh that one would expect from a man who had lost half a million dollars. Neither the bonds nor their cash value was the cause of Cranston's regret.

The Shadow simply regretted that he hadn't stopped Five-face before the master crook had tricked Joe Cardona and led the ace inspector to banish crime's trail.

It meant that special measures would be needed, if The Shadow hoped to meet Five-face again. This evening's events had definitely clarified certain puzzling matters.

The Shadow's laugh changed to a strange comprehending whisper, as this master of the night began to plan his coming ventures, which— he hoped—would lead to the final trapping of Five-face!

CHAPTER XIX
OUT OF THE PAST

ARNOLD MELBRUN was right. The French bonds *were* fraudulent. Count Raoul Fondelac had turned a swindle into whirlwind crime.

As a result, the newspapers estimated that Lamont Cranston had lost half a million dollars. Coupled with thefts committed by Flush Tygert and Barney Kelm, this latest exploit raised crime's recent total above a million dollars.

Still, the public did not connect those deeds with one man. Jake Smarley was practically forgotten; Flush and Barney almost so. All talk concerned Count Fondelac, who had proven himself quite as slippery as his predecessors. From the moment that he had said good-bye to Inspector Cardona, Fondelac had completely disappeared.

The cabby remembered driving to Fondelac's apartment, but the count had left the cab somewhere on the way. There wasn't a scrap of evidence in the apartment itself that offered the police anything resembling a trail.

Three men were distinctly interested in what had become of Fondelac. They were the lieutenants who knew him as Five-face. Grease, Banker, and Clip regarded themselves as very fortunate to have escaped unscathed and unrecognized. Still, they prided themselves on having remembered the importance of a getaway, just as Five-face had.

It was Banker who broached the subject of the future, when the three gathered, at nightfall, in their dilapidated headquarters.

"Four faces gone," tallied Banker, counting his fingers, "which means that Five-face has got just one left; his last one."

"Yeah," put in Grease, "and maybe he's scared to show it. Ever think of that, Banker?"

"He'll show it to us," asserted Clip. "Why shouldn't he offer to divvy, with all the dough he's grabbed?"

Banker began to stroke his chin. Meanwhile, Grease put an answer to Clip's question.

"We've got nothing on Five-face," snarled Grease. "It may look like we have, but we haven't. What if we squeal on him, supposing he doesn't show up? He won't care if people find out that he was four different guys. Any one of the four would be bad enough for him, if the cops put the arm on him."

"Five-face thinks in big terms," insisted Banker, slowly. "Remember, he told us there would be another job. I think there will be. He won't have to show his face."

"Why not?" demanded Grease.

"Because he'll turn the job over to us," explained Banker. "That's when we want to be smart. Unless it's as safe for us as it is for him, we want to say nix."

The three began to discuss the new angle that Banker had suggested. They were in the middle of their parley, when a rap came at the door. All three were congregated close, when Banker opened the door. With one accord, the trio stepped back.

On the threshold stood a man with a face so ugly that no one could have blamed him for changing it whenever occasion offered.

His forehead bulged above his eyes, which were as small as gimlet points; his nose had a sideward twist. His lips were large, but widespread; they showed a clutter of misshapen teeth, that seemed to fill the ugly face.

The lieutenants knew that face. They had never expected to see it in life again. Banker's voice was hoarse, barely audible, as he spoke for his pals:

"Blitz Bell!"

THE ugly man stepped into the room and closed the door. His gait was crablike; one shoulder drooped, as he made his way to a chair. He didn't speak; he simply picked up the greasy pack of cards and performed the flush trick, slicing a fifth club in among four others.

If he hadn't given that demonstration the lieutenants would never have granted that Blitz Bell could be Five-face.

"Go ahead, say it," asserted Blitz suddenly, in a raspy tone. "You thought I was croaked, didn't you? Like everybody else, you fell for that story about the Feds getting me, a couple of years ago. Well, they got Blitz Bell—in a way."

With both hands, Blitz stroked his face; the pressure seemed to mold it into a smoother visage. Then he let the bloated features return, in rubbery fashion.

"Here's the lowdown," he rasped. "I had a face lift, see? Before the Feds caught up with me. They thought I blew myself up along with the dynamite shack, when they surrounded me. But that was because they didn't see anyone around who looked like Blitz Bell.

"I had a good job done on this mug of mine. Ever since then, I've been able to change it into five, including my own. Funny, ain't it, the face I've had the most trouble with *is* my own? Only, I like it, and I don't give a bang if nobody else does."

In his speech, Blitz Bell showed a confidence which the listeners shared. The lieutenants had taken it for granted that Five-face would adopt an unexpected personality for the climax that he had planned. The guise of Blitz Bell fitted the bill to perfection.

Supposedly dead, Blitz was beyond the reach of the law, provided he could keep his secret. Grease, Banker, Clip were seeing a man who had stepped from the past; and even with Blitz's explanation, the thing still awed them.

They would never have dreamed that Five-face could be Blitz Bell, the notorious public enemy that the Feds had supposedly eliminated years ago!

Yet, on the table lay proof that Blitz was Five-face: those outspread playing cards with which he had demonstrated his identity. They were glad that Five-face had used his skill to prove who he was. It was a better token than any other.

To a man, the lieutenants were willing to follow Blitz wherever he suggested. They were anxious to learn what new crime he intended. Remembering Blitz by reputation, as well as sight, they knew that he would not rest on past success. If opportunity offered—and Five-face had promised that it would—Blitz was the man to make the most of it.

With a wide-lipped smile that exposed his fanglike teeth, Blitz Bell spread a newspaper on the table. He pointed to a picture of Count Raoul Fondelac and gave a raspy laugh. He tapped the teeth that bulged from his mouth.

"Plates," explained Blitz. "I had them made to match my own, before I got rid of the real ones. My teeth were bum, anyway. I've been four other guys lately, but I can still be myself when I want."

Blitz thumbed through the newspaper, came to the page he wanted. Then, to the listeners:

"I said we'd pull a big job for a payoff," spoke Blitz. "That's what we will do, but we'll be after more than dough. I'm going to get back at the one guy who was lucky enough to stall us off!"

Alarm showed on the faces of the lieutenants. They thought that Blitz meant The Shadow. They didn't like the idea of hurling a challenge at so formidable a foe, even with Five-face as their leader. Blitz understood.

"I don't mean The Shadow," he asserted. "I mean this guy"—he pointed to a photo in the newspaper—"Arnold Melbrun. He's the bird who outguessed me when I was Smarley, and saved a hundred grand for those friends of his.

"But we're going to get that dough, and a lot more. At the same time, we'll fix Melbrun permanent. Look at what it says here: Melbrun is leaving for South America, tonight, to put over some big business deals.

"He's chartered a special plane for the trip. Do you know what that means? I'll tell you: dough! He's probably carrying a pile of it, because money talks in South America, like it does here. He's taking off at midnight, so we'll show up before then."

SWEEPING the newspaper to the floor, along with the pack of cards, Blitz strode to the door. There, he turned to face his lieutenants and give a final word.

"Get all the mobbies you've got left," said Blitz. "Have them cover the airport. I'll have the take from the other jobs, all packed in a bag, when I meet you guys. We'll ride right through and take over Melbrun and his plane.

"I used to fly crates, years ago. I can handle that plane. I know a lot of landing spots that nobody else ever heard about. We'll grab Melbrun's dough and make our getaway, all in one whack. When we get to where we're going, we can divvy all the swag, including what we take from Melbrun."

The door closed on Blitz Bell. Three astounded men stood silent for a dozen seconds, then went mad with glee. Even Banker, usually reserved, caught the fever from Grease and Clip.

Greater than any of the previous crimes engineered by Five-face, tonight's proposal promised success without a flaw. In this final stroke, Blitz Bell and his lieutenants would move with rapid speed.

It was crime that showed the conniving of a master brain; the sort that would render pursuit impossible, even by The Shadow!

CHAPTER XX
THE FIFTH FACE

GLISTENING under the glare of floodlights, the silvery plane was ready for its midnight take-off. Luggage had been loaded aboard, and Arnold Melbrun was shaking hands with the business associates who had financed his trip to the Argentine.

Very soon, the plane would be carrying the importer on the first hop of this important journey. Melbrun had long looked forward to the trip, and his associates were assuring him that it would result in new and greater trade relations with South America.

There were other men whose plans did not coincide with Melbrun's. If all worked as Blitz Bell had promised, the ugly-faced big shot and his lieutenants would make a flight in Melbrun's stead. So far, however, Blitz & Co. had not appeared.

Among the idlers on the fringes of the airport were hard-faced men who indulged in muttered comment. They were the leftovers of the various mobs supplied by Grease, Banker, and Clip. They hadn't been too eager to take on this job tonight, until they learned that it involved wide-open spaces where flight would be easy.

The thugs had cars available near the airport. All that they had to do was cover the fringes, while their leaders made the real attack. That in itself was a novelty, so the trigger men had agreed to be on hand.

They knew nothing about the intended flight. That would appear to be something produced by necessity. Later, perhaps, the small-fry thugs would be paid off with hush money sent by the lieutenants. But even that detail might be overlooked. Safely gone with Five-face, the lieutenants might dispense with such payments.

Cliff and Hawkeye were with the cover-up crew. They knew that Harry and Clyde were in Moe's cab, which was parked nearby. They were quite sure, too, that Jericho was on the ground. Still, The Shadow's agents were somewhat mystified.

They had learned that strife was due at the airport and had reported the fact to The Shadow. Whether he knew more than they did was a question. Keeping close to the apartment where the lieutenants had their headquarters, neither Cliff nor Hawkeye had seen any sign of The Shadow.

Their report included details of a muffled visitor, evidently Five-face. But they hadn't seen the face of Blitz Bell when the big shot entered and made his departure. As a man returned from the grave, the owner of that face had been very careful to keep it obscured in public.

The agents were sure, however, that The Shadow would arrive before the zero hour of midnight. They knew, too, that police would later be on hand, for Burbank was to phone a well-timed tip-off to the law. Spectacular things were due, and for once, The Shadow's aides were impatient, wondering just what their chief intended.

The plane's big propellers were spinning. Melbrun had turned away from his friends, to enter the ship, when a low-built sedan sped in from a roadway, swerved, and suddenly cut across the field itself.

There were four men in that car: Banker at the wheel, with Grease beside him; Clip in the rear seat, with Blitz Bell.

Crouched low, Blitz was clutching a heavy bag. It wasn't the valise that Five-face had carried from the Diamond Mart, and used later at the Hotel Clairmont. Five-face no longer regarded luck as essential. He considered his plans too complete to be spoiled by anyone, even The Shadow.

While men were dashing out to yell at the crazed car, it came to a stop not far from Melbrun's plane. Looking from the rear window, Blitz Bell gave a raspy chuckle at sight of the approaching airport guards. They looked like pygmies, they were so far away; and in number, they were very few.

"Get Melbrun!" ordered Blitz. "I'll snipe those saps from the hangar, while you're taking over the plane. Then I'll join up with you, bringing this—"

He lifted the bag, let it sag again with a thud that made it bulge. Sight of the bag pleased Blitz's three companions. They liked the way that it was stuffed. Diamonds, cash and bonds could all be unloaded after they were divided. But the boodle from the past did not make them forget the present opportunity.

REMEMBERING that Arnold Melbrun was awaiting them as another victim, the three lieutenants leaped from their car and started toward the plane, only fifty yards away. They didn't care if the floodlights showed their faces and their guns. This attack was to be short, swift, and sure.

Melbrun's friends stood astonished, until revolvers spurted. Then, with one accord, they fled. So did the airport crew around the plane.

Only one man was caught flat-footed where he stood. That man was Arnold Melbrun. He hadn't a chance to flee, and he realized instantly that the gunners were after him.

Other shots were sounding from the car, where Blitz had remained. They stopped suddenly, as the big shot heard the approach of distant sirens. Immediately, shooting began along the fringes of the airport. Covering thugs had heard the sirens, too, and were starting to make trouble.

Of the three lieutenants only Banker sensed what had happened. Letting Grease and Clip dash ahead of him in their quest for Melbrun, Banker looked across his shoulder. He saw wavering figures in the distance, men sprawling, guns in their hands, though the police had not yet arrived!

Instantly, Banker understood. The Shadow must have planted members with the mob! For the first time, Banker realized why other attacks had faltered, particularly that last one, at the Cobalt Club. With a snarl, Banker dashed after Grease and Clip. This job would have to be even speedier than Blitz Bell had ordered.

Arnold Melbrun had taken the only route to temporary shelter. Dodging the aiming guns of Grease and Clip, the importer sprang into the plane. He tried to get its sliding door shut, but by that time the attackers were too close. Melbrun took the only course that offered.

With his luggage was a large wardrobe trunk, which stood on end, just within the plane's door. Ducking beyond the trunk, Melbrun hurled his full weight upon it, shoving it toward the door, as a blockade. Bound on a trip which offered hazards, such as a forced landing in the Amazon Country, Melbrun was equipped with a revolver. He yanked the weapon and began to fire from behind his improvised barricade.

By then, airport attendants, some with guns, had reached the car where Blitz Bell had stayed. The fight on the fringes of the airport had broken all apart. Wild mobsters were in flight, pursued by The Shadow's agents. Police cars were roaring in through the gates; people were guiding them toward Melbrun's beleaguered plane.

There, Melbrun had gained a moment of success. From behind the big trunk, he had nipped both Clip and Banker with quick shots, but the hits were superficial. Grease had escaped bullets by lurching forward, so that he was under the very shelter of the trunk itself. Seeing Grease's move, Banker and Clip copied it.

Viciously, the three grabbed at the trunk and the sides of the doorway, hoping to pull the barrier away and get at Melbrun. The importer was fighting hard to hold out until rescue came. But the trunk was slipping. Melbrun needed quicker aid than the arriving police could provide.

Then, at this most vital moment, came a challenge that made all others puny. Melbrun heard it, a titanic laugh that brought snarls from the three crooks beyond the trunk. Seemingly from nowhere, a black-cloaked figure was sweeping into the floodlights, bearing down upon the three attackers who held Melbrun trapped.

There was no mistaking that mighty fighter, whose big fists wielded huge automatics. He was The Shadow, master of the night, from which he had appeared as suddenly as though projected from an outer space!

FOR an instant, the three thugs outside the plane turned, as though willing to combat this mighty foe. Then, seeing the big guns aim, realizing that they were open targets, they grabbed at the trunk again, madly trying to wrest it free so that they could reach the shelter inside the plane.

Melbrun let them have the trunk, with a shove that pitched it full upon them. The three crooks went sprawling as the bulky object struck them, spinning sideward as it came.

Half lurched from the doorway, Melbrun caught himself. He was an open target, but he didn't care. The Shadow had stopped short, his guns trained on the three sprawled mobsters.

They were the sort, those killers, who could

expect no mercy from The Shadow. Melbrun wasn't the only man who foresaw their instant death. Joe Cardona, approaching in a speeding police car, would have sworn that sure death was due.

Then a strange thing happened. The Shadow faltered, seemed to sidestep, as though seeking shelter. Perhaps he had sensed guns trained from a distance; weapons that no one else guessed about. Such was Cardona's opinion, at the moment; and The Shadow's odd shift startled Melbrun, too.

At the very moment of rescue, Melbrun was abandoned. It didn't seem to matter, considering that he had bowled over his attackers; but there was one point that Melbrun missed.

The Shadow's sudden change of course gave a respite to the three crooks on the ground. Melbrun's own course, his only sensible one, was to dive back into the plane, seeking shelter beyond other luggage, until the police could take over where The Shadow had left off.

Melbrun hesitated only half a second. It was too long. From the ground, half-rising crooks delivered a volley at the plane's doorway. Banker was sagging badly; Clip was wobbly; even Grease had a jerky aim. But the range was too short to matter.

Taking bullets in the chest, Melbrun pitched forward when further shots flayed him. His body tumbled headlong upon the big trunk that lay, half broken, on the ground.

Cardona and others were blasting away. Their shots riddled the three killers, but came too late to save Melbrun. Then, surveying the dying figures on the ground, Cardona left the crooks and their victim to his squad. He hurried over to the sedan from which crooks had attacked.

Puzzled men were staring into the car. It had no occupant; merely an opened bag stuffed with paper, but with a space near the top. With a slow nod, Cardona went over to the plane, to view the result of the battle there.

Melbrun was dead. Of the three who had slain him, all were dying, and only one could talk: Grease Rickel. He was the sort who would believe that he had been double-crossed, if properly questioned; particularly since Banker Dreeb and Clip Zelber could no longer advise him to shut up.

Cardona began his persuasive effort, and Grease responded. He was muttering names of Smarley, Flush Tygert, Barney Kelm, even Fondelac. In between, he kept repeating the name: "Five-face."

"I get it, Grease." Cardona was playing a hunch. "All of them were Five-face. He's the guy who double-crossed you."

"Yeah." Grease's tone was a gaspy sigh. "Blitz Bell... back in the car... with all the swag—"

That was all, but the name of Blitz Bell did not score with Joe Cardona. He couldn't believe that Blitz had come back to life, nor that the fellow could have vanished in mysterious style. Besides, Cardona had seen the present contents of Blitz's bag.

A name sprang to Cardona's mind. He actually voiced it:

"The Shadow!"

That explained it! The Shadow had visited these crime lieutenants as Blitz Bell. He had made the crooks believe that he was Five-face. Cardona didn't know about the gambling stunt that Five-face used to identify himself; if he had, it would have strengthened his opinion. The Shadow was clever enough to duplicate any such trick.

Cardona was thinking of something else. If Blitz was not Five-face, who was? Staring groundward, Cardona saw the answer. It came with a flash, as he remembered the Shadow's strange act when the cloaked fighter had suddenly abandoned the rescue of Arnold Melbrun.

HEFTING the importer's body to one side, Cardona yanked open the broken trunk. He tugged at locked compartments and smashed them.

From one came a flood of diamonds: Breddle's. Another disgorged the cash that the financiers had yielded. Cranston's bonds slid in big batches from the third.

As he gathered up those trophies of supercrime, Cardona stared at the dead criminal. Tense in death, the features of Arnold Melbrun were no longer wholly his own.

His face looked long, gaunt, like Smarley's; wise, like the countenance of Flush. Its grimacing lips belonged to Barney; yet Cardona saw a smoothness, too, that reminded him of Fondelac.

To Cardona, The Shadow's triumph had been a stroke of proper justice, wherein the master fighter had let Five-face find his death at the hands of the very men whom the criminal overlord had sought to double-cross!

Belated on the scene came Commissioner Weston, who had been returning from a late trip out of town. With him was Lamont Cranston, who had met the commissioner at the Cobalt Club. They heard the facts that Cardona had pieced together. It was amazing how smartly Five-face had played his game.

Smarley's crime had failed, so planned by Melbrun to cover up his real identity. He had succeeded as Flush Tygert, then as Barney Kelm, but in the latter case he had been most clever.

Melbrun hadn't called his office from his home. He had made that call from a pay booth in the Hotel Clairmont, where he was in the guise of Barney!

As Fondelac, Five-face had been in a dilemma. Cranston had insisted that Melbrun come to the

Cobalt Club. But Fondelac could not have met Melbrun, any more than Barney could have.

"You didn't realize what a jam you put him in, Mr. Cranston," said Cardona, turning to the commissioner's friend. "But The Shadow must have checked on it, and guessed the answer. What's more, The Shadow figured that Five-face planned a double cross."

"Quite obvious," observed Cranston, coolly, "considering that The Shadow had identified Melbrun as Five-face. Melbrun had already arranged to leave for South America. The stage was set for him to walk out on his accomplices."

"So The Shadow took over," nodded Cardona. "That business of coming in as Blitz Bell was perfect. What a surprise he rigged on Melbrun! Even then, Melbrun didn't guess it. He thought that his bunch were coming on their own. When he saw The Shadow, Five-face actually counted on a rescue!"

Cardona was opening a bundle as he spoke. From it, he took a big batch of sorted securities, that bore figures up in the thousands. They added up to more than half a million dollars, those stocks and bonds that Cardona handed over, with the comment:

"These are yours, Mr. Cranston."

"Thanks, inspector," returned The Shadow, calmly. "I'll put them back in my collection."

"Your collection?" queried Weston. "What collection, Cranston?"

The Shadow's lips showed a Cranston smile.

"My collection of counterfeits," he explained. "Worthless stocks and bonds, from many sources. I was doubtful about Fondelac, commissioner. I thought it best to let him have these, until I found out if his French bonds were genuine."

"Remarkable!" exclaimed Weston. "Remarkable foresight, Cranston!"

REMARKABLE foresight. Cardona agreed with the opinion, as he watched the commissioner and his friend stroll to the official car, with Cranston carelessly carrying the worthless bonds that had been reclaimed from Five-face.

Cardona was wondering if The Shadow had mysteriously warned Cranston to beware of Fondelac. If so, The Shadow must have known much about Five-face, even before he had identified the master crook as Arnold Melbrun.

As Cardona pondered, he heard a parting tone that seemed to quiver in from outer darkness, beyond the floodlights of the airport. Cardona stared.

He didn't realize that the whispery laugh was from the direction of the commissioner's car, where Cranston had gone on alone, while Weston stopped to talk to the airport authorities.

Cardona recognized it only as the laugh of The Shadow—a singular, mirthless note of triumph from the lips of the master fighter who had turned Five-face over to the double-crossed lieutenants, as their victim, instead of their leader.

Five faces. Four had belonged to Arnold Melbrun; but the fifth—that of Blitz Bell—had been The Shadow's. As the false Fifth Face, The Shadow had actually revealed the true one!

A knell, that mirthless laugh, for Arnold Melbrun and three others who had been finally trapped together by the design of The Shadow!

THE END

Coming in THE SHADOW Volume 11:

In a tale of justice, The Shadow becomes the guiding hand of destiny. Follow him on

THE ROAD OF CRIME

a tale of wrong that is righted, and criminals who get their just deserts…where the guilty suffer, and the innocent are given a new chance. Then, see what happens when

CROOKS GO STRAIGHT

When men have served their punishment for crime, how does the world receive them?

It is after prison that the real test comes, and how two men meet this test is told graphically by Maxwell Grant. Don't miss these two book-length novels in the next thrilling volume of THE Shadow™

Only $12.95. Ask your bookseller to reserve your copy now!

SPOTLIGHT ON THE SHADOW: THE SHADOW OF ALFRED BESTER
by Anthony Tollin

Walter Gibson's novels introduced readers to Lamont Cranston and Commissioner Weston, but the characters reached their greatest audience in the famous radio series broadcast from 1937-54 over the Mutual Broadcasting System. Many of radio's top scriptwriters wrote for the series including Edith Meiser, Alonzo Deen Cole, Sidney Slon, Frederic Dannay and Manfred B. Lee (a.k.a. Ellery Queen) and science-fiction great Alfred Bester.

Alfred Bester (1913-87) began his career writing for science-fiction pulps after studying psychology, science and law at the University of Pennsylvania. "Two editors on the *[Thrilling Wonder Stories]* staff, Mort Weisinger and Jack Schiff, took an interest in me, I suspect mostly because I'd just finished reading and annotating Joyce's *Ulysses* and would preach it enthusiastically without provocation, to their great amusement," Bester wrote in *Hell's Cartographers*. "They told me what they had in mind. *Thrilling Wonder* was conducting a prize contest for the best story written by an amateur, and so far none of the submissions was worth considering. They thought 'Diaz-X' might fill the bill if it was whipped into shape. They taught me how to revise the story into acceptable form and gave it the prize, $50. It was printed with the title, 'The Broken Axiom.' They continued their professional guidance and I've never stopped being grateful to them."

Bester's pulp career was short-lived due to the declining market, but he soon found work in a new and expanding field. "When the comic book explosion burst, my two magi were lured from Standard Magazines to the Superman Group. There was a desperate need for writers to provide scenarios… for the artists, so Weisinger and Schiff drafted me as one of their writers. I hadn't the faintest idea of how to write a comic book script, but one rainy Saturday afternoon Bill Finger, the star comics writer of the time, took me in hand and gave me, a potential rival, an incisive, illuminating lecture on the craft," Bester recalled. "I still regard that as a high point in the generosity of one colleague to another." Bester soon succeeded Finger as the primary writer of DC's *Green Lantern*.

In the spring of 1944, Bester's radio-actress wife Rolly (who originated the role of Lois Lane in the *Superman* syndicated series) arranged a meeting between her husband and *Charlie Chan* producer-director Chick Vincent. The radio producer agreed to give Bester a tryout if he delivered a finished script in a week's time. Bester missed the deadline, but returned after an additional week with *two* scripts adapted from his earlier comic book stories. Both sold, and Bester began a new career in broadcasting. "The comic book days were over, but the splendid training I received in visualization, attack, dialogue and economy stayed with me forever."

Bester wrote a dozen scripts for *The Shadow* during the 1944-45 season which starred Hollywood transplant John Archer, who later starred in Robert Heinlein's *Destination Moon,* the film that launched the 1950s science fiction boom.

Bester's Shadow scripts often featured strong psychological and scientific overtones: a psychotic fascinated with destruction seeks fame through terrorist acts in "The Destroyer," while an evil medico induces nightmares through ultrasonic broadcasts in "The Man Who Dreamed Too Much." Many of Alfie's *Shadow* scripts were based on his earlier Green Lantern and Starman stories, including "The Little Man Who Wasn't There" and "The Man with the Missing Memory." Bester's "The Case of the Flaming Skull" and "The Man Who Was Death" were adapted from his 1941 Batman story, "The Strange Case of Professor Radium."

"The Immortal Murderer" reprises portions of Bester's 1941 comic script, "The Man Who Wanted the World." The Green Lantern story introduced Vandal Savage, a Cro-Magnon who had become immortal through exposure to a meteor. Savage was most likely inspired by the character of Cartaphilus in George Sylvester Viereck and Paul Eldrige's 1928 novel *My First Two Thousand Years: the Autobiography of the Wandering Jew,* and also by the curse of immortality imposed in myth upon Ixion, Tantalus and Sisyphus.

In 1963, Bester's former agent and editor Julius Schwartz revived the Immortal Villain (along with the Justice Society) in *The Flash* #137, and Vandal Savage continues as an important supervillain in the DC Comics universe to the present day.

Bester's first novel *The Demolished Man* won the first Hugo Award at the 1953 World Science Fiction Convention, while *The Stars My Destination* is recognized as one of the greatest science-fiction novels of all time. Bester bridged both traditional and new-wave science fiction, and was posthumously awarded the Science Fiction and Fantasy Writers of America's Grand Master Award.

RUTHRAUFF & RYAN Inc. ADVERTISING

RADIO DIVISION

CLIENT: D. L. & W. COAL COMPANY **BROADCAST DATE:** FINAL REV. #206 SUN. 12/10/44

PROGRAM: 'blue coal' **NETWORK:** WOR

THE SHADOW
"THE IMMORTAL MURDERER"
by Alfred Bester

	(MUSIC: "SPINNING WHEEL" - FADE UNDER)
SHADOW:	(FILTER) Who knows what evil lurks in the hearts of men? The SHADOW knows. (LAUGHS)
	(MUSIC UP...SEGUE BRIGHT THEME)
ANNR:	Once again your neighborhood 'blue coal' dealer brings you the thrilling adventures of the SHADOW…the hard and relentless fight of one man against the forces of evil. These dramatizations are designed to demonstrate forcibly to old and young alike that crime does not pay.
ANNR:	The SHADOW, who aids the forces of law and order is in reality Lamont Cranston, wealthy-young man-about-town. Years ago in the Orient Cranston learned a strange and mysterious secret…the hypnotic power to cloud men's minds so they cannot see him. Cranston's friend and companion, the lovely Margot Lane, is the only person who knows to whom the voice of the invisible SHADOW belongs. Today's drama … "The Immortal Murderer."
	(MUSIC UP…SEGUE INTO NEUTRAL BACKGROUND)
ANNR:	Today's story opens in the caveman room of the city museum. A museum guide is explaining the wonders of ancient man to an absorbed audience of (FADING OUT) museum visitors…
	(FADE IN AD LIBS ON ECHO CHAMBER)
GUIDE:	Yes, ladies and gentlemen…this is the museum's famous "Hall of the Caveman"…the most complete exhibit of its kind ever assembled.
	(AD LIBS OF ADMIRATION)
GUIDE:	And this, ladies and gentlemen, is our greatest exhibit. In this case we have a perfect restoration of the ancient Neanderthal Man!
	(AD LIBS)
WOMAN:	Doesn't he look savage, though?
GUIDE:	Note the huge jaw…the small flat skull with the heavy eyebrow ridge. Note also the huge shoulders, chest and torso carried on short bandy legs. The Neanderthal Man has sometimes been called the human gorilla...

Alfred Bester

MAN:	He sure looks like one.
GUIDE:	Yes. And you see him here as he might actually have lived…dressed in fur pelts, carrying his huge club. In fact this restoration is singularly lifelike…
WOMAN:	He does look alive, doesn't he? (GASPS) He is alive! I saw his eyes move!
GUIDE:	Merely an optical illusion, madam…
WOMAN:	(SCREAMS) No! Look! He is moving! He's lifting his club!
	(AD LIB PANIC)
MAN:	He's going to smash that case! Let's get outa here!
GUIDE:	B-but this is impossible!
	(CRASH OF GLASS)
GUIDE:	(CHOKES)
	(AD LIB SCUFFLE. SCREAMS AND SHOUTS)
WOMAN:	He's choking the guide!
GUIDE:	(STRANGLED) Let go of me! Let— HELP! Hel— Ahhhh... (BODY FALLS TO FLOOR)
CAIN:	(ROARS WITH LAUGHTER) He is dead! I kill him!
WOMAN:	No! Don't come near us!
CAIN:	Listen! You shall spread the word of my coming.
MAN:	Wh-who are you…?
CAIN:	My name is Cain. You have read about me. I am the world's first murderer…Let the world beware. I have returned...and I shall kill again!
	(MUSIC BRIDGE)
	(SHOP DOOR OPENS. BELL JANGLES)
CLERK:	Good afternoon, sir. Welcome back to Tripley's. Come for another suit?
	(STEPS. DOOR CLOSES)
MAN:	Yeah. Need something heavy for winter…Mr. Tripley here? He always waits on me.
CLERK:	Mr. Tripley will be out in a moment, sir. He's been outfitting a very odd customer…Very odd indeed.
MAN:	Say, talking about odd things…Did you read in the paper what happened in the museum this morning? One of the cavemen came out of his glass case.
CLERK:	Caveman?
MAN:	Yeah. Murdered the museum guide. Said he was Cain...the original murderer.
CLERK:	Caveman! B-but that's the odd customer Mr. Tripley is waiting on. I…I thought it was was s-some kind of stunt!
MAN:	Yeah. I figured the museum story was a stunt too.
CLERK:	Wait! Here comes Mr. Tripley's customer now. D-does he look like the same caveman?
MAN:	Yeah, only he's all dressed up.
CLERK:	He…He's carrying his club and the skins he was wearing.
CAIN:	(FADING IN) You, clerk…come here.

John Archer (a.k.a. Lamont Cranston) in 1944

CLERK:	Y-yessir. Everything s-satisfactory, sir?
CAIN:	Take club and skins back to museum. Tell them "Cain has no use for them now."
CLERK:	Y-yes, Mr. Cain. Would you l-like to pay for your clothes now?
CAIN:	(FADING-) I already pay…in the coin of Cain.
	(DOOR OPENS AND CLOSES. BELL JANGLES)
MAN:	Holy Smoke! A caveman in striped pants and cutaway and top hat! He looked weird!
CLERK:	Th-this has got me scared. (FADING) I'd better get Mr. Tripley. (CALLS) Mr. Tripley…
	(DOOR OPENS OFF)
CLERK:	Mr. Trip— (YELLS)
MAN:	What's the matter?
CLERK:	Oh, this is horrible!
MAN:	What is it?
CLERK:	(ON) Look…Mr. Tripley…
MAN:	(SICK) His head's been smashed…
CLERK:	So that's the coin of Cain…Murder!
	(MUSIC BRIDGE)
	(TELEPHONE RINGS. RECEIVER UP)
GIRL:	Steel's Sporting Goods…Oh, hiya, May. Yeah, this is Jenny. No, I'm alone. I kin talk. Get a load of me working in a sports store fer men…It's the man shortage. Yeah. Say, ain't it awful about the Caveman from the museum? Two murders already. But how kin a stuffed dummy from a glass case come to life? I betcha it's all a publicity stunt, May…
	(DOOR OPENS OFF)
GIRL:	Oh-oh! Gotta hang up now. Customer just come in. See ya later…
	(PHONE DOWN)
GIRL:	Yes, sir. May I be of assis- (STOPS COLD AS SHE SEES HIM) (FRIGHTENED) Yes s-sir?
CAIN:	You sell guns?
GIRL:	Yes, sir. Rifles, shotguns, pistols, revolvers…
CAIN:	Revolver.
GIRL:	Certainly, sir…
	(CASE DOOR ROLLS BACK)
GIRL:	What caliber, sir?
CAIN:	Big.
GIRL:	Would you be interested in this, sir? Thirty-eight caliber. Hand-honed action. Six-inch barrel. Very fine target gun.
CAIN:	I do not want gun for targets. I want for killing. Give me one hundred shells.
GIRL:	(LAUGHS DOUBTFULLY) Yes, sir…Right here, sir.
	(CLICKS OF GUN BEING LOADED)
GIRL:	Oh! Please don't do that, sir. We don't allow firearms to be loaded here…
CAIN:	This gun accurate?

Judith Allen portrayed Margot in "The Immortal Murderer," succeeding the ailing Marjorie Anderson.

GIRL: Yes, sir. Please, sir. You're pointing it at me. Please sir...stop!
CAIN: Silence!
GIRL: You're...that man I read about in the papers. You're Cain...Cain the killer (BREAKS) Let me out of here. (FADING) (QUICK STEPS) Help! Help!
(SHOT) (TUMBLING BODY FALL) (GIRL WHIMPERS OFF)
(TWO MORE DELIBERATE SHOTS)
(MUSIC BRIDGE)
WESTON: I tell you, I won't stand for this crazy business any longer! What am I running a police department for?
CRANSTON: Now take it easy, Commissioner.
WESTON: It's easy for you to sit there smirking, Cranston.
MARGOT: He's not smirking, Commissioner.
WESTON: My apologies, Miss Lane. I oughta have said...leering. But you people haven't got the papers riding you! You aren't faced with a cockeyed fugitive from a glass case...a maniac who commits three murders and...
CRANSTON: What makes you think this caveman is mad?
WESTON: Don't tell me you believe a museum dummy really came to life? You don't believe he's Cain, the original murderer?
CRANSTON: I don't know what to believe.
WESTON: For the love of Pete! The Neanderthal Man died out years ago...
CRANSTON: Two hundred thousand, to be exact. He lived during the late Pleistocene...that was the great Ice Age.
MARGOT: But this Cain acts just the way you'd expect a caveman to act... I mean, one that's just come to life. He escapes and kills his keeper. First he gets clothes...then weapons, and now...
CRANSTON: Now all he needs is money.
(PHONE RINGS. RECEIVER UP)
WESTON: Weston. Yeah...What!? Get my car ready. I'm coming right down.
(PHONE DOWN)
WESTON: What are you trying to do...Hoodoo me, Cranston?
CRANSTON: What do you mean?
WESTON: Didn't you say now all that caveman needs is money? Well, Mr. Cain's just held up the National Brokerage House...Took a hundred thousand in cash...killed a teller...and set fire to the building!
CRANSTON: Good Lord!
WESTON: I'm hustling down there now. See you later. (FADING) You two better stay outa this. I got enough headaches already from Caveman Cain!
(DOOR OPENS AND SLAMS)
MARGOT: Well, Lamont...what do we do?
CRANSTON: As if you didn't know. Come on. My car's downstairs. We'll see if we can beat Weston to the Brokerage House...<u>and</u> Mr. Cain.

Ted de Corsia costarred as Commissioner Weston during the 1944-45 season.

	(MUSIC BRIDGE)
	(CROWD AND ROAR OF FLAMES IN B.G. FIRE SIRENS SOUND)
MARGOT:	Golly, Lamont! What a blaze…Looks like we beat Weston to it.
CRANSTON:	Four murders, one fire and three robberies so far. Mr. Cain is beating his old crime record plenty.
MARGOT:	Lamont! You don't really think he's the ancient Cain?
CRANSTON:	Well, it's hard to believe, Margot.
CAIN:	You would not say that if you had seen him.
MARGOT:	(GASPS) Oh!
CAIN:	So sorry to frighten you. I could not help overhearing your conversation. I took the liberty of answering.
CRANSTON:	You saw this Cain?
CAIN:	Yes.
MARGOT:	What does he look like?
CAIN:	He is six feet tall. His chest and shoulders are powerful…his legs short and bowed. His face is apelike and bearded…
MARGOT:	Lamont!
CAIN:	He is dressed in top hat, black cutaway, striped trousers. He wears spats and ascot tie…
MARGOT:	Lamont! He's describing himself.
CAIN:	And he carries a loaded thirty-eight caliber revolver. Be very quiet, Miss Lane, Mr. Cranston!
MARGOT:	Y-you know us?
CAIN:	I know everything.
CRANSTON:	What do you want, Cain?
CAIN:	I want to talk. You will both turn around. Get in your car and drive off. I will be with you…watching.
CRANSTON:	All right…Come on, Margot.
	(CAR DOOR OPENS)
MARGOT:	Lamont!
CAIN:	Get in! Be quick!
	(DOOR CLOSES. FADE B.G. SLIGHTLY)
CAIN:	Drive off, Mr. Cranston. Obey orders. Remember I am not afraid to kill.
CRANSTON:	Yes, you've given ample proof of that.
	(CAR STARTS. FADE OUT FIRE B.G. CAR B.G. FOR:)
CRANSTON:	All right. Now what?
CAIN:	Tell me, Mr. Cranston…Do you believe I am a museum dummy come to life?
CRANSTON:	No.
CAIN:	I'm pleased to hear that. You're right, of course. Fortunately, the mass of people have been taken in by my little propaganda campaign. They believe and they will be easier prey because they believe. However, this campaign had another object besides creating terror.
CRANSTON:	What was that?
CAIN:	To get in touch with _you_, Mr. Cranston.
CRANSTON:	Four murders to get in touch with me? Don't you believe in telephones?
CAIN:	I just wanted to be sure you would take my message seriously.

Marjorie Anderson costarred as Margot Lane opposite John Archer (Lamont Cranston) at the beginning of the 1944-45 season, but left the series in December for health reasons.

From the collection of Karl D. Schadow

CRANSTON: What message?

CAIN: This: "Tell THE SHADOW I must see him at once."

CRANSTON: What!?

CAIN: Come, come, Mr. Cranston. I know you are intimate with THE SHADOW. Tell him to call on Adam Cain at his earliest convenience. The address is Thirteen Paradise Road.

MARGOT: How d-do you know Lamont knows THE SHADOW?

CAIN: How I know, Miss Lane, is of no concern at the moment. It is enough that I do know. Carry my message, and I will not trouble you again…

CRANSTON: But Mr. Cain—

CAIN: No buts, my friend. Do as you are told.

(CAR DOOR OPENS. BRING UP WIND)

MARGOT: Lamont! He's going to jump!

CAIN: Keep driving! My regards to… (QUICK FADE) THE SHADOW!

MARGOT: Stop the car, quick, Lamont! Maybe we can follow him.

(CAR SCREECHES TO STOP)

CRANSTON: No use, Margot. He's vanished.

MARGOT: Lamont! Th-this…This is awful.

CRANSTON: It certainly isn't good.

MARGOT: Who is this Cain? How much does he really know about THE SHADOW? What's he after?

CRANSTON: There's only one way to answer these questions, Margot. The Shadow will…<u>have</u> to visit Mr. Adam Cain!

(MUSIC BRIDGE. ORGAN MERGES INTO:)
(PIANO PLAYING CHOPINESQUE MUSIC SOFTLY)

CAIN:	What an exquisite melody this is. How unfortunate that Chopin never published it. The world is so much the poorer for its loss.
SHADOW:	(LAUGHS)
	(PIANO STOPS A MOMENT. THEN CONTINUES)
CAIN:	So you've received my message, my dear SHADOW? Was that laugh directed at my playing…or my sentimentality?
SHADOW:	Leave that piano, Cain. What do you want?
CAIN:	How abrupt you are. Please sit down. I'll be with you in a moment.
SHADOW:	THE SHADOW waits for no man, Cain. You know that. THE SHADOW is a spirit of right and justice, come tonight to collect a debt of murder and destruction that you owe!
CAIN:	(LAUGHS) Dear, Dear…I know all that. But your histrionics are wasted because I also know that THE SHADOW is Lamont Cranston.
SHADOW:	What!?
CAIN:	Do sit down, Mr. Cranston, and stop this nonsense. I can see you, you know.
SHADOW:	You lie, Cain. No man sees THE SHADOW!
CAIN:	But I do. I learned your trick of invisibility many, many years ago. Of course I see you, Mr. Cranston. Look! Here's proof. You're wearing a blue pinstripe suit…gray shirt…blue and gray figured tie. Enough? Or shall I add the white handkerchief in your pocket?
	(STARTS TO PLAY PIANO AGAIN)
CAIN:	Your act is wasted on me, Mr. Cranston.
	(PIANO CONTINUES ALONE FOR A MINUTE)
CRANSTON:	All right, Cain…What do you want?
CAIN:	Ah, that's much better.
	(PIANO CUT)
CAIN:	I want to talk business with you, Mr. Cranston. Important business. I think it's time THE SHADOW put aside his playthings and grew up. And I shall teach you how.
CRANSTON:	Cain…Who are you?
CAIN:	(STRONG) I am the master of THE SHADOW!
	(HAMMERING DISCORDANTLY ON PIANO KEYS TO EMPHASIZE POINTS)
CAIN:	I am Cain…Cain, the immortal murderer! Cain the destroyer! The maker of Dynasties and Empires! The builder and scourge of civilizations. The giant earth-shaker! I am Cain, the immortal! I am a million years old!
	(MUSIC ORGAN STAB INTO BRIDGE)
	(MIDDLE COMMERCIAL)
	(THUNDER ROLLS)
CAIN:	Ahhh, listen to that, Mr. Cranston. A bad storm brewing outside. Nice to sit in here by the fire, eh?
CRANSTON:	Quit stalling, Cain.
CAIN:	You are not polite…but it is because you are bewildered, eh? You don't believe I am a million years old?
CRANSTON:	No.
CAIN:	Yes, it is true. When I slipped into that case in the museum to begin my campaign, I decided to replace the Neanderthal figure because I am a Neanderthal Man.
CRANSTON:	Impossible.
CAIN:	(STRONG) Look into my eyes and say that. Look! Look! I tell you!
	(THUNDER)

CAIN: So...I see you are shaken. Now you begin to believe...You see in my eyes a million years of life...death...of boredom.

CRANSTON: What do you want, Cain?

CAIN: A million years ago I was a savage...a creature that hunted, ate and slept. I was content, then...as a beast is contented. One day...came a catastrophe. A star fell from the skies...You call them meteors.

CRANSTON: Yes.

CAIN: It was a giant mass of metal, glowing white hot...flaming with fierce gases. It struck the earth with a titanic concussion ...

(THUNDER)

CRANSTON: And you lived through that concussion?

CAIN: By some strange freak I lived...lived and breathed those gases. Perhaps they were radioactive...Perhaps of some unknown element. I do not know. All I know is they gave me Immortality.

CRANSTON: I still don't believe it.

CAIN: I did not at first. But I lived...and lived...and lived. Through eons of savagery... Through thousands of Egyptian dynasties...The Assyrian civilization...The Hellenic Age...I lived to watch the rise and fall of the Roman Empire...Spent the Dark Ages in the Orient where I learned your trick of invisibility a thousand years ago...

CRANSTON: No!

CAIN: Yes, Mr. Cranston. I watched and played many important parts in the history of man... until I realized it was wise for me to protect my life.

CRANSTON: Your immortal life?

CAIN: Yes, immortality—barring accidents. A man can live forever; but no immortal can live without a head, or with a smashed heart. One narrow escape during the debacle of the Spanish Armada taught me a lesson I've never forgotten. My life is too valuable to be risked.

CRANSTON: Yet you risked it today.

CAIN: Yes...It was foolish, but centuries of boredom have made me reckless. For I am bored, Mr. Cranston. Unspeakably, incredibly, maddeningly bored. Centuries ago I played an active role in the world's drama. Today, I have decided to begin the game again. It is my only diversion.

CRANSTON: And you have called THE SHADOW to tell him this?

CAIN: I have called THE SHADOW to join me in the most fascinating game on earth...the game of power!

CRANSTON: You're insane.

CAIN: Together we will shake the earth once more. I shall remain behind the scenes while you move our pawns out in the open. Dream your wildest dreams and you shall realize them...I can make you anything you like...king...emperor...president...Even a god!

CRANSTON: Impossible! Cain, do you think THE SHADOW would ever join you in a criminal game worse than anything THE SHADOW has fought? No, Cain, THE SHADOW will not join you...and THE SHADOW will never permit you to play with human lives...with blood and terror!

(THUNDER)

CAIN: (MUSING) So I've misjudged you, eh? You are still a child, clinging to a child's virtues and the morality of infants. Well...don't give your answer now. Perhaps you will change your mind.

CRANSTON: I'm afraid not. You don't change sides when you fight evil.

CAIN: Mr. Cranston, I understand your reactions perfectly. This is a tremendous decision for

THE IMMORTAL MURDERER   125

	you to make. That's why I shall give you until twelve o'clock tonight to decide. By then you will have seen things my way.
CRANSTON:	Cain, I can give you my answer now.
CAIN:	(UNHEEDING) Only don't attempt to bring in the police. I could outwit them so easily, it would be pathetic.
CRANSTON:	You're certainly an egomaniac, aren't you?
CAIN:	(CHUCKLING) Well, I <u>am</u> sure of myself, Mr. Cranston. In fact, so sure, I will give you your <u>first</u> assignment now! Cranston, by twelve o'clock tonight, I want you to find us a headquarters...someplace where we can be completely cut off from the world as we plot to destroy it!
CRANSTON:	And suppose I don't?
CAIN:	(POWERFUL) War between us, Mr. Cranston, will mean only one thing. I am a million years old...a master in the arts of death and destruction. Fight me, and I will crush THE SHADOW under my heel like a rat!
	(MUSIC BRIDGE)
	(DRUMMING OF RAIN. THUNDER)
CRANSTON:	And that, Margot, is the story of my incredible interview with Mr. Cain...I'm sorry I'm so late but I've had a few things to do.
MARGOT:	Lamont! I-I don't know what to say! It's all so grotesque...so unbelievable.
CRANSTON:	Yes.
MARGOT:	It-it's like an irresistible force meeting an immovable object. What's going to happen?
CRANSTON:	Cain's going to be smashed.
MARGOT:	He's a million years old...a million years evil. There are centuries of death and violence in him...
CRANSTON:	That's why he must be stopped.
MARGOT:	What can <u>you</u> do, Lamont? He knows you're THE SHADOW! He knows your secret of invisibility. How can you stop him?
	(CLOCK BEGINS TO STRIKE TWELVE)
MARGOT:	(ON THIRD STROKE) Lamont...it's twelve o'clock.
'	(TWO STROKES IN CLEAR)
MARGOT:	He said to call him by twelve...
CRANSTON:	Yes...
MARGOT:	Lamont...what are you going to do?
	(LAST STROKE TO END HERE)
	(QUICK PICK UP OF PHONE AND DIAL)
CRANSTON:	(OVER DIALING) I'm calling him now, Margot.
MARGOT:	Are you going to tell him you'll fight?
CAIN:	(FILTERED) Yes, Mr. Cranston. You're a little late with your call.
CRANSTON:	I've just reached a decision.

Radio Margot Grace Matthews watches John Archer reprise The Shadow's laugh in 1987.

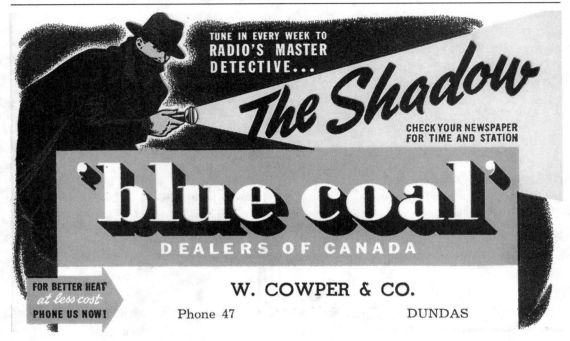

CAIN:	Fine. Where are our headquarters?
CRANSTON:	On Princeton Street. I own a bank building that's not rented at the moment. The bank vault would suit our purposes ideally.
CAIN:	Excellent. I'll meet you there in a half hour.
	(CAIN HANGS UP PHONE) (THEN CRANSTON HANGS UP)
MARGOT:	Lamont, you can't join him…
CRANSTON:	I'm not, Margot. I'm going to stop Cain. I'll have to leave now, Margot.
MARGOT:	I'm going with you.
CRANSTON:	No…Margot, when I learned the secret of The Shadow in the Orient, I swore I would fight crime relentlessly as long as I lived. That was the price of my terrible power.
MARGOT:	But he'll kill you. You can't fight him.
CRANSTON:	I promised I would fight crime as long as I lived!
	(MUSIC)
	(ECHO OVERALL)
	(FOOTSTEPS IN MIKE)
CAIN:	(OFF) Ah, you are here, Mr. Cranston. This is an excellent location.
SHADOW:	It will suit our purposes, Cain.
CAIN:	(SURPRISED) But you've assumed your Shadow role again.
SHADOW:	Yes, Cain.
	(CLANG OF BIG VAULT DOOR)
CAIN:	Why have you closed the vault door?
SHADOW:	To insure our privacy.
CAIN:	(FEELING HIM OUT) You can stop being The Shadow now, Cranston.
SHADOW:	I prefer it this way.
CAIN:	So you've decided to fight me, Cranston?
SHADOW:	Did you really think I would help you?

CAIN: You know what this means, Cranston.

SHADOW: Yes, Cain...death! For both of us!

CAIN: Both of us?

SHADOW: Cain, that vault door is six feet thick...and when it's shut this vault is absolutely airtight. Even you can die of suffocation. Sit down, Cain. You and The Shadow will be here a long time...forever.

CAIN: I don't believe you! You wouldn't make this insane sacrifice just to kill me.

SHADOW: The Shadow has spent a lifetime fighting crime. There could be no better death for The Shadow than this. I will take with me the greatest archcriminal of all time.

CAIN: No, it's ridiculous! We'll make a deal, Shadow.

SHADOW: Tell me, Cain, can you see The Shadow now?

CAIN: Of course.

SHADOW: What am I wearing?

CAIN: Why...the light in here...it's so dim I can't quite make out...(STARTS TO LAUGH)

SHADOW: Why the laughter, Cain?

CAIN: That telephone, fool, that telephone.

SHADOW: It only goes to the outside of the vault.

CAIN: Then I'll keep ringing it. When the watchman comes to investigate, I'm free.

SHADOW: There is no night watchman. This building is deserted.

CAIN: Cranston, I know you know how to open the door from inside. Let me out and I promise to retire for your lifetime. For a century! You can't throw away your life. You can't throw away my immortality!

SHADOW: There is no release, but death!

CAIN: You sniveling canting fool! Would you kill us for a whim of justice...an illusion of right and wrong?

SHADOW: We are here for eternity...

CAIN: Wait! Of course! I, too, know how to open vault doors from inside. Of course! There is always a release from inside. And if I remember correctly, it would be right about here. Yes! (DOOR SOUND) This little door in the wall!

SHADOW: Wait, Cain. Don't touch that handle.

CAIN: So, the one flaw in your scheme. You forgot about this release from the inside.

SHADOW: No, Cain, I didn't forget about it. I've wired that release to the electric circuit. If you touch it, it will electrocute you.

CAIN: Fool! Do you think I believe you? This was to be your escape. But now it's mine!

SHADOW: No, Cain, no! Don't touch that release!

CAIN: (LAUGHS)

(LOUD SPLUTTER OF ELECTRIC CURRENT)

CAIN: (SCREAMS)

(HISS OF CURRENT) (BODY THUD)

SHADOW: So you wouldn't believe me, Cain.

(BUZZ OF TELEPHONE)

SHADOW: The telephone! The telephone from outside the vault!

(PICK UP RECEIVER)

Announcer Don Hancock

SHADOW:	Hello?
MARGOT:	Lamont! Are you all right?
SHADOW:	Margot! Yes, I'm fine <u>now</u>, Margot. Quick—get me out of here!
MARGOT:	But how?
SHADOW:	Listen—here's the combination. First, twice around to eighteen.
MARGOT:	Eighteen, I've got it. (CLICKS)
SHADOW:	Now, once left to thirty-two. (CLICKS)
SHADOW:	Twice right to six… (MUSIC)
MARGOT:	Lamont, I'm so happy I could cry.
CRANSTON:	Go ahead. I guess you have a right to.
MARGOT:	But I can't! I'm too happy!
CRANSTON:	I give up! I can take cavemen, but not women.
MARGOT:	Lamont, was he really a caveman?
CRANSTON:	I don't know, Margot…I really don't know.
MARGOT:	But why did you go into the vault with him? Suppose Cain wasn't ten thousand years old after all?
CRANSTON:	Margot, if The Shadow found that he wasn't what he claimed, I had a secret way of turning off the electric current. Then I would have opened the door and taken him to Commissioner Weston.
MARGOT:	But he would have told that you were The Shadow.
CRANSTON:	It would be his word against mine. Maybe people wouldn't believe that rich boy Cranston could be The Shadow.
MARGOT:	And if you found he was really the original Cain?
CRANSTON:	We would have sat in that vault forever.
MARGOT:	I'm afraid that's the way it would have been. After all, he was able to break down the power of The Shadow.
CRANSTON:	I'm not so sure, Margot.
MARGOT:	But you said he saw you?
CRANSTON:	No, Margot, I said he <u>described</u> the clothes I was wearing. I realized later that when I visited Cain, I was wearing the same clothes he saw when he got into our car.
MARGOT:	Then which was he?
CRANSTON:	Margot, Cain was either the oldest criminal the world has ever known…or one of the cleverest, most ambitious crooks of our time. As to which he was…I'm afraid we'll never know. We'll never know. (MUSIC CURTAIN)
ANNR:	THE SHADOW program is based on a story copyrighted by Street and Smith Publications. The characters, names, places and plot are fictitious. Any similarity to persons living or dead is purely coincidental. Again next week THE SHADOW will demonstrate that…
SHADOW:	(FILTER) The weed of crime bears bitter fruit…Crime does not pay. The Shadow knows… (LAUGHS) •

John Archer and Shadow *announcer André Baruch in 1986*